# AMBULANCE GIRLS UNDER FIRE

Also by Deborah Burrows:

*Ambulance Girls*

*Deborah Burrows*

# AMBULANCE
# GIRLS
# UNDER FIRE

EBURY
PRESS

1 3 5 7 9 10 8 6 4 2

Ebury Press, an imprint of Ebury Publishing
20 Vauxhall Bridge Road,
London SW1V 2SA

Ebury Press is part of the Penguin Random House group of companies
whose addresses can be found at global.penguinrandomhouse.com

First published in the UK in 2018 by Ebury Press

www.penguin.co.uk

A CIP catalogue record for this book is available from the British Library

Hardback ISBN 9781785034626
Trade Paperback ISBN 9781785037764

Typeset in India by Integra Software Services Pvt. Ltd, Pondicherry

Printed and bound in Great Britain by Clays Ltd, St Ives PLC

Penguin Random House is committed to a sustainable future for our business,
our readers and our planet. This book is made from Forest Stewardship
Council® certified paper.

*To the Williams boys: my brothers, Bevan, Mark and Vaughn,
who are and always have been so supportive and loving;
my nephews Dylan and Darcy
and my new great-nephew, Jesse.*

# CHAPTER ONE

*Sunday 29 December 1940*

'Watch out, Ashwin!' Maisie Halliday's voice was thin and high, almost a scream. 'For God's sake, *run*. The whole thing is coming down on top of you.'

I glanced up at the wall beside me. Maisie was right: the bricks were rippling and it was obviously close to collapse, but I hesitated, unsure if I had really heard a voice calling out from the ruins. Then I tasted dust. My heart gave a thump and, acting on pure instinct, I turned and made an attempt at a frantic dash to safety. It was more of a clumsy waddle, as I was weighed down by my heavy waterproof, rubber boots and gas mask, all of which made it difficult to move quickly, especially as the ground was boggy from water used to put out the fire and uneven with rubble from the building's earlier collapse. I staggered through mud, water, cinders and charcoal, slipping and sliding and almost falling several times.

When I reached the roadway I bent over, rested my hands on my knees and pulled in a few ragged breaths. From behind me came the roar of collapsing bricks mingled, surprisingly, with cheers. I realised why when I raised my head. Fires were burning out of control around me and the scene was bright as daylight; my ungainly retreat to safety had been witnessed by rescue workers and firemen. I threw them a grin and a wave and plodded across the road to Maisie, who was standing beside our ambulance.

As I got closer I saw the scowl on her usually serene face.

'Bit of a close shave, that,' I said lightly, and smiled at her as I took off my steel helmet. Smoke swirled around me in a sudden eddy, making me cough as I pulled out my handkerchief. Scraps of charred paper floated past us in the heated air.

'It was far too close,' Maisie replied, in a stiff angry tone.

I didn't reply. Instead I swiped the handkerchief across my sweaty face. When I glanced at the linen it was blackened. *Blackened face, dirty uniform. I must look like a guy,* I thought. *Penny for the old guy?* I gave a laugh at the thought that one national newspaper had described me as 'the loveliest debutante of 1937'.

'How can you laugh, Ashwin? You nearly died.' Maisie sounded close to tears.

I put away the soiled handkerchief. 'But I didn't die. So no need to fuss.'

Maisie's voice rose. 'Why do you always rush into danger? You're not invincible, you know.' She was really angry, which surprised me, as Maisie was usually remarkably even-tempered. 'I don't want to attend another funeral,' she said, her voice cracking. 'Not so soon after David Levy's.'

I no longer felt like laughing. The pain of David's death two months before was as raw as the burns on my cheeks from the falling embers. But Maisie didn't know about David and me, and she never would. I straightened my back, raised my chin and assumed the mask of chilly reserve that served me well in such situations. *Head high, walk tall.*

'I'm sorry to have frightened you,' I said. 'I thought I heard a voice calling out and I simply reacted.'

'Well, it was a daft thing to do. That's what the rescue squads are for.' Maisie tried for a disgruntled tone, but her sunny nature won through and she gave me a smile. 'I'm just glad you weren't hurt.'

I glanced back at the pile of bricks that was all that remained of the wall and raised an eyebrow. 'Well, so am I.'

Maisie laughed. She was nineteen, and a dancer when she wasn't an ambulance attendant. Her slim, tough dancer's body was allied to a face with the dark luminosity of a Raphael Madonna. I liked her, and she was always friendly enough to me, but we weren't close. I suspected she distrusted my class on principle.

'Aren't you ever afraid?' she asked.

'There's no time for fear,' I replied, waving at the scene around us.

The ancient City of London was alight and burning out of control after the night's incendiary attack by the German bombers. Above us, massed battalions of low-flying aircraft were still dropping yet more of the little deadly devices, interspersed with high-explosive bombs that made the ground shake. Firemen, with smoke-blackened faces and dripping uniforms, sweated on the ends of wriggling hoses, fighting a futile battle against the flames. Rescue workers, grey with choking plaster dust and ash, combed through the charred and smoking ruins. Fire engines, trailers and pumps were dotted around, barely visible in the thick smoke.

As usual, the noise was almost overwhelming. The crash of bursting shells, the whine of falling fire-bombs and the scream of larger high-explosive bombs were accompanied by the constant throb and moan of aircraft engines and the shrilling and clanging of ambulance and fire-brigade bells. The thump of pneumatic drills as roadmen worked on a burning gas main that shot blue flames high up into the sky. The song of the guns: the thud of the big anti-aircraft guns, the bark of the smaller mobile guns and the sharp rattle of machine guns firing on descending flares. And behind it all, the roar of fires burning out of control.

With every gust of the breeze great clouds of pale smoke filled with sparks rolled down and burst over those who fought to save what they could. The high roof of a warehouse, burning fiercely, had become a grid of bright beams against the darkness beyond. Leaping flames formed a halo around the dome of St Paul's Cathedral on its hill above us because, amazingly, the cathedral still stood, silhouetted against a blood-red sky. I sent up a quick prayer that it would survive the firestorm.

It was an awesomely beautiful sight, the City of London in flames. I felt humbled, and also terribly sad, to witness it. David had loved the City, with its maze of narrow lanes and all its history. Its annihilation would have caused him terrible grief.

An angry voice cut through the din. 'What the hell did you think you were doing, Ashwin?' Our station officer in charge, Jack Moray, stood in front of me, hands on hips, scowling. 'Getting yourself killed won't help anyone.'

I shrugged. 'I thought I heard someone calling out to me.' I made my tone nonchalant. 'Would you be so kind as to ask heavy rescue to check the area? In case someone is trapped in the ruins. In a cellar, perhaps.'

Moray gave a jerky nod. His lips were thin and flat against his teeth and his face was taut with anger. 'Less than an hour ago, a brick wall just like that one –' he gestured towards the pile of bricks across the road '– collapsed and killed four firemen. If you don't stop taking such insane risks, I'll stop sending you out to incidents. I mean it, Ashwin. You can stay behind at the station and man the phone instead of Fripp.'

I knew it was an empty threat. Nola Fripp was more trouble than she was worth at an incident because she was scared of loud noises and tended to shriek and run for cover when she was needed to tend the wounded. Moray had taken to leaving her at the station and attending incidents himself if required. No one wanted Fripp on the road in an air raid.

I nodded, and said as if repeating a lesson, 'I understand. No more risks.'

*Unless I have to.*

Maisie flinched at the sound of an explosion nearby.

'They're dynamiting the buildings to the south to prevent the fire from spreading,' Moray told her. He shook his head, as if in wonderment. 'Even the roads around the cathedral are on fire. They're wooden block roads and they're burning. An amazing sight. It's like you'd imagine the roads of Hell.'

'Any more casualties for us?' I asked.

4

Maisie and I had been to hospital with three loads of casualties already that night, but we knew that we'd be working until well after daylight.

'Mobile first-aid station in Farringdon Street has four waiting for you. Burns, lacerations and broken limbs…' He gave me a meaningful look. 'From falling walls.'

'I could read a book out here,' said Maisie, as we walked away. 'It's so bright.'

'The pages would be blood red.'

A loud slithering sound came from above and we dodged backwards as a dollop of hot lead from the roof of the old building beside us came down where we had been walking.

'That singed my uniform,' said Maisie. She gave an unconvincing laugh. 'You don't expect to be sent to your maker by a melting roof.'

'I expect just about anything nowadays.'

We collected the patients and carried them in stretchers to the ambulance. It was tricky, as the whole area was boggy and slippery with ice and mud and water, and we were forced to dodge the coiling hosepipes that covered the roads. As soon as we slid the final stretcher into the rails in the ambulance body, Maisie climbed inside and I drove away from the burning City at the regulation sixteen miles per hour. Maisie's voice floated in from the back. She was reassuring our patients.

Fleet Street was on fire and as the warden directed me into a diversion I noticed with a weary sadness that the wedding-cake steeple of St Bride's Church had been hit. The once beautiful church was a skeletal shell and the ruins were burning furiously. The ever-growing inferno lit up the ruined streets so effectively that it was as if I was driving in full daylight. For once it was easy to see my way and I had no need of my ambulance's shuttered headlights to show me the holes and bomb craters in the road ahead.

My ambulance was a tough old bird, and we rolled along uncomfortably through the fire-bright streets. If bomb craters blocked our way, I drove on the footpath. Eventually we arrived and I parked in the hospital yard. When I climbed out to help Maisie with the wounded, flakes of blazing stuff – rags or paper – floated past on the wind like grey snowflakes. They coated Maisie's tin hat and coat.

'What's it from?' asked Maisie, as we carried the first patient to the hospital entrance.

'I think it's all that remains of the books in Paternoster Row.'

At the hospital entrance a medical student was sitting with a pile of large brown envelopes. On these he recorded each patient's number and any identifying information. The young man had a bony, pleasant face, but his eyes were leaden with exhaustion and his voice was raspy as he greeted us.

'I hear they're calling it the Second Great Fire of London,' he said, 'because the entire City is on fire. Is it true?'

'Pretty much,' said Maisie. 'We've lost most of the Wren churches, and Guildhall is burning, which is awful, but it looks like they've saved St Paul's.'

'At least that's something.' He gave a bitter laugh. 'I wonder if they'll make up a rhyme this time around.' At Maisie's look he said, 'You must remember it. *In sixteen hundred and sixty-six, London burned like rotten sticks.*'

As I drove back to the beleaguered City, a searchlight sword struck out across the sky. Others soon joined it, until there was an intricate tracery of light through which flew small objects like ominous black birds, ones that that carried death under their wings.

Beside me, Maisie laughed, which confused me until she said, 'I've thought of a rhyme.'

'A rhyme?'

'A nursery rhyme, like the one the medical student recited. Here goes: *In December nineteen forty, Goering's planes left London in flames.*'

'It doesn't scan,' I protested.

She was silent for a while, then said, 'What about: *In nineteen forty in December, German raiders turned London to embers.*'

6

'That one doesn't really rhyme.'

'Oh, you're a tough audience, Ashwin. *Goering's planes were London's bane*? No. That *is* awful. *Fire. Mire. Byre. Lyre.* Shame there's no spire on St Paul's,' she muttered. 'Then again, all those Wren churches have gone, and they all had spires.'

I parked the ambulance near Ludgate. In our absence, the fires in the City seemed to have increased in intensity. The dome of St Paul's was silhouetted against a sky of yellow and green and red, with great billows of smoke around it. Clouds of sparks fell around us as we headed towards the mobile first-aid post in a haze of smoke, ready to collect our next batch of wounded. The heated air scorched my skin.

To my astonishment, Maisie gave a shout of laughter. 'Got it,' she said. 'Listen.'

And, against a backdrop of roaring flames and billowing smoke, and above the hiss of hoses and the shouts of rescuers and the clanging of fire engine and ambulance bells, Maisie declaimed her poem into the heart of the inferno before us:

> *'In sixteen hundred and sixty-six,*
> *London burned like rotten sticks.*
> *In nineteen forty, it happened again,*
> *The Luftwaffe came and left London aflame.*
> *But try as they might they'll never break her*
> *Just like before, we will remake her.'*

# CHAPTER TWO

In May 1940, not long after my husband, Cedric Ashwin, was incarcerated under Regulation 18B as a Nazi sympathiser and potential fifth columnist, I moved out of the Mayfair townhouse we had shared for the two and a half years of our marriage and into a small serviced flat on the Gray's Inn Road.

My flat was in St Andrew's Court, which had been built only six years before. I liked the clean vertical lines and stark white walls of the building, which were softened by blue metal window frames and delicate iron balustrades on each balcony. As I couldn't boil an egg, I also liked the service restaurant. It was below the street level, so you could only hear bombs that dropped very close by and you hardly heard the guns at all when you were eating. And because St Andrew's had been constructed of tough, modern concrete, the air raids had not caused any real damage to the fabric of the building itself.

Another benefit was that St Andrew's was close to Bloomsbury Auxiliary Ambulance Station, in Woburn Place, near Russell Square, where I worked as an ambulance driver. St Andrew's was also close to my other workplace, the Jewish Children's Placement Board in Bloomsbury House, on the corner of Gower Street and Bedford Avenue. For the past five weeks, on my days off, I had been working at the JCPB as very bad typist and reasonably efficient clerk.

It was to Bloomsbury House that I was heading on that chilly December morning, the day after the firestorm, the last day of 1940. I wheeled my bicycle on to Gray's Inn Road and had just steadied myself ready to push off from the kerb when someone called out my name. I turned around to see Eddie Hollis leaning against the wall of the building next door.

'Good morning, Eddie.' My voice was cold and my face unwelcoming.

Eddie was one of Cedric's most ardent admirers. He was a colourless sort of man, with thinning dark-blond hair and blue, rather protruding, eyes. His neck was thick, but he had surprisingly small ears. Before the war he had been an active blackshirt. As such he had delighted in tormenting those he considered to be his inferiors, specifically any Jew who lived in London. I had not seen him since my husband had been incarcerated and it was not a pleasure to see him now. In the past eight months I had distanced myself from Cedric's followers and I didn't want to encourage visits from Eddie Hollis.

Eddie peeled away from the wall and slunk across the footpath to stand next to me. He put a restraining hand on my handlebar.

'You off to that Yid place then?' Eddie's tone was just as offensive as his words. It was concerning that he not only knew where I lived but also about my work at Bloomsbury House. Had he been watching me, my husband's grubby little acolyte?

'Why do you go there?' he said. 'He doesn't like it. I told him all about it and he's not happy.'

My head jerked up to stare at him in furious amazement. 'You've been spying on me? Did my husband ask you to spy on me?'

He looked down, seemingly embarrassed.

'What do you want, Eddie?'

A note of excitement crept into his voice. 'They're letting him out. Letting him leave the Isle of Man and come back to London. He'll be here soon. The week after next. Thought you'd like to know.'

It was as if he had punched me in my solar plexus, and I couldn't prevent a shocked gasp. So Cedric was coming back to London. Eddie smirked at my response to his news.

*Head high, walk tall.* I straightened my back and raised my chin. I would deal with Cedric when I had to. He knew I wanted a divorce. I had asked him for one in every letter I sent, but so far he had refused to consider it. I could no longer live with him as his wife, which meant he would have to accept a divorce or at the very least a judicial separation.

'How nice for him,' I said, without enthusiasm.

'I've got a message for you. From Mr Ashwin.'

'What message?' Was Cedric going to agree to the divorce? My heart began to race and I began to hope.

'He wants you to find a place for you both to live.'

'What? Well I won't be doing that. I won't be living with him when he returns.'

Eddie shrugged. 'That's the message.' He gave a smile, almost endearing in his obvious delight. 'We have a code. Me and Mr Ashwin worked out how to get past the censor by using a code in our letters.'

'I think you misread your code.'

His sullen, brutish expression returned. 'I'm just giving the message'

'Is that all, Eddie? I have an appointment to keep.'

'At Bloomsbury House? Why do you go there?' He seemed to be genuinely puzzled.

'I do work there helping Jewish children, if you must know. And I'm late. So please let go of my bicycle.'

His pretence of politeness slipped then and his lip lifted in a snarl. 'You're a cold bitch, aren't you? Those bastards have locked him up for eight months and soon he'll be free and you don't care at all.' He spat on the footpath, close to my feet. 'You don't deserve him.'

I looked at his hand on my handlebar. It was very pale and covered with sandy hair. 'Goodbye, Eddie,' I said.

He released his grip, but not before he had given a vicious push to the bike, so that I nearly overbalanced. Annoyed, I rode away without looking back at him.

It was less chilly than the previous day but that meant the snow had melted into mush, so I had to be careful. The wind stung my cheeks as I rode faster, pushing the bike as fast as I could safely go, enjoying the sense of speed, trying to forget that Cedric would be back in London very soon. As I rounded the corner into Tavistock Road I pondered Eddie's words.

Eddie had said I didn't deserve Cedric. Did I deserve a womanising cad who supported the brutality of Hitler's regime? I had been eighteen when I married him in 1937, too young to realise the cost of a decision hastily made. I had thought I was desperately in love with the handsome and sophisticated older man who had steered me through social minefields and treated me with courtesy and gallantry.

Cedric had called me his green girl, his child bride. He said he had chosen me because I was delightfully different from the weary sophisticates he usually squired around. I soon came to realise that he intended me to be a pleasingly naive and socially useful wife who ticked all the right boxes. I had been born into a 'good' family, I made an attractive hostess and, given my background, I could be expected to support his political ambitions. What Cedric did not tell me was that he was incapable of fidelity.

'Everybody does it, darling,' he had replied, with an elegant shrug, when I confronted him three months after our marriage. It was as if my world had shattered into tiny pieces. Recklessly, I had pushed him for names. They were all women I knew. Some had been friends, or I had thought they were. *Did I deserve that, Eddie Hollis?*

I was too young to know how to deal with Cedric's cruelly good-natured cynicism. When I threatened him with divorce, he laughed. 'But darling,' he had said, 'how could you survive if you divorced me?' I didn't know how to answer that. Worse, however, was his insinuation that if I pressed for a divorce then my family and my friends and all of London would assume that it was some fault in me that left Cedric unsatisfied and needing to seek solace in other women's arms. The embarrassment of divorce proceedings would have been too much to bear. Or so I thought. I had only just turned nineteen.

So I had stayed with Cedric. I was faithful to him because I saw no reason not to be. In the years that followed I achieved a degree of sophistication, and some wisdom. I wasn't exactly happy, but London is full of amusements and I made friends there. Cedric was charming and he expected very little from me. I played the hostess at his political dinners, I didn't enquire too much about his political views and I pretended to be deaf to rumours about his constant infidelities. In return he gave me an easy life. What a shallow, snobbish, unthinking creature that Celia had been. Perhaps I *did* deserve Cedric.

Everything changed with the war. My husband – who had spoken at rallies where thousands of men, all dressed in black shirts, had chanted fascist slogans and watched him with shining eyes as they shouted their protestations of allegiance – was declared to be an enemy of the nation. The crowds melted away, save for a few diehards like Eddie.

Cedric was incarcerated and I became the target of hatred and ridicule. Horrible letters arrived. So-called friends disappeared. People I had known since childhood no longer recognised me in the street. When I joined the ambulance service to help the war effort, the press declared it to be a stunt and the numbers of vile letters increased. One summer evening as I left my house in Mayfair, a stranger spat on me and called me a quisling. It was not long afterwards that I moved to the flat in Bloomsbury.

I was no longer the shallow girl who had been content to be Cedric Ashwin's wife. Coming to work at the ambulance station had been a life-changing experience for me in so many ways. Not only did I have to cope with unimaginable horror and sadness, for the first time in my life I was part of a team, working alongside people I never would have otherwise met. In many ways it was humbling. All that mattered in the ambulance station was how you did your job, and you were treated according to how you worked, not how your voice sounded. Any snobbery I may have had soon faded as it became clear that I was no better than my colleagues. When the Blitz began we had to cope with the hideous reality of modern warfare and push fear aside to help those who were injured. It was in the ambulance station that I learned to look beyond someone's class, to see *who* they were and not judge them according to what social stratum they came from.

And then something completely unexpected happened. I fell in love. Desperately, passionately and tormentedly in love with a man who insisted that I think for myself. David Levy told me I was a blank page, a *tabula rasa* with no thoughts of my own, only what I'd been told. David forced me to think about what we were fighting for, about the prejudices I'd accepted all my life. He compelled me to go beyond the limitations of my scanty education and my so-called privileged upbringing, to be more than I had been.

But David died. And no matter how many times I told myself there was nothing I could have done to save him, I returned to that night in my mind over and over, running through the course of events, trying to understand if there was something I could have done differently, if this or that might have affected the final outcome. The memory was like a physical wound that would not heal. I carried it with me always, could not leave behind the pain and regret. My actions after his death haunted me more. I had been a craven coward. When David died I had said nothing and had allowed his body to lie in a bombed building, undiscovered. I had let his parents hope when all hope was gone.

David's parents forgave me, but how could I forgive myself? That was why I worked in Bloomsbury House and helped David's mother deal with Jewish refugee children. I wanted to atone. And that was why I was navigating dangerously slippery roads on a chilly December morning.

My destination, the old Bloomsbury Hotel, was in sight. 'That Yid place', as Eddie had called it. The vast, decaying old pile housed the various organisations, as many as twenty of them, that were engaged in looking after people who had fled the Nazis to seek refuge in Britain. The refugees called it 'Das

Bloomsburyhaus' and the name had stuck, so that it was now officially known as Bloomsbury House.

It was a rabbit warren of little offices containing the various refugee groups. Mrs Levy's organisation was the Jewish Children's Placement Board, which was allied to the Jewish Refugee Committee and was one of several that assisted children who had come to Britain under the Kindertransport scheme.

The activities of the Kindertransport are fairly well known now. In short, when the plight of Jews and anyone else the Nazis deemed unacceptable became desperate, the British government was persuaded to issue permits for 10,000 unaccompanied children to be brought to England. Thousands of children, mostly Jewish or part-Jewish, were evacuated to Britain between November 1938 and the invasion of Holland in May 1940. Once the children arrived they were met by groups of volunteers. These were not just Jewish groups, but also Quakers, Christadelphians and others. They arranged for the children to live with foster-families, or in hostels, schools or on farms throughout the country.

On the whole, the scheme worked well. Of course, some children were unhappy, especially the Orthodox Jewish children placed with Christian families, and we had discovered that some of the older children were being used as servants by their host families, but we did our best. I am pleased to say that every child who came to England under the scheme was alive at the end of the war. Sadly, many of their parents were not.

Since 1938, Mrs Levy's small organisation had managed to place two hundred mainly German children with foster-parents or in hostels across England. It ran on a shoestring, and for the past five weeks I had volunteered my services. I helped to keep track of the refugee children, checked the reports of their progress, and arranged to move them to another placement when required. I dealt with their special requirements and worked out how best to help them survive in a new country. I found the work very satisfying, especially as it had brought out a hitherto unsuspected flair for organisation in me.

I hadn't seen much of Mrs Levy since I had joined the JCPB. She had been badly injured when her home was bombed in November 1940, the same night that David had died. Her legs had been crushed and after several operations she still needed crutches to get around. That meant she had not been able to come to Bloomsbury House very often. In many ways this was a relief to me. I liked and admired Elise Levy very much, but we both knew that given the circumstances of David's death we were unlikely to ever be close friends. It was a shadow always between us.

My cheeks were flushed with cold as I chained my bicycle to a bar set into the wall of the building and hurried up the snowy steps into Bloomsbury House's huge reception hall. The refugees sitting on the uncomfortable benches watched me hopefully as I entered. I walked past them and up the wide staircase to the second floor, where the JCPB had two tiny adjoining rooms.

When I entered the office Lore Rosenfeld, who managed the JCPB under the direction of Mrs Levy, looked up from behind a pile of papers and gave me a smile. Lore was a chatty lady in her late forties with a halo of wiry black hair. Like Mrs Levy, she was German by birth but had married an Englishman twenty-odd years before and had lived in London ever since. Behind her stood a row of metal filing cabinets, each containing a child's file. A life wrapped up in cardboard. Some of the files were pathetically small. The thickest were those of the children who had arrived in 1938. By the time the last children arrived, as Holland fell to the Nazis, there was often very little information to work with and an obviously emotionally damaged child.

'I have a real problem for you today,' she said, as I took off my hat and unwrapped my scarf. 'Leonhard Weitz.'

'Leonhard Weitz? I don't recall that name.'

She handed me a slim file. The photograph showed a boy with a thin white face, round glasses and a mop of dark hair. According to the identity slip he was eight years of age, and had come from Vienna. 'DOES NOT SPEAK' was printed at the bottom of the identification card in damning capitals.

'Is the child mute?' I asked. 'A medical disorder?'

Lore gave a brief shrug. 'Read the attached notes.'

They told a tragic story. Leonhard's father, a professor of anthropology at the University of Freiburg, had been deported to the Sachsenhausen concentration camp in 1937. The boy's mother died soon afterwards of illness and his two older brothers disappeared in unspecified circumstances in 1939. Leonhard had been recommended to the JCPB by his father's cousin, and he had arrived in England in April 1940.

In the view of the psychiatrist who examined Leonhard after his first foster-parents in Manchester sent him back, the boy had been deeply traumatised, possibly by witnessing the death of his brothers. Leonhard had not said a word since his brothers' disappearance, but there was nothing obviously wrong with his vocal cords. The psychiatrist had diagnosed 'elective mutism post-trauma'. It was recorded that Leonhard regularly wet the bed and was prone to outbursts of agitation that could become quite violent. A heart-breaking addendum noted: 'Played violin in the family quartet, and still enjoys listening to music.'

'So he can speak,' I said, 'but chooses not to do so?'

Lore shrugged again. 'The child is damaged in his mind.'

I checked the notes again. 'So... the big problem with him is that he's been sent back from the second set of foster-parents? Are there no other foster-parents available?'

'That's your job. Please go through all the records and see if anyone suitable comes up. Otherwise he must remain at the hostel.'

We both knew it would not be the best solution. A child so fragile would be unlikely to improve as one of many boys in a rowdy hostel.

I took off my coat and sat down at the smaller desk. 'I'd better get to work then,' I said.

# CHAPTER THREE

*Wednesday 1 January 1941*

We shouldn't have been in the house at all. It was the job of
the rescue squads to search bombed houses for casualties, but
during an air raid as intense as that one was, everyone pitched
in. Even the ambulance girls.

'You take her legs.' Maisie hooked her arms under the old
woman's shoulders. 'We should hurry. I think Jerry is coming
around to have another go at us.'

'He always does. So anxious to deliver Herr Goering's little
presents.'

The roar of the German bombers, no more than a few hundred
feet above us, was almost deafening. Adding to the din was the
thunder of the ack-ack guns in Hyde Park, London's attempt to
fight back. I knew Maisie was right: it wouldn't be long before
we'd hear the shrieks of falling bombs.

Our patient was, mercifully, unconscious.

Just as I took hold of the thin, lisle-encased legs, a ghastly
noise, like the sound of an animal in torment, seemed to rip
apart the air. We waited. The house shuddered as the bomb
landed nearby with a crash like thunder.

'That one was too close for comfort,' said Maisie.

'Let's get out, shall we? And at the double.'

We hoisted the pathetically light and fragile body and carried
it in a sideways shuffle towards the hallway. Half of the house
had been ripped away and what was left teetered alarmingly
above us as we picked our way down the stairs, navigating

through the debris by the light of the burning buildings across the street. Their rosy glow revealed a shining dark trickle of blood from the wound on the old woman's forehead, which gave me real concern. Head wounds were tricky, and I would have been happier if she were conscious. It was all too easy for someone to slip gently from a concussion into death.

At last we reached the street where the Air-Raid Precautions warden and our ambulance were waiting. We took care in lowering the old woman on to the stretcher that was laid out on the icy road and Maisie wrapped her in blankets against the chill of the freezing night air. I knelt to check her condition preparatory to placing her in the ambulance.

'Anyone left inside?' The ARP warden was a small man with a large moustache that was white with plaster dust. Under his steel helmet, his face was grotesquely streaked with plaster and sweat, giving him a ghoulish appearance. His breath puffed in the cold air as he spoke.

'I don't think so,' I said. 'We shouted out, but it was too dangerous to do a thorough search.'

The old woman's eyes fluttered open and she said, 'Bobby? Where's my little Bobby?'

Maisie and I exchanged glances and turned to look at the house behind us. It was already tottering. It wouldn't last long, and we both had a horror of being caught in a collapsing building.

'Who is Bobby?' I asked, my voice clipped and urgent. My cousin's six-year-old daughter, Roberta – a charmer with a cheeky grin, and auburn-haired like myself – was always called Bobby. 'Is Bobby your granddaughter? Grandson?'

The old lady's eyes had fluttered shut. I shook her gently. 'Tell us about Bobby.'

'My darling,' she murmured. 'Five years old—'

I was up and had bolted into the building before the end of the sentence, conscious only of one thought: *We had left a child in a collapsing building*. I ran up the stairs as quickly and lightly as I could, guided by the dull beam of my masked torch as it

18

flickered over the white glazed tiles on the staircase walls. When I reached the first floor a voice sounded in the darkness ahead of me.

'Hello, I'm Bobby. What's your name?' It sounded like an old woman, not a child, which was puzzling. My torchlight revealed an empty doorway. The door had been blown out by the blast and the room beyond had a curiously light feel to it, which I suspected meant that most of the walls were gone. So I entered carefully.

'Bobby?' I called.

'Hello, I'm Bobby.'

I ran the beam of my torch around what was left of the room. In a corner was a large cage, in which an almost entirely bald parrot cowered. Great tufts of grey feathers lay on the cage floor, and I assumed they had been plucked out in terror by the creature.

'Bobby?' I asked. I gave the creature a wry smile as I picked my way through the debris on the floor, heading for the cage.

'Hello, I'm Bobby. What's your name?'

'How do you do, Bobby?' I looked around warily. The walls were only just holding together. 'My name is Celia Ashwin.'

I hoisted the cage, which was not heavy but was bulky and difficult to manage, and began to retrace my steps.

The shriek of a falling bomb split the air apart.

We had been taught that a bomb travels at a speed of 150 miles an hour. Sound travels at 700 miles an hour. A bomb dropped from 20,000 feet will take about a minute and a half to land. The whistle we hear as it falls is made by the air resistance and begins about a minute after the bomb is released. So we have thirty seconds to find shelter before the bomb hits. Not enough time to get out of a tottering house carrying a parrot cage. I began to run, hampered as ever by my rubber boots and bulky waterproof. Bobby and I had just reached the staircase leading to the ground floor when the world pitched alarmingly.

*This is death*, I thought, and I fell into a pit of roaring oblivion.

\*

I opened my eyes to darkness, unable to take a proper breath. Something hard jabbed into my back, heavy objects pinned down my legs, chest and shoulders and my head throbbed and ached. At first I thought I must be in bed, having a nightmare. So I tried to sit up and struggle out of the dream, to will myself to wake up, but I couldn't move. Then I had the shocking realisation that the nightmare was real, that I had been bombed or the house had collapsed and I was entombed under the rubble. In that one startled moment everything in my mind was clear and still. *The impossible really has happened. I am going to die.*

Every sense was heightened: the utter darkness, the taste of dust in my mouth, its scent filling my nostrils, the pain in my back and legs and shoulders and head, the heavy silence. I tried to scream, but instead I coughed and gasped for breath.

'Oh God,' I whispered. 'Please don't let me die here alone.'

David had died like this, alone in a bombed house, his body crushed. *No, he had been already dead when the walls caved in on top of him.* I tried to take a breath and again was choked by the dust. *David.* Perhaps this was my punishment for leaving him to die alone.

A new prayer formed in my mind: *If I'm going to die, then please let it be quick.*

I slipped into a jumble of fragmentary dreams. I was in the stable yard at Goddings, my childhood home. It was a place I had loved, only now the horses were crowded around me so tightly that I was being suffocated by their big heavy bodies. I was dancing with David in the flat in Caroline Place, whirling around with him to the scratchy music of the phonograph, laughing and wishing we could dance to a real band in a nightclub because he was handsome and a good dancer and I loved him. But our affair was secret, and we could never be seen together in public. I rested my head on his shoulder and thought, *Just at this moment, I am happy.*

A voice, close at hand, screeched, 'Hello, I'm Bobby. What's your name?'

I seemed to emerge from a great distance. There was a brief sense of dusty blackness all around me and then I was again in the Goddings stables, struggling to escape from the press of horses that were suffocating the breath out of me. I tried to push them away, to shout at them, 'Get off me.' This triggered another violent fit of coughing. Panicked, I fought for breath between the coughs, until I crashed again into the void.

It was a spring morning and shafts of dappled light danced over the bright grass and lit the massed bluebells that marched up the bank into the forest. Sunshine sparkled on the water in front of me. The river flowed swiftly in the valley behind Goddings, the big old red house that seemed as old as time and was my home. Even at six, I knew it was the 'big house', the Manor, and when Father drove through the village the older men would touch their foreheads because he was so important. Father had dark-red hair. So did I, and my brother and my sister.

I had overheard Mr Fettiplace, the postman, say that you always knew a Palmer-Thomas by their red hair and the Devil's own temper. When I had told Nanny, she had said Saul Fettiplace should learn to mind his tongue.

Goddings was not visible from the glade but I knew it was just over the hill. Inside the house were Nanny, who I loved, and the servants, who were my friends. Helen, my sister and my enemy, also lived there. And, when he was not at school, so did my brother Tom. Father and Mummy lived at Goddings, but I feared Father, who was often angry, and I was in awe of Mummy, who was dark-haired and beautiful and always smelled divine. Nanny could be hugged, but Father and Mummy were rarely touched.

I examined the grey thing held firmly in my fist. It had been half buried in the damp earth beside the river. Something, a fox or a badger, had disturbed the soil and brought it to the surface. At first I had thought it was a buckle or a bit of scrap metal, but something drew me to look more closely. So I dipped it into the water and a small medallion was revealed, in the shape of an old-fashioned sailing ship with little people on the deck and on the high prow and bow. There was a ring at the top for attaching it to a chain.

'What's that?' Helen had come up behind me. Her hair glowed red in the sunshine

'It's mine,' I said, in my piping six-year-old voice. My hand closed over it and I raised my chin defiantly.

Helen and I existed in a constant state of war. As she was five years older, Helen usually won but I was not made for capitulation and would fight on until all hope was gone. This was usually when Helen went to Father for support. She was his favourite child. Tom and I knew this and accepted it. It formed a bond between us.

I jumped out of reach as Helen moved to snatch the object, but the stony ground beneath my toes and the cold touch of the water on my bare feet meant I was trapped. The river ran too fast for me to escape that way.

'It's mine,' I repeated, 'I found it.'

'It might be valuable.' Helen's voice was thick with self-satisfaction. 'We should show it to Father.' Quick as a striking snake, her hand darted out to grasp my arm. Helen's eleven-year-old strength was unassailable. Once she had the object she held it up close to her eyes.

'It's mine,' I wailed. 'I found it.'

Now Helen had it, the little grey medallion had become the most important thing in my life and I knew I would die if she did not give it back.

'Why is Celia crying? What is it?' Tom's voice cut through my howls. He slithered down the bank, heedless of the bluebells and of the state of his clothes, and in a smooth, decisive movement he snatched the object from Helen. He stared at it. 'It's a pilgrim badge,' he said.

My tears vanished. Tom was ten and I adored him with a fierce, possessive love. Tom would give the medallion back to me.

'I found it. There.' I pointed to the place to provide proof of its finding and thus of ownership. 'So it's mine.'

'Yes, it's yours if you found it,' he agreed, but he kept hold of the object and was examining it closely.

'What's a pilgrim badge?' Helen's voice was cold. She seemed not to care that Tom had the object, but I somehow knew how annoyed she was. 'It's an ugly old thing anyway.'

'It's hundreds and hundreds of years old,' said Tom.

'We must show it to Father if it's old.' There was a self-important note in Helen's voice. 'It might be valuable.'

I became anxious, fearful again of losing it.

Tom frowned at Helen. 'Celia found the badge and now it's hers. If I hear you've pinched it from her – or if you tell Father about it – then your coral beads will go missing. For ever.'

My hopes rose. Helen loved her coral beads much more than an ugly old pilgrim badge.

'I'll tell Father,' said Helen, through gritted teeth.

Tom shrugged. 'I don't care if you do. All I'll risk is a whipping, and I'm used to those at school. But you'll lose your beads.' His look hardened. 'For ever.'

'It's a piece of silly old junk anyway,' said Helen. As she flounced away she shouted back over her shoulder, 'I'll hide the beads where you can't find them.'

Tom called a warning after her, 'I'll find them.'

He peered down at the badge with a wistful look in his eyes. 'It's grand.'

'You can have it,' I said, because I loved my brother more than anything in the whole world, more even than my pony, Arrow, or my Labrador, Goldie.

'No.' He handed it to me. 'Finders keepers. It's yours, fair and square.'

I took it and held it close to see all the details. Each of the little men on the boat had beards and wore long robes. 'Are they the Wise Men?' I asked.

'They're pilgrims,' he said. 'It's a talisman. That means a good-luck charm. You keep it safe and it'll keep you safe. See you safely home.'

The scene shifted. I was crying in my bedroom. Helen had come in and was screaming, 'Hello, I'm Bobby.'

I didn't want to speak to Helen. She had pinched my arm when we were having tea with our parents and when I screeched Father had called me a stupid little fool and ordered me out of his sight.

'They hate you, you know.' Helen looked smug. 'Father thinks you're stupid and Mummy thinks you're ugly. They wanted another boy and they got a stupid ugly girl instead. Right now – right at this very moment – they are deciding whether to send you away and adopt a boy instead. I think they will.'

'No,' I screamed. 'I won't go.'

'Bye bye, Celia,' said Helen. 'It'll be so nice to have another brother.'

A voice rang out: 'Hello, I'm Bobby. What's your name?'

I emerged from darkness to find myself facing a red-carpeted staircase lined with stern-faced Yeomen of the Guard. I was in Buckingham Palace and it was the evening I was to be presented to the new King George VI and Queen Elizabeth. The royal couple were holding their first Court since the Coronation the month before, in May 1937. I was nervous, and struggled to keep my face fixed in the calm mask I had perfected over the years. *Head high, walk tall.* The bouquet of spring flowers in my right hand gave off a faint sweet scent as I fixed my eyes on the glittering headband of the debutante in front and ascended, step by terrifying step, hoping not to stumble. The gown I wore was beautiful, with broderie anglaise appliqued on a dark cream taffeta underskirt, but the bodice was tight as a corset and I found it difficult to breathe.

The long lace train was looped over my arm and was another worry. It was the veil of Alençon lace that had been worn by our mother at her wedding and it attached to my gown at the shoulders. When I was in the Throne Room it would trail the required eighteen inches along the floor behind me. Helen had been presented five years before and it had been her train also; she had warned me how slippery it was. I found it almost impossible to keep it steady over my long white glove that clung like a vice on to my arm. The kid gloves were an integral part of the outfit, and were designed to fit so tightly that I had despaired of ever getting them on. But Norton, my mother's maid, had the knack. With a fixed grimace, Norton had tugged the fine kid upwards until each glove finished halfway up my upper arms and then she deftly wielded a special buttonhook to close the line of tiny pearl buttons stretching up from each palm.

The slow, stately ascension of young women continued. I was uncomfortably conscious of my ungainly headdress of three ostrich feathers attached to a lace veil. A similar headdress was being worn by each of the two hundred debutantes that evening, but many of the feathers were rented and smelled quite musty. Ahead of me a girl sneezed, which made me want to giggle. The feeling soon passed. My head ached from the pins that kept the horrid thing fastened high and tight, but I kept the slight smile playing on my lips. I shifted my thoughts to imagining the bluebell glade in the early spring. I could almost feel the cool breeze off the river.

Months of preparation had culminated in this evening. It should have been a highlight of my life and yet I would rather have been anywhere else than in Buckingham Palace preparing to curtsey to the King and Queen. I hated that Father had been forced to spend a small fortune on my 'coming out'. He had insisted on telling me the mounting costs every time we had met in the last few months. Society expected him to spend the time and money to launch his youngest child on the world, but he didn't like it and he had made it perfectly clear that if I failed to perform exactly as required, he would find a way to punish me. Father's fits of temper were terrifying, and I was desperately worried at his veiled hints about the decrepitude of my beloved but now very old Labrador, Goldie. I suspected Goldie's life depended upon how I comported myself before the royal couple and the cream of London society that evening.

At the top of the stairs a powdered footman showed me into the White Drawing Room where I joined the other debutantes who sat in rows of gold chairs as they waited to be called. They were seated in order of importance, and therefore in order of presentation. As a mere 'honourable' daughter of a baronet, I was near the middle, and would have to wait while the more highly ranked debutantes were presented. I sat and settled my gown around me to reduce the possibility of creases. A light dance melody was being played by the Guards Band inside the Throne Room and it floated around us like a dream, but the tension in the room was almost palpable.

One by one, gorgeously gowned young women rose and walked self-consciously towards the doorway leading to the Throne Room. Again, I tried to escape in my imagination to the bluebell glade, but worry for Goldie and fear of my father's wrath kept intruding. So I sat still and maintained the slight smile that so infuriated Father when he bullied me, and I mentally practised the deep Court curtsey I would very soon need to perform faultlessly.

My moment came with a nod from one of the footmen. I stood, shook out my gown and walked to the doorway into the Throne Room, where my mother joined me. The Court usher scrutinised every detail of my appearance, and nodded. He lifted the train off my arm and arranged it carefully on the floor behind me. I handed over my pink Card of Command to the Lord Chamberlain, and my mother's name and then my name were announced.

'The Honourable Celia Palmer-Thomas.'

*Head high, walk tall.* The white and gold Throne Room was lit by six enormous rose crystal chandeliers, almost blinding in their brilliance. On either side of me were men in evening dress or uniform and women in gowns of satin, chiffon, tulle, and lace that shimmered with opalescent sequins, crystal and pearls. It was like entering into a dazzling dream. As I began my stately procession towards the dais at the end of the room, I saw a familiar face in the crowd. Cedric Ashwin, handsome in his formal attire, was smiling at me. He was a friend of my sister's and as usual I admired his social ease and effortless confidence. His smile was comforting, reassuring. I gave him a slight nod and continued my slow walk across the room.

The royal couple were seated on gold chairs on the dais. The King wore a scarlet and gold uniform. The Queen's gown was of deep golden brocade and her train of gold lamé and coloured sequins pooled on the floor by her feet. A tiara of diamonds and rubies was set on her dark hair and a necklace of diamonds and rubies hung around her neck.

My social future, and probably my beloved dog's life, depended on how I managed the next few minutes. I took a deep breath and forced myself into a trancelike calm. All that remained now was the curtsey, which I had practised innumerable times in the little dance studio next to Harrods, under the firm instruction of Miss Betty:

*Smile. Holding your bouquet low in front, sink down in front of the King. Put your weight on the right foot and your left foot behind. At the deepest point of the curtsey incline your head. Smile again as you rise, keeping your weight on the right leg. Remember to give a little kick to get your dress out of the way of your foot. Take three sliding steps to the right, all the while looking at the King and Queen. Smile. Repeat the curtsey, this time to the Queen. Give another discreet kick to ensure your skirt is free, then move slowly to a door on the far side of the Throne Room, without ever turning your back to the royal couple.*

I smiled and the Queen smiled back, but as I began to sink into the curtsey, a raucous voice was loud in my ear: 'Hello, I'm Bobby. What's your name?'

# CHAPTER FOUR

The world shifted. It was as if I was underwater, but when I tried to move, my body would not, could not obey me. I floated upwards from a great depth to realise I was not in the Throne Room. I was not in the stables or dancing with David or crying in my bedroom at Goddings. My father was dead. Tom and Nanny were dead also. And David. I lay buried in a bombed house and I was very cold.

As consciousness returned I wondered why I had dreamed of my presentation. How silly it all seemed now, that night in 1937. Now my country was fighting for its life, London was under constant attack and the glamorous world of parties and privilege was an age away, like Ancient Egypt. My presentation at Court was as far from the dirt and blood and human misery I had encountered in the past months as anything could possibly be.

I tried to move my legs. It was no good. I was trapped and most likely going to die. And if I died, who would mourn me? I had lost Nanny to a wasting disease when I was fifteen. She was the only real parent I had ever known, even if the world saw her as a mere servant. My brother Tom had died in June last year, drowned during the evacuation at Dunkirk. And David was gone also.

'Oh, God.' My voice was a sigh into the dusty darkness. 'I loved them best.'

My death would simplify matters. I wouldn't need to divorce Cedric, for one thing, and there would be no scandal. Helen and my mother would be upset if I died, but not heartbroken. *I am not loved, truly loved, by anyone.* The shadows closed in, great cold depths of them swirled below me and I began to drift down, into the velvety blackness.

'*You stop that right now. No defeatism. Don't you dare give up hope. It bloody well comes with the morning.*' It sounded like David's voice in my head, the drawl he adopted when he was supremely annoyed and refused to show it.

'David,' I murmured. Words drifted into my mind: *Weeping may endure for a night but hope cometh in the morning.* David was right. I must pull myself together. No defeatism! So I made a desperate effort to stop myself sinking any further into the abyss of loneliness and self-pity.

'Celia? Are you there, Ashwin?'

It was a woman's voice, coming from far up above me. I opened my eyes. A thin finger of light had pierced the darkness and I had a sharp tug of fear. I tried to call to her, 'Turn out the lights. They'll bring the raiders back,' but I was convulsed with another coughing fit. That caused the hammering in my head to become almost intolerable.

The woman said, 'I think she's down there. I hear coughing.'

With that, the fog in my brain cleared. They must have set up arc lights under tarpaulins. All rescue work had to be done under cover or risk the German raiders seeing the light and bombing the area again. Or was it sunshine? I couldn't hear the drone of aeroplanes. How long had I been trapped?

There was a scraping noise. Then sounds of careful movement, as if someone was cautiously removing rubble, stone by stone. The beam of bright light suddenly shifted to shine directly upon me and I winced and closed my eyes so now there was a red haze against my eyelids. My head was throbbing violently and with each throb an intense pain shot into my neck and shoulder. I felt flattened, swamped by the heaviness of the mud and plaster above me.

'She's here. We've found her.' The woman's voice held a note of triumph, but cracked to finish in a sob.

I recognised the voice. It belonged to Maisie Halliday.

29

'Bobby is a parrot,' I called to her, ignoring the pain it caused me to do so.

Maisie's pretty laugh floated down. Although it ended in another sob, it lightened the gloom.

'We know. The old lady told us just after you bolted inside. Then the house fell down.' There was another laugh, shakier. 'Bobby saved you. When we heard him calling out we knew where to look for you.'

'Hurrah for Bobby,' I said. My tone was mocking, but the parrot's name dissolved into a cough that seemed to split my head in two.

'How are you?' Maisie asked. 'You fell through into the cellar.'

'I'm a trifle hemmed in by masonry.'

'Try not to worry. We'll get you out. And the doctor's on his way.'

The cautious sounds of removing rubble began again. Voices, muttering and grumbling, became men's recognisably ferocious swearing at something that wouldn't budge. The sounds formed a backdrop to my struggle to keep conscious.

From what seemed to be a long way off Maisie shouted, 'Careful. Careful.' And then, 'Celia?'

'Yes,' I whispered.

Maisie's voice sharpened. 'Celia? Are you still with us?'

Ignoring the pain, I raised my voice to drawl, in a fair imitation of David's voice, 'Still here. A trifle bored, though. Send down a magazine, if you'd be so kind.'

Maisie's laugh gave me strength. It sounded so alive in the dusty darkness.

'The *Tatler*?' Maisie's tone was teasing. 'All you posh types devour the *Tatler*.'

'What else? I need to keep up. Oh, and I'd kill for a pink gin.'

'I'll send down some water.'

'Skinflint.'

A muffled conversation ensued between Maisie and someone behind her. There was relative silence for a while, with only little sounds around me, the squeaks and shuffles of shifting masonry, or perhaps rats. There were always rats on a bomb site. Maisie was surprisingly good at ignoring them, or shooing them away; Fripp screamed blue murder whenever she saw one. When I attended an incident I forced myself to imagine Ratty from *The Wind in the Willows*, a book I had loved as a child, and I tried to see the rats as an annoyance rather than a terror. Now I was trapped, the rodents became yet another horror. I didn't want rat bites to contend with on top of everything.

'The doctor's just arrived,' Maisie called out. 'He wants to get down to you, check on your condition. We're going to try to move some of this stuff to make way for him.'

Something shifted. The increased light revealed that I was buried almost to my shoulders in a mess of beams and planks. A big piece of stone or plaster lay across my chest and shoulders, pinning me down. I managed to pull my right arm free and give a smile and a little wave to those above.

'Atta girl,' a man shouted down. 'We'll soon have you out. Soon as we can. That's a promise.'

'Can you move your legs?' This man's voice was clear and cool and public-school inflected. Probably the doctor.

'No,' I called up. 'Has the All Clear sounded?'

'Local All Clear went an hour or so ago,' he replied, 'but they might return. It's only around five, a few hours yet until dawn. Hold on – I'm coming down to you.'

I began coughing again. Each cough brought a sharp, ragged pain that made my head seem to whirl and spin and my stomach lurch with nausea. I drifted into the dream of the horses suffocating me in the stable yard and was jerked awake by more shouts and swearing. I realised that someone, with infinite caution, was lowering himself through the wreckage towards me with the support of a rope fastened around his chest and under his shoulders. He was wearing an army uniform and a steel helmet and he was holding a bag that I assumed held first-aid gear. Inch by careful inch he came down, until at last he crouched beside me.

His face was obscured by the shadow of his helmet, and as he introduced himself there was a loud crash above us and I didn't hear his name.

'May I take your hand?' he asked. Now that he was beside me he sounded surprisingly young. 'I need to feel for your pulse.'

It was as if he were asking me for a dance. Hysteria bubbled up. I pushed it away and held out my arm, coated a chalky white with plaster dust. His touch was firm and sure as he pressed two fingers lightly on my wrist, staring at his watch under the beam of his slim torch.

'A bit quick,' he said, 'but strong.' His voice was briskly encouraging. 'You're doing very well. Now I need to shine my torch into your eyes. It won't take a moment.'

His fingers moved to my chin and he tilted up my head, holding it steady as he shone a bright thin beam into my eyes, left then right. My head jerked at the lancing pain it caused. He made a soft grunting sound and put a cool hand on my forehead. I winced at his touch. Torchlight moved across my head, and as he gently palpated my scalp it was all I could do not to cry out with the exquisite pain of it, but I gritted my teeth and submitted.

'You weren't wearing a tin hat?'

'I was. It must have come loose in the fall.'

'Any vomiting? Tingling in your arms or legs?'

'No. And no.'

'Cold?'

As soon as he mentioned it I shivered.

'Yes.'

'I'm not surprised. It's like an icebox in here.' He pulled a blanket out of the bag beside him and tucked it around my neck and free shoulder, making sure it was tight.

'Thank you.' Despite the blanket, I shivered again. 'Well, what do you think? Will I do?' I tried for a jocular tone but my voice was faint and to my annoyance, it quavered.

'You'll do very well,' he said, with a medical practitioner's impersonal, rather clinical, kindness. 'Your name's Cecilia? Is that right? Pretty name.'

I couldn't be bothered to correct him.

'Can you feel your legs, Cecilia?' he asked. 'Move them?'

I tried to push my legs against the crush of debris and felt the muscles flexing fruitlessly. Each movement caused jagged pain to shoot through my skull. 'Yes. I think my legs are working, but I'm wedged in tight. They are rather numb.'

'I don't think there's much blood loss,' he said carefully, 'but I can't tell how badly off you are without examining you properly. It's clear that you have a head wound and you seem feverish. Are you in much pain?'

'My head throbs a bit.'

'Is the pain very bad?'

'It's just a headache.'

He rooted around in the bag beside him. 'I'll give you a shot of morphine.'

'No.' My voice was sharp, imperative. 'Thank you, but I don't want morphine.'

His hands stilled. 'Why ever not?'

The sharp throbbing in my head made coherent thoughts difficult, so I took a minute before I replied, and hated sounding so hesitant when I did.

'I'd rather face it – death, pain, whatever comes – I'd rather face it head on. I don't want to fall asleep and drift into death without knowing about it.'

'I was only intending to give you enough to take the edge off. I don't want you falling asleep, not if I don't know the extent of your head injury.'

Now I felt like a fool. 'I won't fall asleep?'

He said, after a short pause, 'Many people would prefer to be asleep when it comes. Death, I mean.'

'"To cease upon the midnight with no pain",' I said softly, quoting Keats. 'I'm not afraid of death… In a way, I'd welcome

33

it, but...' My voice faded away as common sense reasserted itself. I could almost hear David's voice saying, '*Honestly, Celia, the role of martyr doesn't suit you at all. Take the bloody morphine.*'

I said to the doctor, 'It would simply take the edge off the pain?'

'Yes.'

'Then please.' I lifted my arm.

'Good decision,' he said, as he pushed back my sleeve. I felt the prick of the injection. 'Won't be long before the pain lessens.'

He had a beautiful voice. He sounded like David, only without the drawl David had often affected. Or was it Tom he sounded like? His voice was lighter in tone than Tom's or David's had been. I wondered how old he was.

A shout came from up above us and he tilted his head to look upwards. At last I saw his face. It was, disappointingly, only a vague outline smothered in plaster dust and I suspected that as long as we were together in the ruins he was destined to remain a ghostly figure beside me, a featureless wraith with a coolly kind voice.

He shouted back, up towards the light. 'She's not too bad, I think, but we'll need the heavy lifting equipment to free her. Let me know when it's all sorted up there.'

'You're sure about this?' someone called down. 'We can still haul you out.'

'I'm sure,' he replied.

'We'll leave one light on, under the tarpaulin. Is that enough?'

'It'll do.'

'Good luck.' The noises above us ceased, and the light dimmed.

'What's that about?' I asked.

'Technical difficulties.'

I had a vague feeling that I should be worried, but the morphine was making my head spin and just then some of the dust in the air caught in my throat. I coughed wildly. The pain it caused pushed all other thoughts out of my head. The doctor rooted around in his bag, brought out a canteen and poured water into a tin cup. He held my hand steady as I drank.

'It's the dust,' I said. 'I'm so tired of brick dust and the smell of cordite. I wish I was at home, breathing clean country air.'

'Where's home?'

I didn't answer for a moment as images of Goddings flooded into my mind. It was more a collection of buildings than a single house, all of them dating from different periods of history and set around two courtyards. The main wing had a Georgian facade, but everybody knew Goddings was much, much older.

'It's a beautiful old pile set up high, overlooking the Kentish Weald.' I took a shallow breath that ended in a sigh. 'The loveliest place in the whole world.'

'I'll take your word for it. I'm a Londoner, born and bred. My parents have a country place in Surrey, and it's pretty enough, but I miss Town like the devil whenever I'm away.'

I laughed. 'You sound like Da— a friend of mine. He loved London more than anywhere.'

'As the cliché says, tired of London, tired of life.'

'I'm a Londoner for the duration, but a Kentishwoman at heart. There is nothing more beautiful than fields of hops glowing gold under a full moon.'

'Oh, yes there is.' I heard the smile in his voice. 'Yellow London streetlights, in that blue hour just before sunset.' His tone became teasing. 'Seen one oust house, seen 'em all.' He was obviously trying to lift my spirits. I'd done the same with my patients in the ambulance. David had been expert at it.

I breathed a laugh. 'But you must admit that the Weald of Kent is utterly glorious.'

'I admit nothing of the sort. What about Hyde Park in autumn?'

'The Blean?'

'The what?'

'It's an ancient forest near Canterbury.'

'I suppose it's filled with fairies? Don't reply to that. If you say "yes" I'll worry. You do have a head wound, after all.'

I gave a gurgle of laughter. 'Canterbury Cathedral?'

'Compared to St Paul's? I think not.'

'Oh – oh, that's just ridiculous,' I said, in mock horror. 'They're apples and pears. What about the White Cliffs of Dover?'

He was quiet for a couple of beats, then said softly, 'I love the White Cliffs.' There was a quick laugh. 'But you can raffle your Kentish Weald. Give me Waterloo Bridge at sunset, when the setting sun sets the Thames ablaze. And all those lovely lines of red buses jammed at Oxford Circus.'

'Accompanied by that delicious reek of gasoline?'

'*Le parfum de Londres.*'

'You *are* mad.'

He gave a short bark of laughter. 'Quite possibly. I'm a Londoner, remember.'

'So you can take it.'

'Whatever Jerry throws at me,' he agreed. 'Bombs, bullets, firestorms, mines floating down on parachutes – all water off a duck's back to a Londoner.'

'Well, as I said, I'm a Londoner for the duration and I have come to love the city, but I miss Kent.' I smiled in the darkness. 'I do love the big red London buses, though. Somehow they are rather *human*, don't you think?'

'That's because they're filled with humanity. Good, bad and in-between. Just like London itself, really.'

He leaned across to give me another sip of water, and I realised the sounds of the rescue party had ceased. There was only the creak and clatter of settling debris around us. What I should have been hearing were men's voices, digging, heavy machinery.

'I don't understand why everyone has disappeared.' I was spooked, but forced myself to ask calmly, 'Why have they gone?'

'Well…' The doctor cleared his throat gently, then spoke quickly, obviously trying to play down the horror of what he had to tell me. 'They found a UXB in the house next door. They're not sure if the bomb is time-delayed or it simply didn't go off. They've called the bomb-disposal squad and I'm sure it'll all be sorted out shortly. That's what brought the house down around you, the impact when it fell. There was no explosion.'

It was as if I had been doused with water. 'Get out of here,' I hissed. 'Go. Now. Get away. Come back if you like, when it's safe. But *get out.*'

'I can't.'

'I'll be perfectly fine alone until it's sorted.' *Or until the bomb explodes and I die.*

'It's too late.'

'This is utter madness.' I said, with an attempt at cool assurance. 'There is no point in you dying here with me.'

His response was equally cool and assured. 'They need to haul me out on a rope and they've all gone away. So you're stuck with me, I'm afraid.'

'Why? Why would you send them away?'

'I'm a doctor,' he said, as if that explained everything. 'I came down to check on your condition. I told them I'd stay with you if you were conscious and in need of attention. You were, so I did.'

'But it makes no sense.' I hated the shakiness in my voice. 'You don't know me. You should have left once you knew I was fine.'

'That's not how it works. You're my patient now and you were in pain. When the morphine wears off you'll be in pain again. If you fall asleep you may not wake. It's better that I'm here.'

'But—'

'No buts. I'm here, and that's all there is to it.'

'Someone to watch over me? Just like the old song?'

He laughed. 'I suppose you could put it that way.'

I felt ashamed to have been ungracious to someone who was risking his life to help me. 'Thank you,' I said.

'Not at all.'

I yawned. 'I'm very sleepy.'

'You mustn't fall asleep. Talk to me.'

'Like Scheherazade? Tell you tales?'

'Tell me stories if that's what you want. Although I'd rather hear about you.' His voice changed, became carefully non-committal. 'Why would you welcome death? You said that, earlier.'

I hesitated, then told him. Perhaps it was the morphine loosening inhibitions, or perhaps it was simply because his voice was sympathetic, but I told him the truth. I hated how pathetic it sounded, but it was the truth.

'Everyone I really cared for is dead. Tom, my brother, last June. My nanny died some years ago, and – and the man I loved died two months ago. Some say we'll meet those we love again after we die. I want to meet them again.' My voice fell away into the darkness and immediately I wished the words unsaid. So I tried to laugh them off. 'That sounded awfully mushy, didn't it? It's this situation. It's playing on my nerves.'

'You have no other family?' There was not even a hint of sympathy in his voice, which was oddly comforting.

'A sister. My mother.' *A husband I despise.*

'They'd miss you.'

'They'd be sad, perhaps, but wouldn't really miss me. Not for long, anyway. Perhaps not at all.'

'Now that does sound like self-pity.' His voice was crisp, matter of fact.

'Actually, it's true,' I said, incensed. My mother had always enjoyed a mindless whirl of social activities more than her children, and I had an odd relationship with Helen.

'But you don't want to hear about my troubles.' My voice had become brisker, no-nonsense, more like myself. 'Might I have some water, please?'

He put the cup to my lips and I sipped. 'Do you love your parents?' I asked him.

'Very much. I had a happy childhood.'

'I rarely saw my parents, but it wasn't an unhappy childhood by any means,' I said. 'I adored my nanny, and I was left to my own devices on the whole because Father had fixed ideas about children, who were to be seen rarely and heard less. And so I spent a great deal of time giving my latest governess the slip and roaming around the Kentish countryside with my dog or on my pony. The servants kept an eye on me when they could.'

What I had hated the most about my childhood was that each afternoon when my parents were at home Nanny would dress me up in my best frock and brush my hair until it crackled with electricity and then I would be trotted out to spend half an hour with Father and Mummy. How I had hated those afternoons.

'Father preferred my older sister Helen to me or Tom,' I went on, 'even though Tom was the heir.'

'I had a brother who was the favourite,' said the doctor, but I could hear the indulgent tone behind the words. 'That was because he was quite ill as a child. I never minded. Just accepted it as the right order of things. My parents tried to hide it, but I knew.'

'Oh, my father made no secret of his preference for Helen.'

He used to say I must be his, with my red hair and blue eyes, but it was a mystery how he could have sired such a gauche and stupid child.

'You were afraid of your father?'

I breathed a laugh and the story came bubbling out, as if I had no control of my tongue. I thought later that it must have been the morphine because I am on the whole a very close-lipped woman.

'Terrified. He died last year, and I really shouldn't speak ill of the dead, but my father could be quite cruel. When I was about eight years old I began to bite my fingernails and he was furious.'

He had raged at me, telling me all a woman had was her beauty and charm, and what hope was there for a scrawny little fool like me, if my hands looked like that?

'So he took to inspecting my hands,' I went on, 'whenever Helen and I joined him and Mummy for tea. And if he thought I'd been nibbling my nails, he would hit me once on each palm with his riding crop. If I cried, he would hit me twice. I learned not to cry.'

Tom had taught me how to hide my fear and misery. 'You can't show him how you feel,' he had told me. 'You have to keep it inside and you have to make your face calm, no matter how bad it is.'

'But I can't,' I had wailed. 'I can't pretend it's not hurting me.'

'He'll just hit harder if you cry or if you seem afraid. What I do when the Head gives me six at school is to pretend I'm somewhere else. Somewhere lovely. What's your favourite place in all the world?'

'The bluebell glade, where I found the pilgrim badge.'

'Imagine you are in the bluebell glade. *Be* in the bluebell glade. Smell the flowers, and the grass, hear the river, feel the wind. And keep your face like this –' he had showed me a very serious, unemotional face '– like a mask. And keep it like that, no matter what.'

Gradually, I had learned not to cry when Father hit me, and over the years I learned to keep my face calm – *head high and walk tall* – no matter what provocation I was given.

Beside me, the doctor shifted. 'Did you stop biting your nails?'

'Eventually.'

'Your brother sounds like a decent sort of chap.'

I gasped. 'Did I tell you that? I can't get clear in my head what I say out loud and what I only think. God, I hate morphine. Tom was more than nice, he was simply lovely. He died at Dunkirk.'

I had given him the pilgrim badge to keep him safe, but it hadn't saved him.

The doctor cleared his throat. 'I was at Dunkirk. Perhaps I treated him.'

'The boat he was on was blown up. He fell into the water and was drowned.'

'The miracle was that so many of us did get back.' The doctor took a deep, shuddering breath that ended in a cough.

'How did *you* get back?'

'I was with one of the last groups to escape,' the doctor said slowly. 'I spent three days travelling with an ambulance-load of wounded. We had missed the last hospital train, so I was trying to keep four men alive without morphine or fresh bandages. We had nothing to eat and little to drink and it was a slow journey along roads choked with burnt-out vehicles and civilians, mostly women, some old men, children. All fleeing the Germans.

'We ended up at La Panne,' he continued, 'which is a beach a little to the north of Dunkirk. It was choked with British and French soldiers, on the sand and in the water, waiting to be evacuated. The Messerschmitts and Stukas were relentless, dive-bombing, machine-gunning us.'

His voice rose, became angry. 'They said I had to leave my wounded patients for the Germans to find. I was told they'd be taken prisoner, but they'd be looked after.' He paused, went on almost in a whisper. 'I have no idea if those men lived or died. We'd spent days together and I'd kept them alive, and then I had to leave them to the mercy of the enemy.'

I could hear the pain in his voice and I wanted to comfort him somehow, but I didn't know what to do. There was a moment of silence, until he cleared his throat. 'And that was my time at Dunkirk,' he said.

'How did you escape?'

'In a grubby oyster dredger called the *Valiant*. It was built for six men to haul in the nets, but the crew shoehorned dozens of soldiers into her and we set off for England. She wasn't built for the open sea and rolled like a pig, so we were all seasick. Then the engines went dead halfway across the Channel and I thought the game was up...'

'What happened?'

'Along came the Ramsgate Lifeboat and it towed us back to England. Out of the mist loomed the White Cliffs, and it was as if I'd been reborn.'

'And because of that they are the only bit of Kent that you love.'

'I was teasing you. Kent is very beautiful. It's just that I like London best.'

I drew in a breath to speak but choked and coughed instead. He poured water into the tin cup, took my chin in one hand and held the cup to my lips with the other. His hand on my face was cool and steady, and as I drank I thought that I had not felt as comfortable with a man since David had died. I felt as though I had known this doctor all my life.

And then I told him who I was.

# CHAPTER FIVE

'I didn't quite catch your name before,' I said. 'Mine's Celia, actually, not Cecelia. Celia Ashwin.'

'Celia Ashwin?'

All at once it was as if a distance had opened between us, far more than the few inches that separated our bodies. Ashwin was an uncommon and damnably well-known name.

'Cedric Ashwin is my husband,' I said flatly. Over the years I had perfected a facade of indifference. I made my voice expressionless as I said, 'I don't agree with my husband's politics.'

The doctor replied in a brisk and business-like tone, 'I'm glad to hear it, because his views are abominable.' He paused, and said, 'Please, call me Simon.'

'Dr Simon? Or just Simon?'

He gave a soft laugh. 'Just Simon. Everyone uses first names nowadays. It's all quite informal and comradely in the Blitz … Celia.'

'Except in Air-Raid Precautions. We use surnames only.' The pain was easing, and left me light-headed and dizzy in its wake, so I spoke without thinking. 'I wish my name wasn't Ashwin. I want to divorce Cedric, but he won't let me. He should damn well let me divorce him.'

The sharp indignant note in my voice made me sound like my mother, I realised with some horror. David had called that tone my 'hoity-toity' voice.

'Because it doesn't suit you any more to be married to a well-known fascist?' There was contempt in Simon's reply and it enraged me.

'Because I don't agree with any of Cedric's views,' I retorted. 'I don't know I ever did agree with them, not really. But I certainly don't agree with them now.'

I found myself talking in a fast, high voice as the morphine again released my inhibitions.

'I don't love Cedric. Not like David. And I'd never – not until I met David – never – despite Cedric running around with half of—'

I stopped speaking, horrified at what I'd said.

'Oh, God, I hate morphine,' I drawled, trying to sound coolly indifferent to what I'd revealed. 'That was all tommyrot, of course. Please forgive me, I'm raving.'

'Not at all,' he murmured.

We were silent for a while. My eyelids drifted shut and my head began to whirl. 'You lied,' I said. 'I'm falling asleep.'

'Don't do that. You must try to stay awake. Talk to me.' His voice became sharper, more insistent. 'You're a young and beautiful woman with a life ahead of you and I'm not about to let you die here. Keep talking, dammit.'

'What do you want me to talk about?'

'Anything. But don't fall asleep.' His tone was again coolly unemotional, entirely professional.

'Thank you for staying with me,' I said. 'I'm glad I'm not alone. David died alone.' My voice became bitter. 'And I let his parents suffer for weeks, not knowing what happened to him. I'm trying to atone for that. I try so hard. I work with his mother's charity, and… Oh, I *am* raving.'

Silence fell between us again, but I was more awake now and I listened to the little sounds of the wrecked house. The small slithers and the creaks of settling debris. I thought again of rats, and shivered.

'I should have brought another blanket,' he said. 'I could give you my tunic.'

'No. Please. I'm fine. It's not the cold, it's something else. Thank you for being here with me, Simon.'

Again there was silence.

'Why did you say I'm beautiful?' I asked, to take my mind off the rats. And to hear his voice again because it was lonely, when he was silent. 'You said I was a young and beautiful woman. My face is smothered in plaster dust and you've shone your torch exactly once in each of my undoubtedly bloodshot eyes. How could you possibly know what I look like?'

He breathed a laugh. 'You're quite famous, you know. Cedric Ashwin's young and beautiful auburn-haired and aristocratic wife, the darling of the social set, who drives an ambulance in the Blitz.'

There was contempt in his voice, or I thought there was, and suddenly I was furious.

'You don't know me,' I said hotly. 'There's no need to be unkind, just because of my husband.'

He said nothing for a little while and the silence settled around us like a shroud.

'I didn't mean to be unkind,' he murmured. 'You are well known, though. And much photographed.'

'When I was presented in 1937 my photo appeared in most of the newspapers,' I admitted. 'I was Celia Palmer-Thomas then. Cecil Beaton photographed me holding a dove and the picture showed up everywhere.'

'How glamorous.'

I gave a little choked laugh. 'Not really. The blasted dove wouldn't keep still. It may have looked angelic, but let me tell you, that bird had a devilishly nasty bite. I've a scar on my finger I'll carry for life.'

There was amusement in his voice as he replied, 'I'm sure it was worth it for the picture.'

'I hate that picture. I look like a halfwit, with my mouth slightly open and gazing rather vacantly into space. The worst of it was that it turned me into a commodity.'

The *Sunday Express* had dubbed me 'The Loveliest Debutante of 1937', writing: 'The Honourable Miss Celia Palmer-Thomas enjoys the twin blessings of beauty and elegance; with a classic oval face, dark-blue eyes and auburn hair, her smile is like a Lely court beauty.'

My sister had been annoyed by the articles, my mother embarrassed, and my father enraged. Tom had laughed and said it would have been more honest to have written: 'Miss Celia Palmer-Thomas is now on the marriage market. Who's the first bidder? Old family, well connected, but not much money. How much for her pretty face?'

'A commodity?' Simon asked.

'People asked me to allow my picture to be used to sell things in magazines. Face cream, stockings, lingerie, even marmalade.'

'And did you?'

'Of course not. I don't like marmalade.'

'I must say, yours sounds like a charmed life,' he said. 'Being presented at Court before the King and Queen, dancing with the good and the great at balls and receptions, attending Ascot, Henley.'

'Don't forget Finals Day at Wimbledon, the Eton and Harrow match at Lord's, the Air Pageant.' I made my voice light, flippant. 'And every first night on the West End, with dinner somewhere first and supper somewhere else afterwards.' I gave a laugh that became a cough. 'I can't believe I managed to survive it all.'

How could I explain, especially to a man, how much hard work it had been, that frenzy of carefully organised gaiety? I had been a gauche country girl, who had felt out of place and unhappy throughout the seemingly endless round of social events, and who had been given little support by her mother or sister. Helen had been seeking a husband of her own and didn't want me around her when she did so, and my mother felt that she'd 'done her bit' merely by presenting me at Court.

'It sounds more exciting than it was,' I said. 'I was scared to death I'd do something wrong.'

Men told me I was beautiful. Beautiful! I had grown up being told I was scrawny and stupid and unwanted. Nanny loved me, but she detested vanity. She would say if she saw me looking at my reflection, 'Who would want to look at *you*, my girl?'

I had felt I was a fraud. I had been terrified the mask would drop and they would all realise I was not elegant or self-assured. And then they would laugh at me and I would be sent away in disgrace. As a result, my manner was stiff and coolly reserved and I had not 'taken'. Apparently I have a stare that can freeze a man at ten paces and I was soon dubbed 'the Ice Queen'. That was why I had been drawn to the older men, who were not put off by my cool exterior. Cedric was soon my favourite because he never once told me I was beautiful. His nickname for me was 'Funny Face' and I had liked him for it.

'How old were you?'

'When I came out? Eighteen. I was presented at the first evening Court of 1937, to the new King and Queen. That was my first disappointment. I had so wanted to meet the Prince of Wales – I mean King Edward – but he had abdicated in December.'

'Why ever did you want to meet *him*?'

I laughed. 'Oh, I don't know. Because he was charming and handsome, I suppose. And it was so romantic that he gave up so much for the woman he loved.'

'He was an idiot,' said Simon.

'Don't you believe in that sort of love?' I was genuinely curious.

'What sort of love?'

'Oh… the selfless sort, I suppose. Where you'd risk anything, give up everything for the one you love. He gave up the crown, after all.'

'He had a more important duty to his people, and he chucked it all away for that American divorcee.'

'For love,' I insisted. 'He did it for love.' I raised my voice slightly to declaim: '"I cannot carry the heavy burden of responsibility and discharge my duties as King as I would wish to do without the help and support of the woman I love."'

'You memorised his abdication speech?' Simon didn't bother to hide his amusement.

'I have that sort of memory.'

An image of David came unbidden, along with the sharply painful realisation that our love hadn't been strong enough to cope with the difficulties we faced. We had been unwilling to contend with social and family disapproval. *We were together only two months.* Maybe with more time I would have found the courage. But it was not only me who was unwilling. David had not wanted to face his family's displeasure at finding out he was in love with a Gentile. *We were both cowards in our way.*

'I disagree.' Simon's tone was sharp. 'Was it cowardly for David to put his family first?'

'I spoke out loud?' I said, horrified.

'David was Jewish.'

'Yes.'

Simon's face remained hidden in the gloom, but his voice was crisply insistent. 'It would have been more than *difficult* to explain you to his family. You are a Gentile who is married to a notorious fascist. How could your love affair ever have ended happily? Did you expect him to abdicate from being Jewish?'

'Of course not.'

The quaver in my voice must have given me away. Simon lifted the cup of water to my lips and again held my face in a cool, steady grip as I sipped. A memory came of a conversation I'd had with David about his religion, a week or so before he died.

'My family attends synagogue on the high holidays,' he had said, 'but it's more for social reasons. We've never been devout or particularly observant.' He'd smiled then, the smile that made my heart sing. 'We have raisins only in our Christmas pudding.' Then he'd shrugged. 'My parents sent me to Harrow, remember, not to a yeshiva. I don't wear the yarmulke except in synagogue, and I haven't been to synagogue for over a year.'

'But, although you don't go to – to synagogue very often, you still feel Jewish?'

'I *am* Jewish. It's not about religion so much as—'

'Don't say race,' I had interrupted him hurriedly. 'That's how Hitler justifies his treatment of your people.'

'I was going to say it's about belonging. But you put it neatly: they are my people.' He had shrugged and repeated, 'I am Jewish.'

I pushed away the tin cup. 'Anyway, that's enough of me. Tell me about yourself, Dr Simon.'

'It's you who are supposed to be talking. I need you to stay awake.' He paused. 'My brother – my parents' favourite – he died recently. We were very close, only a year apart in age. More like twins.'

'I'm sorry to hear it. Really, I am so sorry.'

We were silent for a little while, both lost in memories.

'It's an odd relationship, isn't it?' I said eventually. 'Siblings, I mean. So much shared. So much of who you are comes from your childhood, and you spent it with your siblings. Tom was four years older, and all my life he was my steady guiding light. My Pole Star. I miss him terribly.'

'And David?'

I jerked in surprise at the question, then said slowly, 'David was a new sun in my sky. He outshone everything. It was so intense. I had never…' I said, with an attempt at flippancy, 'Oh, I don't know how to describe what I felt for David. It all seems like a dream now. Adoration? Love is too steady a word for what we had.' The pain of the memory was suddenly overwhelming. 'Please, I don't want to talk about David.'

'Talk about Cedric Ashwin, then.'

'He is a womanising bully. Just like my father, I now realise, except Cedric's bullying is through charm and my father rarely bothered. Cedric played me for a fool and I let him do so because I didn't know any better.'

'Oh, come off it, you married the man.' Simon's voice was harsh, and the bitterness in it shocked me. 'You can't tell me he didn't discuss his political views with you. They were a part of the man he was. The man he is still, because those vile pamphlets he wrote keep popping up all over London. You were eighteen – yes, that's young, but the soldiers I treated in France, and more recently in North Africa, were just as young and they had volunteered to be there. Eighteen-year-olds are fighting the Nazis as we speak. Eighteen-year-old Jews are being shot by the Gestapo in Poland. Even at eighteen you should have known what sort of man you were marrying. You can't—'

Simon fell silent. I was stunned at his vehemence, and hated my own vulnerability, trapped in the dark with him, unable to move. It was obvious that he hated all that my husband stood for and, by default, he hated me, too. The pamphlets Simon had spoken of were ones Cedric had penned before the war and his supporters continued to publish them. 'This is a Jews' War', 'The Jewish Conspiracy Against You' and 'The British: A Hoodwinked People' were some of the titles.

I tried to move my legs but they were still trapped, and my left arm and chest were similarly held in a vice grip by the ruins.

Simon gently cleared his throat. 'That *was* unkind and I apologise.' His voice was hesitant, contrite.

I drew in a breath, and although I wasn't sure why I should do so, I tried to explain.

'What Cedric was saying – about Jews, about the best way to run Britain – it was no different from what my father had said when I was growing up. What Cedric believed was what I had been taught to believe. I was young, naive, and Cedric seemed to be everything I wanted... And then I met David.'

Again Simon cleared his throat and seemed about to speak, but I forestalled him.

'In two months with David, all I thought I knew about the world, all I thought I was, had changed. It was David who changed me.'

Simon gave a bark of mocking laughter. It was shocking after my confession.

'Don't make more of it than it was,' he said. 'You were a married woman who had a fling with a good-looking man. It was a tawdry affair. That's all.'

My chin came up and there was as much ice in my voice as I could manage: 'It was not tawdry. You don't know me, or David. How dare you judge us?'

A cracking sound rent the silence and I flinched, certain the bomb had exploded. Instead, light poured in from the widening hole above us.

'All sorted next door?' Simon called out.

A northern-accented voice replied, 'Aye. All sorted. It was a big 'un. Thousand pounder with a delayed fuse. Bomb squad fixed it. Nowt to worry about now, Doc.'

Relief threatened to overwhelm me, but I was determined not to cry. Not in front of the doctor, who had been so cruel. *Head high, walk tall.* Only I couldn't help flinching when bits of plaster showered down on top of me, dislodged by rescue workers as they removed lumps of rubble and bricks. I flinched again as Simon leaned towards me.

'Not long now,' he murmured. He used his body to protect me from the falling debris.

More rubble fell, and the noise of the rescue increased. Northern voice called down, 'You all right, Doc? How's the patient?'

'We're both fine. Keep going. The sooner she's out now, the better.'

Simon took hold of my wrist and rested two fingers lightly on my pulse. I closed my eyes, too exhausted to keep them open.

'Try to stay awake,' he said. He was still holding my wrist, but I could not summon the energy to tell him to let go.

'Hurry up, if you can,' he called out sharply to those above.

'Doing our best,' was the gruff reply. A London accent this time. 'You don't want the whole blooming lot down on top of you, do you?'

I began to drift. Simon pinched the skin between my thumb and forefinger.

'Ouch!'

'Keep awake.'

'You enjoyed doing that.' My voice was indignant, and he gave a low chuckle as he shook his head.

The noises around us increased. Simon moved away to allow the rescuers to crouch beside me and begin the slow process of lifting bomb debris off my body. Chains attached to a portable crane were let down and used to lift away the heavier pieces.

'I'll see you up top,' Simon said, and gave a shout to the men above, who pulled him up the pile of wreckage, using the rope that was still looped around his chest. He was heading for the light. I felt surprisingly lost and alone without him.

'Nearly there,' said the northern voice, who was now a burly shape beside me in the gloom. 'Nearly free, lass.'

The pieces of debris that pinned me down were removed, one by one. When the final, largest piece was pulled away from my chest the sudden sense of lightness and freedom made me feel as if I had been reborn.

Then I was lifted up and passed from one pair of arms to the next until I was shivering on a stretcher in cold morning air, surrounded by men in dusty overalls, who smiled at me and told me everything was grand.

'You were near to heaven last night, love,' said one of them. 'I bet you heard them harps playing.'

Pale sunlight lit the scene. Hope had indeed come with the morning. Maisie Halliday was there, tucking blankets around me and wiping my face with a damp flannel. She had been crying but was trying valiantly to smile.

'You're a lucky one,' she said, as she turned her head away to dash away the tears. 'I'm sorry to be so sloppy, it's just that...' She sniffed, and turned back towards me with a smile.

I managed a smile. 'You look rather blurred, Halliday. And what's more, you appear to be bobbing up and down. Or is that me?'

She managed a laugh. 'It's you. The doctor will be here soon, for a last check-over and then I'll get you to hospital.'

'The doctor...' I paused, unsure what I wanted to ask about the doctor called Simon.

'Oh, isn't he simply marvellous? Went down to check on you even though he'd been told about the bomb in the next house. And then he refused to leave you there alone. He's an army doctor, helping out.' She smiled. 'And what an amazing coincidence—' Maisie glanced up. 'Here he comes.'

My heart raced as I watched him walk across the rubble towards us. Things did seem rather blurry but they sharpened as he approached. My rescuer was revealed to be a man of average height, dark hair, slim build. His thinnish and finely boned face had an air of frowning abstraction I was willing to put down to tiredness. This slender, studious-looking man had stayed beside me for hours in the face of an unexploded bomb. War made unlikely heroes.

'How's the patient?' he asked Maisie. His eyes were dark and straight black eyebrows lent him a stern expression.

'She says things are a bit blurred.' Maisie gave him a bright smile that he did not return.

Instead he nodded, knelt beside me without a word and took my hand to check my pulse. Again he shone his torch into my eyes, but this time I did not flinch.

Maisie smiled, touched my shoulder and stood up. 'I have to check on the ambulance, but I'll be back in two ticks to take you to hospital.'

As she walked away the doctor and I regarded each other. His eyes were grave, sombre even. I said, simply to say something, 'I want to thank—'

'Please don't,' he interrupted. 'I was just doing my job.'

I realised then I would know his voice anywhere, after so many hours together in the dark. It was a little rougher after our ordeal, but still cool and professionally disinterested. My gaze fell to the Royal Army Medical Corps insignia on the shoulder of his khaki tunic, which sat below the two pips that showed he was a lieutenant. The caduceus, a pair of snakes entwined around a winged staff, had been the doctors' emblem since the time of ancient Greece. *That's why he stayed with me. Because he takes his calling seriously, even if he despises me.*

'How many fingers am I holding up?'

'Three.' I looked up at him, into a face I had never seen before. 'And you have two eyes and one nose, all in correct position. Nothing is blurred any more.'

A faint smile touched the corner of his mouth and suddenly I realised what the frown and professional detachment had disguised before. He was young, only a few years older than myself. A newly minted doctor. Although he had the face of a stranger, there was something familiar in the curve of his lips, the wry, self-mocking expression, the shape of his nose and the angle of his jaw.

My heart thumped painfully. Maisie had mentioned a coincidence. David had two brothers... and Simon had spoken of his brother.

'Simon?' I whispered. 'Simon Levy?' That was the name of David's brother, the youngest of the three, the one who had joined up in 1939 as soon as he finished his medical training.

'Yes,' he said, before standing in one quick movement. 'David mentioned me?'

I nodded and tried to swallow, but my mouth was too dry. 'He was very proud of you,' I croaked. 'Simon, I am so sorry. So very sorry.'

His eyes were fierce, his mouth set in a firm uncompromising line. Then he looked away and drew in a deep breath. 'My parents tell me they've forgiven you. That you've sincerely and honestly apologised for the hell you put them through and you are attempting to atone by helping my mother with her refugee children. They said I should forgive you also, with a sincere mind and a willing spirit, as we're taught to do. I – you have no idea how much I hated you.'

I tried to reply, but no words came. Simon Levy turned to survey the destruction around us. There was tension in the way he held his shoulders and a tightness around his eyes. He cleared his throat.

'The Talmud says, "Whoever saves one life saves the world entire." It is ironic that I should, perhaps, have saved yours.' He looked down at me, frowned. 'I thought you'd be older, or at least seem older. I thought you'd be...'

'You thought I'd be a *femme fatale*?'

Again, a smile touched the corner of his mouth. 'Perhaps I did. I still wish to God David had never met you, but at least some good has come out of the night.'

'What good?' I whispered.

'I don't hate you any more.' He called out, in a brisk voice, 'She's ready for transfer.'

The stretcher-bearers hoisted me up with a cheery, 'Thanks, Dr Levy.'

'You're light as a feather, miss,' the one at the front said as they carried me to the waiting ambulance. 'Makes a pleasant change.'

'Dr Levy?' I let my voice trail away.

'Marvellous feller, Doc Levy. Got sent home from North Africa some weeks ago – he's with the Medical Corps, of course – but he's always helping out at these incidents. D'you know him, miss?'

'I knew his brother.'

# CHAPTER SIX

'Will there be a scar?' My sister gestured towards the bandage on my head.

'I have no idea.'

'Shame if it does scar,' said Roly, her husband. 'Couldn't wear those pretty hats you gels seem to like so much.' He nodded at Helen, who was wearing a little straw number perched on the side of her head. 'No use at all on a windy day, but dashed pretty, what?'

Brigadier Roland Markham, currently serving in the War Office and a close friend of Winston Churchill, was some twenty years older than Helen. He delighted in treating women with the sort of gallantry that had been outmoded even when he was a young man. He had always been more our father's friend than ours, but when Helen failed to snare a suitable husband by the time she was twenty-five she had accepted Roly's offer and their elaborate wedding had taken place two months before war was declared. They seemed happy enough together. Roly adored Helen, who bossed him relentlessly and spent his money freely, but in return gave him a comfortable and well-managed home. I knew that she tried her best to be her idea of the perfect wife.

They had offered to put me up until I was fully recovered, but I had steadfastly maintained that I wanted to return to my flat. And so they had dropped me back when I was discharged from hospital two days later.

Helen and I had never been close – she was too bossy for that – but it was hard to shake off twenty-two years of sibling rivalry and, I suppose, sisterly affection. She liked to keep an eye on me, and I allowed her to do so. When Cedric had been imprisoned, most of my friends had slipped away but Helen, and Roly at her insistence, had continued to support me publicly.

'I don't know why you insist on remaining with the Auxiliary Ambulance Service,' said Helen peevishly. 'Roly can easily get you a position with the Princess Royal's Volunteer Corps.'

I glanced at Roly, who had turned away to stare fixedly out of the window. I put him out of his misery.

'You know I applied to the FANYs, but they rejected me because of Cedric,' I said. 'I asked if I could join the ATS to drive ambulances. I applied to the Wrens and to the WAAF. Everyone rejected me. Oh, they gave me various excuses, but clearly it was because of Cedric.'

But, Roly could—'

'No, Helen,' I said sharply. A thin, needling pain began to drive into my head like a dentist's drill and I lost my patience. 'He can't. It's unfair to expect Roly to compromise himself to get me into a service that doesn't want me. The Auxiliary Ambulance Service is doing a marvellous job in this Blitz and I'm staying put.'

'Cedric would not be compromising himself. Everybody who counts knows how silly it was to incarcerate Cedric. Locking him up like a common criminal, simply for holding beliefs that all of our friends held before this war. It's outrageous.'

'But Cedric *continued* to hold those beliefs,' I replied wearily, because Helen and I had had this conversation innumerable times before, 'even after it was clear that Hitler was a dangerous lunatic and Mussolini a pompous braggart. Even once war had been declared, Cedric still wanted an alliance with Germany and Italy. How could the government ignore that?'

Helen sniffed. 'At least Cedric is not a hypocrite,' she replied, and tossed her hair in a gesture that was so like her when she was a fractious child that I couldn't help smiling.

'I don't see what there is to grin about,' she said. You scarcely bothered to put pen to paper for poor Cedric. He's been terribly upset about how little you contacted him. You'll have to work hard to regain his affection when he returns.'

'I want to divorce him,' I replied flatly.

Roly continued to stare out of the window.

'Don't be ridiculous,' said my sister.

I had been discharged from hospital upon the firm instruction that I rest in bed for a week. After Helen and Roly left the flat I sat on the couch and stared at the wall for a moment or two. Next I picked up a novel that Helen had lent me and flicked through a few pages. Then I telephoned Jack Moray at the ambulance station, to tell him I was fit for duty and would be returning to work the following day.

I am not sure I can explain why I did so. Someone who knows about such things told me some time later that I was probably still concussed. Maybe so, but I suspect it was because the idea of a week to myself in my flat, tormented by the vivid memories of the time I had spent trapped in the darkness, was intolerable. I hated to be inactive. Since David's death, I had been unable to sleep unless exhausted by physical effort. And I felt peevish after Helen's visit.

Looking back, all I can say is that I was not thinking clearly enough to accept I was not fit to work. So I decided to carry on. 'Business as usual', just as Churchill required. It was a decision I came to regret.

At seven o'clock the following morning, I pulled on a knitted helmet and wrapped a thick woollen scarf around my head to cover my mouth and nose as some protection against the cold. The All Clear sounded as I collected my bicycle from the shed at the rear of the building, and I set off along Gray's Inn Road heading for the Bloomsbury Auxiliary Ambulance Station in a light, freezing mist.

My journey to the ambulance station took longer than usual that morning because I fought a bitter wind the whole way. On Sidmouth Street, just past the ruined hotel, I had to stop and push my bicycle through the banks of piled-up snow. The Georgian terraces that overlooked Regent Square gardens had been badly bombed and the whole area had an air of desolation. At the Hunter Street dogleg I skidded on several patches of black ice, but with some effort managed to keep the bicycle upright. A minute later I was at the ramp leading to the basement garage of Russell Court, but by then I was chilled through, my legs were shaky and the wound on my head throbbed.

Bloomsbury station was located in the basement of a large mansion block called Russell Court, about half a mile from my flat. Before the war the place had been filled with young men about town who took advantage of the serviced apartments with meals provided. Now the young men were all in uniform and the building stood nearly empty.

I free-wheeled down the ramp and rode over to the place where we propped our bicycles, beside the green five-gallon cans containing the station's precious petrol. In front of me were the station's ambulances, and also the cars we used to transport the 'sitting' wounded. The cars all had large white crosses painted on their bonnets and the ambulances had crosses on their roofs, but that didn't stop over-enthusiastic Messerschmitts from using them as target practice.

I dismounted, propped my bicycle against the wall and stood quietly to catch my breath as I glanced at my watch. Seven-fifteen. My shift started at seven-thirty, and because the station had moved to alternate twenty-four-hour shifts with the New Year, I would be spending the rest of the day and all of the coming night either at the station or out attending incidents.

The previous shift were working on their vehicles, cleaning them after a hard night and readying them for the day ahead. Some ceased their scrubbing to wave at me. I waved back and walked over to an old Studebaker that had been converted into an ambulance by welding a box van body to the back. It was the ambulance that was usually assigned to me. Inside the body were fittings for stretchers and I now knew from bitter experience just how uncomfortable a ride it afforded for our patients. A pair of long legs encased in ugly brown trousers protruded from the back of the ambulance. Only Maisie Halliday had legs that long.

'Good morning, Halliday,' I sang out.

The rest of Maisie appeared and beamed at me. 'Ashwin. You're back.' Her smile faded. 'All better, then?' Maisie seemed unconvinced.

'Well enough to work,' I replied, touching my bandaged forehead. 'Slight concussion. Otherwise only minor injuries, cuts and bruises.'

'Gosh, you're lucky.' Maisie turned away to fuss around in the ambulance again. It was clean, because the previous shift had done its job, but Maisie's duties as attendant required her to make sure all the first-aid equipment, bandages and blankets were there, ready for a call-out. Her voice floated out of the vehicle. 'You were out of hospital quickly. I didn't even have time to visit you.'

'They needed the bed, so they chucked me out yesterday and I went back to my flat.'

Maisie reappeared. 'I was so scared when you were buried. Thank God for Dr Levy. He's not much like our Levy to look at, is he? Even though they were brothers.'

I shook my head, managed a smile. 'No. He's not much like our Levy.' I gestured towards the ambulance. 'I'd better check the old girl before they send us off.'

'And I need more blankets,' said Maisie. She ran off, heading for the storeroom.

I opened the bonnet to check the water and oil and made sure the petrol tank was full and the lights were working. Next I examined the tyres, which were in reasonable shape after a night on the glass-strewn roads. All of this information was entered into the logbook. My head was still throbbing, but I could cope with the pain when I was busy.

'All shipshape?' asked Maisie, a little later.

'And Bristol fashion.'

Maisie nibbled at her lip, seemed about to speak, but stayed mute.

'What is it?' I asked.

'Did you hear that the old lady died? The one with the parrot.'

I hadn't heard that, and I sighed. 'It must have been the shock, poor old thing.'

'But – well, I'm worried. Whatever happened to Bobby? I know they rescued the bird.'

A vision came to me of a parrot cage in my sitting room, and of the company a talking parrot would be. It might fill the blank, silent hours I spent there alone.

'I'll see if I can find out,' I said.

She motioned towards the stairs that led to the common room and kitchen. 'And now I think we both deserve a nice cup of tea.'

The common room had acquired a few comforts in the sixteen months since war was declared, including a card table, a dartboard, a bookcase and books and even a piano, but the room was always chilly, despite the oil heater and the rugs that covered the concrete floor. One end had been partitioned off into two rooms, a small storeroom and the office, from where 'reports of incidents requiring assistance' were telephoned through from Central Control. A window with sliding panes had been set into the wall between the office and the common room. Through this window the officer in charge for the shift would shout out instructions or hand over the chits detailing the incidents to the drivers and attendants. There were ten of us on each twenty-four-hour shift, including the station leader, Jack Moray.

In my time at the ambulance station I worked closely with my colleagues but I knew very few of them at all well. I was not invited to anyone's home, or to meet anyone's family. Lily Brennan and Maisie Halliday were my friends. The rest were comrades. We depended on each other to get a difficult job done and did so on the whole with grace and good humour, but we were not friends. This means that when I describe those who worked with me in the station I am at a disadvantage. If those descriptions seem shallow, it is because I am unable to flesh them out.

Moray was in the office on the telephone when Maisie and I entered. He gave me a wave through the window. Moray at that time was a dark-haired man in his thirties and attractive in a wolfish sort of way. He ran the station well but I had long suspected he was secretly as fascist as my husband, Cedric. It was something in his expression when Oswald Mosley or Cedric Ashwin were mentioned, and his refusal to publicly denounce Hitler. Of course, he was as appalled as the rest of us at the devastation wreaked by the Luftwaffe and he had risked his life on many occasions to save air-raid victims. But he did not seem to detest Hitler – known generally as *that man* – as passionately as did most Londoners.

Nola Fripp looked up from the book she was reading when Maisie and I entered the common room and she gave us a tight-lipped nod. Fripp is difficult to describe, mainly because she was so very drab. Picture a rail-thin, rather mousy woman in her early twenties who dresses very well but wears her clothes badly. Someone who speaks in a quick, breathy voice, as if determined to get out all she has to say before the listener becomes bored. The type of person who avoids eye contact but gives the impression of always covertly watching you. Her father worked in the War Office and occasionally she made announcements about the state of the war that she ascribed to him.

Fripp was not among my favourites at the ambulance station. For one thing, she was an anti-Semite who had made her dislike of David embarrassingly and publicly apparent. For another, when she had arrived at the station the previous July, she had pulled me aside to express her extreme admiration for Cedric and her horror at his incarceration.

'It's so unfair,' she had declared. 'England never recognises true genius. They lock away a visionary like Cedric Ashwin and I just know they're going to appoint Winston Churchill the prime minister.' Her tone became chatty. 'My father can't see

Churchill lasting more than a few months if they do. Says he's a warmongering firebrand.'

My response had been less than enthusiastic, which had disappointed her. I had rebuffed any other attempts at friendliness and now we were simply acquaintances.

When Fripp had first spoken to me, Cedric had been in gaol for two months. For the first time in our marriage I was free of his influence and I was beginning to realise how tightly he had controlled my life. It's a heady thing, freedom at the ripe old age of twenty-one. More importantly, my views on Cedric's politics had begun to change. My brother had just died, and I could not allow myself to accept that he had died for nothing. Especially as the aerial battle between the Luftwaffe and the RAF, which we came to know as the Battle of Britain, was in full swing in the skies above us. We all knew that if our pilots lost that battle, German invasion would soon follow, and reports of the Germans strafing fleeing civilians in Europe, and murdering Jews and those who did not agree with Hitler meant that we had few illusions about what would happen in Britain if the Nazis arrived. So it was becoming crystal clear to me that Cedric had been wrong about Hitler and the war. What else had he been wrong about, I wondered? Less than two months later, David Levy transformed my views utterly.

'Ashwin,' Squire's voice boomed out. 'Glad to see you back, Duchess. Bee-yoo-tiful as ever.'

I smiled at the man who, as usual, was hunkered over the oil heater. George Squire was a former boxer, not tall, but with big hulking shoulders and enormous hands. When we had first met, some seven months before, he told me that he had been brought up in Seven Dials.

'I think you'd be more of a Belgrave Square beauty,' he had added, 'but I won't hold that against you.'

And, to my astonishment and my delight, he had taken a breath and sung out in a deep baritone voice:

'*Hearts just as pure and fair*

*May beat in Belgrave Square*
*As in the lowly air of Seven Dials.'*

He sang well, in an accent from the streets of that once notorious slum. I loved Gilbert and Sullivan operettas, and *Iolanthe* is one of my favourites. So I had smiled at him and sung in reply:

'*When virtuous love is sought*
*Thy power is naught,*
*Though dating from the Flood,*
*Blue blood! Ah, blue blood*!'

When I finished Squire had clapped a hand over his heart and swept me a low and flourishing bow. As he bent over his left ear was clearly larger than the other, and the cartilage was red and thick and deformed. I had seen my first cauliflower ear.

'Ah, Duchess,' he had said to me when he was upright, 'I've a feeling that if we nicked you, you'd bleed blue.'

'Not at all,' I had replied. 'It's just as red as yours.'

He had grinned and shaken his head. We'd been allies from that moment on. Another reason I disliked Fripp was that, although she rarely looked directly at anyone, she ostentatiously avoided looking at Squire as if the sight of him gave her pain.

A chorus of voices joined his that morning and I was greeted with smiles and sympathy. I found myself a little overwhelmed by this show of support and affection, as I knew I was not one of the more popular members of the team.

'I'm fine. Really.'

'I hear it was Levy's doctor brother who kept you alive.' Doris Powell raised her head and darted me an inquisitive look. Curly-haired Powell loved to gossip. 'Now that's a turn-up for the books.'

'I thought Levy's brothers were with the army in North Africa,' said Alma Harris, glancing up from the mess of khaki wool on her lap. Harris was in her fifties, a brisk lady with iron-grey hair, a forthright manner, lots of pep, and a flair for organising things. She spent all her spare time knitting for the troops, when she wasn't volunteering on a mobile refreshment car that provided tea and refreshments at a bomb site. That morning she was knitting a service helmet, with earflaps.

'He told me his other brother is still in Africa with a tank squadron' said Maisie. 'But Dr Levy had a bad bout of typhoid and then pneumonia and was sent home to recover just before Christmas. So now he's working at the Queen Alexandra – you know, the military hospital in Millbank – but he put his name down to help out with ARP in whatever spare time he has.'

'You're a full bottle on the bloke,' said Sadler, who was playing patience in the corner. 'Fancy him, then?' He regarded Maisie with an appreciative eye. She returned his look coldly.

Sam Sadler was an East London spiv, a wide boy with slicked-back hair and fingers in many pies, including the black market. Aged in his forties, he moonlighted as a dance-band leader at a nightclub in Soho, and apparently he was an excellent trombonist. In looks he was scrawny, with sharp features and plenty of nervous energy that kept his hands busy and his watchful eyes darting around.

Sadler had avoided being called up because of an irregular heartbeat, a 'dicky ticker' as he called it, and I had overheard him tell Squire that he loved wartime because of the many opportunities for easy money to be made. A couple of months before, his best friend had been dismissed from the ambulance service for looting, and although it was widely assumed that Sadler was involved, he had never been charged. He seemed to have a steady supply of black-market goods and I suspected him of looting when he could get away with it.

'Is he handsome as his brother was?' asked Powell with a raise of an eyebrow.

Maisie thought about it. 'To be honest… no, he's not.'

*Which is hardly fair*, I thought, *given that David was so ridiculously good-looking*. Simon wasn't unattractive, but his frowning intensity could be off-putting, I supposed.

'Nice, though,' Maisie went on. 'He managed to make me laugh, even though I was so frightened for Ashwin.'

I looked at her. 'Made you laugh? He seemed awfully serious to me.'

Then I recalled that Simon Levy had made me laugh, too. But that was before he knew who I was.

Maisie smiled. 'Well, I suppose there wasn't much to laugh about when you were both trapped in the dark with a UXB next door.' Then she said, with a touch of concern, 'He's getting a bit of a reputation for reckless bravery. One of the lads on the site told me.'

The conversation shifted and I leaned back in my chair and closed my eyes, trying to ignore the pain in my head as the voices rose and fell around me.

Doris Powell was engaged in Careless Talk, as usual. 'They say fifth columnists had spread petrol all around the City and that's why the buildings went up so quickly.' Powell was always mentioning fifth columnists, or spies, or was promoting some outrageous theory.

'Nah. There weren't enough fire-spotters.' Sadler's cockney accent was unmistakable. 'The City was almost empty and incendiaries were able to take hold without hindrance. It was neglect that did for the City.'

'It's very easy to criticise,' said Harris.

'At least St Paul's is still standing.' That was Stephen Armstrong, a spotty seventeen-year-old who was waiting to be called up and was ruthlessly mothered by the older women in the station.

There was a chorus of assent to his comment.

'A land mine was dropped on the Temple, though. Did an awful lot of damage.' Rupert Purvis was the station's 'conchie', a conscientious objector. He was a pleasant-looking man of around thirty – an artist – with very bright blue eyes and a close-cropped beard that lent him a naval air. He had been raised as a Quaker and that was why he steadfastly refused to take up arms. I knew him to be a brave and careful ambulance attendant.

'The guns went all night but not one raider was brought down,' said Armstrong.

'They do what they're supposed to,' said Purvis, 'which is keeping the bombers high and forcing them to dodge and swerve and change their speed and altitude, so they can't bomb accurately. It's because of the guns that none of the bridges across the Thames has been hit as yet. Nor Battersea Power Station just across the river, or any other military objectives.'

'Yeah, yeah,' said Sadler. 'And so Jerry hits the East End docks instead. Because it's an easier target. It's just tough luck for them what live there.'

'They knock down more pubs and churches and houses than factories,' said Harris, 'and more biscuit factories than arms factories.' She sighed. 'I suppose that's good for the war effort.'

'They always seem to manage to hit the City,' said Maisie.

Powell spoke up. 'I heard that's because fifth columnists placed a special box under the Bank of England. It lets out a magnetic ray so that the raiders know when they're over the City.' Any further comments were drowned out by groans.

'Why's it only work on moonlit nights, then?' said Sadler. 'Eh, Powell? I'll tell you why. You're talking a load of old cobblers.'

'No need for nastiness,' said Powell, obviously aggrieved. 'We've not seen the worst tricks the Germans have up their sleeves. You know what's coming next, don't you?'

'What?'

She lowered her voice and said, in a hissing whisper, 'Mustard gas.'

'Honestly, Powell…' Maisie's tone was exasperated.

'You just wait and see. That's why I carry my gas mask everywhere. Everywhere. Always.'

'Tell you something,' said Sadler. 'I heard that the best thing a woman can do if she's caught without her gas mask in a gas attack is to drop her knickers.'

There was general laughter and some outrage at that, but Sadler spoke across it. 'Nah. Minds out of the gutter, please. You soak 'em in water and then put them over yer head. Works a treat apparently. My old Aunt Millie said so.'

'What a load of—'

'Those Messerschmitts are bad enough,' said Harris firmly. 'The other day saw me running along the Putney High Street dodging machine-gun bullets, with no protection other than a shopping basket.'

The thump of a distant explosion cut through the chatter, and sudden silence fell.

I felt a quick stab of anxiety and opened my eyes to see Jack Moray enter the room. He was holding chits in his hand. Another explosion sounded.

'Heavy rescue are dynamiting parts of the City to make it safe,' he said. 'Nothing to worry us. There's a motor vehicle accident in Leigh Street that needs an ambulance. Harris, Squire, it's yours. Take the old Ford.'

Harris thrust her knitting down the side of the chair, rose and collected the chit. She left with Squire.

'Armstrong, you go with Fripp in the Buick – I've a mortuary run for you two.'

During the day the ambulances were often sent out on 'mortuary runs' to transport bodies or body parts to the hospitals for identification and preparation for burial. Sometimes there was little left to bury, just fragments of what had been a human being. Sometimes we picked up bodies that were untouched, that looked as if they were sleeping. Blast will do that. It destroys the lungs and leaves everything else intact. I found that to be worse, in a way. To be confronted with what appeared to be a sleeping child, knowing that it would never wake, is truly awful. Surprisingly, Fripp managed the mortuary runs with remarkable ease. It was loud noises and personal danger that she couldn't bear.

Moray's gaze flickered to me, and passed on. He handed out the rest of the chits, but gave no duties to me. I suspected that he wanted to let me rest until the inevitable night raid. Daylight raids had almost ceased because the RAF was so efficient at bringing down the bombers. It was a different story when the sun went down. The RAF had lost too many pilots and planes trying to find and then fight the Luftwaffe at night. Now it was rarely attempted. German bombers came in the darkness, when London and the other cities were wide open to them, protected only by the barrage balloons and ack-ack guns. And the English weather.

After checking my ambulance's engine yet again and making the old machine shine, I revised my first-aid training. Next I volunteered to mop the floor of the common room. I did so whilst listening to the Harry Engleman Quintet on the forces radio. They were belting out 'The Desert Song', which pepped me up. I needed pepping up, because I was beginning to flag.

And so, at around three o'clock I went to one of the uncomfortable bunks that had been put in once the station moved to twenty-four-hour shifts. I had a feeling it was going to be a bad night, and I'd need my wits about me. I fell asleep as soon as my head touched the pillow.

# CHAPTER SEVEN

The banshee wail of the Warning jerked me awake at five o'clock, pulling me into an unwilling consciousness of my throbbing head wound. My entire body felt prickly and sore and cold, but my face was burning. I went to the washroom and splashed cold water on my cheeks before I entered the common room.

'Nothing to worry about,' said Armstrong, looking up from the book he was reading as I entered. 'They're only lighting up the raid.'

He meant that planes had come over to drop incendiary bombs, hoping to start fires that would guide the bombers to their targets when the real action began later that night. I spared a thought for the fire-watchers. All over London men and women were up on roofs, waiting in the dark, unprotected except for their tin hats, watching for the first signs of fire and then having to deal with it using stirrup pumps or sand.

When the Warning sounded again at nine o'clock my heart thumped painfully. I wondered if anyone had suffered a heart attack just from hearing the long drawn out wailing of the siren.

The boom of ack-ack guns was followed by the throb of aeroplane engines. We could all now tell the difference between an English and a German plane. The German Dorniers and Heinkels were two-motored planes that hummed loudly then faded and then hummed loudly again, almost as if the motors were pushing forward, taking a breath and then pushing forward again. These were definitely German bombers and it was clear that they were flying very low. Wave after wave of planes flew over and soon the basement shook with each thudding vibration of exploding bombs.

'They'll be after Euston Station,' said Armstrong.

'Yeah, yeah,' snarled Sadler, throwing his cards down in disgust on to a rocking table, 'they always are. Only they tend to miss, don't they, mate? And they hit houses instead.'

Moray appeared in the doorway, and looked around. 'I've been told Jerry's going to put on quite a show tonight. Observers reckon planes are coming over hot and strong.'

'We're ready for them,' said Harris. Her resolute voice and firm expression was at odds with her clicking knitting needles and the fluffy mass of wool on her lap.

'Ashwin, you're teamed with Halliday in the Studebaker,' said Moray. 'She's driving. I don't want you behind the wheel with that head wound. Next week will be soon enough.' He turned to look at Harris. 'You'll be driving the Buick, with Squire attending. I'll take the older Ford with Purvis. Sadler and Powell, you're in the other Ford. Armstrong, you choose one of the cars.'

The telephone rang in the office. Moray turned and went in to pick it up.

My stomach clenched painfully. *Please don't let me be buried alive again. If I have to die out there, please let it be quick.* And now there was a new prayer. *Please stop Simon Levy being recklessly brave. His parents cannot lose another son.*

Moray had said it was a major incident. That was obvious as soon as Maisie pulled into the devastated street and we saw the trucks, cars and heavy machinery that had been brought in. A mobile canteen was off to the side, serving tea and soup. The rescue gangs were already at work, combing through the rubble, ignoring the flash of explosions that lit the sky like summer lightning.

Raiders skimmed above us like black bats, dodging the quarter moon. The drone of their engines filled the air in a continuous maddening roar that competed with the frenzied whoosh of a broken water main and the roaring inferno of the ruptured gas pipe in the next block. Great gaps had been blasted into the terraces. The remaining buildings were licked by flames that lit the scene in a flickering red-and-gold light. Men were busy, spraying water on the fires and looking for survivors. The usual bomb-site smell of cordite, brick dust, gas and smoke hung in the icy air.

It was bitterly cold. Frost lay thick on the ground, shimmering white and treacherously slippery. More so was the black ice, and my feet slid underneath me as I followed Maisie to where the burly warden was standing. I managed to keep my balance by concentrating on the white-painted 'W' on his helmet, which was clearly visible in the firelight. He stood in front of an avalanche of roof tiles, walls, floorboards, pitiful odds and ends of furniture, battered beds, pictures, toys and books, bricks and mortar and broken beams, the remains of a four-storey house that until an hour ago had stood in this Pimlico terrace for a hundred years.

'Those we found alive have been taken away already,' he said, speaking loudly to be heard over the noise around us, 'but you'll need to wait. They're still looking for other survivors. Might have heard something out back, they think, and at the moment they're trying to work out what it is without bringing the rest of the house down.' He raised his voice. 'Trouble is hearing anything in this din.'

'What do they think they've heard?' asked Maisie. In the ruddy glow of the flames her face was gaunt and shadowed.

'A man is missing in that house. They're hoping it's his voice calling out from the cellar, but it's a fearful mess.'

My steel helmet hid the bandage around my head, but the wound underneath throbbed. It was hard to concentrate on my steps as I followed Maisie and the warden on to the bomb site. The ruins were in a parlous state and we had to negotiate the litter of twisted steel and piled heaps of rubble. Each step I took caused glass and board and slate tiles to crack under my feet.

Without warning something gave way and my leg sank, almost gracefully, into the mess of debris. Unable to keep my balance I keeled over so that the rest of my body was sprawled uncomfortably on the wreckage. When I tried to pull my leg free, I could gain no purchase.

Maisie wheeled around and choked back laughter.

'Sorry, Ashwin,' she said. 'But you do look a sight.'

'You all right?' The warden asked.

'I seem to be wedged in tight.'

'Let's see what we can do.' He knelt behind me, put his hands under my arms and pulled. As my leg dislodged, he tumbled backwards, carrying me with him and we landed together in a jumble of limbs and torsos. The warden gave a roar of laughter, and the men around us joined in. After a few seconds of embarrassment, I laughed also.

'It's like Laurel and Hardy.'

'Oi, hands off the ambulance girls, Bert.'

'Don't you put up with his liberties, love. He's a right one, that Bert.'

'Cheeky beggars,' said Bert.

We stood up shakily, clinging to each other for support, but immediately lost purchase on the slippery ground to fall in an ungainly tangle. Again there was laughter. Although it was a strange sound on a bomb site with people trapped in the wreckage and raiders still in the sky, I thought it wasn't so bad to be the cause of a light-hearted moment among such misery. Only, I wished my head hurt less. The fall had exacerbated the pain.

A voice I recognised cut through the frivolity.

'Is medical assistance required? Or am I interrupting a moonlight tryst?'

Bert squinted into the gloom. 'That you, Doc Levy?' He chuckled. 'Moonlight tryst indeed.' His voice rose. 'Ee, you lot. Don't stand round gawping. Help us up.'

My arm was encircled in a tight grip and I was hauled upright, but it was almost impossible to keep my balance on the icy ground. Again I felt myself slipping, and my rescuer's grip tightened to hold me steady. I grabbed at his shoulder and clenched the rough wool of a military greatcoat. It was Simon, of course. I wondered if I was destined to meet him now at every incident I attended, as some sort of uncanny punishment for my affair with his brother.

'Thank you, but I can stand by myself.'

'I doubt that, it's like an ice rink.'

'I'm perfectly able to stand.'

'As you wish.' He released my arm. Almost immediately I slipped and began to fall. Again I was caught in his hard grip.

There was no point in being ungracious. 'Thank you.'

'Lean on me and I'll get you across.'

Slipping and sliding and clinging together, we stumbled over to an area of asphalt, where he released my arm.

'You shouldn't be back at work.' His voice was accusing. 'It's too early.'

'I felt well enough. I prefer to be busy. Useful.'

He touched my helmet. 'Let me know if it begins to bleed again. Or if you feel nauseous or dizzy.'

We walked carefully across to join Maisie, the warden and a group of heavy-rescue workers, who were standing under a great ragged length of wall that loomed at least twenty feet above them. It was all that remained of the house and it shook with each percussion of gun or bomb.

'What's the situation?' asked Simon.

'We've a man trapped down here.'

The warden gestured towards a narrow hole in the bomb debris, from which smoke was rising into the freezing air. Simon walked across to lean over it and peer inside. I joined him, coughing a little at the reek of wood smoke. A network of bricks and beams underneath was revealed by the red glow of burning timbers.

Suddenly, I was almost overwhelmed by the vivid memory of my own ordeal, trapped and immobile, buried in similar deep pit of debris. I began to sway. Again it was Simon's firm grip on my arm that held me upright.

'Sit down and put your head between your knees,' Simon hissed into my ear. Then, to Maisie, dismissively, 'She's faint – look after her.'

'I'm fine,' I protested. 'Really, I'm perfectly all right. It was the smoke.'

Simon regarded me for a second or two. I met his examination steadily, determined to remain, daring him to try to send me away. He turned away from me to crouch at the edge of the hole and peer in again.

'Any idea who it might be?' he asked the warden.

'Joe Gardiner lived in the house and he's missing.'

I knelt beside Simon and squinted into the narrow hole. By the light of a burning jagged beam inside I could make out a man's head, twelve to fifteen feet down, surrounded by debris.

'Joe Gardiner,' Simon shouted. 'Are you conscious? How are you?'

A voice floated out, weak, but steady. 'I'm trapped down here. God help me, I can't move hand or foot.'

All the weakness and terror that had so consumed me a moment before had now disappeared. Feeling alert, excited, I moved closer to Simon.

'Are you injured?' he called down.

Again the voice floated out of the darkness. 'Something's gone through my leg and I've been bleeding, I think. Hurt like hell at first, but now it's becoming numb.'

'Can't do much for him, I'm afraid, sir,' someone behind us said. 'It's too risky with that wall hanging over. It's about to topple.'

There was a loud explosion some distance away and the ground shook. A man standing nearby called out in alarm. 'Watch out, sir – it's coming down.'

As those nearby moved quickly to stand out of harm's way, I looked up. The wall stood black and jagged against the leaping flames behind it and its dark bricks were rippling. I felt a moment's panic and glanced at Simon, who was asking Joe more questions about his leg. I looked up again at the wall. The bricks had become still, but it was clearly only a matter of time before it fell to pieces.

Simon reached into his bag, took out a morphia syringe and filled it.

'I'm going down there,' he shouted to the warden, who threw a wary glance at the wall and joined us by the hole.

'You'll never do it,' the warden replied. 'It's too narrow.'

The warden was right, I thought. Even if Simon managed to get in he would not have the slightest chance of bending down to attend to his patient. He wouldn't even be able to gain a foothold at the bottom without setting his feet on the trapped man's head.

'I'll have to go in headfirst.'

'You can't do that,' someone shouted. 'Just look at that bit of wall, won't you? It's about to fall.'

'Shut up about the damned wall,' muttered Simon. He gestured to his right and raised his voice. 'Bring that crane here, please.'

It was not a request.

The warden looked at me. I shrugged and nodded, wondering why they thought I had any say in it, when Simon was so obviously determined to risk his life to help a man he'd never met before and who was likely to die anyway. If the wall toppled, then Simon would die too, down there in the darkness.

They wheeled the crane over.

Simon took off his greatcoat and laid it on the ground by the opening. Next he removed his tunic, folded it, and handed it to me.

'Would you mind standing away over there,' he said. 'They're right about the wall.'

'And you're rather partial to this tunic?'

'It's the pipe in the inner pocket, actually,' he replied, his voice deadpan. 'My favourite. I'd hate it to be smashed.'

*You don't need to do this,* I wanted to say. *Please, think of your mother, she can't lose another son. There's no need to be so reckless.*

Instead, I gestured to the hole. 'It'll be a snug fit. Good thing you're slim.'

He almost smiled. 'Despite my mother's best endeavours.'

I hugged his tunic to my chest and walked away to stand out of reach of the tottering wall.

Simon rolled up his sleeves and lay on his greatcoat.

'Fasten it on my feet,' he said quietly.

They hooked the chain around his feet and turned the wheel so that he was drawn, feet upwards, into the air. Presently his head was clear of the ground and he dangled upside down, a slim figure silhouetted against the light of the burning buildings behind him.

'Right, swing me round and lower away,' he said.

Steadily, spinning a little on the end of the chain, he was lowered head first into the hole until he had disappeared entirely.

'Stop,' he called abruptly.

I couldn't stand the suspense. I glanced at the warden, who gave a quick nod, and we both walked over to peer into the hole. The top of Simon's head was poised above Joe Gardiner and the burning beam that lit the scene was close enough to frizzle Simon's hair and singe the shoulder of his shirt. Simon paid it no mind and was engaged in conversation with Joe. Then he extended his arm to place his left index finger on Joe's neck.

'What's he doing?' whispered the warden.

'Feeling for the jugular vein.'

Simon lowered his right arm, which held the syringe. He eased the needle into the flesh of Joe's neck and with even, unhurried pressure, drove the plunger home.

The warden looked at me. 'Why hasn't he extinguished that ruddy beam? His shirt'll be up in flames soon.'

'I think he needs the light to work by,' I said.

Simon withdrew the syringe and swung himself around towards the burning wood. With his bare hand he steadily crushed out the flame and the scene fell into darkness.

'Right,' he called out. 'You can pull me up now.'

I moved back to stand by the crane. Relief, or something, was making me dizzy. I leant against the machine for support as the short nuggety man who drove it turned the wheel to wind up the chain and pull Simon out.

'By God,' muttered the crane driver as he did so, 'I've seen some heroes. But he takes the cake.' His voice became indulgent. 'Ruddy madman, is young Doc Levy.'

At last Simon emerged, spinning a little on the end of the chain, and the onlookers gave a subdued cheer. He was lowered to the ground and once the chains around his ankles had been released the warden helped him to his feet.

I took his tunic across to him. 'How's the patient?'

'He'll do, for a while.' Simon thanked me and put on the tunic. He glanced up at the wall before bending to pick up his greatcoat.

'Allow me, sir,' said the warden, and held it for Simon as he shrugged himself into it.

'Thanks. He'll need a top-up in four hours. I'll be back unless I get word that he's already out.'

Simon walked away. I watched until he disappeared into the darkness.

'Right, lads,' said the warden, 'we've got four hours to get Joe there out of the hole before Doc Levy has to do that all over again. Let's save the doc the trouble, shall we?'

'What about that wall?' asked one, gesturing to the mass of masonry. 'One decent shake and down comes the whole lot.'

The warden looked at the wall for a moment, then called over a young man who was with the squad. He handed him a whistle.

'Now look here, Charlie Pratt,' said the warden, 'I want you to watch that wall as we work. Don't you take your eyes off it. First sign you see of it shifting you blow the whistle. The lads'll get clear if they're nippy.'

On the sharp eyes of Charlie Pratt, I thought, rested the lives of a dozen rescue workers.

The men in the rescue team nodded, picked up their tools and set to work. They were digging and levering and shovelling dirt as I left to find the mobile canteen for a cup of tea to warm me, settle my stomach and perhaps help the headache.

78

# CHAPTER EIGHT

Two talkative, cheery young London women ran the mobile canteen that night, one with a head of frizzy blonde hair, the other a red-lipped brunette. They were there to serve tea and sandwiches and soup to ARP workers, but as I approached it was clear that at the moment they were serving one British army doctor. Simon was leaning against the counter, chaffing the women as they poured tea into a thick brown mug. I lurked in the shadows to watch.

Scarlet lips handed him a plate with a piece of cake. 'Have some cake, too,' she said, in an attractively husky voice. 'It's little enough for a hero like you.'

'Just doing my job.'

'That's not what I hear. You're getting quite the reputation.'

He laughed and it transformed his face. I was watching an entirely different Simon to the one who had just been talking to me.

'As a mad fool? I only do it to impress pretty girls, you know.'

Frizzy blonde emitted a high-pitched giggle that set my teeth on edge, but the brunette's low chuckle was infectious. 'Go on with you.'

She pushed a mug of steaming tea towards him. He downed it in a few gulps.

'That one didn't touch the sides, did it?' she said. 'Here, let me pour you another.'

Simon smiled his thanks and took the tea, lingering over the second cup, and eating his cake in quick, neat bites.

When he pulled out some coins to pay for the tea and cake, the brunette said, 'Just a penny for the tea. The cake's on us. I'm Kitty and this is Joan.'

'Thanks. It hit the spot, Kitty,' he said. 'Just what I needed.'

'You know how sailors have a rum ration issued to them,' Kitty replied musingly, 'well, it seems to me that civilians are the soldiers of this war – at least in London – and their ration is tea. Hot, strong and sweet tea.'

'Provided by Kitty and Joan in the tea car,' he said, still smiling.

'Do you like to dance, Doc?' asked Joan.

'When I can. I used to go to the dance halls every week when I was younger.'

That surprised me. I found it hard to imagine Simon Levy at a dance hall.

'Jitterbug? Swing? Kitty may look like butter wouldn't melt, but you should see her on the dance floor. It's a treat.'

'Joan,' said Kitty warningly.

Simon took another mouthful of tea. 'I bet Kitty looks simply lovely on the dance floor. Where do you go?'

Kitty had recovered her poise and her smile was an invitation as she smoothed her dark hair. 'The Paramount Dance Hall. I'll be there Friday night.'

Simon smiled again. 'The Paramount? Tottenham Court Road? I used to go there before the war.'

Kitty threw him a sly smile. 'I know you did. I remember you.'

'So we'll look out for you, shall we?' asked Joan.

'Can't make Fridays, I'm afraid.'

'Saturday, then. Or Thursday. Let us know and we'll be there.'

He drained the mug and put it back on the counter. 'What's the band like nowadays?'

'The band is brilliant. And if there's a raid on you can rent a bunk for the night for a shilling.'

'We'll be waiting,' said Joan.

Simon smiled again. 'I've a tight schedule, but I'll see if I can make it one day soon.'

He turned around, gave me a brief nod and walked off. My face became even hotter as I realised he had known I was there, spying on him, like a schoolgirl with a crush. I gave a mocking smile to the darkness. I had thought Simon's frowning intensity could be off-putting, but apparently his frowns were only for Celia Ashwin. He might no longer hate me, but it seemed clear he did not like me either.

Kitty gave Joan a shove. 'I can look after my own love life, thank you very much.'

Joan giggled. 'No point just gazing adoringly.'

'I don't—'

'Whenever you catch sight of the doc, it's like this.' She opened her eyes wide and let her mouth drop open.

For that she got another shove from Kitty.

'I admire him. He's brave. Nice.' Kitty smiled as she swiped a cloth over the counter in front of her. 'And nice-looking.'

'You'd better hope he doesn't turn up at the Paramount,' said Joan. 'Your dad'll flay you alive if you take up with a Jew, even if he is a posh one and a doctor to boot.'

Kitty shrugged theatrically. 'Dad doesn't rule my life. Anyway, I'd not be looking to marry him. Just to have a bit of fun. Dance. Have a laugh. You know, that's the best thing about the Paramount, it accepts everyone, black, white, yellow, Christian, Jew or whatever. There's no prejudice there, and there should be more of that, I say. We're all the same deep down.' She sighed. 'He always turned up at the Paramount in a group, and they only danced with each other.'

Joan turned away to get something from the back and I only caught the words 'broken heart'.

'*You* can talk,' said Kitty. Then she caught sight of me. 'Sorry, miss. Didn't see you there. It's a nasty night, isn't it? Care for a cup of tea? Bovril? Or some nice vegetable soup?'

\*

Just under four hours later, I was back at the bomb site. It was even colder than before. Maisie, swathed in rugs, had refused to leave the ambulance, telling me to call her when we had a patient who was above ground. Charlie Pratt was still on watch, staring at the wall with the whistle in his mouth, ready to blow a shrieking warning if the bricks began to move. The men had been working without respite, and were now using mobile cranes to shift large pieces of masonry and steel. An enormous girder swung up and over my head. The warden shone his torch into the hole, turned and grinned at the men with a 'thumbs-up' sign.

'Got him, mates.'

Joe Gardiner was eased out of the hole and on to a stretcher. He lay there, gazing upwards with a weary smile, as if he'd never seen anything as beautiful as a sky leaden with low cloud. The men had let out a cheer as his head appeared, but they were so exhausted that most of them were sitting or lying on the frozen ground while Kitty and Joan moved around them handing out yet more mugs of tea. The All Clear had not yet sounded because the Luftwaffe had not disappeared, but the drone of their engines was some distance away. It seemed that they were bothering another part of Greater London.

They'd done enough damage here, I reflected. Fires lit the scene with a fierce red glow as rescue workers desperately tried to locate other survivors in the street behind us. They were using dogs now, but no one else had been found alive.

It was bitingly cold. My feet were numb, but my hands tingled with the heat of the mug of tea I held. I felt queasy, which I ascribed to drinking too much tea made with chlorinated water and dried milk. Worst of all, the pounding in my head was almost overwhelming. I consoled myself with the thought that it was only another five hours before I was off-duty and perhaps I could snatch some sleep at the station.

Two men, who introduced themselves as Bob and Noel, brought Joe Gardiner over to me on a stretcher and laid him at my feet like a trophy. I quickly checked the man's vital signs, which were not bad, considering his ordeal. The main problem was the severe penetrating wound to his right thigh, which needed bandaging to ready him for the journey to hospital. He groaned as I did so.

'Doc's right on time,' said Bob, smiling at something behind me.

I twisted around to see Simon walking towards us. I checked my watch. It had been exactly four hours since he had hung like a bat above Joe's head and administered morphine to him.

'No need for acrobatics this time, Doc,' called Noel. 'We got him out to save you the trouble.'

Simon flashed him a smile and his voice was warm with approval. 'You all did a splendid job.'

He barely spared me a glance as he knelt beside the stretcher and took hold of Joe's wrist to check his pulse. The impression Simon gave was one of friendly competence, and Joe visibly relaxed.

'Good morning, Joe,' he said. 'I'm very pleased to be able examine you in more comfortable circumstances.'

'I owe you a pint, Doc,' he said, and Simon rewarded him with a quick grin.

'I'll hold you to that.' At last he looked at me, and asked in the pleasantly professional voice I remembered from our time together in the dark, 'How's the patient, Mrs Ashwin?'

'Tired. He has a nasty leg injury and appears to have lost a fair amount of blood.'

Simon drew up a dose of morphine. 'This'll make you feel more comfortable, Joe.' He had just lifted the needle when a tremendous roar sounded behind me.

'There she goes,' Joe whispered.

I swung around as the wall collapsed, shifting down heavily like some bricked monster lumbering to its knees and thickening the frosty air with a cloud of brick dust that made me cough. A ten-foot-high mound of rubble and smashed wood filled the hole from which Joe had been plucked only fifteen minutes before, and where Simon would have been at that moment if Joe had not been rescued.

'You're a lucky one, Joe,' said Simon. He administered the morphine with a steady hand and checked the man's pulse. 'He's fit to be transferred to hospital,' he said to me.

I nodded and pushed myself up, ignoring the nausea roiling in my stomach as I did so. Once on my feet, the scene seemed to sway and the sick feeling increased. Thankful for the concealing gloom, I stood still to allow the dizziness to dissipate and my stomach to settle.

'I should get Halliday – my driver – to help with the stretcher,' I said.

'Allow us, princess,' said Noel. 'I hear she's asleep in the ambulance.'

He and Bob hoisted Joe on the stretcher between them and began walking. I followed behind with Simon.

'How's the head?'

'Better,' I lied. 'Really, I'm perfectly fine.'

He seemed to consider this, but as we reached the mobile canteen he halted abruptly and put his hand on my arm to stop me walking. He gave me a look, slow and appraising.

'I think you've come back to duty too early. I'd like to take a look at the wound, if you don't mind.'

I said, with an attempt at levity, 'I'm a shade tougher than Dresden china, you know. I swear, I'm fine.'

The girls leaned over the canteen counter to call out greetings.

'Hello, Doc,' said Kitty.

'Another cuppa?' asked Joan.

Simon smiled at them in response. 'Are you able to help me?' he asked. 'I need somewhere under cover, but with good light. I want to take a quick look at this ambulance officer's head wound.'

'Come into the tea car if you like,' said Kitty. 'There's plenty of room and lots of hot water.'

'Sounds perfect.'

'Thank you for your concern, Dr Levy,' I said. It was my hoity-toity voice, borrowed from my mother for the occasion. 'But I haven't the time for this. I must get my patient to hospital.'

He ignored me and spoke to someone over my shoulder, presumably to Joe. 'Can you wait five minutes, old man? Good.' His glance shifted to the right. 'Would you put him in the ambulance, please? I want to check her head wound. Won't be a minute.'

I twisted around to see Bob and Noel heading away with Joe and made a move to follow, but was stayed by Simon's hand on my arm.

'Celia, I've seen you almost faint three times now.' His voice was calm, infuriatingly reasonable. 'To be frank, you look terrible. I want to check the wound for infection.'

My indignation disappeared. I felt deflated, like a balloon that had lost its air. Small and ill and helpless. Although my face seemed to radiate heat, I was suddenly cold and shivery. I clutched at my coat and clenched my teeth. And all the while Simon watched me.

When the shivering fit had passed, he ushered me into the van, which was larger inside than it looked. Counters ran along both sides. The front counter lay behind the hatch from where tea and soup were served, and on the back counter was the urn with hot water for the tea and a couple of spirit stoves. A large kettle steamed gently on one; the other held a large saucepan of what looked like vegetable soup. I took one look at the bubbling mess in the saucepan and gagged. A small canvas stool had been unfolded for me to sit on. I moved it closer to the doorway, away from the soup, and sat down, ignoring Kitty and Joan, who stood outside, watching. I removed my helmet.

Simon washed his hands, then unwound the bandage that swathed my head. He made a small grunting sound when the wound was revealed.

'Ooh, that looks nasty,' said Joan.

'Who's been looking after you?' he asked.

'I can look after myself.'

He placed a cool hand on my forehead. 'It's clear the wound's become infected. What did they tell you at the hospital? I'm surprised they said you could go back to work this quickly.'

'I felt well enough to return to the station. I prefer to work.'

He rebandaged my head swiftly, competently. 'I can't clean the wound properly here. When do you go off-duty?'

'Seven-thirty this morning.'

'You work twenty-four-hour shifts?'

'Yes.'

He turned away to wash his hands again, then glanced at his watch. 'It's almost three now. That wound needs to be cleaned and disinfected and you need to rest. It's too long until you're off-duty. I'll see if Noel or Bob can go with your driver in the ambulance.'

'I can't just slope off in the middle of a shift.'

'I'll fix it with the station officer. Right now you need to rest more than they need you to work. I'll see you home, I've—'

'There's not the slightest need to see me home.'

'—got a car. I can clean the wound at your flat.'

I picked up my satchel and stood, carefully. My head throbbed and the nausea had returned, but I managed a smile. Nanny's voice was ever in my ear: 'Never show you are annoyed, no matter how tiresome anyone may be. It's ill-bred.'

'You've been most kind, thank you,' I said. 'I'll return to the ambulance, now. The wound can be bathed and re-dressed at the station.' My voice hardened. 'I will finish my shift.'

His eyes, amused, met mine. 'It hurts like hell, doesn't it? And how were you intending to get from the station to your digs at the end of the shift?'

'Bicycle.'

His eyes flickered and he frowned. 'You can't ride a bicycle in this weather and certainly not with an infected head wound. I'll drive you home now.'

Kitty had joined Joan at the doorway. Joan's look at me was calculating, but her voice was honey as she said to Simon, 'So, you'll drop by the Paramount Saturday night? Kitty's always there by eight.'

'I'll be there, unless I'm on duty,' said Simon, smiling at them both. 'Save me a dance. Thanks for the tea and cake earlier, and for the use of the van. Goodnight.'

We emerged to find that snow had begun to fall steadily. Thick low clouds pressed down on us and an eerie yellow light lit the scene as rescue efforts continued. The throb of plane engines was faint and far away, over to the north.

When I stumbled on the icy ground, Simon's grip on my arm was hard, steadying and annoying. It was all I could do not to shake off his hand. I knew my reaction was childish and ungrateful, but he had been officious and intrusive. Even if the wound was infected, I did not need a high-handed doctor telling me what to do. Even if he was David's brother. Especially if he was David's brother.

The ambulance was in sight. Maisie had already started the engine and Bob and Noel stood at the rear, presumably chatting to Joe. Smoke from the exhaust swirled around them, lending a gothic feel to the scene.

'Thank you,' I said to Simon, as graciously as I could manage. 'I *will* get some rest, I promise. Someone at the station can easily deal with the wound tonight, and I – I will ask my friend, Lily Brennan, to check it when I return to my flat. She drives ambulances also, and she knows first aid.'

'Vassy's girl?'

'Yes. She has a flat in my building.'

Lily Brennan was an Australian who had worked with me at Bloomsbury until a few weeks before, when she had transferred to the big Berkeley Square Station. I was surprised Simon knew her, until I remembered that Jim Vassilikov, Lily's fiancé, had been at school with David and presumably with Simon also.

I steadied myself, drew in a breath, and raised my chin. 'So, although it's kind of you to offer, please don't bother. I live only a quarter of a mile or so from the station. Really, there's no need to see me home.'

'Really,' he replied calmly, 'there is every need.'

'I will ask someone from the station to see me home at the end of the shift,' I replied, with equal calmness.

'Except you will be going home now.'

My composure – usually so reliable – faltered, and broke. 'You are infuriating,' I hissed. 'Lily is perfectly capable of looking after me. Why are you doing this? To prove you don't hate me any more?'

He gave a short bark of laughter. 'No, I don't hate you any more. I'm not sure I like you much, but I'll be damned if I'll let you die. A few days ago you told me you don't care if you live or die, and the way you've been acting proves that.'

I tried to speak, but he ignored me, listing my infractions in a hard, cold voice. 'You've come back to work too early, you've let your wound become infected and now you insist on refusing medical care. Although it's obvious you have a fever, you say you'll walk or bicycle home. In a snowstorm—'

Again I began to interrupt but this time was silenced by a sharp cutting gesture. There was a pause as we glared at each other. He shut his eyes, but almost immediately opened them again and continued more calmly.

'I don't have to prove anything to you, Celia Ashwin. But continuing on in this way could have serious consequences. I've seen too many people die in the past year and I do not intend to allow any patient of mine to die needlessly through stubborn bloody stupidity. So, I'll drive you home. And I'll do whatever it takes to make you well.' The cool ironic smile returned. 'Whether you like it or not.'

The trip home in Simon's little Austin took us through detours and dead ends. He drove in a silence as cold as the swirling snow outside the windows. The thin shafts of light from the car's taped headlights could not illuminate all the potholes and debris caused by the raid, so it was a bumpy drive. Each bump caused pain to shoot through my head and I shivered, despite the blanket Simon had begged for me from Maisie.

I slipped into a reverie and was jolted back to reality as I realised that the walls of Coram's Fields loomed palely beside us. We were driving along Guilford Street. I never went that way any more. I would cycle the long way to and from the Ambulance Station rather than pass by Caroline Place, the short shattered row of terraces opposite the old Foundling Hospital grounds. The flat where David and I used to meet had been in Caroline Place. It was there that David had died.

I hugged the blanket close around me and closed my eyes, trying to force away the vision that flashed into my mind: David lying still and cold on the floor of the flat.

The car slowed and stopped.

'That's where he died, isn't it?'

I opened my eyes. Caroline Place was in almost total darkness, but the vague shapes of ruins could be discerned through the falling snow.

'Yes.'

*My brother – my parents' favourite – he died recently. We were very close, more like twins.* I closed my eyes. Simon released the brake and we moved off slowly, bumping over some rubble on the road. I didn't open my eyes again until the car came to a final stop outside St Andrew's Court.

Simon, holding his doctor's black bag, came around to open my door and assist me out of the vehicle. I leaned on him as we walked slowly up the front step, but once he had pushed the doors open and ushered me into the lobby, I shook off his hand. Standing without support, the room seemed to sway and I was forced to cling to the doorjamb until the dizziness resolved. I looked up at Simon, who offered me his arm. I hesitated, then gave way under his sardonic gaze. Accepting the inevitable, I took hold of his arm. Ahead of us were the stairs, which swept around the small but elaborate lift that dominated the centre of the lobby. Leaning heavily on him I walked towards the lift.

The lift stopped at my floor with a jerk that seemed to split my head in two and I led him along the narrow passage to my door. There I tried and failed to insert the key with hands that shook like those of a drunk with the *delirium tremens*. Simon waited with a kind of neutral patience.

'Please,' I said, 'would you? My hands are stupidly unsteady.'

He took the key from me, opened the door and followed me inside. My flat was small, but the sitting room was a good size and I loved the balcony that was reached through French doors from the bedroom. There was also a tiny kitchen – more a kitchenette – and a small bathroom.

The blackout blinds were still in place from when I had left for work early the morning before, so I switched on the light. It revealed a neat sitting room, one with few keepsakes or indicators of my taste. A bland, careful room. One that kept its secrets. When I had moved there from the town house in Mayfair, I left behind anything that had belonged to Cedric, almost everything in the house. I should have taken more, because a bomb hit the house four months later and what wasn't destroyed in the blast was burned in the resulting fire. Since joining the ambulance service I'd had no time or inclination to shop for personal items.

'There's a first-aid kit in the bathroom,' I said.

He gestured towards his black bag. 'I've got all I need. Please sit down. I'll be ready in a minute.'

The bag was deposited in the bathroom and he went to the kitchen. I sat quietly, trying to ignore the throbbing in my head, concentrating on presenting an unruffled demeanour. *Head high and walk tall.* Inside, I was squirming with embarrassment. I knew I had behaved badly, and I was ashamed of myself. Simon Levy had been trying to help me and although I found his concern intrusive, I should have responded graciously.

Simon was opening cupboards and moving around in the kitchen. There was some hesitation, where he obviously had to search for an implement or vessel, but on the whole his movements were sure and unhurried. Then the sound of water filling a pot and the crump of the gas being lit. After a while he emerged with a saucepan of boiling water and carried it into the bathroom. A second or so later he appeared in the doorway.

'Please, come in,' he said.

I entered the bathroom. Simon was standing by the washbasin in his shirtsleeves. He had laid out gauze, bandages, tweezers and a small pair of scissors. A basin of steaming water that smelled of antiseptic was in the bath. Its metallic smell competed with the sulphurous odour of the open bandages. I sat down carefully on the edge of the bath.

He unwound my bandage and, with painstaking care, cut away the stitches and washed the wound with warm water. He was a careful, gentle nurse, but it was all I could do not to scream with the pain he caused.

'This may sting,' he said, turning away to drench a piece of gauze in a liquid I assumed was antiseptic.

'Why do doctors, nurses and ambulance officers always say that,' I replied tartly, 'when we all know perfectly well that it will hurt like blazes?'

He smiled as he picked up the sodden gauze with the tweezers.

'This *will* sting,' he said, and laid it on the wound. I had gritted my teeth in anticipation of the pain, but could not help flinching. He pulled back and paused, until I nodded to indicate that he should continue. Fifteen minutes later it was done, and I was a shaking mess. Simon's hands were steady as he restitched the wound and rebandaged my forehead, but he was holding his lips tightly and a sharp crease had appeared between his eyebrows.

I raised my hand to the bandage. The wound was at the scalp line, on the left side, where I usually parted my hair.

'Will I be I scarred for life?' I asked. I said it lightly, meaning it as a joke.

Simon closed his black bag with a snap. 'I think you probably need a scar.'

'Why? Whatever do you mean?'

'For your own protection.'

'What?'

'Don't they say God dislikes perfection?'

When he looked at me his expression gave the game away.

'You're joking, you beast.' Without thinking I playfully punched his arm.

He smiled at me as he rubbed the spot. It was a sudden, very attractive smile similar to that he had given the tea-car girls. It lit his face with mischief, so that he looked like a schoolboy caught out in a joke who was a little abashed at his temerity. I realised with some surprise that it was the first time he had ever smiled at me.

And then – it was as if I could read each thought as it came into his mind – he remembered I was not simply an ambulance girl, ripe for teasing and sharing a light-hearted moment in dark times, I was his dead brother's married lover, who had been the last person to see David alive and whose cowardice had caused such grief to his parents. The shutters descended and his expression reverted to the rather sullen wariness he had always displayed towards me.

'No need to worry,' he said briskly. 'There will be a slight scar, I expect, but you'll still be a beautiful woman.'

It took talent to make the compliment sound so insulting.

'Come back into the sitting room,' he said. 'I'll dissolve an aspirin powder in water for you. It should help to relieve the fever and headache. Then you should go straight to bed.' Then he added, without any inflection at all in his voice, 'And get your beauty sleep.'

He disappeared into the kitchen and returned a moment later, holding a glass of water that was opaque with dissolved aspirin.

'Here,' he said, holding out the glass. 'Drink this. You'll feel better for it.'

I sipped the mixture, coughing a little as small particles caught in my throat. When I looked up Simon was leaning forward in his chair, regarding me with a frowning intensity, looking much like a younger version of his father. David had taken after their beautiful mother.

'Thank you,' I said. 'For…' I lifted my hand to brush the bandage. Then, for a reason I didn't stop to analyse, I held out my hand to him.

'Pax?' I said, invoking the schoolboy's way to show hostilities had ended.

He sat still, looking at my outstretched hand. It trembled a little, but I did not pull back. Eventually he sighed and took hold of it. His handshake was firm, formal, uncompromising. He had not said 'Pax' in reply, and I felt like a fool.

We sat in silence as I finished my drink.

'I must be going,' he said, rising in one quick movement and reaching for his black bag. 'I'm due at the hospital in a few hours. Be sure to go straight to sleep.' A pause. 'Any scar on your forehead will soon fade. Really, it will be nothing to worry about.' His voice took on a brusque note. 'That is, if you take care of yourself and get rid of that infection. No, please don't get up. I can see myself out.'

The aspirin did take the edge of the pain in my head, but I found it hard to sleep that night, and I found myself fervently hoping that I would not meet Simon Levy again at an incident. Or anywhere else for that matter.

# CHAPTER NINE

Lily Brennan and Jim Vassilikov arrived the following evening with first-aid supplies and Lily announced that she had spoken to Simon Levy, who had asked her to dress my head wound.

Australian Lily was a tiny sprite with brown curls and a delightful smile who seemed delicate but was tough as steel. She was one of the few people who know about my affair with David. Jim was around a foot taller than Lily, a tall, fair-haired man with a strong, aquiline nose, obvious intelligence in his deep-set grey eyes and the bare hint of the Slav in his cheeks. Although he still wore the blue-grey RAF uniform that Londoners so loved, he no longer flew due to injuries sustained when his Hurricane was shot down in November 1940. Without knowing his surname, it was difficult to pick his antecedents, as his type of blond diffidence was as equally common in Berlin as in London. In fact, he was a White Russian aristocrat who escaped Bolshevik Russia as a small child and spent the next two decades becoming as English as John Bull.

I had known and liked Jim since I was fourteen, when he was at Cambridge and stepped out with my sister Helen. I was there when Jim first met Lily in the St Andrew's lobby three months before. Lily had tumbled inside on a gust of wind, soaked to the skin and shivering with cold. Her face had been grimy after a hard shift, but she lit up the room with her hundred-watt smile. Jim hadn't been able to take his eyes off her. It was obvious to everyone there that he was besotted. Except Lily, who could be remarkably obtuse on occasion.

'This may hurt,' said Lily, as she pulled away the bandage. She grimaced apologetically at my gasp of pain. 'Sorry. Let's have a closer look. My word, it looks a lot better than Simon led me to believe. I think it's healing nicely.'

'Of course it is,' I said. 'Dr Levy made a terrible fuss over nothing.'

Lily exchanged a look with Jim, and then they both looked at me. I had an impression of Lily's eyes, that always seemed to sparkle, and Jim's measured grey gaze. I looked down, annoyed at myself for my rudeness about Simon and wondering why he brought out the worst in me.

'Well,' said Lily, picking up the soaked gauze, 'I'm very pleased to see it's healing. Simon told us you were barely able to stand up.'

I gasped at the pain as she laid the iodine-soaked gauze on the wound, then said hotly, 'That's sheer exaggeration. I could have finished my shift, but he was ludicrously insistent. He'd do much better to mind his own business in future.'

'You really don't like Simon, do you?' said Lily.

I looked up and held her gaze. I remembered how brave Simon had been to insist on being lowered into the narrow hole to administer morphine to Joe Gardiner, and his kindness to me when I was fractious and ill. *His refusal to acknowledge my offering of peace. His comments just before he left.*

'Oh, I know I owe him a great deal and he's obviously a good man. But he dislikes *me*. I think he can't forgive me for David's death.'

'Give him time,' said Jim, reaching into his tunic. 'We picked up your afternoon post downstairs.'

He handed me two letters. One was from Moray. The other from Cedric, sent from the Isle of Man, where his internment camp was located. The postmark was dated three weeks earlier and on it was stamped 'Delayed due to Enemy Action'. I set it aside to read when I was alone. In all of my now irregular letters to Cedric I asked him for a divorce, but he had remained implacably opposed to the idea and I did not hold many hopes that he would have changed his mind.

The usual form in a divorce case was for the husband to admit to adultery in an affidavit. Just one of Cedric's many affairs would form the basis for a divorce, but without Cedric's affidavit I had no proof that a court would accept. I did not want to admit to my affair with David. If Cedric divorced me on that basis it would be embarrassing for the Levys and humiliating for me, and there was no guarantee that Cedric would bring divorce proceedings against me even if I did. If I refused to return to Cedric then he could divorce me for desertion after three years, but I doubted that he would do so unless he wanted to remarry. I had no grounds to seek a divorce for cruelty. There were no other options open to me. My greatest fear was that Cedric would never allow me a divorce and I would be married but not married, unable ever to get on with my life.

'Do you mind?' I asked, holding up Moray's letter. At their nods, I opened it. Moray wrote that he had spoken to Dr Levy that morning, who said I was not to return to work until Saturday at the earliest. Although Moray appreciated my devotion to the ambulance service, if I came back any earlier I would be sent home immediately. Which was annoying, as I felt remarkably improved after a long sleep and a day spent lounging around my flat.

The upward wailing notes of the Warning split the air.

'Do you want to take shelter?' I asked.

They shook their heads. I knew why. St Andrew's was a solid building, we were sitting away from the windows and, like me, Lily and Jim preferred to remain put rather than scurry down to the basement shelter during an air raid.

'I'll make a pot of tea,' said Jim. He held up a paper bag. 'Brought our own supply.'

'And we've brought biscuits,' added Lily.

Jim disappeared into my kitchen and a short while later, as the roar of German aircraft competed with the thump of the guns and the crump of falling bombs, we were sipping tea and munching biscuits and discussing a parrot.

'I simply can't believe it,' I said. 'You've found Bobby?'

'Not quite yet, but we will,' said Lily. 'The parrot deserves a good home. After all, he saved your life by calling out and letting the rescuers know where you were.'

I gave an involuntary shudder at the memory of those long hours in the darkness. 'So he should have,' I said. 'I was trapped only because I'd tried to save the bird. But how—'

Jim smiled. 'You know what Lily is like once she gets the bit between her teeth. She went to the ARP warden – dragging me along with her – and demanded to know what he'd done with the thing.'

Lily laughed. 'Jim loomed over the poor man and cross-examined him until he admitted he'd sold it to a bird seller in Club Row.'

'The bird market?' I had visited Club Row in Shoreditch as a child. Images came to mind of birds squawking and tweeting in cages piled up along grimy stone-fronted shops. 'That can't still be operating, not with the bombing.'

'Apparently the little shops are still open,' said Jim, 'but the street market has shut for the duration. According to the warden, Bobby is at the shop of Ephraim Tulloch.'

'Well, I doubt Mr Tulloch has sold the bird,' I said. 'Poor Bobby was practically bald.'

Outside, the raid had increased in intensity. A loud explosion shook the room, and we all flinched. I put my cup and saucer on the small table in front of me. 'That was close.'

Jim shook his head. 'At least a mile away. Jerry's hitting the City again, I suspect.'

'What's the point of that?' said Lily. 'It's all gone.'

'It's not been utterly annihilated,' protested Jim.

'Give them time.'

I decided to bring the conversation back to more cheerful matters. 'What on earth are you going to do with the parrot if you do get hold of it?'

Lily shrugged. 'I'll have to find it a new owner. Fancy a parrot?' Her accent broadened. 'It'll make a bonzer pet.'

'You don't want to keep it yourself?'

She threw Jim a sly smile. 'Jim says a mouthy parrot is not conducive to marital bliss. His words, not mine.' Her smile became wider. 'And we'll be married in less than three weeks. Someone will take Bobby, I'm sure.'

Without giving the matter any real consideration, I found myself saying, 'I'll take him.'

Lily threw Jim a look as if to say, 'I told you she would.'

To me she said, 'Good-oh. Bobby will be company for you. No one can mope with a parrot around. We had a gorgeous cockatoo in Kookynie when I was a child and it picked up all sorts of funny sayings. I'll teach Bobby some Australian slang and you'll laugh—'

'Like a parrot at a bagpiper,' said Jim.

Lily and I both stared at him.

'Shakespeare,' he said, with more than a little smugness. '*The Merchant of Venice.*'

'Don't show off, darling,' said Lily.

Three whistling, ripping noises cut through the ceaseless drone of German aircraft, and a minute later the room shook three times in quick succession. A stick of bombs had landed, much closer than before. When I lifted my teacup to my lips my hand trembled. This worried me. I had always found air raids exhilarating, rather than terrifying. Had my time buried underground turned me into a coward?

Then I realised what Lily had said.

'Why did you say, "mope"?' I asked, putting the cup down. 'Do you think I've been moping?'

Lily looked at me. 'You suffered a terrible loss only two months ago. No one could get over David's loss quickly. Of course you are still unhappy. Last week you were trapped for hours and hours, not knowing if you would live or die. Then you discover that the man who saved you is David's brother, which must have made it all even worse.' She leaned across to touch my hand. 'I think you are sad, Celia. But I know you will find your way back. In your own time.'

It was as if my mind was blank, and I had no reply. People who don't know Lily well see her only as a pretty, curly-haired bundle of energy with a lovely smile. They see a small Australian whirlwind who sweeps everything up around her and never seems to relax, but Lily has a core of solid nurturing affection and tough common sense. And she was right, of course.

'Anyway,' Lily added, 'I never said you were moping. Just that any tendency in that direction would be prevented by the company of a parrot.'

Another explosion, this time much nearer, shook the room. Lily smiled at me. Lily's smile is impossibly infectious and I found myself smiling in return.

I said, teasingly, 'Any tendency towards moping…?'

'Will be prevented by the company of a parrot. *Everybody* knows that. It is a truth universally acknowledged.'

'So you're allowed to quote, but I'm not,' said Jim, in an aggrieved tone.

'If you feel well enough, please come with us to Shoreditch tomorrow afternoon,' said Lily, pointedly ignoring him. 'Jim has the day off because he worked all weekend. We're determined to find Bobby.'

They stayed until the All Clear. As Lily picked up her coat and hat she asked, 'By the way, who is your doctor?'

'Dr Cameron, in Gower Street. Right now he's away with the army and his father is looking after the practice for him. Why?'

'You'll need those stitches out in a couple of days.'

They left. I made myself a cup of Horlicks and sat on the couch to read Cedric's letter, which had been marked as passed by the censor. We were at war and all mail was read and censored, but it was galling to know that strangers were allowed to read my pleas to my husband for a divorce and his flippant refusals.

I tore open the envelope and extracted the two sheets of flimsy blue paper. *Darling, great news. I am to be let out of this place…*

So Eddie had been right after all. It was likely that Cedric's father had had a hand in his release. My father-in-law was a Member of Parliament and a friend of Churchill's, and he had been campaigning for months to have his son released from prison.

I carried on reading, scanning Cedric's thick, left-slanted writing. It was heavily censored, but what remained was sufficient to dash my hopes of freedom. *I will never agree to a divorce. Really, darling, you'd hate being a divorcee. The invitations would dry up. Remember, divorcees are not allowed into the Royal Box at Ascot. Much better to keep things as they are.*

Invitations? Royal Box? I wondered if spending time on the Isle of Man had addled his brain. Most of our friends had dropped me cold, and there was no longer any social season worth mentioning.

*You must know I adore you. I tell you, darling, all our dreams may soon come true. Let's begin again, shall we?*

So Cedric thought that if he told me he loved me and snapped his fingers I'd come running back to him. I shook my head. He was in for a nasty surprise.

# CHAPTER TEN

When I came downstairs early the following afternoon Jim was waiting with Lily in the lobby. Lily was telling him some story as he gazed at her with the slightly dazed expression he always seemed to exhibit when he was looking at his fiancée.

Their registry wedding was to take place in a little under three weeks and a Russian Orthodox ceremony would be conducted later, once Lily had finished her conversion. This consisted of lessons once a week with a Russian priest. Lily had told me that the conversion process was hard-going and would take some time. When I asked her if she minded having to convert, she said that as it mattered a great deal to Jim she was happy to do it. I wasn't sure that I could be so accommodating. The subject had never arisen with David.

'Ready for Operation African Grey?' said Lily, turning at my greeting.

I laughed. 'Operation African Bald, more like.'

'Jim says we shouldn't offer any money for Bobby as the warden had no right to sell him in the first place, but we'll see.'

'Him? Are you sure Bobby is a boy?'

'It's hard to tell the sex on an African Grey,' said Jim.

'Until it lays an egg?' I suggested.

Lily shrugged. 'Bobby's a boy. I'm sure of it. Will you teach him any words or phrases?'

'I think parrots pick things up without you even trying.'

'Tell you what,' said Lily. 'I'll teach him how to sing "Waltzing Matilda" and he'll liven up your flat with swagmen, billabongs, coolabah trees and jolly jumbucks. A touch of

Australia in Bloomsbury.' She gave a gurgle of laughter at my expression.

'There will be no singing anywhere near my parrot,' I said, sternly. 'I mean that.'

Jim broke in. 'If you don't mind, I'd like to visit the City before we head off to Shoreditch. I want to see what sort of damage the firestorm caused. I know you were in the City on the night it burned, Celia, but I've not had a chance to get there yet.'

'The main problem will be finding the right bus,' said Lily. 'With all the roads blocked by "No Entry" or "Unexploded Bomb" signs, the 63 bus now curls about in all sorts of back streets. The other day I met one going east and west, got on and ended up heading north when I wanted south. I felt such an fool, but the conductor said it happens all the time nowadays.'

Despite Lily's concerns, we managed to catch a southbound bus to Ludgate Circus, and marched up the left side of Ludgate Hill towards St Paul's under a leaden sky that suggested it would soon be snowing. The streets were filled with people, apparently all as anxious as Jim was to view the fire-ravaged City on this grey day. The mood of the crowd became sombre as we got closer to the cathedral and saw the extent of the damage caused by the firestorm.

Ancient alleys and courtyards were flattened areas of ash. Buildings were empty shells that had burned from the inside out. Ave Maria Lane was closed, and when we peered down the little crooked street, the fire appeared to have left nothing in its wake. All around was a wasteland of charred ruin, yet ahead of us St Paul's stood proudly in the centre of the blighted City, serenely beautiful as ever.

'Paternoster Row's a complete ruin,' said a warden who was directing a heavy-rescue team. 'Terrible shame. They say we lost six million books in the flames.' He sighed, then raised his chin and straightened his shoulders. 'We must always remember, we'd be much worse off under Hitler.' His voice strengthened. 'It's true, you know. You have to think of that when all of this gets you down.'

We wandered on among the sightseers. The buildings on the left side of Watling Street were mostly ruins. Jim sighed to see the utter destruction.

'So many Wren churches,' he muttered.

I was startled when Lily gave a short laugh.

'Oh, look at this,' she said, pointing to the window of a little stationer's shop. All the plate glass of the windows lay in glistening fragments on the shelf behind and the place was in a terrible state with the counter smashed and stock scattered over the floor. A couple of workers were doggedly putting it to rights. In the windowsill, a board with a bit of handwritten doggerel verse had been set up under a Union Jack. It said:

> *'Hitler dropped a bomb on Hart's,*
> *and knocked it all to bits,*
> *but if he saw us carrying on,*
> *he'd have blue pencil fits.'*

It was signed 'Professor Bush'. Next to it another board proclaimed: *'We're open and still going strong'*.

Lily called out 'Good on you' to the workers who were cleaning up inside.

They smiled at her, and one of them said earnestly, 'None of this matters, so long as we beat *him.'*

Hart's was not the only bombed shop to have a defiantly funny notice in its window, and we managed to laugh despite the devastation.

*'We are open for business. Oh, boy, are we open for business'* was in the shattered windows of a haberdashery shop that had had a wall blown out. And around the corner, a fishmonger had put up: *'Jerry tried to jump the queue and cut up rough when we wouldn't serve him'*. We passed two shops, both practically demolished with their roofs off and no glass in any window. One had a notice up, *'Open as Usual'*, and the one next door had gone one better and put a board up, *'More Open Than Usual'*.

We continued on our trek, up Bread Street and into Cheapside as the snow began to fall. It was a nightmare scene. Building after building had been reduced to a scarred and blackened shell. It was a relief to see the steeple of St Mary-le-Bow. We walked up to the old church, standing before us on its slight hill. It was black with soot and gouged by shrapnel but rendered picturesque in the falling snow.

'They used to say that you weren't a true cockney unless you're born under the sound of the Bow bells,' said Jim to Lily.

'I know that,' she replied. 'Squire told me.

Jim gazed at the blackened walls and sighed. 'I wonder if the old church will last the war.'

'If it survived this,' said Lily, waving at the destruction around us, 'I'm confident it'll survive whatever Hitler throws at it.'

As we continued our walk I watched the crowds milling around. Not one word of anger or fury had I heard, no railing against Hitler or the Luftwaffe. Everyone looked serious, but there was a quiet dignity about the people as they slowly paced through the devastation, as though awed by the magnitude of the loss of the City.

Jim and Lily turned into a narrow laneway, and I followed them, shuffling through the banked-up snow. On either side were ruined shops and houses.

'Where are we?' I asked.

'Old Jewry,' Jim replied. 'Now the headquarters of the City Police, but London's Jewish ghetto in medieval times.'

'Really?' said Lily. 'David never told me about this street.'

'It's not a place that has pleasant memories. There was a massacre of Jews here, in the late twelfth century, during the coronation of Richard the Lionheart. I suppose they thought it was a patriotic gesture,' he added drily.

'Was that when the Jews were expelled from England?' asked Lily.

Jim seemed to search his memory. 'No. That was a century later, in 1290. The Edict of Expulsion.'

It sounded all too similar to what was happening in Europe under Hitler, where Jews were again being exiled and killed.

Looking at the narrow laneway with its charred buildings, I tried to imagine the crowded streets of medieval London. Here in this ruined little street had lived black-gowned men who perhaps looked like David or Simon. They had watched in despair as their homes were destroyed and their people killed. And a century later, they had been forced into exile across the Channel.

Jim led us out of Old Jewry and into Coleman Street, now a wasteland of ashes and blighted walls, charred rubble and bricks, a tangle of steel girders twisted into tortuous shapes. Ahead of us was a little ruined church. Only its blackened walls remained, still reaching for heaven.

'St Stephen's,' said Jim. 'A Christopher Wren church, built after the last Great Fire. So many of the Wren churches have been destroyed. All of them masterpieces.'

'Will they be rebuilt, d'you think?' asked Lily.

'God, I hope so,' said Jim.

'But the City isn't a residential area any more,' I pointed out. 'It doesn't need a church on every corner. If they're complete wrecks, shouldn't the sites be sold to help the City repair the churches that are less damaged?'

'No,' said Jim firmly, ever the traditionalist.

Eventually we reached our destination, the devastated Guildhall. The richly decorated council chamber had been burnt out. The giant figures of Gog and Magog – London's ancient guardians – were no more. The roof had been blasted open and the painted ceilings destroyed. The building was roped off and men were working hard to secure the ruins. Someone had hoisted the Union Jack but there was no wind and the flag drooped disconsolately. Snow began to fall again, deadening the sound of machinery and men, carpeting the scene of desolation in an austere white beauty.

Jim gestured towards the shell of yet another old church that stood next to Guildhall.

'St Lawrence Jewry. An incendiary took hold there on the night of the bombing, the fire spread to Guildhall and this is the result.'

I looked at the ruined church. *St Lawrence Jewry. Old Jewry Street.* Even after seven hundred years, the memory of the medieval Jewish ghetto still lingered in the names. Amongst this charred destruction were the ghosts and shadows of David's people. I had a sudden image of his brother's thin face with its dark intensity. They were Simon's people, too. And what happened to them in this place seven hundred years ago was only a pale shadow of what was happening right now, just across the Channel.

'There should have been more fire-watchers,' said Jim. His face was flushed and angry. 'The City was criminally understaffed with fire-watchers. That's why the incendiaries took hold.'

'At least they saved St Paul's,' said Lily.

'If I hear that one more time, I swear I'll do something violent,' he said. 'Look around you. Look at what's been lost. Most of Fleet Street. The Temple northwards and eastwards beyond Fountain Court is gone. Charles Dickens would weep to see it.'

I thought of the Temple Church, where the effigies of the Crusaders lay with their crossed legs, and also felt like weeping.

'It'll be rebuilt.' Lily took hold of his arm. 'This is beyond the worst I could have imagined. But I refuse to cry, because it will be rebuilt.'

Jim took a deep breath. 'You keep saying that, Lily. But it won't be the same.'

I cleared my throat, unsure if I should speak. Jim knew a great deal more than I did about London's history, but it was a story that David had told me, and it had given me hope on a night when we clung to each other as the bombers came in low and the scream and thunder of their falling cargo seemed to tear apart the air.

'After the first Great Fire,' I said, 'when Sir Christopher Wren was laying out the centre of the new cathedral—'

I saw Jim's expression soften and he smiled. He obviously knew the story, but I didn't think that Lily did, so I went on.

'—he asked for a stone to mark the centre of the dome, as a guide for the workmen. Someone brought him a piece of old tombstone they had picked up at random from a heap of rubble in the ruins of the old cathedral. And when Wren looked at it he found that it was engraved with the Latin inscription "*resurgam*", which means "I shall rise again". So he placed the stone in the new cathedral, beneath a carved phoenix. I suppose it's still there.'

Lily's smile lit up that gloomy day as she turned to Jim. 'See,' she said.

'See what? It changes nothing.' But he smiled at her in return, reached out and touched her hair.

It seemed clear that they had forgotten that anyone else existed, so I turned and walked a little distance, leaving them alone while I watched the heavy-rescue crew secure the ruins of the once-beautiful Guildhall. And as I mourned the City's destruction in my own way, I felt cheered to remember Maisie's bit of doggerel:

*'But try as they might they'll never break her*
*Just like before, we will remake her.'*

'*Resurgam*,' I said, and the word slipped away into the wind.

# CHAPTER ELEVEN

A short while later Lily, Jim and I were on a red London bus trundling through the snow along Bishopsgate towards Shoreditch. As I watched the scarred face of London pass by the window I remembered my conversation with Simon when I was trapped and reflected that London buses *were* somehow comfortingly human. Perhaps it was their sheer normality amid the chaos.

Then a blue bus passed us and reminded me that nothing in wartime London was normal. Emergency bus services were used to ferry passengers whenever a railway line was incapacitated. As a result, London's fleet of buses was over-stretched and buses were being brought into London from all over the country. I watched it drive away and wondered where the blue bus had come from.

We got off at Bethnal Green Road and walked along Club Row towards Arnold Circus, looking for the birdseller who might have poor Bobby. I had come to the live animal market in Club Row with my godmother as a treat one Sunday morning when I was ten years old and visiting her in London, and I had looked in wonderment at the caged life before me. There had been birds of all kinds, cats and puppies and more exotic beasts in cages outside the shops. The vendors' cries matched those of their wares, as they called and cawed and bellowed in the frosty air. One fellow in a striped waistcoat and a spotted handkerchief knotted around his sinewy neck had jumped in front of us and thrust a kitten into my face. 'Kitten for the pretty little girl?' he asked my godmother, before grinning at me. 'I'll have to call you Penny, luv. Coz your hair's the colour of a new copper penny.'

I had longed to take the small bundle of squirming black-and-white fur from him, but my godmother batted away his hands. 'Oh, no,' she had said, in her regal manner, 'that will simply not do.'

Now I walked through a shadow of the busy market I remembered. The air did not ring with shrieks and calls and barking and mewing and the shouts of cockney vendors. Some cages lined the roadside as before, but their few occupants sat miserably huddled on perches, obviously cold and dispirited. I saw lorikeets and budgerigars and poultry and pigeons, but no parrots. It was all much more subdued than I remembered and more than a little sad.

'Here it is,' said Jim, waving at the sign outside a brick shop front with birdcages in the window. 'Ephraim Tulloch, Birds Rare and Exotic.'

Mr Tulloch was a little man with a large round stomach that strained his waistcoat, and his eyes sat in his fleshy face like two blackcurrants in a pale, doughy bun. He laughed when we said we had come for Bobby.

'You're welcome to him,' he said. 'He's not a handsome bird and he doesn't say anything. Knew I'd never be able to sell him, but Syd would have wrung his neck if I didn't take him.' He leaned towards us and said, in a more confidential tone, 'I've a weakness for parrots, so I couldn't allow that. Almost human, they are. Especially African Greys. Ferociously intelligent are the African Greys.'

'So it *is* a male parrot?' said Lily. 'I thought so, but we weren't sure.'

Mr Tulloch winked. 'He's a boy all right. Now, let's talk turkey.'

Jim might be a barrister in peacetime, but Mr Tulloch was able to comprehensively out-argue him to strike a bargain to his advantage. We took ownership of Bobby for what Mr Tulloch

109

had paid the warden, plus the price of the bird's food over the past week and 'a little something extra for my trouble'.

The problem that faced us then was how to transport Bobby and his cage to my flat. Taxis were in short supply so we decided on the tram. After negotiations with the conductor, Jim bought Bobby his own ticket and the parrot sat next to me in his large, blanket-covered cage.

The other passengers were naturally curious and, after some encouragement, I pulled away the blanket to reveal my new pet.

'That's one ugly parrot,' said a sailor who was sitting in front of me.

Heads nodded in agreement. I looked at Bobby, who was indeed a sorry sight with his three large bald patches revealing wrinkled grey skin underneath the feathers. But his bright red tail feather still curled proudly and his yellow eyes had a glitter of knowing intelligence.

I replied, stiffly, 'He looks remarkably well, I think, given he was dug out of a bombed house a week ago. He is still recovering.'

'Does he talk?'

'Sometimes.'

I hoped Bobby would not announce himself to these people as repetitively as he had done when we were trapped together. I did not want to hear again the voice of the old woman who had loved him enough to think of him as she was dying.

'You know,' said a middle-aged man in a brown suit, 'one of my earliest memories is being taken to see a lady who lived in Highgate by the cemetery. She had a parrot, and the parrot used to say, "I'm pretty witty Nell, who the devil are you?"'

There was laughter around us. A motherly-looking woman in a felt hat leaned across to say to Bobby, 'Who's a pretty boy, then?'

Bobby regarded her lugubriously through one round eye, but did not reply. When he continued to make no sound, interest in him lapsed. I kept the blanket off the cage, however, thinking he might enjoy seeing what was going on around him.

A few minutes later, just as we had swung into Clerkenwell Road, we all flinched as the upward wailing notes of the Warning filled the tram. There was a general groan of annoyance.

'It's only four o'clock. Jerry's early today.'

Then the shriek of a falling bomb rent the air. There was no time to take cover or prepare for eternity. In the seats around me people screamed and ducked down, terror distorting their faces. Lily grabbed Jim and buried her head in his chest as his arms tightened around her. Time seemed to slow. I had a moment's sharp panic followed by resignation. *At least I am facing death in the light, in the open air.* For some reason that was important to me. Simon Levy's face flashed into my mind. Would he be sorry that he had refused my offer of peace? Or merely annoyed that all his efforts to save me had failed after all.

There was a sound like crashing thunder as the bomb exploded.

I felt no thump of impact. No pain.

Nothing happened at all. The tram continued rattling along on its journey. Almost immediately, the All Clear sounded.

Around me exclamations and sobs resolved into swearing and angry muttering.

'Oh, you clever bird,' said Lily, pushing herself out of Jim's tight hold and staring at the parrot with an expression of bewilderment. She shook her head. 'Crikey.'

'Bloody thing almost scared the wits out of me,' said the sailor who had called Bobby ugly. 'It oughta have its neck wrung.'

I threw the blanket over Bobby's cage and silently dared anyone to try. My hands were shaking, so I held them tightly together in my lap.

'Leave it alone,' said the man in the brown suit. 'Bird was only mimicking what it's been hearing. Just be thankful it wasn't real.'

'Why don't you teach him something nicer, dear?' said the woman in the felt hat. 'A song, or a nursery rhyme, perhaps.'

'"London Bridge is Falling Down"?' suggested brown-suit man.

And the laughter started. It may have been slightly hysterical but it was, on the whole, good-natured. I caught Lily's eye and we laughed together until tears were streaming down our faces.

Jim deposited Bobby's large cage in a corner of my sitting room and he and Lily left me alone with the bird. When I removed the blanket Bobby bobbed his head and walked sideways along the perch, all the while regarding me with a grave, knowing frown. Mr Tulloch had said that parrots, and especially African Greys, were extremely intelligent. Bobby certainly seemed to ponder deeply upon life. *Bobby*. The name did not suit the gravely dignified bird that was subjecting me to such unwinking scrutiny.

Mr Tulloch had suggested that I let him wander about. 'Get him used to your flat,' he had said. 'Bit of bird dirt never hurt anyone. Mind you, he's a clever feller in that department. Been trained, you see. Goes in the morning, and won't go again unless he's really scared.' So I opened the cage door and gestured towards the room.

'Come out if you like,' I said. 'This is your new home.'

Bobby hopped from his perch to the floor of the cage and stepped delicately out into the room. He waddled across to the bookcase that stood under the window, gave a gentle squawk and flapped up to land on the top of a pile of books. From this vantage point he looked around the sitting room and at the closed window. Bobby peered out over London, fluffed up his feathers and turned around to face me. Again I was subjected to that dark lugubrious gaze. Did the answers to all the questions of the universe lurk deep within those round yellow eyes?

'Hello, I'm Bobby,' he squawked. 'What's your name?'

'Good God, Celia. A parrot?'

My sister ran a pocket-comb through the long shining bob of her auburn hair and adjusted the mink cape she wore over her evening gown. Helen had dropped in to see me on her way to dinner at the Ritz.

'I like the parrot. He's company,' I said, too defensively.

'Cedric won't like it.'

'Well, it's none of his business. As I've told you, I want to divorce Cedric.'

Her mouth tightened. 'You can be very worrying, Celia. It's as if I don't know you any more. You always have been out of the usual, but now...' She waved her arms in a gesture of annoyance. 'It's this war. It's changed you. It's changing everything. Girls are quite above themselves nowadays, off to work in the factories, or in uniform and walking out with the young servicemen. I shudder to think what they'll be like after the war. And look at you, cool as a cucumber, telling me you want a divorce. It's utterly ridiculous. I remember how happy you were when you were first engaged, when you—'

'I was eighteen years old. I had no idea what marriage, or Cedric, was really like.'

'A husband isn't something you can throw away like a – a faulty gas mask.' She paused, as if to admire her simile. 'A husband is for life.'

'Gas masks aren't for life, and neither is Cedric.'

She firmly changed the subject. 'So Jim really is intending to marry his colonial?'

'In less than three weeks now.'

'What a waste of an impressive title. She won't appreciate the honour.'

'Oh, for goodness' sake, don't be such a snob, Helen. She's marrying Jim, not his title. Not only does she not appreciate the title, Lily honestly doesn't give two hoots about it.'

Helen raised an eyebrow. 'As I said, a waste.'

She moved across to the parrot's cage and stood for a while, looking at Bobby and he walked slowly up and down his perch and watched her back with his soulful eyes. *A cat may look at a king*, I thought, *and a parrot at a brigadier's wife.*

'Will you put Cedric up here when he's released?' she asked, still looking at Bobby.

'No. Of course not. He can stay with his father or in an hotel.'

'His father doesn't want Cedric to move in with him for political reasons.' She gave an elegant shrug. 'I'm sure the Dorchester or somewhere similar will have room for him. Actually, he mentioned it in his last letter.'

'It's supposed to be bomb-proof, earthquake-proof and fire-proof.' I flicked away a mote of dust from the side table. 'So you've been corresponding with him?'

'More regularly than you, he informs me.'

'I write to him only to ask for my freedom.'

She swung around to face me at that, and I caught a glimpse of fury in her eyes, soon damped down. 'How melodramatic you are sometimes, Celia,' she said lightly. 'You'll see things differently once he's back.'

Dr Cameron senior was a genial Scotsman of around seventy with shaggy white eyebrows and a twinkle in his pale blue eyes. When I asked after his son he replied, 'Och, Alastair's getting quite a tan in the desert sun, I believe.'

After he had removed the stitches in the head wound and given me a thorough check-up, he told me I was fine to report for duty.

'It all looks ticketyboo to me,' he said, 'but wait one more day before you go back.'

He wrote me a note to take to Moray, which said I was fully fit for duties in two days.

'I'll let your Dr Levy know,' he said, as he handed me the note. 'He was insistent that you should not return to work as an ambulance driver until you were quite well.'

I stared at him. 'How…' And then, annoyed, 'He's not *my* Dr Levy.'

Dr Cameron peered at me from under his shaggy brows. 'Now you just climb off that high horse, madam. Dr Levy wrote to me, explaining about the circumstances of the injury and the infection. It's usual to do so if you treat another doctor's patient.'

I wondered how Simon knew that I was Dr Cameron's patient. Then I realised. *Lily.* She had asked me who my doctor was, and must have informed Simon. Were my friends spying on me? I told myself not to fall prey to paranoia, but it was disconcerting to know that Simon Levy was keeping an eye on me.

I decided that if I couldn't return to work at the station, then I would spend the following day at Bloomsbury House instead. My accident and recovery meant that I hadn't appeared at the refugee centre for more than a week, and I missed the work.

I had some qualms about leaving Bobby alone, so I put his cage by the window to allow him to look out, and I left the wireless on, tuned to the BBC, reasoning that if he picked up any words, they would be acceptable in polite company. Despite my best efforts over the past two days, I'd not been able to teach him any words or phrases at all. Or, at least, none that he was willing to repeat. And yet, I found his silent company cheering, especially when he let me hold him close and he tucked his feathery head under my chin. Maybe it was simply having a living creature in my flat to look after.

'Now you be a good boy,' I said to him as I left.

I laughed at myself as I negotiated the stairs. Was I at risk of becoming one of those lonely women who talked to their pets as if they were human? And yet … there was something about Bobby that did seem almost human. I laughed again. *Don't become eccentric,* I told myself. Then I wondered whether, if Cedric could be convinced that I had become an eccentric embarrassment to him, he would want to be rid of me. *Was it worth a try?* Cedric was cunning and could be charming but he wasn't all that bright. I was laughing as I opened the door.

I decided to walk to Bloomsbury House, rather than cycle. It was a clear morning, although very cold. During my walk I looked – really looked – at London. It had a very different appearance to the grand cosmopolitan city I had moved to after my marriage.

There were gaps where buildings that had stood for centuries, or as little as decades, were now just rubble on the ground. Windows that still had glass in them were criss-crossed with paper in various designs, or stuck over with a muslin or net curtain to prevent splinters. Nearly every house had a wall of sandbags against a window or a front door. Buckets of sand and water were in most doorways to deal with incendiaries and large water tanks stood in parks or wherever there was space for them. The kerbs were painted white, and thick yellow bands on the pavements pointed to the fire hydrants. White signs showed the way to air-raid shelters.

Chillingly, on the corner of Bedford Avenue was an object that resembled a large bird table. The square top was painted yellowish-green. These tables had been placed throughout London and they were supposed to change colour from green to red in the presence of mustard gas. I patted my gas mask, safe in its natty leather case. There had been talk of gas attacks lately, as a precursor to invasion. Then I remembered Sadler's Aunt Millie's gas-beating knickers trick, and I laughed.

Lore examined me closely as I walked into the JCPB office, and said in her accented English, 'Celia. Why are you here? I heard you were ill – injured, I mean. Injured in a raid. Are you well enough to be here?'

'I'm fine. Really. Got my All Clear from the doctor this morning.'

She seemed unconvinced. 'Simon – I mean Dr Levy – he seemed to think you—'

'*Dr Levy?*' Was there a person in London who had not been told my entire medical history by Simon Levy? I took a breath and consciously relaxed my jaw. 'Dr Levy is an excellent doctor, but he is excessively cautious. I am absolutely fine.'

Lore gave me a bright smile. 'I admit that you do look very well indeed. Apart from the bandage, of course.' Her eyes became dreamy. 'Isn't Simon a lovely young man? Such a caring doctor. He came to us for the Seder on Friday.' Dreaminess gave way to a slight look of calculation. 'He is partial to my Miriam, and it would be an excellent match.' Then she made a face and laughed. 'All the women wanted a Levy boy for their girls, but Elise Levy is like a guarding dog over her sons.' A querying look. 'Is it terribly rude to call Elise a guarding dog?'

'It is, rather. Better to say that she's vigilant in looking after their interests. Or, that she's a careful mother.'

Lore looked down at the desk. 'I worry about my Miriam. Especially after... You knew David?'

'Yes... I did.'

She sighed. 'Such a shame. Miriam adored him.'

I picked up the day's mail and began to leaf through it. 'And did he...?'

'Sadly, no. He liked her, but not, you understand, like that. David kept his private life very private. Even from his mother. It must have been so much easier for parents in the old days, with *shidduch.*'

She must have seen my look of incomprehension.

'Matchmaking. Such things were arranged in a civilised manner in past centuries.' She gave me a wry smile. 'Not that we had *shidduch* in modern Berlin. Like my father, Mrs Levy's was *ein Deutscher, aber ein Jude.* That means, a German, but Jewish.' Her expression became bitter. 'Of course, the Nazis see us only as Jews. It doesn't matter if we are devout or liberal or atheists. Or if we were born and raised as Christians. To them we are Jews if only one grandparent was Jewish and all the rest were Aryan.'

'Mrs Levy must be very worried about her family.'

Lore sighed. 'She has heard nothing for some months. It is very distressing. I am lucky to have no family in Germany. Not any more. I persuaded them to come over here to join me in England when that evil house painter came to power. The Levys sponsored them. All of them.' She looked at me and raised her hands. 'And so, Elise and Jonathan Levy probably saved the lives of my entire family.'

'Surely it's not that bad in Europe,' I said, falteringly.

Lore gave me a wistful smile. 'My dear, it *is* that bad. We Jews know what is happening over there, but who will listen?' She seemed to recollect where she was and shuffled the papers in front of her into a neat pile. Her tone became brisk. 'But you and I cannot solve the problems of the Jews in Europe. We must consider only the problems of the children we managed to bring across to Britain.' She looked down at the papers in front of her. 'And here is a small boy who is a very big problem.' She pointed to a small photograph. 'Leonhard Weitz.'

'But we placed him. Last week. I finished the paperwork.'

'No,' said Lore. 'The foster-parents you identified refused to have him. And now he is in trouble at the hostel for fighting.'

I frowned down at the picture. 'I'll find someone to foster him. I'm sure I can find someone.'

She gave me a rueful smile. 'We have an offer to foster him from a wealthy and loving Jewish family.'

'Then what is the big problem?'

'The big problem is that it is Elise Levy who is determined to take in the boy. And her husband and son are just as determined not to allow her to do so. And you and I are in the middle of it all.'

# CHAPTER TWELVE

Mrs Levy shook her head. '*Alles ist gut*, Celia. The boy could not stay in the hostel. He was being bullied.'

I was in the Levy's new home, a Georgian townhouse in Montague Street, behind the British Museum and close to Bloomsbury House. Lore had insisted that I walk over to see Mrs Levy that afternoon. My instructions were to convince Mrs Levy to return Leonhard Weitz to the hostel and allow us to find other foster-parents, but since my arrival Mrs Levy had been firmly and gently refusing to consider giving Leonhard up.

She gave me a sceptical look. 'Are you sure you are well enough to be working? Simon seemed to think—'

'I am perfectly fine.' I sounded sharper than I had intended, and softened my tone. 'I was entirely recovered four days ago, but Si– Dr Levy told my station officer I wasn't allowed to return to ambulance work until tomorrow.'

'Simon is a tyrant sometimes,' she agreed. '"Mutti," he says to me, "you must rest. You look haggard." I know that a hag is an old and ugly woman, so I take to my bed. Then he orders me up. "Mutti, you must exercise. If you don't, you'll never walk without crutches again." So I do his horrible exercises, and when he sees me next it's, "Mutti, you look terrible. You must rest." He is impossible.'

Her indulgent smile took the sting out of her words. The smile reminded me so much of David that I had to look down to hide hot tears. With her delicate features and luminous dark eyes, anyone less like a hag than Mrs Levy would be hard to find.

I decided to bring the conversation back on point. 'I don't understand how you found out about Leonhard Weitz.'

'I telephone the hostel regularly to see if they are in need of anything. Food, books, supplies, anything they might need. Florence mentioned Leonhard, and she told me that the other boys were shunning him. What is your English expression? Ah yes, sending him to Coventry. An odd expression, I think. Apparently he had struck a boy when he was being teased, and broke his nose.' She smiled. 'It's exactly what my Simon did, at Harrow.'

'Simon did that?' My voice was high and shocked.

Mrs Levy smiled at this. Embarrassed, I said, more moderately, 'It's difficult to believe.'

'Oh, yes. It shocked me, too, at the time. Simon was my shy boy, not a fighter like his older brothers. We found out later that Saul, my oldest, had taught both Simon and David how to box and fight before they went to school because he thought it was necessary that they knew such things.' Her eyes misted, and her lips trembled as she said, 'All through his time at Harrow, my hothead, David, was in trouble for fighting. I did not expect it of Simon.'

I nodded. I didn't expect it of Simon either.

'The other boy was quite badly injured and Simon was almost expelled.'

'Almost?'

'When Jonathan went to the school he found that they had decided to give Simon another chance because he had behaved so well after the fight.' She gave a soft laugh. 'Simon had taken care of his victim very efficiently, Jonathan was told. He stopped the nosebleed, and bandaged the boy's injuries with a handkerchief. He was found out because of the boy's two black eyes and his handkerchief-splinted broken arm. The other boy bore him no rancour and they became fast friends afterwards.' She laughed. 'Boys.'

I couldn't help but laugh as well. 'So he broke the boy's arm as well as his nose? How old was Simon?'

'He was thirteen years old.' She smiled. 'He told me later that he decided then and there that it was better to look after injuries than to inflict them. But he also told me it had felt good to punch the boy who had called him a filthy Yid.' She sighed. 'All my boys were bullied at Harrow, because they were Jewish. I wanted to take them out, but Jonathan said they had to learn to cope with it, because they would find it everywhere.'

'And that is why you want to help Leonhard? Because he was being bullied at the hostel? I'm sure that we can find an excellent set of foster-parents for him.'

'No. No,' she said firmly. 'Now we are settled in the new house it is right to foster a child. This boy needs mothering.' Mrs Levy frowned. 'He came here with nothing, absolutely nothing.' Her expression lightened. 'I will need to buy him clothes, toys, everything.'

'But—'

'It will be good to have a young boy to fuss over again. He reminds me of my own boys in his looks, particularly my Simon, but I fear the boy is indeed ... damaged. In his mind, you understand. He will need patience and love. I hope it is enough.'

'And he won't talk at all?'

'Not a word. It is very sad.' She looked up at me and smiled. 'You should meet him. We are about to take tea. Please join us. I will fetch Leonhard.' Her smile dimmed. 'You will find my mother-in-law, Mrs Cora Levy, in the drawing room. Please introduce yourself. She has just arrived to stay with us for a few days. Although she has moved to the country for the duration, she finds it difficult to be away from London.'

When I entered the drawing room I saw a small, dark-haired old woman seated by the window, who was busily knitting something in khaki wool. The tea trolley was near her, and plates of cakes and sandwiches had been set up on it, next to a silver teapot and cups and saucers made of china as delicate as eggshells.

I walked across and introduced myself.

'Celia Ashwin?' She scowled a little as she considered my name. I waited for her to realise who my husband was, and for her manner to change when she did. It took a minute or so, but then she gave a slight start and looked at me closely.

'Your maiden name was Palmer-Thomas.'

'Yes,' I said, surprised.

'And your mother was a Beaumont?'

'Yes.' My shoulders relaxed as I realised that Mrs Levy apparently had no interest in Cedric, but was engaged in the game of 'where are you placed among the county families'. It was a common game with the older generation of my set if they met anyone new, but I had not expected a little Jewish matriarch to be interested in my family.

Mrs Levy nodded again. 'And *her* mother was French. Célia Bernard, from Toulouse. Is that right?'

'Yes, that's right. I was named after my grandmother.'

She looked hard at me, pinning me with the full force of her shrewd gaze, and apparently expecting me to say more. When I remained silent, she sighed. 'Please tell Elise that I am tired after my journey and have gone to my room.'

The old woman rose and walked a little stiffly to the doorway. There she turned and said to me, 'You seem a nice enough girl. How silly you were to marry that nasty man.' Before I could reply she had opened the door and was gone.

Five minutes later Leonhard Weitz entered the drawing room with Mrs Levy.

There was something about the boy that tugged at my heart. He had outgrown the jacket he was wearing and thin childish wrists and hands hung limply by his side. His head was pulled down into his shoulders, as if waiting for a blow to fall and there was a quality of watchful, fearful silence around him. A mop of black hair framed a pale face with big dark eyes that regarded me from behind his spectacles with wan hopelessness. No child should look so defeated, I thought, and felt suddenly angry.

After our introductions – I said hello and he gave me a formal little bow – Mrs Levy led him across the room to the tea trolley by the window and offered the boy a glass of milk. He shook his head. She cut a piece of cake and placed it on a small plate. Although he accepted it, he made no move to eat. Mrs Levy lifted her eyes to mine and shrugged delicately before smiling at someone behind me.

I turned to see that Simon had entered the room. He greeted me with an expression of studied indifference rather than hostility. I saw it as indicating an improvement in our relations, so I gave him a smile. He looked away and went over to his mother, who had poured him a cup of tea. Then he walked across the room to stand by the fireplace. Somehow I knew he wanted to talk to me in relative privacy and, after accepting my own cup of tea, I joined him. I saw Mrs Levy's small smile as I did so, and suspected she was well aware of the fact that Simon and his father did not approve of her taking in the boy.

'His name is Leonhard Weitz,' said Simon, in a low voice. He pronounced it the European way, Ley-a-nard.

'I know that,' I said.

'And he doesn't talk.'

'I know that, too. According to his notes, he hasn't said a word since he arrived here in England last year.'

Leonhard had shifted his surprisingly adult and intense gaze away from Mrs Levy to look out of the window. The cake on his plate remained untouched.

Simon frowned. 'Do they know if he speaks English?'

'According to the notes, he complies with directions given in English. But his first language is German. He comes from Vienna. It may be comforting for him if your mother speaks to him in German.'

'My mother said his foster-family was unkind to him and he was bullied at the hostel. That's all she's told me.'

'She probably didn't want you to worry. Actually, he's been returned by two foster-families. They found him morose and uncooperative, sometimes aggressive. He was in trouble for fighting at the JCPB hostel. Your mother insists that he was bullied, and is determined to care for him.' ˙

We both looked at Leonhard. The fixed immobility with which he stared out of the window was difficult to witness in a child of eight. I have never been sentimental about children generally, but suddenly, and indeed almost violently, I wanted to help this child.

Simon shook his head. 'He'll be difficult to look after and she's not robust. Her legs are not healing as quickly as we had hoped.' Our eyes met, clashed, and we turned again to look at the boy who, at Mrs Levy's urging, had taken a small sip of milk.

'My father and I are both worried that it will be too much for her, looking after a child like that.'

'Perhaps it will do her good to cosset him.'

'I doubt he will let her, and it is dispiriting never to get any response, any gratitude for kindnesses one performs.'

*Was this a sly dig at me*? I didn't answer. Instead I walked across to Leonhard and sat beside him on the sofa. He turned his head to regard me gravely.

'Hello, Leonhard,' I said, saying his name the English way.

'It's pronounced Ley-a-nard,' said Simon again. He sat on a chair opposite and picked up a sandwich.

'We pronounce it Lennard in England.' I looked at the boy. 'You'll have to get used to people saying it like that. A new name for a new country.' I smiled. 'Do you mind? Or...' My smile widened, and I said, 'What about Leo? Leo Weitz. I like the sound of that. Would you like to be known as Leo, here in England?'

He looked at me unblinkingly for a full minute before he nodded his head.

'Leo it is then,' I said. 'Leo the lion.'

A thought suddenly occurred to me. My stomach clenched at the impudence of it and my heart raced. Could I? The child seemed so lonely. And children needed animals. Especially emotionally disturbed children. I couldn't imagine how I would

124

have got through my childhood without my dog and pony. Not to *give* him Bobby, not yet anyway. But the boy, like Bobby, was all by himself. Perhaps Leo Weitz simply needed something to take care of, to cosset. After all, it was a truth universally acknowledged that the company of a parrot could prevent moping. Lily Brennan said so.

I asked Simon, 'What's the German for parrot?'

He stared at me. '*Papagei*. What are you—'

'Leo,' I said, 'I have a *papagei*.' I glanced at Mrs Levy, who was watching me with interest. I raised an eyebrow and she made a moue that I interpreted as permission to proceed. So I ignored Simon's sharp movement and went on quickly, before he could interrupt.

'He is an African Grey *papagei*. His feathers are grey but he has bright red tail feathers. Actually, at the moment he's rather bald. That's because he's been very frightened by the bombs and when he's scared he plucks out his feathers. Would you like to meet him? He talks sometimes, and he also makes bomb noises that are quite realistic and can be frightening. His name is Bobby. Perhaps you could have him come and visit you here once he is recovered. But you should meet him first.'

'Bobby? From the bomb site?' Simon's face lit up in his sudden transforming smile. 'Your saviour?'

'And the reason I was buried in the first place. Yes. The very parrot.'

Leo stared at me. His eyes were dark and fathomless behind his spectacles. My voice faltered under the intensity of his gaze. 'Would you like that, d'you think?' I mumbled.

But when I caught the spark of interest in his eyes my skin prickled again. Leo moved his head into the slightest of nods.

I smiled at the boy, and he almost smiled back. Mrs Levy's smile was seraphic. I did not look at Simon.

'A parrot?' said Mrs Levy. 'How splendid. I had a parrot when I was a little girl in Berlin, and I loved it very much.' She glanced at me. 'Another cup of tea, Celia?'

At my nod she took my cup and picked up the teapot.

'We will arrange for Leo to visit the bird at your flat to meet your parrot,' she said. 'He will enjoy it, I'm sure.

Simon showed me to the door after we had finished our tea.

'Good God,' he said, unknowingly echoing my sister. 'A parrot?'

'He's company. Lily thinks he prevents me from moping. I think he'll be good for Leo.

His smile was sceptical. 'I wonder if you really just want to rid yourself of an annoying pet.'

'Not at all,' I said, incensed. 'I like the parrot. Very much. But I think Leo needs something to think about. Perhaps to care for eventually.' I looked straight into his eyes. 'And I think your mother needs Leo. I think she's bored and desperately needs to feel needed.'

'Let's say you're right about that, is *this* boy is the right one for her? I'm worried that she'll end up frustrated and unhappy when she can't help the child. He needs professional care, not a well-meaning woman who wants to mother him.'

'He needs love,' I said. 'And your mother can give him that.'

He lifted his hand in a gesture of defeat. 'When can I bring him to your digs to meet the bird?'

'*You* don't have to bring him.'

He shrugged. 'Who else is there? You're working tomorrow?'

'Yes.'

'We'll be there Sunday afternoon.'

It must have been a small devil that prompted me, because the words were out before I could think. 'Don't forget your date tomorrow evening. With Kitty at the Paramount.'

Immediately, I wished the words unsaid. Simon was silent for a few seconds that seemed to stretch into minutes. Then he smiled gently. 'You know, I'd completely forgotten about that. Thank you for the reminder.' He opened the door. 'I'll see you Sunday. Three o'clock.'

# CHAPTER THIRTEEN

The following morning I arrived at the ambulance station early and found most of the shift in a sombre mood. London had had a quiet night, with only a few raiders coming over, but the morning news revealed that it was because the enemy had attacked Portsmouth instead. The city had suffered its most severe raid of the war, with hundreds killed and injured. It was a matter of pride that the capital could take whatever the Luftwaffe threw at us and Londoners hated to hear that the smaller cities and provincial towns had been badly hit.

'Your Dr Levy was here Thursday morning,' said Powell, as I entered the common room.

I answered with a non-committal, 'Really?' But then, stupidly, I added, 'He's not *my* Dr Levy,' which made Maisie smile.

'He asked after you,' said Sadler to me.

To my horror I felt my cheeks become warm. I assumed an indifferent tone. 'Really?' I repeated.

Sadler laughed. 'Yeah. He said –' He changed his voice to parody Simon's public-school accent. '"Mrs Ashwin isn't on duty, I trust."'

I raised my eyebrows and gave him a look that I hoped registered chilly disinterest. 'Well, I wasn't, so I assume that put an end to any further discussion.'

Sadler's smile broadened. 'Nah. It didn't. He told Moray you were to be on light duties for a week. So it looks like you'll be manning the phone while Fripp drives a car, coz no one's willing to go with her in an ambulance.'

'That's not true,' said Fripp, who had slipped in behind me. Her voice was high and incensed, but it was true, and we all knew it.

Sadler shrugged and said without any indication of remorse, 'Sorry, Fripp, didn't see you there.'

He stood and held up a canvas bag.

'Now we're all gathered together, is anyone interested in a few knick-knacks?' He upended the bag. Various odds and ends tumbled out and scattered on to the table.

'Where did they come from?' asked Harris.

'From a man who bought them from a bombed-out chemist,' he said, assuming a pose of righteous indignation. 'It's all entirely above board, I can assure you. Take your pick. As you are aware from past experience, my prices are always reasonable.'

We all had a look and the pile gradually diminished. I chose a tube of toothpaste, two cakes of scented soap (one for Lily) and a tub of cold cream. His prices were high, but not extortionate, and at least I didn't have to spend hours queuing for the items. Even Moray came out of the office to buy razor blades and toothpaste.

'I hope you don't have any tins of toffee,' said Powell.

'Don't ask her,' said Sadler, rolling his eyes. 'It'll be another of her loopy rumours.'

'Why is toffee suspect?' asked Purvis with a smile and a wink for the rest of us.

Powell frowned at Sadler. 'You may not believe it, but this came from an impeccable source. Enemy aeroplanes are dropping tins of toffee. They have a tartan design, and on the lid they're marked Lyons' Assorted Toffee.'

Maisie gave her a sceptical look. 'And these toffees are bad because… ?'

'I'm not sure,' said Powell. 'But if the enemy dropped them they must be dangerous. Maybe they're poisoned.' Her eyes became wide. 'Or there are little bombs in them that go off when you open the tin.'

'I know,' said Sadler with a wry smile. 'They're toffee bombs. Like heartburn, only much, much worse.'

'Those Germans and their nasty plots,' said Purvis, smiling widely. 'What will they think of next?'

Just after darkness fell, the Warning sounded. A few minutes later came the booming of the guns, followed by the drone of aircraft.

'Sounds like a fair few aircraft,' said Squire.

'I've just been told that it's another fire-blitz, like December twenty-nine,' said Moray, coming out of the office holding a handful of chits. There was a chorus of groans, and sighs.

'They're dropping mainly incendiary bombs, but interspersing them with high-explosive bombs, like meat in a sandwich. Most of Holborn is already in flames, and that's where most of us are going. Also, there's big fire in Guilford Road, on our own doorstep.' He looked around, assessing those who were in the room, then held out a piece of paper. 'Harris, you're driving with Sadler. Powell, you're attending Armstrong. Squire, take the Buick. I'll go with you.'

He looked at me. 'You're on the phone tonight.'

'I'd rather be on the road.'

Inwardly I was cursing Simon Levy. I felt perfectly well and hated the thought of being safe inside when London was again in flames.

Moray shrugged. 'Next week is soon enough for that.'

He turned away to hold out a chit to Purvis. 'You're attending Halliday tonight. Fripp, take the Ford sedan. We'll go in convoy. Squire and I will go first. Follow us closely. The warden will direct us once we're there.'

Within minutes I was the only officer left in the station and seething with frustration. Outside, the raid had increased in intensity and the cup I'd placed on the desk vibrated noisily in its saucer. My ears felt heavy, as if I had dived deep underwater and was staying there with the pressure of heavy waters on me.

Every few minutes now came the whistling, shrieks of high-explosive bombs ripping through the air and the crumping sound they made as they landed. The station rocked and shuddered as if London was experiencing an earthquake.

An hour into the raid I was startled when the door to the common room was flung open. Fripp ran in, tears streaming down her face and shrieking hysterically.

'I can't do it,' she said, sobbing. 'Moray knows I can't. *You* go out there. You enjoy it. I know you do.'

'Does Moray know you're here?'

'No.' She sniffed and raised her chin, but didn't meet my eyes. 'But he *knows* I can't be out in a raid as bad as this. You take the sedan. I'll mind the phone.'

The telephone rang and when I picked it up a voice echoed into my ear.

'Any spare vehicles?'

'Only a sedan car at the moment. The rest are all out at the Guilford Street and Holborn fires. Has something happened?'

'High-explosive shell hit Bank Underground Station. Bloomsbury is now on diversion to Bank. All of the central ambulance stations are on diversion to Bank.' The voice, usually so calm, cracked as it said, 'We've hundreds of casualties and we need as many cars and ambulances as we can muster. Send all your ambulances and cars there as soon as they return.'

I gave Fripp the message and ran down to where she had abandoned the Ford sedan in the middle of the garage. It had been donated to the station at the start of the war and I had driven it often during the past months. The once shiny paintwork was pitted and dull after months of service, but it was a reliable vehicle and comfortable to drive.

The engine roared into life when I pressed the starter and I slowly drove up the ramp towards the red glow in the street outside. The Guilford Street fire was burning seemingly out of control and it lit my way all along Woburn Place as I drove past the trees of Russell Square and the extravagance of the Russell Hotel.

The roar of plane engines was a constant drone above me, punctuated by the guns' thunder, the scream of falling bombs and the sound of explosions. Gun flashes and exploding high explosives lit the sky like an aurora. It was like Guy Fawkes Night, and also nothing like it at all. In front of the car the searchlights struck out in crazy arcs and in their crossed beams a swarm of shining gnat-like planes moved slowly, with little puffs of what looked like cotton wool below them.

The planes followed a deadly pattern as waves of bombers dropped small bundles of incendiaries and flew off. They were followed by planes dropping high explosives. Then came more planes that dropped incendiaries. I was dismayed to see the red haze in the direction of the City, where I was heading. I could only hope that St Paul's wasn't in flames.

A swarm of incendiary bombs fell around my vehicle. The little phosphorous-filled cylinders hit the roof of the car with a clatter and bounced on to the road, erupting into white flashes as they flared up and then dozens of sizzling bluish-white flames illuminated the street. Dark figures flitted around with sand buckets and stirrup pumps and the flaring lights suddenly ceased. Choking smoke whirled around the dim beams of my masked headlights, and there were suspicious red glows behind the windows of too many buildings as I drove past.

I had just turned into Southampton Row when, over the thud of the guns and drone of planes, a more sinister noise could be discerned. A mosquito whine was growing louder and becoming closer to a shriek. It was a noise I had heard several times before. I jammed on the brakes and pulled over, glad of the blackout and the sedan's concealing black paint, praying that the white cross that had been painted on the roof at the start of the war had faded enough or was covered by concealing dust. We had told the ambulance authorities that we'd rather be inconspicuous, but they had refused to allow us to paint out the white crosses. 'Geneva Convention,' had been the reply. 'They can't shoot ambulances.' We knew better.

The screaming, tearing noise in the sky above me intensified. Two Messerschmitts were coming in low to power-dive the buildings ahead. The screech of their engines rose to a frightening crescendo. I crouched down by the steering wheel and flinched at the sound of thudding bullets hitting masonry and glass and then the road in front of and beside the sedan. Tar flecked my windows, but no bullets hit the car. The planes flew up and away, and in a few seconds were gone. I sat up and sucked in one deep breath and then another and in my mind I entered the bluebell glade. When I grasped the wheel a minute later my hands were steady.

I started the engine and continued my journey. The amount of debris on the road meant I couldn't go fast and I was forced to divert into a side street every block or so because of the fires around High Holborn. Just as I reached Queen Victoria Street the sound of the bombers overhead seemed to diminish and fewer bombs seemed to be falling. And then, there was the shocking absence of aircraft noise above me. As I reached the barrier that marked the entrance to the incident, I heard the steady note of the All Clear.

Bank Underground was, I knew, a popular shelter. There would have been thousands of people in there. I steeled myself to cope with what was obviously a disaster and parked the sedan next to a group of ambulances, empty and awaiting their loads.

A mobile canteen was nearby, and I walked over to it. This one was run by the Salvation Army. Instead of Joan and Kitty, three 'soldiers' in their snappy uniforms were serving tea to what seemed to be a multitude of rescue workers, firemen and first-aid workers. I refused a cup of tea and asked if they knew where the Incident Officer or a warden was, or failing that if they could direct me to the mobile first-aid post.

'The Incident Officer's awfully busy, but the first-aid van is over there, off to the left.' She pointed to a spot obscured by smoke and I set off.

My masked torch showed me enough of the potholes and debris to allow safe passage. The last thing I needed was Dr

Simon Levy being called in to treat me for a turned ankle. It was Saturday night, though. He was probably dancing with red-lipped Kitty at the Paramount. *And what if he is?* I told myself sternly. *It's not your business, Celia.* And then I remembered that the Paramount Dance Hall was on Tottenham Court Road, and I sent up a quick prayer that it had not been hit, because I had liked Kitty and Joan and it was horrible to think of people being killed while dancing.

Like all major incidents, this one was a hive of frenetic activity in the firelight. Men and women were running and shouting. Firemen's hoses hissed and wriggled as they sprayed water on flames. Water trickled along the road in thin rivulets that reflected the rosy firelight and turned the smashed streets into muddy tracks. Cranes had been brought in and were lifting large pieces of masonry, directed by shouts from heavy-rescue men. Teenaged messenger boys whizzed by on their bicycles, their eager young faces set and determined as they dodged the debris to carry messages between the wardens. A couple of stretcher-bearers passed me, carrying an unconscious man whose face was sticky with blood and whose clothing was in tatters, followed by another pair carrying a woman who was conscious and crying out in gulping sobs.

I picked my way through the water and rubble and mud, until I was brought to a halt by the scene before me. I gazed, shocked, at Bank Junction. It had been where nine busy London streets converged in front of the Bank of England and the Royal Exchange. Now it was an immense crater containing great slabs of roadway and lumps of rock enmeshed with twisted iron girders, lamp posts and the remains of a traffic island. Fiercely burning fires in the buildings around it bathed the scene in the pink of a shepherd's delight sunset, but firelight glow could not disguise the horror of what had happened earlier that night.

'What—?' I turned to a man, obviously part of a heavy-rescue squad, who had paused to wipe his face with a grubby handkerchief.

'Looks like a bomb somehow got into the station and exploded underground.' His voice was brusque, and sounded raspy. 'The blast lifted up the whole roadway and then it dropped back again. Problem is working out how to get through the mass of concrete lying between us and those in the tunnels.' He looked at my uniform. 'You want the first-aid station?'

'I can't seem to locate it.'

'Behind you. They parked the van in Poultry.'

As I retraced my steps, stumbling on the rubble on the road, snatches of conversation came to me through the smoke.

'They must have thought they was safe.' The voice floated out from somewhere over to the side. 'All them people. Must've thought it was safe as houses, sheltering down there.'

'Just goes to show,' said another voice. 'If the bomb 'as yer name on it, yer a gonner. No matter what ye do, yer still a gonner.'

The mobile first-aid post was hard to miss once I knew which street it was parked in, because it was a large furniture removal van that had been turned into a travelling hospital. A doctor was inside, stitching wounds with the aid of one nurse while a second nurse sorted the patients into those needing an ambulance and those who could go in cars. She looked up as I came closer.

'Ambulance or car?'

'Car. I can take four.'

'Oh, good. All of these are ready for transfer. Take your pick.'

She nodded towards a small crowd of people who were standing or sitting on makeshift chairs near the van. They were bloodied and had the dazed look of those who couldn't quite work out what had happened to them, but knew it had been dreadful. Around each left wrist was a handwritten tag, on which was written the name, address, place of injury and a summary of the wounds. I chose four patients and we slowly walked together to the car.

There was no point taking them to hospital, because the hospitals were reserved for the severely injured. Instead I drove them through detours and roundabout routes to a first-aid post that occupied a corner of a vast underground casualty depot near the river. After I dropped them off I drove back to the horror that had been Bank Underground Station to pick up more wounded. And over the next five hours this journey was repeated over and over again, until I could have driven the route blindfolded.

# CHAPTER FOURTEEN

I parked in what had become 'my' spot, next to the Salvation Army tea car, and walked to the mobile first-aid station to collect another group of sitting wounded. As I picked my way through the rubble, the fluting voice of a child cut through the dust and the smoke.

'Hitler won't make me cry.' The declaration ended on what sounded suspiciously like a sob. 'He *won't*.'

A voice I knew answered. 'Good for you. Now this may sting a little.' Simon laughed. 'A friend of mine says I shouldn't say that, and I should be truthful. You're such a brave girl that you deserve the truth. This *will* sting. But if Hitler won't make you cry, I don't think a little iodine will.'

*A friend of mine?*

The yelp was muted, as if emitted through gritted teeth. 'Didn't hurt a bit,' she said.

When I rounded the corner Simon was sitting on a box outside the mobile first-aid station bandaging the arm of a girl who looked to be around ten years of age. Her face was bloodied but she stood calmly as he wrapped the cloth around her thin white arm. As I drew closer the smell of the iodine he had put on the wound mingled with that of the thick smoke from the burning buildings around us.

He looked up as I walked towards them, nodded to me and smiled at the child. 'Here comes your lift to the first-aid station. Mrs Ashwin will take you there in her big black car.'

The girl swung around and looked me up and down. 'I didn't cry,' she said.

'Good for you,' I replied and gave her a smile. 'We'll be off in a few minutes, once I have a couple more patients to come with us.'

'My name is Sally,' she said. 'Gosh, you're pretty.'

'Thank you.'

'My mum's gone to hospital,' she volunteered. 'But Dr Levy says that they'll get Aunty Patty to pick me up from the first-aid depot. I'm being very brave. Mum told me I had to be.'

'Good girl,' I said, exchanging glances with Simon. He gave me a slight smile and a nod, and I took it to mean that Sally's mum would make it.

'I thought you were supposed to be on light duties,' Simon said to me.

'Needs must, when the Devil drives,' I replied, and he rolled his eyes.

Sally walked over and took my hand. She stood quietly next to me as a man in a dusty overcoat brought a thin elderly woman to Simon. Her face was powdered white with plaster dust and the elaborately curled wig she wore was askew.

'Mrs Goldman, isn't it?' said Simon, 'I'm sorry to see you've been hurt. Is there any pain?'

She replied in a language that sounded like German.

'English please,' said Simon, glancing up at the man who had accompanied her.

'Mam, you know we speak English here,' he said. His accent was pure East End. He said to Simon, 'My mother hurt her shoulder. Falling masonry. It was bloody mayhem down there.'

'Simon Levy,' said the old woman, in a thin gasping voice. 'Your brother died. Such a lovely boy.'

'Mam,' said the man impatiently. 'Hush.'

'He died in November,' said Simon evenly. 'It was very sad. Where does it hurt?'

After examining her and giving her morphine Simon wrote on the card around her wrist, and called to me, 'She can go with you to the first-aid depot.'

He turned to the next patient, a woman in a fur coat.

With the assistance of her son, the old lady walked over to me. Sally was still grasping my hand in a hot, moist grip and shrank back a little as the woman approached. Mrs Goldman stared at me for a good minute and then said something in the German-sounding language.

Behind me, Simon gave a short bark of laughter, but Sally gazed at her wide-eyed. 'Is that German? Are you a spy?'

'Not German,' said her son. 'Yiddish.'

'What did she say?' I asked.

'She thinks you are Jewish.'

'I don't have that honour,' I said, bewildered.

Mrs Goldman had a dazed look that I associated with shock, so I simply smiled at her.

My fourth and last patient was a woman in her thirties, who wore a very good fur coat over a smart woollen outfit. Many shelterers wore their best clothes to the underground in case a bomb hit their home and destroyed all their possessions. The woman seemed unhurt, but she had a wide-eyed, unfocused stare that worried me, and she seemed confused.

'I'm Mrs Whitely,' she said. 'I do feel queer. I think I'm going to die.'

I made the usual soothing noises. 'Dr Levy has checked you over and he thinks you're well enough for the first-aid centre. You're not going to die, Mrs Whitely. Now, hold hands with Sally here, and with Mrs Goldman. Mr Goldman, please take your mother's hand. It's rather schoolyardish, I know, but it means we'll all keep together. The sedan is a good hundred yards from here and it's rather dark.'

Sally's grip on my hand increased as we groped our way through the controlled chaos of the bomb site. I used my torch to point out obstacles on the muddy ground, assisted by the light of Mr Goldman's torch. We had walked about half the distance when Sally shrieked and pulled hard on my hand. Mrs Whitely had fallen.

'What's the matter with her?' Sally's voice held a note of hysteria. Mr Goldman came over to her, crouched down and spoke to the girl in a low, comforting tone.

I knelt by Mrs Whitely, and gave her a cursory examination by torchlight. She was conscious, but her breathing was rapid and her eyes were fluttering.

'Oh, I do feel queer,' she repeated, and sighed. 'I don't want to die.'

'You are not going to die,' I said, looking around. I would need to ask a rescue worker to carry her back to the van to be assessed.

Then a voice I knew came out of the darkness, a deep voice, born in the Seven Dials slums. 'Looks like you've got a bit of a problem, Duchess.' Squire knelt beside me and muttered, 'I've lost blinking Armstrong. We was down there together – down in the bombed station. It's a right mess, and he took it hard. He's only a nipper, really.' He smiled at Mrs Whitely. 'Feeling poorly, love? How's about I carry you back to the doc?'

She managed a smile. 'Not just yet, if you don't mind. Let me catch my breath.'

So he knelt beside her and took her head on to his lap and rubbed her hands. 'Yer hands are cold, love. I'll warm them for you.' Squire looked up at me. 'Best take your lot to the car and get them to the depot. I'll see that she gets to Doc Levy or Doc Hamble in the van.'

I nodded, and took hold of Sally's cold little hand. Mrs Goldman took the other and we set off. No one spoke as we trudged to the car. Beside it, the mobile canteen was like a beacon of warmth and good cheer. I said to Mr Goldman, 'Look, I really want to check on Mrs Whitely before we go. Could you ask the tea-car ladies to give everyone a cuppa? I'll be back in a minute.'

I barely gave him time to reply before I dashed into the darkness, heading for where I had left my patient. Squire was still kneeling on the ground, holding her head cradled on his lap, but now Simon squatted beside them. He appeared to be feeling for a pulse in Mrs Whitely's wrist.

Simon shook his head and, very gently, lowered Mrs Whitely's hand to lie on her chest. He shone his torch into her eyes, prising open each lid in turn with his finger and thumb. And then placed his fingers over her jugular vein. That would be just to make sure, I thought. Simon would always want to make sure, because he so hated to lose his battles with Death.

'Is she—?' My voice was raspy, and louder than I had intended.

It was Squire who answered. 'Afraid so, Duchess. Internal injuries, the doc thinks. Very sad. She slipped away just after you left.'

*Slipped away*. He made it sound so peaceful, her death. Made it sound the antithesis of what had happened to cause it. Mrs Whitely, who was someone's wife and someone's daughter and maybe someone's mother and who had not wanted to die, had *slipped away* into the darkness.

Simon remained motionless beside her, seemingly fixated on Mrs Whitely's pale face. Then he swayed and almost toppled. Squire put out a big hand and grasped his arm to hold him upright, then glanced at me.

'Why don't you take the doc home, Duchess? Take him with you in the car, drop off your patients and then drop him home on your way back to the station. He lives in the Bloomsbury area, told me so earlier tonight. He was with us, down there, earlier. It was... as bad as it gets, down there.' He looked at me for a few seconds, and it was shocking to see the misery in his eyes. Squire was stolid, always utterly dependable no matter what horrors we faced. I wondered what he and Armstrong and Simon had seen in the devastated underground station.

I nodded.

'All he really needs now is a good kip,' said Squire.

Simon shook his head, but slowly as if he found the movement to be a challenge. 'The patient...'

'Now don't you worry about the poor lady, Doc,' Squire assured him. 'I'll carry her to the van. Doc Hamble can certify her.'

I walked over to them and knelt beside Simon. 'How long since you last slept?' I asked.

His eyes were bloodshot and his face drawn, but he managed a slight smile. 'Was at the hospital most of last night and all day. Then I heard of this disaster and came over to help.' He raised his shoulder in a slight shrug. 'Two days? I've been catnapping, though.'

I took hold of his arm and pulled him with me as I stood. Squire helped and together we got him upright.

'Come on, Simon,' I said. 'I'll take you home.'

He made no demur as I led him to the sedan. I was pleased to see that my three patients were standing beside the tea car, sipping hot drinks. Sally was munching a cookie.

'Mrs Whitely won't be coming with us,' I said. 'But we've got Dr Levy instead. He's along for the ride.'

By the time I'd dropped off the Goldmans and Sally at the first-aid depot, it was close to seven on a cold, wet morning. It was a while yet until dawn, though, as with the continuance of summer time we didn't see the sun until around nine o'clock. I headed for Bloomsbury with Simon stretched out along the back seat. When I pulled up outside his parents' house I twisted around to him, lighting his form with my dim torchlight.

Simon was fast asleep, sprawled across the seat. His arms were crossed over his chest in a protective gesture, but the lines of worry and responsibility in his face had been smoothed by unconsciousness. His dark hair was messy and dusted with plaster and his face was streaked with blood and dirt and ash. Asleep, he looked absurdly young, far too young to be a doctor with all the responsibility that came with that knowledge and training.

David had been so proud of his doctor brother. Simon was only eleven months the younger, and David had said that they were as close as twins. 'Simon's the family dreamer,' David had said. 'He wants to save the world and that's why he took up medicine. You'd love him, Celia. He's so damn *good*.' He had laughed then, and said, 'I make him seem like a prig, and he's not. Actually, he's such a casual-seeming devil, it takes a while to realise that he's tough as they come.'

*Tough as they come.*

'Why do you take so many risks, Simon?' I whispered. 'Is it because you had to leave those wounded men behind at Dunkirk? You can't save everyone, no matter how much you try. I wish you'd realise that.'

I stared at him by the light of my masked torch for longer than politeness allowed but could see nothing more than a hint, if as much as that, of his brother in his face. He slept so peacefully that I was sorry to wake him, but I had to return the sedan to the station and have it spick and span before the next shift arrived at seven-thirty.

'Simon,' I hissed. 'Simon, wake up. You're home.'

Nothing. He did not so much as twitch.

'Simon,' I said, in a louder voice. 'Wake up.'

Again, nothing. So I climbed out of the car, marched around to the rear door and pulled it open. If I couldn't wake him I'd either have to knock up the Levys, which I did not want to do, or comb the streets for a policeman or milkman or someone who could help me to drag him up to the front door. Then we'd have to search him for his key and get him inside. A light rain was falling, which added to my impatience.

I leaned across the seat, took hold of his shoulders and shook him vigorously. 'Simon, *wake up.*'

His eyes fluttered open and he blinked a few times. Then he saw me, hovering over him. If I had had any doubts about how Simon Levy thought of Celia Ashwin, they were dispelled by his look of utter contempt and loathing.

'Good God,' he said, 'can I never escape you? Leave me alone, why don't you. *Go away.*' He raised his hand as if to strike me.

I dropped him on to the seat as if he was electrically charged and pulled myself out of the car. On the way I bumped my head and hot tears filled my eyes at the pain. I blinked them away furiously and stalked around the car to stand by the driver's door where I waited for Simon to emerge. There was no point in driving off if Simon had not fully extricated himself from the vehicle.

In a few clumsy movements Simon twisted himself out of the back seat and slouched against the side of the car, knuckling his eyes and shaking his head.

'I am so sorry,' he said. 'That was insufferably rude. I wasn't awake... I thought ... didn't realise...' He sucked in a breath. 'Please, Celia, forgive me.' He looked around and shook his head again. 'What am I doing here?'

He looked so exhausted, and so unhappy that I couldn't remain angry. I had always known how he felt about me. It shouldn't have been a surprise, but I had not expected such an unguarded look of raw anger and loathing as the one he had just given me.

'Are you all right to get into the house?' I asked, keeping my tone cool and disinterested. 'You were dead on your feet, and Squire – he's the big ambulance driver who was with Mrs Whitely, the woman who died – he suggested that I drop you off on my way back to the station.'

He pushed a hand over his face and took a shuddering breath. When he looked at me his utter misery and guilt were clear in his face. 'I certified her fit to go to the first-aid depot rather than to hospital. I should have realised.'

'How could you have known? You had no X-ray machine. It was too dark to properly examine her. It's not your fault, Simon.'

'I should have known how seriously injured she was. I do, sometimes. I just *know*. I can't explain how.'

'It was her time to go. You can't save everyone.'

'I can try, can't I?' he said sharply, then moderated his voice to repeat, 'I am so very sorry about... I thought it was a dream.'

'You thought it was a nightmare, obviously,' I snapped.

He flinched at that. 'How many times do I have to apologise? I didn't strike you. I would never strike you. I was asleep. I thought you were...' His voice trailed away.

'Celia Ashwin. You thought I was me.' My voice was dry. Simon may not have struck me, but he had wanted to do so.

His voice hardened. 'I've sincerely apologised. What do you want from me? Blood?'

We glared at each other. His eyes were bloodshot and unutterably weary, but had a spark that showed his annoyance. I preferred annoyance to the utter defeat of the minute before. Blood? There was a trickle of dried blood running down his neck. Something must have nicked him in the darkness.

I tried to enter the bluebell glade; it eluded me, but again my anger drained away. Simon had been working without respite for the past two days. He had gone into the devastated underground station and dealt with who knew what horrors. And then his last patient of the night had died, after he had declared her to be well. He may not like Celia Ashwin, he might even hate her, but Simon Levy had behaved, as usual, with utmost bravery and concern for his patients and he deserved my respect.

*Head high and walk tall.* I raised my chin. 'Think nothing of it. As you say, you were asleep.' I managed a smile and looked straight into his eyes. 'I've forgotten about it already.'

He opened his mouth as if to say something, but obviously thought better of it and just nodded.

'Are you all right to get into the house?' I asked.

'Yes. I have a latchkey.' He grimaced. 'Celia... Thank you for the lift home.'

'Please, don't mention it. I'd best be off. I need to report back to the station and clean the car before the next shift arrives.'

As I drove away he was still standing in the middle of the road, watching me go.

# CHAPTER FIFTEEN

I arrived back at the Bloomsbury ambulance station in time for breakfast. All of the officers in my shift had returned, but everyone was picking listlessly at the watery scrambled eggs. I had never seen the group so miserable.

We had all become expert at black humour, because otherwise we would never have been able to cope with the daily horrors we experienced. My time in Bloomsbury ambulance station had been a time of laughter as well as tears. I could not attempt to reproduce the humour we used to 'carry on', as Churchill demanded, because it was often questionable. Black humour is of the moment, and is usually childish and sometimes crude, and not at all amusing unless nerves are stretched to breaking point and need release. But it was important to us, and when I think of that time it is as if a ribbon of laughter wound around us, binding us together, keeping us whole. They were some of the happiest months of my life.

That morning, however, it seemed that what had happened at Bank Underground was too distressing for the usual jokes. It was unusual for ambulance crew to enter a bombed building to collect wounded, as this was the job of light-rescue recovery teams, but the scale of the disaster last night was such that everyone had been expected to help. So the Bloomsbury men, Moray, Squire, Armstrong, Sadler and Purvis, had gone underground to assist the rescue teams and work as stretcher-bearers. And now they could not stop talking about the night's horror.

'I heard the bomb fall into the booking hall,' said Squire, as I sat beside him with my plate. 'They reckon at least sixty died at the scene, and others in hospital afterwards.'

'Casualties were high because it fell right at the entry to the concourse,' Moray explained. 'That meant most of the blast went down the escalator shafts and straight on to the platform areas. Most of those sleeping at the bottom of the escalator were killed outright, and also others who were sleeping on the platform.'

'Some were blown on to the electric line and killed that way,' said Armstrong, who was very pale and had not looked up from his plate. He picked at the food without any enthusiasm.

'Dr Levy and I were sent on to a train that had stopped halfway into the station.' Purvis shook his head and I caught an echo of the horror in his eyes. 'Mercifully it was almost empty. Dr Levy did what he could, but…' He sighed. 'We took out five, but all the rest were dead. We had to leave the bodies for the clean-up crews.'

'Lights went out, of course,' said Moray. 'The air was so thick with dust on the Central Line platform that our torches were of little use. It was utter chaos.'

'There should have been emergency lighting,' said Harris. 'It's disgraceful that you had to feel around for casualties in the dark.'

'Things got better once the soldiers arrived,' said Armstrong, looking up at last. 'They had arc lights. Hundreds of soldiers came to clear the debris.'

'They pulled out a little girl, just like my Alice at that age,' said Squire, in a tight thin voice that I'd not heard before. 'She'd lost her mother and she just kept calling, "Mummy. Mummy." And then there was that poor woman what just up and died in my arms. Doc Levy was devastated. First time I'd really seen him close to cracking.' He looked across at me. 'That's why I sent him home with you, Duchess. Had to get him out of there. No, I'll never forget last night.' He dashed a hand across his eyes, and frowned down at his breakfast.

Moray spoke up. 'The deaths at Bank Underground Station just go to prove that being underground isn't necessarily a safe haven.'

'Tell us something we don't know,' said Sadler. He had a fixed look, as if he were holding back pain, and his lips were flat against his lips. 'I know you lot think I'm – well, maybe I am, but this is *London*. Those people last night, they were my—' He looked up, directly at me. 'It's a good thing your Hitler-loving old man is in quod. Because I'd like to lay hands on that New Order bastard.' His hands closed into fists.

'Language,' said a shocked female voice.

I said nothing, but stared at Sadler until he looked down at his plate. My relationship with my husband was none of his business, nor was the fact that Cedric would soon be out of gaol.

Squire patted my shoulder as if I were one of the greyhounds he had bred before the war and Moray went on as if Sadler hadn't spoken.

'And because being underground is not necessarily safe, I'll arrange for you all to start revising your first-aid training.' He looked across at me. 'Another thing. When I say that an officer is not fit for duties, I expect that the officer will stay here in the station.'

I opened my mouth to remonstrate, but before I could speak he went on, 'May I see you in the office, Fripp. Now, please.'

Fripp followed Moray into the office with dragging feet and trembling lips as Powell unwittingly cheered us up with her latest rumour.

'My Aunt Glad told me that they were using a new weapon last night,' she said, in the confidential tone she used for her more outrageous theories. Aunt Glad was often the source of such rumours. 'It uses vibration to disintegrate buildings. And that's why there was such a strange glow in the sky.'

'What poppycock,' said Harris dismissively.

'No,' said Purvis, in a low and suspiciously sombre voice. 'Powell's absolutely right. There *was* a bright glow all around us last night. I heard that the Nazis even have a word for it.'

'What do they call it?' asked Powell, her eyes wide.

'*Mondlicht.*'

Even Powell could work out the German for moonlight. She flounced out of the room followed by laughter. My mood lifted. If we could laugh, we could get through the worst Hitler threw at us.

'When in doubt, brew up,' said Harris, getting to her feet. 'Who wants another cuppa?'

I had a tailwind as I rode my bicycle back to St Andrew's Court. It was the first nice thing to have happened in the past twenty-four hours, I thought. The second nice thing was seeing Lily as I emerged from the basement where I parked my bicycle. She was coming out of the service restaurant with her friend Katherine Carlow.

I was a trifle wary of Katherine, who was clever and sarcastic. More than that, she was always so beautifully attired that I felt like a positive dowd beside her. Katherine had been a junior couturier at one of the big fashion salons in London before the war and now was Deputy Station Leader in the Berkeley Square Depot, to where Lily had transferred before Christmas. Katherine's husband was in the army and stationed in Egypt.

Lily caught sight of me and said, in a sing-song voice, 'Thirteen days. Thirteen days. It's only thirteen days.'

I feigned ignorance. 'Thirteen days? Whatever do you mean?'

Katherine smiled at Lily's outraged expression. 'Celia's joking, Lily. How could anyone forget when you remind them constantly?'

Lily and Jim were to be married in the Westminster Register Office on the twenty-fifth of January.

'Do you have your outfit all ready?' I asked.

Lily had told me that Katherine had used her contacts in the fashion world to obtain a length of robin's-egg-blue silk and had spent the past two weeks making Lily's wedding dress. 'It's not a long dress,' Lily had assured me. 'There's a war on, and ostentation is infra dig nowadays. It's a day dress that I can wear afterwards.'

148

Katherine smiled. 'It'll be ready by the day, and she'll look divine.' She glanced at her watch. 'And I must love and leave you both. Family duties. My mother-in-law is coming up to Town to buy linen. She does it every year, and *that man* is not going to stop her this year, no matter how many bombs he drops. Or so she informed me in her last letter. She's arriving from Tunbridge Wells on the ten o'clock and my job is to settle her into her hotel.' She laughed. 'She'll be shocked at the state of Selfridges. I'll get yet another lecture about the perfidy of *that man*.' And with that Katherine hurried away up the stairs.

I looked at Lily. 'I have some scented soap for you. Sadler got it from a man who...' I touched the corner of my nose and Lily laughed.

'How sweet of you. Thanks so much.'

I began to root around in my satchel for the soap, when Lily put a hand on my arm.

'Actually, I need a quick word with you, Celia. I know you're probably dead on your feet, but could I pop up to your flat for a minute?'

Once we were in the flat I offered her tea, which she refused, saying, 'I'm only staying for a minute.' She looked at my face. 'No bandage? Looks like your wound is healing well. I doubt there will be much of a scar at all.'

'Yes,' I said coolly, 'Simon Levy stitched it beautifully. I owe him a great deal.'

Lily turned away to smile at Bobby, who was in his big cage on the table in the corner, watching us. The black iris was tiny in his yellow eyes. 'The bird's settled in well? He looks a lot healthier than when we got him. I think he's getting some new feathers.'

I turned a sceptical eye on the bird. 'I think it takes a while for feathers to grow back. He seems happy enough, though.'

'Still not talking?'

'Very occasionally he says he's Bobby and asks my name, but otherwise, not a word. What did you want to tell me, Lily?' I didn't want to be rude, but I could scarcely stand upright, I was so tired.

She gave me a wary smile. 'It's just that…' She paused, then said, 'I thought you should know that Simon Levy will be part of the wedding group.'

'Simon Levy,' I muttered. My voice became louder. 'Simon Levy. *Simon Levy*. I cannot seem to go anywhere or do anything without *Simon Levy* being there. And he positively hates me.'

Lily laughed. 'He's lovely. Apart from the fact that he's lovely, I wanted to invite him to … well, to stand in for David, really.'

I swallowed, and turned to look at Bobby. 'Yes, of course.'

'I think you exaggerate how much he dislikes you. He's said only nice things about you to us.'

'What things?'

'Oh, about how brave you are.'

'To a foolish degree.'

She laughed again. 'Well, he did suggest that we try to convince you to take fewer risks.'

'He can talk. He takes appalling risks all the time.'

'You're as bad as each other, Celia.'

I ran my finger along the bars of Bobby's cage. 'He had to leave some wounded soldiers behind at Dunkirk, and I think he now feels compelled to try to save the world.' I shrugged. 'He might think I'm brave, but he doesn't like me.'

Bobby walked along the perch and surveyed me closely. He stopped, bobbed up and down a couple of times and then stretched out his neck and squawked, 'Simon Levy. Simon Levy.'

Lily gave a peal of laughter as a black wave of horror engulfed me. I would never be able to invite anyone to my flat, not ever again. Could I ship Bobby to Scotland? I had cousins in Mull. Was that far enough? How could I introduce the bird to Leo Weitz now? *Leo*.

'Oh, dear Lord,' I said, in tragic tones, 'he's coming here this afternoon.'

'Who is?'

'Si— him. He's bringing Leo to meet Bobby.'

'Who's Leo?'

'An Austrian refugee boy who's staying with the Levys.'

Would Leo believe that Bobby had died? No, I couldn't do that. It would be too cruel. My mind whirled through the possibilities. Leo had never seen Bobby. He wouldn't know if I substituted another parrot. But where could I get another bald parrot at such short notice? The truth was like a drench of cold water. I couldn't find another parrot by this afternoon. It had to be Bobby, who would squawk out Simon's name and I would simply die.

'No, Bobby,' I said, in a tightly controlled voice. 'Please don't say that. Try to repeat this. *God Save the King.* Come along, Bobby, say God Save the King. God Save the King.'

'That's a good one,' said Lily, who was still laughing. 'God Save the King. You can do that, Bobby, God Save the King.' Then, to me, 'Bet you wish you'd let me teach him Waltzing Matilda.' At my look, she grinned and turned to the bird. 'C'mon, Bobby, God Save the King.'

Bobby bobbed again on his perch and opened his beak. 'Simon Levy' he said. 'Simon Levy.'

I whirled around to plop down on the sofa beside Lily who was again in whoops. 'Oh, *bloody hell*,' I said.

'Celia!' said Lily.

'Bloody hell,' said Bobby. 'Bloody hell, Simon Levy.'

# CHAPTER SIXTEEN

'*Simon Levy*,' I bellowed as I opened the door later that afternoon. 'Look, Bobby, it's *Simon Levy*. And Leo Weitz. They've come to see you.' I ushered Simon and Leo inside as Bobby watched, and listened, from his cage.

After Lily left I had fallen into a deep and much needed sleep and had awakened six hours later with a Plan, one that was quite brilliant in its simplicity. I would tell the doorman to let Simon and Leo come straight up to the flat, and that would mean I could greet Simon by his full name when I opened the door to him. And I would repeat Simon's name when he was in the flat. That way, if Bobby squawked it out, the obvious conclusion would be that the bird had just picked it up.

'Celia Ashwin', responded Simon, polite but obviously bemused. Leo gave me his formal little bow.

Simon gestured towards Bobby's cage. 'Look, Leo, there is the parrot.'

Leo walked over to Bobby's cage. He stood absolutely still and solemnly stared at the bird. Bobby's yellow eyes with their ink-dark pupils, set deeply in concentric circles of grey wrinkled flesh, observed Leo in turn. I went across the room to stand beside the boy. Bobby's glittering gaze moved to me and he bent his head at an enquiring angle, as if to ask, 'Who is this you have brought to see me?'

'Bobby,' I said in a ceremonial kind of address, 'this is Leo Weitz.' I half-turned and waved at Simon, raising my voice slightly. 'And this is *Simon Levy*.'

I glanced back at Simon, who was observing my antics with a perplexed smile. So I added, with an attempt at light-heartedness, 'One should always treat parrots with dignity.'

I looked down at Leo, who was now regarding me, rather than the parrot. His expression, I thought, reflected Simon's bemusement. So I continued the theme with a touch of desperation, 'Rather like bees, really. Our head gardener would always introduce new members of the household to the bees, and whisper any family news to the hive. "We must always tell the bees", he would say, "Whisper it to the bees".'

Leo continued to stare at me. His unblinking dark gaze was as intimidating as the parrot's. 'I think parrots deserve as much consideration as bees,' I finished limply.

Inside, however, I exulted. I had conceived and executed the Plan without any hitches. The bees embellishment had come to me in the moment, but I thought it was a good one. The Plan had worked! If Bobby said Simon's name now, it would surprise no one.

I turned and smiled at Simon. In fact, I positively beamed at him. His look of bemusement turned to alarm. I moderated the wattage and nodded at him.

'Just like the bees,' I said, and turned to Leo, who was again watching the parrot. Bobby walked along his perch, back and forth in a slow, stately manner, but always keeping a beady parrot eye on the boy.

'Celia,' Simon had come up to stand directly behind me, and I started with surprise.

'Sorry,' he said. Then, with one eye on Leo, continued in a low voice, 'Please accept my apology for my behaviour earlier this morning. I was fast asleep and when you shook me awake I was dreaming of – of something – not you. I wasn't thinking clearly.'

I said, graciously, 'Please don't concern yourself with it.' Then I gave a short laugh. 'Poor you. I know I'd be furious if some annoying ambulance girl ripped me out of my dreams into a chilly morning after too little sleep.'

Simon smiled. It was an open, attractive smile, the sort of smile you'd give a friend. I smiled back at him. Our eyes met. All at once, the room seemed smaller, as if it had contracted to the space – not more than two steps – between us and my heart gave a painful little jerk.

A sharp rap sounded at the door, and we both started with surprise. Simon turned abruptly towards Leo and put a hand on the boy's shoulder. I had the sense that the world had spun away from me and I shivered, as if I had been doused in cold water. When I glanced again at Simon, he was standing very still beside Leo and watching Bobby's slow pacing up and down his perch. All I felt now was a slight feeling of embarrassment, although I wasn't sure why. Confused, and more than a little angry at myself, I marched to the door and pulled it open.

Cedric was standing in the doorway.

My first thought was anger at Cedric for arriving without any warning at my door. Then I noticed the small hold-all Cedric was carrying and my skin prickled. I put an arm across the doorway, symbolically barring his entrance.

My tone was coolly polite as I stated what Squire would have called the bleeding obvious. 'So you're back.'

I was determined not to invite him in, no matter how rude I might seem to be. Cedric had never been in my flat, because I had leased it after he had been arrested, and for some reason I simply could not bear the thought of him coming inside the first home I had ever had to myself. Somehow if he could do that then it was tantamount to giving him leave to enter my life again.

'I'm back,' he said with a smile. 'Aren't you going to invite me in?'

'I'm sorry, Cedric, of course it's marvellous that they've released you, but I'm awfully busy just now.'

Cedric's smile became fixed and his glance flicked past me to settle on Simon and Leo, who were still standing by the

154

parrot cage. Simon kept his back to us, but Leo twisted around to look at us.

Cedric raised an eyebrow. 'A Jewish boy?' His voice was low, for me alone. 'The child looks Jewish. I know you work with them, but really, darling. Letting them in your home?'

'They are my guests.'

'Get rid of them, darling. We have things to discuss.'

'Ye-es. We do have things to discuss, but not now. Could we meet later in the week? Lunch?'

He lifted the small bag he was carrying. 'But darling, I was hoping to stay with you here, at least until we can find somewhere more suitable.'

'*No.*' My voice was louder than I had intended and in my peripheral vision I saw Simon stiffen. I moderated my tone and lowered my voice. 'I cannot put you up here, Cedric. The flat is too small, and – and I don't want to.'

His expression was amused rather than annoyed. I was angry with myself. I should have said that I didn't want him to stay with me before I made the silly 'flat too small' excuse. Knowing Cedric and his supreme self-confidence, he would think that I might have taken him in if the flat had been bigger. But Cedric had always made me tongue-tied. If I had known that he would turn up that afternoon I would have prepared a dignified little speech about how it was over between us and that I was determined to divorce him, no matter what.

Instead, I spoke in a strangled voice, falling over my words and not making anything clear. 'I don't – we're not – I mean, it's not—' I faltered under Cedric's amused look and finished with a hissing whisper, 'It's different now. I'm different. I told you in my letters. I want a divorce.'

Behind me, Simon was talking to Leo in a low, measured tone. It was something about parrots and what they ate, and how they should be looked after. I strained to catch his words and missed some of Cedric's reply.

'...as Helen suggested. As for the divorce, darling, we will talk about that later, when we're alone. All will be well, I promise. But now, I'll leave you to your guests.' He picked up his case, turned around and sauntered away down the corridor.

I closed the door and turned around. Simon was still looking at Bobby, but from the stiff set of his shoulders I thought he was angry. I said, more to myself than to Simon, 'Why would he come here?'

Simon twisted around to glare at me and reply, in a hard, sharp voice that was utterly unlike his usual tone, 'How the devil should I know? You married the man.'

There was not a hint of the light-hearted friendship Simon had displayed earlier.

The boy must have picked up the anger in his voice because his eyes were wide with distress. I flashed Simon a look. He put a hand on Leo's shoulder and said, 'Don't worry, Leo. Celia and I are discussing adult matters. We are not annoyed with you or Bobby.'

I smiled reassuringly at the boy and said in as calm and pleasant a voice as I could manage, 'Of course not. Why don't we let Bobby out for a walk?'

I saw a question in Leo's eyes, so I went on. 'Bobby likes to wander around the flat. And he especially likes to look out of the window. Once he climbed up my sleeve and stood on my shoulder.' And what a terrifying experience *that* had been. I finished brightly, 'Shall I open the cage door?'

Leo nodded. There was a spark of interest in his eyes that made me happy, so I pushed thoughts of Cedric, and of Simon, from my mind and walked over to Bobby's cage. I opened the door.

'Stand back, and give him some room,' I said.

Bobby dropped down from his perch and waddled over to the doorway, where he stood, gazing at the three of us. Leo moved closer, then leaned towards the door to the cage and put out his arm. I was about to tell him to move away when, to my surprise, Bobby left the cage and stepped up on to the sleeve of Leo's coat. The boy stood with his shoulders braced and his head held high but a quiver of excitement ran over him as the parrot ascended.

Bobby walked solemnly, in a swaying gait, up the length of Leo's arm. As he did so his sharp claws gripped the material as if it were a perch, but Leo did not flinch, so it seemed that only the material was being nipped. At last Bobby came to rest on the boy's shoulder, from where he surveyed the flat. Then he turned his beady little eyes on Leo for a few seconds, before leaning down and whiffling the boy's black hair with his big beak. It was a gentle gesture, nuzzling Leo just above his right ear.

Leo smiled then, a real, boyish smile of delight, and one I had never seen him give before. He beamed at me, and then at Simon, and for once there was no shadow in his dark eyes, only pure happiness.

'Simon Levy!' Bobby squawked into his ear. Leo flinched at the sound, then his smile widened as he realised what he had heard. He turned towards Simon and his mouth was an 'O' of shocked delight.

Simon looked shocked also. He glanced at me. 'Why would the bird…?'

And then Leo laughed. It was a rusty sound at first, as if he was out of practice, but it strengthened as Bobby spoke again, in his little-old-lady voice.

'God Save the King!' said Bobby.

Leo's soft, rusty-sounding laugh transformed into the high, infectious giggle of an eight-year-old boy. Simon smiled at him, then gave me a quizzical look.

'Simon Levy,' said Bobby. 'Simon Levy. God Save the King! Bloody hell!'

'Really, Celia, that bird is the absolute limit. Did you teach it that appalling language?'

Helen turned away from the cage and began burrowing in her small evening purse. It was Tuesday evening, and she was on her way to dinner at the Savoy, wearing a blue chinchilla stole that would have cost the equivalent of a year's salary for an ambulance girl.

'No.' That wasn't a complete lie. Some of the unsavoury words Bobby had come out with in the past few days had not been taught to him by me. At least he had not mentioned Simon's name since Helen had arrived.

'The horrid thing sounds like a Liverpool sailor,' said Helen with a sniff of displeasure as she extracted a lipstick from her purse.

I went across to Bobby's cage and covered it with the blanket, which silenced him.

'Thank you,' said Helen, in a martyred tone.

'I like that the bird's talking,' I responded defiantly.

'Cedric called by,' she said, as if I'd not spoken. 'He was devastated at your attitude towards him on Sunday afternoon. There was no need for rudeness.'

'I wasn't rude. I had guests and he appeared in the doorway, unannounced.'

'He's your husband, you silly girl.' She pulled out a compact and peered at her reflection.

'Not for long. Not if I can help it.'

Helen's reply was muffled, as she was reapplying her lipstick.

'Must you be so ridiculously dramatic?' she said at last, and smoothed the colour by rubbing her lips together sensuously. She smiled at her reflection. 'You married him, Celia. You cannot simply throw him away now you've tired of him, or are embarrassed by his incarceration.'

'It's not—' I took a calming breath. 'He didn't treat me well, you know. He ran around with half of London. The female half.' *There. I had told her.*

'They all do it,' she replied serenely. 'Not my Roly, of course. But husbands in our set often have other … interests.

158

You married too young, Celia. You were naive. But that doesn't alter the fact that you married Cedric and you cannot simply rid yourself of him on a whim.'

I stared at her. 'It's not a whim.'

Now she was combing her hair. 'Of course it is. Marriage means loyalty and forgiveness. To be perfectly frank, I think working for that ambulance organisation has changed you.' She glanced up at me. 'For the worse. The people there have filled your head with bourgeois ideas. And why must you work at Bloomsbury House? It's ridiculous when you know I'm desperate for help at Comforts for the Bombed.'

Helen managed a small charity that distributed clothing and household effects to those who had been blitzed. She knew nothing about David, or my reasons for working with Mrs Levy.

I took a cigarette from the box on the windowsill, but I didn't light it. I was trying to reduce my smoking, but speaking to Helen always made me desperate for a cigarette. 'Even if I could forgive Cedric's almost constant infidelity,' I said, 'I cannot condone his fascist views now we are at war with the Nazis.' I shook my head. 'Hitler is a murderous monster. Cedric supports a murderous monster.'

She paused. 'Yes. I think Hitler really is as bad as you say. But who could have guessed it in the thirties?'

*The Jews*, I thought. David had told me that they had known from the early 1930s what Hitler was doing to the Jews in Germany and Austria. Cedric had visited Berlin and had actually met Hitler around that time. He had once told me that only someone like Hitler could sort out the mess that Britain had got itself into. At one of his blackshirts meetings – I heard him say it – he suggested that the best thing for Britain would be a pogrom, and the following day his followers had dutifully smashed the windows of Jewish shops. His eyes had sparked with amusement when he was told about the incident. When I had told him how appalled I was he had cut me off, saying that he was not responsible for the actions of his followers if they took too literally what he said.

'*Anyone* could have known,' I said to Helen, 'if they had bothered to read Hitler's awful book or really listen to what the man was saying and take note of what he was doing. And Cedric was his apologist. What Cedric did before the war was unforgivable.'

'What his followers did was questionable,' admitted Helen, 'but *he* did nothing except expound on his views of what Britain needed to do in order to be great again. Yes, Cedric admired Hitler. Well, so did many in our set. But only Cedric was willing to stand in front of crowds and tell them what he thought. I think it was brave of him to do so. And you supported him too, as I recall.'

'I should have realised what it actually meant, and I hate that I didn't.'

Helen ignored me, continuing to pull her comb through the shining sweep of her hair. When she had finished she shrugged on the chinchilla.

'At least speak to Cedric,' she said. 'He adores you. Let him explain. You owe him that. Why not come over to our place for coffee one evening and meet him there, on neutral ground? When are you next on duty?'

'I'm on duty all week.'

'What about Saturday evening? Roly and I will be out until around midnight, so you and Cedric can talk in peace. Say nine?'

Helen was right. I did need to meet Cedric.

'Very well,' I said.

When I arrived at the offices of the JCPB in Bloomsbury House two days later, Lore jumped up from behind her desk and gave me a hug. I was becoming used to the exuberance of the German and Austrian women I met, but I found it hard to accept uncomplicated physical affection. I stood still and let her hug me, then gave a shaky laugh.

'What's that for?'

'For Leonhard Weitz,' she said, smiling. 'Elise Levy is beside herself with joy. He came home on Sunday afternoon, ran up to her and whispered in German that the parrot knew Simon's name.' She laughed. 'And also that, according to the parrot, Simon is King of England.'

'He talked? Leo talked?'

'Leonhard talked. He has a rusty little voice, she tells me, but he is using it.' She gave me a narrow look. 'He has learned an interesting expression, also. One that will not be repeated in polite company.'

I laughed. 'Then please don't,' I said, and added lightly, 'Who knows where parrots pick up such things? Oh, how marvellous that Leo is talking.'

'I think you will have a visitor again soon. It was love at first sight with that parrot.'

'The parrot seemed to like Leo, too. Of course he can visit the bird whenever he likes. I'll write to her and suggest next Sunday afternoon. He can come every Sunday. It's my day off.'

Lore was in a chatty mood that morning and hovered near my desk. Although it made it almost impossible for me to work, I found myself encouraging her to talk about the Levy family.

'Elise is like a new woman now she has the boy to care for,' she told me. 'After she was injured in the air raid and David died, it was as if she had no joy in life. Leonhard cannot be a replacement for David, of course, but Elise told me that having the boy in the house gives her a reason to get up each morning.'

'He's a nice little boy,' I said. 'I'm surprised that he was sent back from two foster-homes and was considered to be a troublemaker at the hostel.'

'I think it is being in a real family again that has made the difference. Elise is like a mother to him, and she tells me that he has even won over Jonathan, who plays chess with him. He has become particularly close to Simon and follows him around like a puppy when he is in the house. Simon puts up with it good-naturedly, although he is so busy with his duties at the hospital and in the Blitz that he is not home often.' She gave me a self-satisfied smile. 'But still Simon manages to take my Miriam out dancing and to restaurants when she has leave in London.'

'How nice of him.' I began to shuffle the papers on my desk. 'I really do need to get on with—'

'I think they would make an excellent match, although I suspect that Elise would like a girl of higher social status for her youngest.'

I put the papers down. 'The oldest son, Saul, he's married, isn't he?'

'Yes. It was a good marriage, to a Rothschild connection. His wife has evacuated to a house in the country, far from the bombing. Elise was hoping for a grandchild before Saul was posted away, but it was not to be.' She gave a decided nod. 'Miriam would not be a bad match for Simon, and Elise and Jonathan would accept it, if Simon was in love with her. Our family is respectable. And, of course, Miriam is Jewish.'

'So the Levys would never accept a non-Jewish girl for Simon?'

She frowned. 'If he fell in love with a girl who was not Jewish and wished to marry her they would not be happy, but they would not cast him aside. They would find it hard to accept, though. I do not think that Simon would do it to them.'

'Lore...' I hesitated, unsure if I should ask, but it had been worrying me. 'Does it bother you to work with me? Because of who I am. Cedric Ashwin's wife.'

Lore considered this for a long few seconds. 'To be honest, I was not happy when Elise told me you were coming to work here. It was an odd choice for you, to work for a Jewish charity. And then I thought that you must wish to atone for what your husband had done before the war. So I said I would accept you cheerfully.'

I felt the heat in my cheeks. 'That was one of the reasons.'

'Then, when you arrived, you were very stiff and seemed proud. I told Elise that I couldn't work with you after all, but she asked me not to judge you too soon.'

My cheeks were now flaming.

'After a week or so I realised that the pride and stiffness was your English manner, not your personality. I know now that you are a kind woman who cares deeply about our poor children.' Lore gave a soft laugh. 'Your sense of humour is so very English, though. You make jokes that do not seem to be jokes and it is only after I have thought about them that I laugh, sometimes long after you have left.' She smiled. 'Miriam says Simon is the same and it drives her mad.'

She bent down to put an arm around my shoulder and she kissed my cheek. 'I like you, Celia Ashwin. No, it does not bother me who your husband is. You do not share his beliefs and you cannot be held responsible for the actions of Cedric Ashwin.'

I desperately hoped Lore was right, especially as Cedric Ashwin now was back in my life. I was soon to discover that life is seldom so simple.

# CHAPTER SEVENTEEN

At eight-thirty the following Saturday evening I stepped out from St Andrew's Court into a squally gust of wind and rain and ran across the road to the taxi I had ordered. I wiped my face with my handkerchief and gave the address of Helen and Roly's villa in St John's Wood.

'It's as black as the Earl of Hell's waistcoat tonight,' said the cabbie as he set off along Gray's Inn Road. 'You'd never believe there's a moon floating somewhere up above them clouds.'

'I just hope the weather keeps the raiders away,' I replied.

'Well, it seems to me that, if they've not come over yet, they won't come at all tonight. Thank Gawd for the English weather, I say.'

He turned into the Euston Road. The thin shuttered headlights lit just enough of the road ahead to allow him to avoid the major potholes, but the roads were so pitted that the journey was a juddering one, splashing through puddles. He drove part of the way on the footpath. And as we headed west along the dark streets, twisting and turning through detour after detour, I tried to think of nothing and let the sweep of the windscreen wipers lull me into a sort of peace. I hoped to prepare myself for what I knew would be a difficult meeting with Cedric.

'Queer stuff, these German high explosives,' said the cabbie after a while. 'See that building there? It's wrecked from top to bottom. Just an empty shell, it is. And yet the house next door hasn't a scratch.'

'Mmm.'

'You go down the shelters?' he asked.

'Not usually.'

'You really should, miss. My missus goes off to the Piccadilly Tube Station each evening. When I'm not driving I go too. Quite good company down there. All very merry and bright, bar the squalling babies and those what snore in their sleep. Last week a silly blighter fell out of his bunk when he had a bad dream. Laugh? We all laughed fit to bust ourselves. He came down wallop.'

'Was he hurt?'

'Only his pride.'

'So you drive even during a raid?'

'Unless the raiders are directly overhead, I'm out there on the streets. What's the good of getting scared? If you're for it, you're for it, and that's all there is to it! No use worrying, is it?'

As we headed further westward and then north the extent of the bomb damage decreased. Houses were down, as J.B. Priestly had said in his wireless broadcast, 'like gaps amidst teeth', but it was nothing like the devastation of the West End or the City or the Docks. We were getting nearer to St John's Wood and Cedric. My heart began to thump, which annoyed me

'Funny how this area's not copped it so badly,' said the cabbie. 'Someone's looking out for them. Not fair, really. But that's life, isn't it?'

He pulled up outside Helen's house. I took a deep, calming breath and prepared myself to meet Cedric.

'Bless you, miss,' he said, as I handed over the fare. 'Now you take care of yourself, and you get to the shelter when the raiders come over. You're much too pretty to be blown up, if you don't mind me saying so.'

I smiled at him. 'I don't mind. Could you be here, waiting for me, in two hours?'

'I'd be delighted. Victory at all costs,' was his patriotic parting comment.

'At all costs,' I replied. How was the cabbie to know I was referring to the expected tussle with my husband?

I held my raincoat over my head and dashed for the front steps, counting each as I ran up to the portico. One, two, three, four, five. Then I was at the front door. A gust of wind whipped my face, almost as if something were flying past me, chilly and invisible. A ghostly warning, perhaps? I pulled the doorbell. *Head high, walk tall.*

The Irish maid showed me into the drawing room, where Cedric stood to greet me. I was so used to seeing men in uniform that it was slightly shocking that Cedric was dressed in a dinner jacket and white tie. It spoke of a time before the war, before all of the misery and destruction of the past year and a bit.

It is hard for me now to describe Cedric, but he was generally considered to be a fine-looking man, with the sort of regular features that women liked, allied to a pair of strikingly pale blue eyes. His mouth was thin-lipped but somehow sensual, and he wore a carefully cultivated pencil moustache on his upper lip, like Errol Flynn. There were other similarities to that handsome and athletic actor. Cedric was a superb boxer, as well as a crack shot with pistol and rifle. There was a catlike grace in his movements and he was very proud of his athletic prowess. In short, his moustache was trim, his nose shapely, his teeth white and perfect, his profile aristocratic.

Although his outward appearance was that of the man I'd seen taken away by police eight months previously, and imprisonment had obviously failed to dent his supreme self-confidence, I had the unsettling feeling that a smiling stranger stood before me. If so, it was a stranger who was regarding me with a look that spoke of ownership.

Once I had been awestruck by this man, but in the last eight months I had grown up. I was no longer Cedric's child bride, grateful to him for helping me to escape from a difficult home. I had been tempered in the fires of the Blitz, and had experienced life in a city under constant attack. I had fallen in love, and I had suffered great loss. I had moved beyond him. Looking at Cedric now, I was more determined than ever to find a way to end our marriage.

I managed to dodge a hug, but Cedric took hold of my shoulders and kissed my cheek, then held me out at arm's length to look at me with a smile. I smelled alcohol on his breath as I shrugged myself out of his grip and sat on an armchair by the fire. He regarded at me with amusement. His manner – almost light-hearted – worried me, and I decided to proceed cautiously.

'I'd kill for a cigarette,' I said, just for something to say.

Cedric laughed and pulled out his silver case, holding it out to me as I extracted a cigarette.

'Would you believe that when I was on my way here from Liverpool my train was strafed?' he said, as he lit my cigarette. He used the lighter I had given him as a present on our second wedding anniversary.

'How ironic,' I said dryly, and it earned me a sharp look. So his Nazi friends had strafed him. A few bullets had hit the roof of his train. Had he any idea what we'd been suffering in London?

'I thought it was an exhilarating experience,' he said. 'It's a powerful machine, the Messerschmitt. Deadly and beautiful.'

I drew on my cigarette and leaned back in my chair. The familiar gesture gave me confidence and I said, in a seemingly careless voice, 'I prefer Spitfires. You've returned to a very different London from the one you left.'

'There's less of it,' he said, with what appeared to be a degree of satisfaction. It infuriated me and I had to work hard at not showing it.

Then his hands closed into fists. 'Stupid fools brought it on themselves. There is no need for any of this. We should be allied with the Nazis against Russia. The Soviet Union is a far greater threat to British freedom than Hitler ever could be.'

'I don't recall Stalin sending bombers over the Channel.'

He frowned. '*We* declared war on Germany, remember. Hitler thinks very highly of the British. He wants peace with this country.'

'He's going about it in an odd sort of way, then. Peace? The way he enforced peace in France, you mean? No thank you.'

'The German people under Hitler are contented and happy. And so will be the people of France and the other countries now under his guidance, eventually. Don't believe the stories you hear, darling. Hitler has done a great deal of good for Europe.'

'Really, Cedric.' I was exasperated. 'The man murders his own people and locks them up in concentration camps.'

'And so does Churchill,' he snapped. 'He insisted that I be locked away, although I've never had anything but the best interests of this country in my heart.' He looked at me, held my gaze. 'I was trying to lead a cavalry charge into the future. I wanted to dissipate our fears and put them to flight. Churchill knew I was a rival to be feared, and he made it his business to destroy me.'

He took out a tobacco pouch and stuffed his pipe, jabbing angrily at the strands of tobacco as he walked across to the fireplace. Once there he took a wooden spill from the container on the chimneypiece, lit it and applied the flame to the bowl of the pipe, puffing until it drew and the rich scent of his tobacco filled the room. When he spoke again his voice was calmer.

'Hitler locks up Jews and communists. Well done, I say.'

'He's also invaded and subjugated most of Europe. He'd do the same here.'

'Individual freedom is overrated. The rights of citizens must always be subordinate to the needs of the state. The Third Reich is powerful and it is fearsome to its enemies, but it is kind to those who support it. And that's why most of its citizens are jolly happy with their state of affairs.'

'Spoken like a true fascist.'

He bowed his head, as if I'd made a good point.

There was a knock on the door. It opened and the maid entered, wheeling a trolley on which were the coffee pot, cups, saucers and a plate of pastries. I let my mind drift away from anger as I poured the coffee. I needed a cool head.

He smiled at me as he accepted his coffee, the charming smile of our early courtship. 'Thank you, darling.'

The coffee was thick and black and very good. Once I had drunk some I felt able to mention my reason for coming.

'Cedric … as I said in my letters, I want a divorce.'

His smile didn't waver, and his voice was even as he replied. 'No you don't. You want to punish me for my indiscretions. I *was* indiscreet and I'm sorry to have hurt you, but let's hear no more of this divorce nonsense.'

I refused to despair, because I had known he would resist. My brief conversations with Helen had made that clear, as had his letters. But I decided to press the point, as an opening sally in what I suspected would be a long and drawn-out campaign.

'I do want a divorce, Cedric.' Perhaps, if I repeated the words enough, Cedric would really hear them.

He said, sharply, 'Don't be ridiculous.'

'It's not ridiculous.' I had to work hard to keep my voice calm and even. 'I've changed, Cedric. I'm nothing like the girl you married. Our marriage cannot continue.'

'It can, and it will. You are my life, Celia. My world. How could I let you go? We are married. We will stay married.'

I sipped my coffee and let my gaze fall away from him, disliking the intensity he was showing. It was a worrying development.

His tone sharpened. 'I will *never* agree to a divorce.' His tone softened, became caressing. 'I adore you, my darling, and I will not let you simply walk out of my life. But it's more than that, you silly child. The marriage is to your benefit as well. There will be changes in this country come spring, and you will need me beside you when they come.'

'What changes?'

He showed the ghost of a smile as he turned away from me to pick up his cup, and he took a sip before he replied in a tone of gentle amusement, 'Nothing for you to worry about. Nothing at all to *worry* about. Quite the contrary. But believe me, darling, you will glad to be married to me then.'

'I don't understand.'

When he turned to me his eyes shone with the light of fanaticism. 'I'm talking about the invasion, darling. When Germany invades, being married to me will be most advantageous.'

'Germany won't invade.' I spoke cautiously, worried about his mood. 'The RAF was victorious against the Luftwaffe. Germany won't invade this country while we have control of our skies and while we have the Royal Navy to protect us.'

His smile was now that of an adult at a child speaking nonsense. 'The story about the RAF defeating the Luftwaffe was unadulterated propaganda. And the Royal Navy is being decimated by German submarines. You expect the remnants of your tattered army and a few Canadian regiments to prevail against thousands of crack German paratroopers? How naive you are to believe anything Churchill reports. German troops will be marching down the Strand come June, and Hitler will be enjoying the amenities of Buckingham Palace.'

My face must have given me away, for he said quickly, 'Don't worry about the Royal Family. We have assurances as to their safety.' He took another puff of his pipe, as if this were normal after-dinner conversation.

*We have assurances*? Was he in contact with Germany? How many were involved in this mad scheme? Or was it just wishful thinking? I felt suddenly very tired; the conversation had slipped away from me and nothing made any sense. Cedric and I should be discussing our divorce, not a Nazi invasion of Britain. Why had he mentioned it? Did he really believe it? And why was he referring to 'your' army, when the word should have been 'our'?

'I'm not sure…' I began, cautiously, but paused because I had no idea what to say. So I picked up my cup and sipped Helen's coffee. For the first time I wondered if Cedric were mad.

He gave a sigh of satisfaction. 'Cedric Ashwin and his beautiful wife will be the epitome of the New Order in this country. We – you and I, Celia – we will be its golden couple. We will set standards for the rest to emulate.' There was something nasty lurking behind his ice-blue eyes, something quick and sinuous as eels squirming in clear river water. 'They will regret locking me up on that godforsaken island.' His expression hardened. 'Especially Churchill. And so, my dear Celia, there can be no talk of divorce. The Fuhrer detests divorce among those he favours. Oh, how he will adore you. You will be one of his favourites.' Puff. Puff. The swirl of smoke rose and dissipated above his head.

'And another thing. He sees children as an important part of marriage. We both wanted to wait, but now I think that the time has come.'

I put down my coffee cup with a slight jerk, so that the dark liquid swirled up and nearly spilled. It took real effort to keep my voice calm, but I managed to do so. 'There will be no talk of children, Cedric. I want a divorce.'

His lips compressed, but when he spoke it was in a voice of utmost reasonableness. 'I am being patient with you, Celia. More patient than most men would be. But there are limits. Please understand. I will not divorce you. You have no grounds upon which to divorce me. Those ... peccadilloes of mine took place discreetly. You have no evidence and will never have evidence that would be accepted by a court. Even if *you* have strayed in the past eight months – and you must be aware that I have never inquired – then I'll put it down to loneliness and we'll never speak of it.'

I became very still. Had Eddie been spying on me when I met with David? On reflection, I thought not. I doubted that Cedric would forgive an 'indiscretion' with David Levy. To buy some time I picked up my cigarette from the ashtray, tipped off the excess ash, and put it to my lips. As I drew in the smoke I gathered my thoughts. I could not convince Cedric tonight, and there was nothing to be served by allowing the conversation to degenerate into an argument.

I didn't think that Cedric would seek to enforce his legal 'rights' as a husband to ensure I was carrying his child when

Hitler goose-stepped down the Strand. It would prick his vanity too much to force a woman. And he had no real financial control over me. Even if he shut off the allowance he had given me during his months in gaol, I still earned a small amount as an ambulance driver. With careful management it would be sufficient to pay for my rent and food. I had never been extravagant and that would not change, especially if I had to count every penny.

'I won't change my mind about the divorce,' I said, carefully, 'but let's not discuss the matter any further tonight.'

More than anything else I wanted to leave the man to his fantasies and go home. But Cedric's talk of invasion and 'we have assurances' about the welfare of the Royal Family after the invasion were concerning. I owed it to my country to find out if Cedric was any real threat. I needed to discover if he was in touch with the Nazis and assisting them in any way.

I wondered how to raise the vexed subject of treason.

'Cedric, it's unwise to say such things – about Churchill and about the invasion – nowadays.'

'Unwise?' A fanatical glitter appeared in Cedric's eyes, but his voice was pleasant and measured, which was disconcerting. Again I wondered if he were quite sane. He gave a soft laugh. 'I still have supporters. True patriots, who know that this country has been sold down the river by Jews and communists and their acolytes.' His voice had risen, and he was now the orator who had held thousands in sway by the power of his voice. '*They* know that only the fascist ideals of discipline and military leadership can lead this country into a new order of social and economic prosperity and hope. And they know that is why Hitler has succeeded.'

'Hitler hasn't succeeded here,' I said brusquely. 'Britain still stands for Democracy, the rights of the individual and the Rule of Law.'

Cedric jumped out of his chair and rounded on me. For a moment I wondered if he was about to strike me. Then his face changed, from anger to contempt to amusement.

'As you have often admitted, you know very little about politics, darling.' He turned towards the fireplace and tapped out his pipe against the grate. 'I hear that you spend far too much time at that Jewish refugee organisation. That has to stop.'

I ground out what remained of my cigarette in the ashtray beside me, watching until every last spark was extinguished, because there was no point in showing my anger. When I was calmer I stood.

'I enjoy that work, Cedric. I help children and it gives me pleasure to do so. Let's say no more about it.'

Anger sparked in his eyes. 'Do not try my patience, Celia.' He softened his tone. 'We won't speak of this any more tonight. You must be exhausted, unable to think clearly. I heard that you had been badly injured not long ago and I can see that nasty scar on your forehead.'

'Slight concussion, that's all.'

He smiled. 'I heard it was much worse than that. Poor darling. More coffee?'

I shook my head. 'I'll leave now, I think.'

He saw me to the taxi and paid the cabbie. His tip must have been generous, because there was real warmth in the cabbie's voice as he said, 'Thank you very much indeed, sir.' And he added, 'Victory at all costs.'

'At all costs,' repeated Cedric.

The taxi moved away, down the dark, deserted streets. As the cabbie had predicted the rain, or something, was keeping the Luftwaffe away that night. I hugged the comfort of my coat close around me and leaned back in the seat. I felt as if my nerves were stretched so tight they were close to shattering. After a moment I shook my head and sucked in a shaky breath. I'd told Simon Levy I was no Dresden china lass, and I couldn't let one meeting with my husband put the lie to that boast. *Head high, walk tall, Celia.* Somehow I would convince Cedric to divorce me.

The taxi lurched to one side as it hit something on the road, and the cabbie swore softly under his breath as he corrected the vehicle.

'Sorry, miss. There's debris everywhere. Have a nice evening?' he asked in a lighter voice.

'An interesting one.'

'That feller what paid for your fare. He reminds me of someone. Can't place who, though.'

My laugh was bitter. 'Hitler? Goering? Mussolini?'

'Now, miss,' he said in an indulgent tone, 'don't be like that. You two have a lovers' tiff? You see all sorts in this business, and I can pick 'em. I knew right away about that one. A right proper English gentleman he is.'

I did not reply. There was no point.

At three the following afternoon Leo arrived to visit Bobby. I opened the door to see Simon with one hand on Leo's shoulder and carrying a basket covered with a striped tea towel in the other. He nodded to me with his usual rather guarded expression. Leo gave me his little bow and looked past me into the flat.

'May I leave Leo with you for the afternoon?' asked Simon, as they entered. 'I have to go in to the hospital.'

Leo went across to Bobby's cage where he whispered something to the bird, who responded by saying, 'Hello, I'm Bobby. What's your name?'

At that Leo giggled and whispered, 'Leo Weitz.' He gave his formal bow to the parrot.

'God save the King!' said Bobby, and Leo giggled again.

Simon smiled at the pair. 'My mother is trying to get Leo to speak more. She wonders if you could encourage him.'

'I'll see what I can do.'

'And this is from my mother.' He handed the basket to me. 'We don't want you using your ration on the boy. It's milk for Leo, and some stollen – fruitcake – for you both. Don't ask me where she gets it from, as it's a closely guarded secret.'

174

When I was alone with Leo I sat down near Bobby's cage. I picked up a pair of laddered stockings and began to darn them.

Leo pointed to the cage door.

'I'm sorry, Leo,' I said, 'but I'm not sure what you want.'

Leo gave me a considering look and said, very softly, 'May I open the door, please?'

'Of course. And I'm sure that Bobby would love to hear what you've been doing this week.'

He opened the cage and Bobby climbed up his sleeve as before. Leo turned away from me and began to speak softly to the bird in German.

'Watch this, Leo,' I said. I went across to the wireless and pretended to turn it on.

The sonorous tones of Big Ben's chimes filled the flat. After nine chimes a familiar voice announced, 'Here is the news and this is Alvar Lidell reading it.'

Leo was delighted and announced to Bobby, '*Du bist ein kluger vogel.*' He glanced at me. 'A clever bird,' he said shyly.

We had a peaceful time as Leo spoke to Bobby and I caught up on my sewing. With clothes rationing just around the corner, we were all forced to 'make do and mend'. Leo spoke only to the parrot, and only in German. I wondered if I should tell him to speak to Bobby in English, but I was too worried that he might stop talking completely if I insisted. At four o'clock we snacked on stollen. I had tea as Leo drank his milk and surreptitiously fed cake to the bird, which I ignored.

At five o'clock there was a rap at the door. I opened it to find Simon standing there. He smiled at Leo, who was standing by the window with Bobby on his shoulder.

'Thank you for looking after him,' he said, then called to Leo, 'Time to go home.'

Leo ignored him. After a minute or so Simon strode across the room with heavy steps, saying 'Fi fi fo fum', in the deep voice of a pantomime villain, which made Leo laugh. As Simon approached, Bobby fluttered off his shoulder to perch on the bookcase, which was just as well, because Simon picked Leo up, turned him upside down and held him dangling by one ankle as Leo shrieked with laughter and tried to keep his spectacles from falling off. I assumed it was a game they'd played before, and I smiled to see them both so relaxed.

'When I say it's time to go,' said Simon in mock annoyance, 'what do you do?' He gave Leo's leg a shake.

'*Ich komme zu dir*,' squeaked Leo.

'English,' said Simon, in the deep giant voice.

'I come to you.'

'And at the double,' said Simon. He turned, still holding Leo's ankle, so that the boy's inverted face was towards me. 'Now thank Celia for a lovely afternoon.'

'*Danke* – I mean, thank you, Celia,' replied Leo obediently, and wriggled. 'Put me down, Simon. *Bitte*.'

Simon righted him, and Leo bowed to me. He glanced at Simon, then said quickly, '*Bitte* – I mean, please – may I come again soon. For Bobby.'

Simon raised an eyebrow at me.

'Of course,' I said. 'Next Sunday afternoon?'

'*Gut*,' said Leo. 'I mean, good.' He turned to the parrot, now settled on the bookcase. 'Goodbye, Bobby. I will see you soon.'

# CHAPTER EIGHTEEN

It was, of course, nothing like my wedding in 1937.

That had taken place in St George's, Hanover Square and we had three hundred guests. Lily's wedding to Jim was at the local register office and their guests numbered ten. My gown had been of parchment moiré with a beautiful lace veil that had swept the aisle behind me; Lily wore the blue dress that Katherine had made and a chic little blue-and-white hat. I had carried a huge bouquet of orange blossom; Lily's small posy was lily of the valley and its scent filled the room. Six bridesmaids wearing white net frocks with crimson velvet sashes had attended me; Lily walked in alone to join Jim, who stood tall and handsome in his RAF uniform, at the registrar's desk. His only sign of nervousness was the imaginary tune tapped out by his fingers on his leg, but when Lily entered the room it was as if he had seen a vision. And when she smiled at him...

It was not in the slightest like my wedding, because it was so very much nicer.

The guests were a mixture of British and Australian. Katherine Carlow, the Matron of Honour, was English. The Best Man, Peter Creighton, was Scottish and looked dashing in his Scots Guards dress uniform, complete with sword. The other Australians were Pamela Beresford, the daughter of an Australian bishop and a close friend of Lily's who also had a flat at St Andrew's, two Australian pilots from Jim's former RAF squadron, Fred Harland and Mike Corrs, and Fred's wife, Frances. Mike's wife, Annette, was English, as was another of Jim's pilot friends, Gerald Wilde. He was a slightly built young pilot officer who hailed from Manchester and took an immediate and obvious fancy to Pam. As for me, save for my little French grandmother, my family had been British since the Conquest. The final guest was the very British, Harrow-educated Simon Levy.

After the wedding we were invited by Jim and Lily to join them for dinner and dancing at the Dorchester.

'It was where Jim took me for tea, the very first time we went out together,' Lily said, laughing, as we gathered around them on the steps of the register office in the lengthening gloom of a January afternoon. Beyond the portico, snow had begun to fall steadily.

'How romantic,' said Frances, the Australian RAF wife.

'Not really.' Lily exchanged glances with Jim. 'I thought he was boring and he thought I was in love with Da— with someone else. Not an auspicious beginning.' Lily threw him a cheeky smile. 'And he didn't even kiss me goodnight.'

'I wanted to,' he replied, bending down and pulling her close. 'Will this make up for it?' He kissed her for what seemed a long time, to the sound of whoops from the Australian airmen.

'Not quite,' she said, when she came up for air. 'The matter requires further negotiation.'

'I married a barrack-room lawyer.' Jim raised an eyebrow and gave a look of mock horror. Then he glanced up at the darkening sky. 'Let's head off to the Dorchester. At least there will be three feet of concrete between us and the raiders.'

'Think they'll come over tonight?' asked Annette, the English RAF wife. 'It's been the quietest week since the night blitz started in September.'

Jim shrugged. 'I assume they'll come every night. Sometimes not many of them, but every night.'

'Pessimist,' said Peter Creighton. 'We're in a lull in the Blitz, didn't you know? Or so they say. D'you agree?' He looked at the RAF pilots.

Mike Corrs shrugged. 'I think it's the weather. The aerodromes in Europe are sodden and they've had a lot of fog.'

'Well I'm happy about it,' said Lily. 'I don't want an air raid on my wedding day.'

She was to be disappointed.

When we emerged from the taxis, Park Lane was darkly elegant in the blackout. All around was shimmering white with fresh-fallen snow and a light mist gave the situation a sensation of unreality. This was not dispelled when almost immediately the Warning sounded. We stared at the sky, watching silvery barrage balloons float upwards to swim above us like a school of tethered silver fish. Searchlights raked the low clouds, backlighting the grandeur of London as they swung to and fro in frenzied geometric arcs. The anti-aircraft guns in Hyde Park began their deafening thump-thump-thump, pounding against my ears, and I flinched as the sky to the south lit up, momentarily exposing the buildings, the puddles on the road and our startled faces in a garish, yellow-white light.

Lily, who was holding Jim's hand, took my hand with her other and we ran across the road together, with the others close behind, dodging falling shrapnel. The hotel's entrance doors had been painted over in dark blue to comply with the blackout and were covered with anti-shatter netting. Behind them hung the heavy blackout curtains.

Once we had pushed through, we were in a bright sanctuary of luxury and glamour. It was like entering another world, a beautiful fantasy world far from the war and rationing and air raids and death beyond its blacked-out doors.

The women all headed straight for the cloakroom, where we tidied hair, reapplied lipstick and gently chaffed Lily, who seemed almost to be floating.

'Now, ladies,' she declared, as she drew a comb through her curls and smiled at her reflection, 'did I or did I not marry the most gorgeous, handsome man in the entire world?'

We made the right noises. Pam, ever the cheeky one, began to hum 'Someday my prince will come' from *Snow White.*

Lily ignored her. Instead she turned towards the very young cloakroom assistant and gave the girl a brilliant smile.

'Hullo, Doris,' she said. 'Remember me? I've just been married.'

'That's lovely to hear, miss,' replied Doris patiently. 'Would you like me to assist in any way, miss. I mean, madam.'

'She's more than just madam,' said Pam. 'She's the—'

'Madam will do,' said Lily, freezing her with a look. 'I'm plain old Mrs Vassilikov, and very happy to be so.' She applied lipstick, smoothed her lips and smiled at her reflection happily. 'Wasn't it the loveliest wedding?'

Frances and Annette looked down, avoiding her eyes. Outside the register office I had heard them whisper that it was the plainest wedding ceremony they had ever attended. Katherine and Pam exchanged looks. Only last week Katherine had said how unhappy she was at the thought of Lily not being married in a proper wedding dress with a veil.

Katherine needn't have worried. Lily had another wedding when the war was over, and it was the most elaborate I have ever attended. It took place in a glittering Russian Orthodox Church. Wedding crowns were held above their heads. Lily and Jim sipped wine from the one cup, and walked together around the Gospel on its elaborate stand. The priest bound their hands with his stole. A pair of crystal glasses was smashed into smithereens. There was music and dancing and many toasts. And Lily wore an exquisite gown and a long lace veil.

But that was years away, after the war and all its enmities were over but not yet forgotten. In the cloakroom of the Dorchester that evening, with the muted thunder of the Hyde Park guns as a backdrop, I sat on the chair beside Lily and smiled at her.

'It was a lovely wedding,' I said, and meant it. 'It was absolutely perfect.'

We followed the waitress through the crowded room to our table, which was near the dance floor. Around us was a sea of uniforms. Jim ordered champagne, and when it arrived we toasted the couple. He stood, looked at his bride and cleared his throat nervously.

'I don't want to make a speech. You all know very well how jolly lucky I am to have convinced Lily to marry me. Lily Vassilikov, would you do me the honour of accepting our first dance?'

Soon they were whirling around the dance floor. Jim was a good dancer and managed the height difference well. The two married RAF couples soon joined them. Then Peter Creighton asked Katherine to dance, and Gerald Wilde asked Pam. That left me alone with Simon.

He looked at me across the table. I met his gaze with what I hoped was cool indifference. He met mine with what I knew was amusement.

'Your name's Cecilia?' he said. 'Is that right? Pretty name.'

He had called me that when we were together in the dark, ruined cellar, before he knew who I was. It was an olive branch, I supposed.

'Actually, it's Celia,' I replied, and smiled a little.

'Still a pretty name.' He gestured at the dance floor. 'Care to dance?'

'Thank you. Yes.'

He took my hand, led me on to the crowded floor and swept me into a waltz. I looked past Simon's face at the dancers in the room and saw Peter steer Katherine into another couple. Her frown of annoyance was quickly suppressed. I couldn't stifle a laugh, because poor Peter had always been an awkward dancer.

Simon's eyebrows rose at my laugh, and I flicked a glance towards Peter and Katherine. 'I have the better dance partner,' I said, and he gave me a smile in return. Then I remembered his look of contempt when I had woken him after the Bank Station disaster and looked over his shoulder again.

I had eaten very little that day and the champagne I had drunk made me feel a little dizzy as I relaxed into the dance. Being held in the circle of Simon's arms felt surprisingly comforting. I supposed that was because he had looked after me when I was ill. And because he was a giver of life, rather than a taker. Most of the men around us had been trained to kill and wound in our fight against Hitler. Simon, however, had been trained to defeat Death, rather than the Nazis. I glanced at his hand, holding mine with just the right degree of firmness, and remembered how cool it had felt on my feverish skin, how gently he had dealt with my wound.

'It's Cesia in Yiddish,' said Simon. He pronounced the name T-sees-i-yah.

I dragged my mind into the present and regarded him with surprise. 'What is?'

'Your name. In Yiddish it's Cesia.'

'I like the sound of it.' As I repeated 'Cesia' I felt the tap of my tongue on my teeth, the small exhalation, the sibilant and the satisfying yah sound to end it. It was a tactile name; Celia was a smooth name.

Simon whirled me around with dizzying precision, out of the path of a very large man in a kilt, whose partner wore a long-suffering look.

I laughed. 'My full name is a mouthful, actually. I was christened Celia Rosamond Constance Grace Irene Palmer-Thomas.'

'Plain old Simon Maximilian Levy am I,' he said.

'When I was ten, a man with spotted handkerchief around his neck told me my name should be Penny.'

'Because of your hair? It's the colour of a copper penny.'

'Yes.' I made a face. 'I hate the colour of my hair. Reminds me of dried blood.'

Simon hesitated, as if searching for the right words, then he looked at me and shook his head. I thought I saw a smile behind his eyes.

'It's nothing like dried blood, and I'm an expert, remember. Spotted-handkerchief man was right. A new copper penny. You must know how beautiful it is.'

It was warm on the dance floor, which probably accounted for the heat in my cheeks. Simon cleared his throat slightly and changed the subject.

'So, you're a girl of many names.'

'And I'm not defined by any of them.' I went on without thinking. 'And certainly not by the name Ashwin.'

For a moment his grip tightened, then it relaxed.

'Glad to hear it,' he said.

I pondered this as my body followed his in the steps of the waltz and the music rose and fell around us. Could I change my name back to Palmer-Thomas when, or if, Cedric divorced me? Perhaps I'd remarry and change it that way, but remarriage seemed improbable. Anyway, I reasoned, it was crazy to think of remarriage before I was actually divorced.

'My mother adores you,' he said, breaking into my thoughts.

I laughed. 'Because of Leo? It's Bobby she should adore.'

'It's good of you to let Leo visit.'

'It's really no bother. Sunday always is my full day off.'

'I suspect my mother will be begging you to let Bobby go.'

'No need to beg. I think that he and Leo are made for each other.'

It was worth losing Bobby for the look of gratitude in Simon's eyes.

'But we should wait until the bird is entirely recovered before Leo takes him for good,' I said.

When the dance was over his arms fell away from me, and I felt almost bereft. As he led me back to the table, threading through the crush of people, a man barrelled into me. Anger flared in Simon's eyes, as he pulled me away from the clumsy fellow.

'Are you all right?'

'I'm fine,' I said. 'A shade tougher than Dresden china, remember.'

'I do remember that.' He smiled. 'You're more than a shade tougher than most soldiers, actually.'

I stopped walking and let the crowd jostle its way past us as I gave him a straight look. 'I'm sorry I've been such a rotten patient. I must have seemed shockingly ungrateful. It's just that – well, I despise weakness and inactivity.'

'I didn't take it personally,' he said. 'In truth, I suspect you were still suffering from concussion, which meant you weren't thinking all that clearly.' His voice became brisk. 'And as I recall, I was rather brutish towards you at times.'

His mouth firmed, as if he had made a decision. Then he held out his hand to me.

'Pax?'

My heart lurched and heat flooded my cheeks as I took hold of his hand. His grip was firm, and his hand cool.

'Pax,' I repeated, smiling.

He gave me a firm nod and a slight smile in reply. For the second time that day I felt completely happy.

It lasted less than a minute.

'Unhand my wife, varlet.'

It sounded good-natured. I knew better. There was real anger behind those six syllables, said in that voice with its drawling vowels and air of command. And yet, Cedric had never commanded anything other than some brigades of black-shirted boys and men, who saw in him a way to recover Britain's lost glory.

Simon's hand dropped away from mine. His face resolved into what I can only describe as a mask. There was a cool remoteness now in his expression and watchfulness in his eyes. I assumed my own disguise before I turned to face my husband. *Head high, walk tall*. My shoulders straightened and my chin went up and in my mind I disappeared into the bluebell glade by the river, where no one could hurt me.

'Darling,' Cedric's smile was forced.

I remembered the look on Jim's face when he saw Lily come into the register office, and Lily's smile in response. I'd promised to love, honour and obey the man who stood in front of me, but never had Cedric looked at me the way that Jim had looked at Lily this afternoon.

Cedric turned to Simon and his jaw tensed before he gave him a charming smile. 'I don't believe...'

How instinctive is politeness, that need to behave like a civilised person. 'Excuse me,' I said. 'Allow me to introduce Dr Simon Levy. Simon, this is Cedric Ashwin.'

Neither man put out a hand to the other; instead a very masculine staring match ensued. Some devil prompted me to take hold of Simon's arm. I ignored the flash of annoyance in Cedric's face, and tried not to feel slighted by Simon's flinch as I did so and the tensing of his muscles.

'Levy?' said Cedric. He was too well bred to sneer, but somehow it was there in his voice, the acknowledgement that Simon was Jewish and that Cedric did not approve of him at all.

Simon's bland mask remained firmly in place. He lifted his hand to cover mine, and tucked it more securely into the crook of his arm. Cedric frowned as he did so, but his face quickly reverted to polite good humour.

'Yes,' said Simon. 'Levy.' He gave my hand a little pat, just to make the point.

Cedric flicked a glance at me. 'You work with a man called Levy, don't you? Is this he? I thought he died.'

Simon's hand tightened on my arm. I replied with what I hoped was chilly politeness. 'That was Dr Levy's brother, David. He – he died in November.'

There was a slight hesitation as I mentioned David's name and I knew Cedric would pick it up. Because my husband was a past master at deception he easily recognised it in others. So I added, 'Dr Levy saved my life a few weeks ago, when I was trapped in a bombed building.'

Cedric inclined his head and gave Simon a smile of great charm. 'Then I am greatly in your debt, Dr Levy. Celia is very precious indeed.'

'Celia exaggerates,' said Simon. 'I did very little.'

Again there was a staring match between them.

'We should return to our table,' I said to Simon. Then to Cedric, 'Jim and Lily Vassilikov's wedding party.'

'Please give them both my very best wishes,' said Cedric. The charming smile shifted to me, but his eyes were pale shards of ice. 'I was intending to drop by your flat tomorrow. We need to have another discussion, darling.'

Did he want to discuss divorce? I hesitated. 'I'm sorry, but I can't see you tomorrow. I have plans.'

'Monday?'

'I'm working all day Monday. And all night.'

His mouth tightened. 'Tuesday then.'

'I'm very sorry, but I'm busy all week. I work shifts, Cedric. Twenty-four-hour shifts. And I also work at the charity. The evenings I'm not working I'm exhausted and, of course, it's difficult with the night raids.'

His expression hardened. 'Really, darling. Dr Levy will think you're avoiding me. You must have some time off. Are you free next weekend?'

'Yes.'

'Saturday evening. Eight o'clock.'

I did not want to go to dinner with Cedric. Dinner was too romantic, too intimate. 'Let's make it a late lunch. Where should I meet you?'

'I would prefer dinner.'

'And I would prefer a late lunch. Where should I meet you, Cedric?'

'But, darling, Quag's does dinner so well.'

'I'm sure Quag's lunch menu is more than adequate. I will meet you there.'

'Lunch, then. Quag's at two. I will count the hours.'

I smiled politely. He gave a slight, stiff bow and walked away into the crowd. Why did he want to meet? It had always been difficult to read Cedric. I wished I could talk it over with Lily, but Jim was a complicating factor. I let out a breath I hardly knew I'd been holding and released Simon's arm. He cleared his throat, and when I turned to him, I found him glowering at me.

'I would prefer not to be used as a stage prop next time we meet your husband.'

I dragged my thoughts away from Cedric and blinked at Simon. 'Oh, and you'd never stoop so low yourself?' I said, annoyed. 'Patting my hand in that odious manner, just to annoy him.'

He stiffened. 'Odious. You find it odious when I touch you?'

'When you misrepresent the situation, I do.'

'Then it won't happen again.'

'What won't?'

'Anything.'

He swung around and stalked through the crowd towards our table. I couldn't work out what had just happened, but it seemed that Simon and I were, yet again, at odds with each other. The band began to play a new tune and couples were streaming on to the dance floor, so it took me a while to push through. When I reached the table Katherine was sitting there alone.

'I decided to save my poor toes and encouraged the Honourable Peter to ask a young thing sitting at another table for a dance,' she said, with an amused grimace. 'Let her suffer, I say. I'm already married and don't need to pretend it's an honour to be asked.'

'Simon is an excellent dancer,' I said, hoping I had hit the right tone of amused indifference. 'Where is he?'

'He found a friend,' she said, and gestured towards the dancers.

Simon was dancing with a slim girl in a blue WAAF uniform. She had a bright smile and crisp dark curls and they were chatting animatedly together. I flicked them a glance and sat beside Katherine.

'What's the matter?' asked Katherine, who was always quick as a cat at picking up social nuances. 'You and the charming doctor have a tiff?'

I assumed a look of boredom. 'We barely know each other. I met him less than a month ago.'

She smiled. 'It can happen in a minute. I knew it was Harry for me within five minutes of meeting him. He says he knew even sooner.'

My answering smile was rather a brittle one. 'It's not like that with us.'

Simon returned to the table when his dance finished and began to chat with Katherine. Peter returned and I talked to him. The others joined us and the meal was served. Simon and I doggedly chatted to everyone but each other.

'Were you speaking to Cedric?' Jim asked me over dinner.

'Yes. I think he's staying here, at the Dorchester. My sister mentioned something of the sort and I'd forgotten until he presented himself on the dance floor.'

'Forgotten where your husband was staying?' murmured Simon.

I looked around at the table. Everyone seemed to be watching Simon and me with varying degrees of fascination.

'I wasn't really listening when my sister mentioned it,' I said.

The waiter was at my elbow and I smiled when he offered to fill my glass. I downed the champagne with gusto. And the next glass, until I felt as fizzy as the drink. Jim asked me to dance, and I kept the conversation firmly on innocuous subjects. Then I danced with Peter, who was as clumsy as I had remembered from my coming-out balls. I danced with both the Australian airmen, and with young Gerald Wilde. I flirted outrageously with all of them. The champagne helped.

Simon danced with all the women and he made them laugh as he whirled them around the floor. I did not dance again with Simon, who seemed to be matching me drink for drink. At one stage I caught Katherine's eye and her wry smile. She looked at Simon, then at me, and raised her glass in a mocking salute. In response I downed more champagne.

\*

Jim and Lily had taken a suite in the hotel for the night, and left us soon after the local All Clear sounded, just after midnight. The Australian airmen and their wives departed soon afterwards. I was about to leave when Peter spoke in glowing terms of a 'little place nearby' that was 'great fun', and suggested that the rest of us head over there. Katherine demurred, but Pam and Gerald Wilde agreed at once and somehow Simon, and then I, said we would join them.

My memory is a little hazy after that. I remember following the group out of the hotel into the darkness of the London blackout and shivering in the cold night air. I remember laughter and shouted directions and movement. I remember tottering off after merry voices that were receding at a fast pace, then clinging to a wall, shaking my head to try to clear the fog that was making the world spin around me, and wishing it were less dark.

And that is how I ended up alone with Simon on Park Lane.

'Where are the others?' I asked. 'I can't see a thing. It's as black as – as the Earl of Hell's waistcoat.'

'That's an odd expression,' said Simon.

'Cabbies use it. Where have the others gone?'

'I think they headed off down Deanery Street. What was the name of that nightclub again?'

'Wasn't it the Pam Grove?' My voice sounded thick, and it was difficult to enunciate my words, so I spoke more slowly and a little louder. 'I mean the Palm Grove.' *Too loud.* I moderated my tone. 'The Tropical Room? I'm sure it's something to do with the tropics. Or was it Africa?' I tipped my head back. 'Is that the sound of planes above us? I didn't hear the Warning sound again.'

'Jerry's having another prowl around,' he said. 'Nothing to worry about.'

'No use worrying is it?' I said, again rather too loudly. 'If you're for it, you're for it, and that's all there is to it. '

'What?' said Simon.

'Cabbies say that, too. And they say "Victory at all costs".' I shook my head. 'Cedric says it also, but he doesn't mean it.' I shook my head again, and immediately wished I hadn't. 'Goosestepping down the Strand. Never!'

Park Lane began to tip and spin alarmingly and Simon snuck an arm around my shoulders. I had a vague feeling that I should be outraged, but actually I was grateful for the support.

'I think you're a bit under the weather, Cesia,' he said.

As that was a pompous statement, I had to reply with indignation. I took great care to speak very clearly as I did so.

'Hah. Oh, no, Dr Levy. You are a doctor and you should know – you must know that one cannot become drunk on the best French champagne. Doesn't happen. One simply becomes merry. Life of the party. Never intoxicated.'

He laughed. 'Cesia – I mean Celia – I'm sorry to inform you that champagne is particularly intoxicating.'

'Not the best French champagne.'

He was holding me very close now and I felt his chest rise and fall in a laugh, and then a sigh. He breathed into my hair, 'How could you have married him? Why did you do it?'

I leaned into his chest and said, softly, 'Because I thought he was ... not what he was.' Then I lifted my head, sucked in a breath of cold London air and said, 'I am not intoxicated. A lady must never become intoxicated. Nanny was very clear on that.'

Someone was giggling. It was such an irritating sound that it took me a while to realise it was me. Simon's hold on my shoulders intensified as I began to slide. I hauled myself upright, put my back against the wall and turned to face him. In the utter darkness I couldn't make out his features, so I raised a hand and traced them with my finger. Down his forehead, then his nose, over to the dent at the top of his lips and down further. My finger caught a little on his bottom lip. Then his chin, rough with stubble. He had become very still and I could hear each quick breath he took, and each exhalation.

'And another thing,' I whispered, 'you're only human, Dr Simon Levy. You can't save everyone, no matter how hard you—'

I was intending to say more, but Simon pulled me hard against his chest and somehow my arms were around his neck and we were clinging to each other in the darkness, kissing with a fevered intensity. And for the first time in many long, lonely months everything felt *right*, as if this place, at this moment with this man was exactly where I was supposed to be. As if all that had happened before in my life had led to me kissing Simon Levy in Park Lane on a frosty winter morning with the rumble of planes overhead and distant crash of bombs falling somewhere else.

We were startled into awareness by a motorcycle roaring past.

Simon pushed away, muttering, 'I am so sorry. Too much to drink...' His voice faded and he turned abruptly. 'I'll find a taxi.' And he was gone.

I stood, back against the wall for support, shivering. My mind had gone blank except for the vivid memory of the heavy weight of Simon's greatcoat, his lips on mine, his hands in my hair and the heat of his body pressed against me. The world was still spinning, but I felt horribly, embarrassingly sober, and the last person I wanted to see was Simon Levy.

Who was suddenly looming in front of me.

'Got one,' he said, and gestured towards the road where a taxi had pulled up. Its masked headlights cast a slim beam on the tarmac. He helped me across to it and opened the door. I got in alone.

He said, 'If you don't mind, I've got to... Are you all right to see yourself home? I've given him the address.'

'Of course.'

'I'll – I'll bring Leo around to see the parrot tomorrow afternoon. I mean, this afternoon. I gave him my word. Three o'clock?'

'That's fine.'

He shut the door firmly and slapped the window to tell the cabbie to drive on.

The trip took a while because of the many detours. At every corner it seemed there was a rail blocking the street and a sign pointing down a small side street.

I spent the journey replaying the last half hour over and over in my mind. *He was drunk. That's all it was. We were both drunk. That's all it was.*

# CHAPTER NINETEEN

I awoke with a vague sense that something was wrong. The headache hit me like a thunderbolt when I lifted my head off the pillow. For a while I sat on the side of the bed cradling my aching head in my hands, trying to work out if assuaging my thirst was worth the agony that would be caused by a walk to the kitchen for a glass of water.

*So this is a hangover.*

Nanny's advice never to drink to excess had been proved incontrovertible and I became a little teary as I thought of her. I tottered towards the kitchen and gulped down water. It helped a little.

*Oh, God. Last night.*

I had heard that intoxicated people forgot what had happened while they were drunk. I had no such luck. Everything was there, replaying in my mind in clear, humiliating detail. I had imbibed too much champagne. I had flirted with every male present. I had kissed Simon. Or he had kissed me. I let my memory slip quickly past the more humiliating aspects of the time alone with Simon, touching his face, being held upright by him, telling him silly things in such a loud voice, and my fevered response to his kiss. Giggling.

I tried to fill my mind with thoughts of David, but the memories of David's face, his scent, the feel of his skin – once so vivid – now slipped away from me like smoke into the air. Instead, unwelcome recollections of Cedric kept intruding. Simon's voice came into my head: 'How could you have married him? Why did you do it?'

I thought of Nanny. Would she have liked Cedric? I had asked myself this many times. He had excellent manners, so perhaps he would have won her over. And, of course, my father had adored Cedric and Nanny would have liked that. I think my marriage to Cedric was the first time my father was actually pleased with me. Tom had never liked Cedric over much. David had hated him, although he had never met him. Apparently Simon hated him too.

I tried again to think of David, but all that came to mind was the feel of Simon's face as I had traced it in the dark. His utter stillness and the sound of his breathing, fast and a little ragged. How my finger had caught on his lower lip.

I stood abruptly and the thudding pain in my head pushed thoughts of Simon out of my mind. A bath helped, and I walked into the service restaurant downstairs feeling a little more human than I had done an hour before. Pam and Katherine waved me over to their table.

'I do like your Dr Levy,' said Pam, as I seated myself.

I froze her with a look. 'He's not *my* Dr Levy. I barely know the man.'

She stammered out an apology. 'It's just that I thought... You seemed to know each other so well. And then you left together and—'

'We left at the same time. We did not leave together.'

'—and you didn't join us at the Tropical Palm Palace.'

'Dr Levy was kind enough to fetch me a taxi and I came back here. Alone.'

Katherine's cool voice cut through my icy response. 'Pam was saying that young Gerald Wilde asked her out dancing tomorrow night. I liked him *and* Dr Levy. I liked everybody, actually. Didn't Lily look happy! I thought it was a lovely evening, even if my poor toes got a workout from the Hon. Peter Creighton.'

'The Hon.?' asked Pam. 'Jim introduced him to me as plain Peter Creighton.'

'He's the son of the Earl of Morran.'

Pam's eyes widened. Then she laughed. 'Well, Gerald is not honourable, except in personality.' She laughed again, this time at her weak joke. 'In Civvie Street he's a bank clerk. Jim's friends certainly come from all over the place. I like that about him.' Again she laughed, and the sound seemed to slice into my aching head. 'Weren't the Aussie airmen good value? It was just like being home. I'm meeting Frances – she's the RAF wife from Sydney – for afternoon tea on Wednesday.'

The conversation flagged as Pam and Katherine were served their porridge. I waved mine away and settled for coffee. It was weak, but hot and reviving and I was able to face the scrambled eggs – made with dried eggs, of course – and thin strip of bacon with composure.

I glanced at the clock above the doorway to the kitchen. Nine o'clock. Only six hours until Leo was due to arrive to see Bobby. Only six hours until I had to face Simon.


Promptly at three o'clock, Simon banged on my door. When I opened it he was standing beside Leo with a hand on the boy's shoulder. Leo was jittering with excitement and grinning at me. I smiled at the boy.

'Come in,' I said. 'Bobby's waiting for you.'

Leo barely paused to take off his coat before he pushed past me in his eagerness and rushed over to Bobby's cage, just like any other excited eight-year-old would do. I heard his soft little voice say, '*Guten tag*, Bobby.'

The parrot said, 'Hello, I'm Bobby. What's your name?'

Leo replied softly, 'Leo Weitz.'

I looked up at Simon. 'Please, come in.'

His smile in response seemed muted. Or was that my own sense of embarrassment?

'Headache?' he asked, as I helped him off with his coat. 'Nausea? Gaps in memory?'

'Not at all. Never with the best French champagne.'

'Compulsion to lie about physical state?'

I laughed. 'Headache,' I admitted.

'Me, too.'

'No?' I looked at him. 'Really?'

'Splitting.'

'I suspect mine's worse.'

He laughed and rolled his eyes. 'There would be short odds on that.'

'Remind me never to do that again.'

'Celia, never do that again.'

We turned to look at Leo. He was standing by the cage, and Bobby, to Leo's obvious delight, was emitting a series of whistles and shrieks. The sounds played havoc with my throbbing head. The bird squealed and I winced. Simon reached into his jacket pocket and silently handed me a paper containing aspirin powder.

'Enough for two?'

He nodded, and I slunk into the kitchen to make up the preparation in two glasses.

And that was that. It appeared that there were to be no recriminations or difficult conversations, just uncomplicated friendship, as he had offered on the dance floor before Cedric arrived. I felt the tension in my body ease as if I were a taut spring that was slowly unwinding.

The aspirin helped the headache to lift and a little later I allowed Bobby out of the cage. As before, he walked the length of Leo's sleeve, to perch on his shoulder and survey the flat in his solemn, dignified manner.

'Bloody hell. Simon Levy,' said Bobby.

Leo's giggle rang out and the boy flashed a delighted smile at Simon.

'Don't repeat that,' said Simon hurriedly, as if to the bird. We all had begun speaking to Bobby as if he understood every word. 'Mutti will not be happy if you do.' He looked at Leo. 'She may forbid us to bring the parrot to the house for a visit.'

Leo's eyes became wide.

'It's not a nice thing to say,' Simon explained. He added, 'It's amusing, but not nice.'

The boy nodded, and turned his face to the bird, whispering to it in German.

'Try to speak to him in English, Leo,' I said, worried that it might cause problems if the bird started to come out with German phrases. 'He's an English bird.'

Leo's whisper was barely audible, but the gist was that Bobby spoke German, too.

'I'm sure he does,' I replied. 'He's a very intelligent bird. But it's best if Bobby speaks English.'

Leo nodded sagely at that, and said quietly, '*Wegen des* – because of the war.' Then he looked at Simon. 'Watch, Simon,' he said. 'I have told you of this.'

Leo marched across to the wireless with the bird and pretended to turn it on. Bobby gave his Big Ben and Alvar Lidell impersonation, at which Simon gravely informed Leo that he was amazed at Bobby's genius. Then Leo turned towards the window and whispered again to the bird.

'He's been talking about that bird all week,' said Simon to me, smiling.

'I'm so happy that Leo's found his voice. Has he spoken about his experiences in Austria?'

'No and I doubt he ever will, except to the parrot perhaps.'

'I don't know if I'd entrust any secrets to that parrot.'

Simon laughed, then threw me a shrewd look. 'I'm still not sure why Bobby feels the need to shout out my name. Especially as there is always more than a hint of exasperation, or even downright annoyance, in the way he says it. Why do you think that might be?'

'Would you care for tea?' I asked, with what I hoped was an enigmatic smile.

Simon and I drank our tea and ate Mrs Levy's cake watching Leo and Bobby. They didn't do much. Leo spoke softly to the bird. The bird ruffled his hair, just above his ear, and the boy giggled. After a while, Leo walked over to the window, moving carefully so as not to disturb Bobby on his shoulder. Once there, they looked out over the gardens and over London. Bobby snuggled under Leo's chin, and Leo cuddled him. Occasionally Bobby made a whistling sound, or said a phrase, and Leo whispered to him, but on the whole they simply communed with each other.

And so, for want of any better entertainment, Simon and I talked, just as we had in those hours I had been trapped in the bombed house, four weeks before. At first we kept rigidly to uncontroversial subjects, ranging from the weather and the likelihood of a raid that night, to what would come under the ration next. Even in the empty courtesy of small talk, Simon's humour and a quick intelligence were apparent.

'The news from Romania is very bad,' I said, when we had moved on to the war. There had been reports in the newspapers of Jews being slaughtered in the streets of Bucharest by the fascist Iron Guard.

Simon glanced at Leo and lowered his voice. His eyes were bleak. 'It was a full-scale pogrom. Synagogues were destroyed, hundreds killed, some brutally tortured.' He glanced again at Leo, who was busy with Bobby. 'Women, children too.'

'I'm so sorry, Simon,' I said.

'It will continue to happen as Hitler consolidates his gains in Europe. All Britain can do to end it is to win the war decisively.'

'We will,' I said earnestly, and wondered how to change the subject. 'Think we'll take Tobruk?'

He nodded. 'Hope so. Bardia was a huge loss for the Italians. If we win the battle for Tobruk we could be looking at the expulsion of the Italians from North Africa.'

'But won't the Germans come to support them? Take over the fight?'

He took another sip of tea and sighed. 'Probably. And that will change the game entirely. Most of the Italians are conscripts who don't want to be there. That's why we were able to take so many of them prisoner. The Germans are a very different matter.' He replaced the cup in its saucer. 'Unlike the Italian conscripts, I'd give anything to be back in North Africa.'

'Because you so enjoyed the experience of typhoid and pneumonia?'

'I had hoped to sample all the diseases on offer there. Typhus, malaria and dysentery are as yet unexplored delights.'

'Beastly unfair of Army Command to keep you here in London in the circumstances.'

'It really is. I'm fully recovered from the typhoid now, and from the pneumonia, but they're not willing to declare me fit for active service overseas. Instead they want me to do special training in the treatment of traumatic injury.'

'How long is the training?'

'I'll be at the Queen Alexandra Hospital for the next few months at least. What about you? Are you intending to keep driving ambulances, or will you join one of the women's services?'

My laugh was forced. 'The services won't have me.'

He raised an eyebrow.

'Cedric,' I explained.

'Is that the *Radio Times* on the table?' It was an obvious change of subject. 'Should we try listening to the wireless?'

We pored over the listings. Radio National had '*Gallows Glorious*, a play by Ronald Gow'. On Forces Radio was, 'A Grand Concert for members of H.M. Forces from a West-Country concert hall'.

'I think we've suffered enough already without either of those,' said Simon. 'Shame it's not Monday. We could have listened to *Ack-Ack Beer-Beer*.'

'You listen to that show? Last time I looked you were neither an anti-aircraft gunner nor a barrage balloon operator.'

'I've been known to have a go at the Luftwaffe with the guns in my spare time.'

I gave him a sceptical look and he laughed. 'I really did, a couple of weeks ago. A gunner was injured – he was in the wrong place and was hit by the recoil. I set his arm and he invited me to come and see the big guns in operation. The crew were very welcoming and even let me have a go during a raid. Entirely against the rules, I'm sure. But terrific fun.'

From bomb victims to heavy-rescue men, and tea-car girls to anti-aircraft gunners, Simon had 'the knack' with people, I thought. He had a rather chameleon-like ability to fit in with any group he was with. Even his accent changed according to his company. Mine resolutely remained the clipped pronunciation I had learned from governesses and parents, and it meant I stood out in a crowd as 'upper class' and different.

'Would you really have gone dancing at the Paramount with Kitty and Joan?' I asked.

'Of course. Whyever not? I used to go there with my chums before the war. It's jolly good fun. Actually, I'm intending to drop in on the Paramount next time I've a night off. I gave the girl a promise, after all.' He threw me a sly smile. 'What's the matter with that? You're not a snob, are you?'

I thought about it. 'I hope not,' I said, very seriously. 'I'm fairly sure I'm not. I enjoy the company of everyone at the station and I certainly don't think any less of any of them because of their accents or schooling or anything.'

'Then why would you not go to the Paramount?'

'I suppose I feel that I'd not fit in there.'

'Come with me. In a group, I mean. I'm free next Thursday night. You choose the group.'

'I can't stay up late. I'm on duty at seven-thirty the next morning.'

'It doesn't have to be a late night. You could leave by eleven or so.'

'I don't know anyone to ask,' I replied feebly. *Me, at the Paramount?*

'I'm sure you can find others to come. What about that tall dark-haired girl at your station. Halliwell, is it?'

'Maisie Halliday. She's a dancer. A real dancer, a professional dancer.'

'All the better.'

'I don't think Kitty and Joan would be pleased to see you turn up with two females.'

'Invite a man as well, then. Or, even better, a couple of men. They'd be pleased about that.'

'I don't know any single men. Or … I suppose Purvis is a single male. He's the station's conscientious objector. Rupert Purvis.'

'Invite him. Anyone else?'

I laughed. 'There's Armstrong. But he's not even eighteen yet.'

'Is he the one who watches you with a face like a whipped puppy.'

'Oh, he does not.' I laughed at Simon's expression. 'Well maybe he does. But he looks at Halliday that way, too. I think he's at the age where he looks like that at any young woman because he's too shy to do anything about it.'

'Invite him along. Give the boy a thrill.'

I thought about the people I knew. 'There's Pam Beresford – you met her yesterday – she has a flat in this building. She and that young pilot, Gerald Wilde, they seem to be quite smitten with each other.'

'The more the merrier.'

'You really think I should?'

'Goodness, woman, take pity. You don't expect me to turn up to the Paramount alone, do you? If I don't arrive in a group I'll be fair game for Kitty. And to be frank, she terrifies me.'

I gave a bark of indignant laughter. 'Oh, you're impossible.' I made my voice gruff, in an approximation of Simon's deeper voice, '"What's the matter, Celia? Surely you're not a snob?" And it's all a plot to get company for your blinking Paramount expedition.'

I threw a cushion at him and he ducked it with a yelp that made Leo and Bobby turn away from the window to look at us.

'God Save the King,' said Bobby. 'Simon Levy.'

'Quite right,' said Simon, standing up and holding the cushion like a shield. 'As monarch appointed by parrotic decree, I expect to be treated with appropriate dignity.'

He lobbed the cushion back at me and I ducked it with a laugh as Leo gave his soft giggle. Then Bobby opened his beak and gave voice to an ominous roaring whistle, exactly like the sound of a dive-bombing Messerschmitt. Simon cringed in an exaggerated fashion at the noise, hit the floor and held up his hands as if facing bullets.

Leo's laughter became louder. 'Bobby,' he said to the bird, '*Du bist ein* ... aeroplane.'

'A scary aeroplane,' said Simon and frowned at Bobby. 'Bad bird.'

That caused Leo to dissolve into a fit of giggles. His shaking shoulders meant that Bobby's perch had become precarious and he stepped on to the pile of books on my bookcase. From there he surveyed us with a dignified air, opened his beak and squawked, 'Bloody hell.'

I fell back on to the sofa, laughing uncontrollably. Leo's giggles intensified and he joined Simon on the floor, rolling around and holding his stomach. He looked so much like a normal, happy eight-year-old boy that I was exhilarated. I exchanged glances with Simon and I knew he felt exactly the same.

I wasn't really sure why, but as I was showing them to the door, I asked Simon, 'Why isn't Miriam Rosenfeld part of this Paramount expedition?'

In reply I received a slight enigmatic smile. 'So Lore has been telling you about Miriam, has she?'

'She says you two are close.'

'That's one word for it.' As he helped Leo into his coat he said, 'Miriam will be at the airfield all week, but who knows?

Perhaps she could get away to join us. Actually, it's a splendid idea. I'm meeting her tonight and I'll ask her.'

As I closed the door behind them I turned to Bobby, who watched me with his fathomless gaze.

'So I'm off to the Paramount,' I said to the bird. 'However did he get me to agree?'

'Leo Weitz,' said Bobby. 'God save the King.'

# CHAPTER TWENTY

'I can't understand why they're not here,' said Pam, as she walked into my bedroom the following Thursday evening. I presented my back and she zipped me up. My green frock seemed wrong, somehow. I hadn't worn it for almost a year and it hung loosely on me. I'd lost weight.

'They'll come,' I said.

'Well, they didn't last night. Or the night before. I can't sleep when they don't come. It's too quiet.'

'I think the weather's been too bad for night raids,' I said.

'And so they inflict daylight raids on us instead. Just as I'd popped out at lunchtime today the siren sounded. Then the guns started up and I had to dodge shrapnel. And when I was on my way back to Australia House after lunch, a raider swooped out of a cloud and began machine-gunning the street. No one got hit, but everyone was really angry and I laddered my stockings when I hit the ground. It was so annoying. How do you like my outfit? It's an old dress, but Katherine jazzed it up for me.'

She gave a twirl and the red fabric flared out around her knees.

'She did a marvellous job. You look lovely.'

'So do you,' she said.

I frowned at my reflection, wondering if I looked scrawny, and whether I'd made too much of an effort with my outfit, hair and make-up. I didn't want Simon to think that I cared about this evening at the Paramount. In fact, I wasn't entirely sure why I had taken such trouble, other than that I so rarely went out nowadays it was a special occasion for that reason alone. I had heard that the West End still buzzed with people determined to have a good time, despite the Blitz, but I was too tired with my ambulance duties and then Bloomsbury House to make an effort to socialise with the few friends I still had.

'You look like Rita Hayworth,' said Pam. 'I know he's bringing his girlfriend, but I don't think your doctor will be looking at anyone but you.'

Annoyed, I snapped, 'He's not *my* doctor.'

She gave me a cheeky smile. 'Yes he is. He treated you, didn't he?'

I had to laugh. 'Yes. He treated me when I was ill. And that's all.' The memory of Simon's urgent kiss in Park Lane, and my fevered response, came into my mind. I looked away, hoping I hadn't coloured.

'I loved her in *The Lady in Question.*'

'What? Who?'

'Rita Hayworth. She has a new one out, *Angels over Broadway.* Gerald is taking me to see it next week.'

'I do not look in the least like Rita Hayworth,' I said, with a touch of petulance.

Pam shrugged. 'Well, Rita has red hair, and so do you.'

'I don't believe she's a real redhead. Do you compare everyone you meet with motion picture stars?'

She looked hard at me, head over to the side, frowning. 'On second thoughts, you are absolutely right. Not Rita Hayworth, but Greer Garson. She's also red-haired and you look a lot more like her than Rita. You've a very English look.'

'I am English.'

'And you look it. Yes. Definitely Greer Garson. I think her eyes are green, though, and yours are that dark blue. I loved her in *Goodbye Mr Chips.* I wept buckets when she— did you hear? She's going to star in the new *Pride and Prejudice* with Laurence Olivier. Gosh, I dote on him. Don't you think that Gerald looks a bit like Laurence Oliver?' This last sentence was uttered in a dreamy voice.

I shook my head, thinking Pam could be rather trying sometimes.

'No? Well, I suppose I've looked at him more closely than you have. I definitely see Olivier in him. Definitely. He's so nice. Gerald, I mean. He said he'd come to the shelter with me on Saturday. It'll give the shelterers a thrill to see a Spitfire pilot. And I thought it was a good way to spend more time with him.'

Pam volunteered as a shelter officer at the big Gloucester Road public shelter twice a week. As such, she was responsible for up to a thousand people a night. Nanny would have called her a flibbertigibbet, but Pam could be very level-headed and conscientious when required.

'I think we won't have a raid tonight,' she said firmly. 'I think the All Clear at five was the last we've seen of them for today.'

'It's only eight o'clock. Plenty of time for a night raid.'

'You sound as if you want one.'

'Might be better than attending the Paramount Dance Hall.'

She laughed. 'You're the one who arranged it.'

'No. I was manoeuvred into it by the very sneaky Simon Levy.'

'It'll be fun.' She glanced at her watch. 'He's probably downstairs by now. We'd better go and meet him and … Miriam, isn't it?'

Simon had offered to drive us to the Paramount. There were few private cars left on the streets but, as a doctor, Simon was entitled to a small petrol allowance. At the dance hall we were to meet Gerald Wilde, Maisie Halliday and Rupert Purvis. I was looking forward to meeting Miriam Rosenfeld, Lore's daughter, who 'wanted a Levy boy' and who had adored David, although I felt mildly annoyed on Simon's behalf that he should be seen as second best to his brother.

At the door I paused. 'Who do you think Simon looks like? Which movie star, I mean.'

She laughed. 'Errol Flynn. *Definitely.*'

206

'He does not,' I said sharply. Errol Flynn was not one of my favourite actors, because I had always thought that Cedric rather resembled him.

Pam seemed surprised at my vehemence.

'Simon doesn't have a pencil moustache,' I said by way of explanation.

She screwed up her face as if she was trying to visualise either Flynn or Simon. 'Well, obviously Simon doesn't have a moustache, but neither did Errol Flynn in *The Sisters*. But I really think Simon does look like Errol Flynn. He has a lovely smile and nice even teeth, and a dent in his chin, just like Flynn has. And there's something about Simon's manner—'

'His manner?'

'He's fun and easy-going.' She smiled. 'You know, Simon could almost be an Aussie.'

'The highest praise imaginable.'

'No need for sarcasm. You did ask.' She turned to me in the doorway and said, with a cheeky smile, 'Want to bet the girlfriend doesn't turn up?' I ignored the comment.

We joined Simon in the lobby. 'You look lovely,' he told Pam and she gave him a mock curtsey.

When he turned to me I thought his smile looked a little ironic. 'As do you. The Paramount won't know what has hit it.'

'You make us sound like bombs,' said Pam, laughing.

'Not bombs, bombshells,' he countered, visibly relaxing. 'They'll think you've come to the Tottenham Court Road straight from Hollywood.'

'Hah,' said Pam, now obviously flirting. 'Via Tasmania, in my case. Mind you, isn't Merle Oberon supposed to be from there? Not that I believe it. Tasmania's a small place and we'd know if she was a local girl.' She touched her nose and flashed me a look. 'Errol Flynn, now, he's definitely from the Apple Isle. He's as Aussie as they come. True blue, dinky di, as they say.'

'Shouldn't we be going,' I said. 'Is Miriam meeting us there?'

'She's busy. Attending a training course somewhere in the country.'

'What a shame,' I said, ignoring Pam's wink.

We emerged from St Andrew's into a pungent fog that enveloped everything like a thick blanket, and made it difficult to breathe.

'It's no wonder we had a day raid,' said Pam. 'They can't come over at night in this sort of weather.'

The mist swirled around Simon's Baby Austin, which Pam eyed critically. 'It's not exactly roomy,' she said.

'Runs for miles on a mere sniff of petrol,' said Simon.

Pam shrugged. 'I think I'd better go in the back. I'm smaller than Celia.' She clambered into the back seat and I sat beside Simon. He pressed the starter and we headed off into the foggy darkness.

'I hear you're quite the dancer.' As Pam leaned forward to talk to Simon I felt her hair brush my face.

'I used to be,' he said, without turning his head. He was concentrating on the thin line of headlight on the road. It wavered in the fog and seemed to be sucked away before it could assist Simon to avoid potholes. As usual, the journey was made longer and more roundabout by the detours into side streets.

'I've never danced the jitterbug,' said Pam.

'You'll love it,' said Simon. 'Be sure to save me a dance. Or is your card only for Spitfire pilots?'

'Oh, I'll dance with anyone.' She laughed. 'That came out wrong. I meant, I'd love to dance with you. Especially if you know how to jitterbug properly. Do you really?'

'I've danced it once or twice, but very badly, I'm afraid. I was there at the Paramount for the first British jitterbug competition in 1939, before all this madness.' He laughed. 'Now *that* was madness. But in a good way.'

'I sort of know how it goes,' said Pam, 'the jitterbug, I mean. It does look mad, though. Aren't girls thrown over their partner's shoulder?'

Simon laughed again. 'That's not required.'

'What about you, Celia?' asked Pam. 'Are you willing to give it a go?'

'Sounds a little too lively for me,' I said.

'Don't worry, Grandma,' said Simon, 'I'll go easy on you.'

Music spilled out from the ballroom as we entered the lobby of the dance hall. It was a lively dance number and Simon tapped his foot in time as we stood together, trying to find our friends among the crowd. Pam gave a muffled cry of delight when she caught sight of her Spitfire pilot and she pushed her way through to capture him. As she brought him to us I looked carefully at Gerald Wilde. He was a little below average height and very slender, and his long face reminded me more of Fred Astaire than Laurence Olivier. I snuck a look at Simon. Maybe he did look a little like Errol Flynn. He caught me looking and I turned away to scan the crowd.

'I don't see Maisie or Rupert Purvis,' I said.

'We're a little early. I don't see Joan or Kitty, either. They were on the tea car Monday night and I mentioned we'd be here.'

'Are you really intending to jitterbug?' I asked him. 'The way they do in those American films?'

He took my arm and we followed Pam and Gerald into the ballroom. 'I'm really intending to *try* to jitterbug,' he said teasingly. 'Game to give it a try?'

'I'm not a confident dancer.'

'You danced perfectly well at the Dorchester. It'll do you good to try something different. We all need to be shaken up every now and again.'

Inside the ballroom was a sea of people of all shapes and colours, in uniform or in their best clothes. Simon led us to a small table and Pam, Gerald and I sat and watched the organised mayhem on the dance floor as he went off to order our drinks. The music was lively and the dance was livelier. Dancers seemed to throw each other away and swiftly come together again, as if magnetically attracted. The actual steps were quite simple, but improvisation thrived as dancers kicked their legs, extended their arms and almost distorted their bodies in a shivering ecstasy.

'Want to give it a go?' asked Pam to Gerald. He smiled, nodded and they rose and entered the fray. Gerald was up to the challenge, gamely trying to swing Pam around in the crowd. She lost her footing a couple of times, but they didn't seem to mind and were laughing together.

'What are you doing here?' The voice was sharp and angry and familiar. I turned to see Eddie Hollis standing behind me. A lit cigarette clung to his bottom lip, and his upper lip was lifted in a sneer.

'Hullo, Eddie,' I said pleasantly. I did not want a scene, and so I was determined to meet Eddie's rudeness with politeness. But I looked around furtively for Cedric. Although I doubted he'd come to the Paramount dance hall, I wasn't sure of anything about him any more.

Eddie repeated his question: 'What are you doing here?'

'I'm here because I am intending to dance.' Cedric was nowhere to be seen, so I replied calmly, but with a note of irritation that I hoped would serve as a warning.

'It's not your sort of place at all.'

I attempted to freeze him with a look. 'Well, obviously it *is* my sort of place, because I'm here.'

He moved closer to my chair. 'You've never been here before.'

'No,' I agreed. 'It's my first visit.'

'Mr Ashwin won't like it.'

I raised an eyebrow and tried to register cold annoyance at the statement. That had no effect at all on Eddie.

'He won't,' he repeated. 'You shouldn't be here.'

My patience and politeness fled. 'It's really none of Cedric's business. Nor is it yours. I can go anywhere I wish.'

'Of course you can,' said Simon, who was now standing beside the table, holding a tray of drinks. 'It's still a free country.' He put the tray down and remained standing, watching Eddie with a slight smile as Eddie glared at him.

'Push off, won't you,' Simon told him airily. 'Let Celia enjoy her drink in peace.'

Eddie wheeled around and left in a frenzied haste, rudely thrusting people aside as he did so.

Simon sat down and picked up his glass. 'Your good health,' he said as a toast, and took a swig. 'I really don't like that man.'

'Well, neither do I, and I think he's taken a dead set against us both. He's a follower of Cedric's,' I said, by way of explanation.

Simon shrugged. 'Let's not talk about him. Instead...' He rose and held out his hand 'C'mon, Celia. Let's cut a rug.'

'But I can't—'

'It's easy.' He pulled me up out of my chair and then on to the dance floor, and stood in front of me a little to the right. I stared up at his face and he winked. He put his right hand on my shoulder blade and laughed at my expression. 'I promise you'll survive the jitterbug.'

I surrendered my right hand to him. When I put my left hand on his shoulder I felt the fine wool of his tunic under my fingers and I watched his chest move in and out with his breath as the band gave a few exploratory bars and began to play.

Although the dance started slowly it soon heated up. He pushed me away and pulled me towards him and we stepped and shuffled and kicked and turned. As I started to move more easily in time with the music, my body loosened up. And I found myself smiling because it was *fun* to dance with Simon. I'm not a bad dancer if I am able to trust my partner and stop worrying about the steps. I could do that with Simon and it wasn't long before we began to really let go. He dipped me, threw me out and pulled me in. We rocked our hips and kicked out and stepped back and turned again, and soon there was nothing beyond the music and following Simon's lead.

I was almost bereft when the music faded and stopped. My heart was pumping and it felt as if something within me had been released. I realised that what I was feeling was happiness, simple, uncomplicated happiness, something I had not felt for a long time.

The band moved into a slow number. Simon pulled me close and I concentrated on getting my breathing back to normal.

'See,' whispered Simon, 'told you you'd survive.'

I laughed into his chest. 'What was that music? The beat is different to anything I've danced to before.'

'Madam, that's jazz, in quarter time with syncopated rhythm. May I say that you jitterbug with style.'

'You may. And may I respond that you are a – what's the term? – a hep cat?'

He gave a shout of laughter, and moved us into a space on the dance floor where we weren't so crushed by the crowd.

'I'll take you to some of the clubs I know and you'll see who the real hep cats are. But thank you for the compliment. It helps to have a good partner.'

I settled into the slower steps and we danced for a while without speaking. I breathed in the scent of his woollen uniform and a not unpleasant whiff of perspiration mingled with the general fug around us of oiled wood, alcohol, stale perfume, cigarette smoke and human bodies. The ropey muscles in Simon's back moved under my hand and the space between our bodies was hot, but not uncomfortable. I was wrapped in his arms and I felt utterly safe, and so my thoughts drifted. When the music faded I realised, with some embarrassment, that my head had come to rest on his shoulder and his arms were tight around me, so that I was pressed against him. We had been dancing like lovers. I pushed away with as much grace as I could manage.

'Forgive me. I've been woolgathering, as usual.'

'You seemed relaxed. Always a good thing in these anxious times. They're preparing for another swing number. You game?' He gave me a searching look. 'Or would you prefer to sit this one out with a drink?'

I laughed. 'I'm game.'

'Stout fella,' he replied, smiling.

Simon swung me away with a flourish and pulled me back hard against his chest. I looked up into his face, laughing and breathless. *I am happy*, I thought. *Right now, I am happy*. Then he twirled me around and we lost ourselves in the steps and the rhythm of the music.

When we returned to the table we found that Maisie and Rupert Purvis had arrived and were sipping their drinks as they watched the dancing.

'You're a good dancer, Celia,' said Maisie.

I was flattered. 'High praise, coming from a professional,' I said, and glanced at Simon. 'You should try dancing with Maisie.'

'She's already taken,' said Purvis. That earned him a cool look from Maisie, but she took his hand and he led her to the dance floor.

Simon looked at someone over to his right and laughed. 'I'm being waved at. I think it's Joan from the tea car.'

I looked where he indicated. Joan was smiling and waving at us. 'England expects every man to do his duty by our tea-car girls,' I said.

Simon stood and turned to me with a mock-heroic look. 'I'm just going outside and may be some time.'

I rolled my eyes and made a shooing movement with my hand. 'Off with you, Captain Oates. You know you're looking forward to it, really.'

He *was* away some time. I saw him dancing with Joan. I wasn't spying on him, it's just that he caught my eye as I danced with Rupert Purvis. And I saw him again when I danced with Gerald, and this time he was dancing with Kitty, who was looking very pretty in a cream-and-pink frock with embroidery on the skirt. I think he danced with Kitty again, and perhaps a third time. I wasn't checking, but her dress was easily identifiable.

He rejoined us after an hour or so, just as we were talking of leaving.

'Enjoy yourself?' I asked him.

'Had a marvellous time. They're very lively girls. Great fun.'

'Kitty looked very pretty tonight,' I said, as Simon drove slowly along Tottenham Court Road. The darkness seemed to press in on us, outside the narrow headlight beam. We were alone in the car, as Pam and Gerald had decided to go on to another club.

Simon laughed. 'She did, didn't she. I like Kitty a lot. And Joan. They're bomb girls, you know. They work together in a munitions factory on the outskirts of London, and they volunteer on the tea car on their nights off.'

'So Miriam didn't mind you going out dancing tonight without her?'

He smiled. 'Of course not. She says I need to relax more. Says I work too hard and worry too much.'

It was just after midnight when he parked outside St Andrew's and I was yawning and longing for my bed. I had to be at the station at seven-thirty that morning, and I suspected that Pam was right, and we'd have another day raid to deal with.

'I'm not used to the social whirl any more,' I said, as he saw me to the door. 'Or to dancing so much. I'll be stiff tomorrow. Let's hope there are no air raids, as I won't be at my nippiest.' A thought hit me and I groaned. 'Oh, God.'

'What's the matter?' asked Simon.

'I'm lunching with Cedric on Saturday. Which is now officially tomorrow.'

He frowned. 'Good luck with that.'

'Oh, I can deal with Cedric,' I said airily.

I really should have known better than to tempt fate with such a stupid remark.

'Thanks for inviting me last night,' said Maisie, when I met her in the kitchen the following morning. 'I really enjoyed it.'

'Simon pushed me into it,' I said. 'You should thank him.'

'He's lovely. Has a girlfriend, you said?'

'Yes. Her name is Miriam Rosenfeld. I know her mother, but I've never met Miriam.'

She laughed. 'Can't be too serious if she lets him go out dancing with you. You looked gorgeous last night. I saw you getting admiring looks from all over. Including Simon Levy, I might add.'

I decided to change the subject. 'I'd have thought you'd prefer to keep away from dance halls in your spare time. Sort of a busman's holiday for you.'

'Lord, no. I'll dance anywhere, any time. I love to dance. Can't not dance, really.'

'Have you always danced?'

'Professionally, since I was nine years old.'

'Nine years old!'

Maisie laughed. 'In local pantomimes. My family needed the money.' She must have seen something in my face, for she laughed again. 'For heaven's sake, don't pity me. I may have done it for money, but dancing's always been my delight. Apparently, from the time I could walk, I danced.'

She took a sip of tea and her eyes became dreamy. 'When I dance it's as if the rest of the world is halted and I'm in my own world of music and rhythm. My concentration on the steps distracts me from all my worries, and my delight in the movement of my body means that I enjoy the moment completely.' She made a face. 'You did ask.'

'I envy you your passion for it,' I said.

'I started learning ballet when I was four.' There was real pride in her eyes now. 'When I was dancing in pantomime I was seen by Italia Conti. She allowed me to train at her Academy in Lamb's Conduit Street at a discounted rate, and then I danced all over England in her productions of *The Rainbow's End*.' Her smile became mischievous. 'Bet you can't work out where I'm from originally. Elocution lessons were part of Miss Conti's curriculum.'

'Where *are* you from originally?' She was absolutely right. I had no idea.

Maisie smiled and shook her head. 'One day I'll tell you. Anyway, I joined the Tiller Girls when I was seventeen and danced with them here in England and in the Paris Folies Bergère for a year. When that fell through I stayed in France and ended up exhibition dancing at smart hotels on the French Riviera.'

'The French Riviera? How glamorous.'

'It was fun. Those Frenchmen are slippery beggars, though. You can't trust them an inch.' She hesitated. 'Oh, I did meet a dreamy Frenchman on the Riviera, but I don't speak much French and he didn't speak much English, so that led nowhere. I didn't really care. He was nice, but awfully intense. Any man I end up with must to be able to make me laugh. Then again, I'm not interested in romance.'

I was sceptical. 'Really?'

'Not at all interested. All the girls in the troupe did was complain about their blokes and how awfully they were treated by them. First thing we had to learn as Tiller Girls was how to deal with unwanted advances. Some of the men backstage behave disgracefully. Comedians and comperes are the worst, and the married ones worst of all. It really puts you off men. Don't get me wrong. I like to have a good time, but nothing serious for me.'

'So you don't have a boyfriend?' It seemed amazing to me that a girl as sweet, pretty and capable as Maisie didn't have a man in her life.

'Nope. Pure as driven snow, that's me. Never had a real boyfriend.' She gave me a straight look. 'My father died when I was a tiny tot, so I didn't have a father in my life. My mother and I lived with my grandparents for a few years and not once did I see Nan and Pop be affectionate to each other.' She sighed and her eyes became suspiciously bright. 'I suppose I don't know much about affection, plain and simple affection, between a man and woman.'

'It's different when you fall in love,' I said. Then I wanted to laugh at myself, because my own experience in that department was not the best.

Maisie gave a shrug. 'Trouble is, I'd really like to have kids one day and you need a man for that. But he'd have to make me laugh, and let me keep dancing.' She raised the cup to her lips and took another sip, then smiled. 'Anyway, to finish the story, I came back here at the start of the war. There's not much call for dancing girls at present and I wanted to stay in London. So I joined the Ambulance Service.'

'And you're nineteen?'

'Almost twenty.'

She turned as the door opened to reveal Jack Moray, and began to chat to him.

I thought that Maisie's little speech – the most she'd ever spoken about herself to me – told more in what had been left out than what had been said. Where had she been born? Her accent gave nothing away. I'd assumed she was middle class and from London. Earning money at nine years old and needing discounted rates at the Academy. That indicated she came from straightened circumstances. I mentally shrugged. Halliday's secrets remained her own.

As did mine.

# CHAPTER TWENTY-ONE

Most Londoners have heard of Quaglino's, the icon of style and gourmandry in Bury Street, Mayfair, and much-loved haunt of the smart set before the war. The Duke and Duchess of Kent, and Earl and Lady Mountbatten were regulars at Quag's, as were the Prince of Wales and his American divorcee in the thirties.

Cedric and I had gone there often after our marriage. That was before the war, when he was still accepted in the best drawing rooms in London. Since his arrest I had not dined out very much, and I had not set foot in Quag's for over a year. Even so, when I arrived that Saturday afternoon to meet Cedric, I was personally greeted by the maître d', Signor Quaglino. His bald head gleamed dully as he leaned down to kiss my hand. When he smiled at me from behind his black-framed spectacles his accent and manner were as resolutely Italian as they had been before we had declared war on Italy.

'Signora Ashwin, it is so good to see you again. And as beautiful as ever. Please allow me...'

He led me down the stairs to what he told me was now known as the Meurice Restaurant, but had been formerly Quaglino's downstairs grill room. Much like Signor Quaglino's head, the famous copper dance floor shone dully under its chandeliers.

He told me that Cedric had not yet arrived. This was surprising, as I was on time and Cedric was well aware how rude it was to keep your guest waiting. Upon consideration, I suspected that his late entry was for tactical reasons. It would mean he was spared the embarrassment of being snubbed by the 'smart set' while sitting alone at his table waiting for me. And it would show me, his recalcitrant wife, that he did not feel bound by manners when dealing with me.

'The whole room has been strengthened, you understand,' said Signor Quaglino, throwing his arm up in an expansive gesture, 'and it now serves as an air-raid shelter for my diners.' His face showed his delight. 'There are special shelves in the cloakrooms for everybody's gas masks.'

He settled me into a chair at a table near the back of the room, quite a distance from the dance floor. Signor Quaglino was no fool. It would not be to his advantage to exhibit Cedric Ashwin to the other diners, almost all of whom – men and women – were in uniform.

'We have always been full, you understand,' he confided, smiling with quiet confidence, 'even throughout this Blitz. But luncheon is our busiest time now, because of the air raids.' He frowned. 'They should come in the evening. Even if a raid lasts until morning, my guests are safe and comfortable. They stay here in my Meurice, entertained at an all-night cabaret. When the All Clear sounds, it is time for breakfast.' He leant in and whispered, 'On the house, you understand?'

I smiled. 'However do you manage, with the rationing?'

He spoke to me in confidential tones. 'We, the Quaglino's, are rationed, yet unrationed. We have a thousand people here each day. Yes?'

I felt myself unable to contradict, although the figure sounded astronomical, considering the astronomical charges he levied.

'And so we want two hundred pounds of butter a week,' he continued. He peered at me through his thick spectacles. 'Do we get it?'

Apparently a response was expected. 'Yes?' I ventured.

He nodded vigorously, and said with a note of triumph, 'Quaglino's gets its butter.'

Although I strongly suspected that it was butter mixed with margarine, I smiled and radiated my admiration at his resourcefulness. Actually, I was wondering about the source of the meat served at the Meurice, and thinking that Signor Quaglino and Sam Sadler from the ambulance station had more in common than either might realise.

'Isn't Lord Woolton bringing in new restrictions very soon, to regulate what food restaurants may offer their patrons?' I asked, with a disingenuous smile. 'And then both restaurants and diners alike will be liable to fines for excess food consumption.'

Signor Quaglino stiffened and his smile became fixed. 'Quaglino's will still offer its diners the best. Now, if I might leave you…'

Personally, I thought that the proposed new rationing regulations were fair. The Royal Navy and the Merchant Marine faced terrible danger to bring much-needed food from the Dominions to England through the German blockade, and everyone knew it was not being fairly distributed. The ordinary people were having a hard struggle to get bare necessities, or were going without, as they were forced to rely on their ration tickets to obtain meat, while those rich enough to dine in the smart restaurants still lived luxuriously. The *News of the World* had reported the previous week: 'Never in the history of a nation faced with famine could so much be eaten by so few'. I smiled to myself. Cedric would no doubt consider my views to be scandalously close to communism.

He arrived a few minutes later and so began one of the strangest and most disturbing experiences of my life. The two hours I spent in Cedric's company that afternoon are seared into my memory. Even now I can still vividly recall the slight scent of the red rose in the little vase on our table, the fleur de lys pattern in the damask of the tablecloth, the Viennese waltz played by the small orchestra as Cedric arrived.

My husband was full of apologies for his tardiness, and he had just sat down when a waiter hovered at his elbow.

'If I may suggest,' said the waiter delicately. He paused, then continued at Cedric's nod. 'For luncheon today, grapefruit, then grilled lemon sole followed by Kebab d'Agneau Orientale with aubergines frites and pommes macaire. And to finish, Zabaglione au Marsala.'

I raised an eyebrow. 'You can offer all that? Even with the rationing?'

'Madam,' the waiter seemed affronted, 'the Duchess of Kent is dining here this afternoon. Quaglino's can offer *anything* when Caldaroni is head chef.'

'That will be fine,' said Cedric.

I gave a laugh once the waiter had left. 'I wonder if the kebab will be *agneau* or *cheval*?'

Cedric frowned. 'If Quag's says it is lamb, it will not be horse meat.'

I shrugged. 'I'll reserve judgement until it arrives. And all those eggs in the Zabaglione? Not even Quag's can provide that many eggs for this many diners. Must be dried eggs.'

'Don't be ridiculous, Celia. This is Quaglino's.'

I couldn't immediately reply because a waiter had appeared with the white wine. We paused as he poured it into our glasses and after he had left I raised my glass in a provocative toast. 'Victory at all costs.'

'At all costs,' he replied, and took a sip of wine. 'I suspect, however, that we refer to a different sort of victory. Mine is victory over that bombastic fool, Churchill.'

Shocked, I glanced at the tables around us. No one appeared to have heard. 'You can't say that, Cedric.'

He gave me an irritatingly indulgent smile. 'This is England. Quaglino's. No one here would be impolite enough to listen to the conversation at a neighbouring table. And really darling, you'd be surprised how many agree with me.'

'Yes, I would be surprised,' I said tartly. 'I've been in London since the Blitz began and you've been here, what, a week? I think I'm aware of the popular mood and believe me, it's not in favour of the Nazis, no matter how much you might like to think it.'

Cedric was quiet as our grapefruit was served.

'I only want what's best for my country,' he said, once the waiter had left. 'All this destruction, death and misery could cease in a moment if England would just listen to reason. It's Churchill's insane stubbornness that is the sticking point.' He paused to spear a piece of grapefruit and eat it. Then he laughed, a bitter sound. 'The man sees himself as an absolute monarch.'

'Unlike Hitler?' I asked sweetly.

Cedric threw me an irate look. 'Churchill has never ridden on a bus, you know,' he said. 'He never carries money. The man is perpetually drunk. He's a throwback to an earlier century but we're stuck with him. And he's letting London burn to bolster his own megalomania.'

I took my time in sprinkling my grapefruit half with sugar, trying to work out how to reply. Personally, I thought that Churchill was the very prime minister we needed at this moment in Britain's history, and I was grateful for his speeches and his dogged determination to win at all costs.

'Darling, obviously I can't discuss it here,' Cedric went on. He took a mouthful of wine. 'Just be aware that the invasion is coming. And when it happens this country will be open and ripe for the picking, laid out just like that delicious grapefruit.'

There was an almost boyish air of excitement about him. It showed in the flaring of his nostrils and his small, cruel smile when he asserted that my country would be invaded and subjugated within months.

'Why are you telling me this?' I speared a grapefruit segment and popped it into my mouth, enjoying the tart-sweet flavour.

'You're my wife. There should be no secrets between us, darling.' His voice was muffled by a mouthful of grapefruit. 'Our marriage will be the envy of England, and Hitler will adore you.'

'You've said that before,' I said sharply. 'I'll never meet Hitler, Cedric. There will be no invasion. Not now. We have control of our skies, and of our shores. Britain can defend itself.'

I wished I really believed it. We were all worried that the invasion would be on us as soon as the weather improved. Hitler had taken all of Western Europe and it was well known that he wanted Britain as well.

Cedric's face became vexed. 'Look around you. Look at the ruins of London.' His expression intensified. 'Control of the skies? What nonsense. Germany will be here come spring, and a good thing too.' He finished his glass and poured more wine for himself.

My heart began to thud in my chest. What Cedric was saying was treason. If I reported him he would be questioned and probably locked up again. Or would he simply deny it all? As his wife I couldn't give evidence in court against him, which would mean that there could be no proof that this conversation had ever occurred. I wondered if Cedric were mad, drunk or simply deluded. I decided to treat it as a joke.

'Honestly, Cedric, you sound like Fumf, when he says, "Fumf has spoken."'

He looked puzzled, then frowned. 'Fumf?'

'The German spy on *It's That Man Again*.'

His frown became petulant. 'The silly wireless programme?'

'The Royal Family listen to it. Just about everyone does. And Fumf is a marvellous caricature. He makes pronouncements and says "Fumf has spoken" as if that's all it takes to carry them out.'

He regarded me with a narrow look. 'You've changed.'

I took a sip of water. 'Of course I've changed.'

'You've lost something. A certain sweetness.'

My patience with him fled. 'Of course I've changed,' I repeated. 'In the past months I've driven ambulances in the middle of the worst aerial assault in history. I've had to treat shockingly injured people – ordinary people – and I've held their hands as they died. Last night I took a woman to hospital who had been trapped for several hours beneath her dead husband's body in a buckled Anderson shelter. I've recovered bodies and parts of bodies from bomb sites. Children, babies. How can anyone go through that and not change, Cedric?'

We were both silent as the waiter returned to whip away our grapefruit. It was replaced by lemon sole, swimming in a buttery sauce. The waiter topped up our glasses and left after Cedric ordered another bottle of wine.

'Eddie Hollis does not approve of your work at Bloomsbury House. Nor does he approve of the company you keep.'

'It's none of Eddie Hollis's business what I do in my spare time.' *Or yours.* 'I don't like being spied upon by that man, Cedric.'

Cedric gave me a long look, as if summing me up. 'Eddie can become a trifle overenthusiastic about what he thinks are my best interests,' he said, as he picked up his cutlery. 'I really don't think you need to go to Bloomsbury House any more. It won't be long until the Germans are here and it would be better if you were not associated with a Jewish organisation when they arrive. I understand that you want to help children, but there are other, better ways to do that, ones more in keeping with your position in society.'

I put down my fork. 'I don't have any social position, Cedric. Not since your arrest. And I don't care if you or Eddie or Adolf Hitler himself doesn't approve of my work at Bloomsbury House. I'm not about give it up.'

He smiled again, but this time it was with an obvious effort. 'I'm trying to be patient. Let's be civilised, please.'

He began to eat. I stared at my plate, wondering if I should even attempt to eat the fish through my rising nausea. What Cedric was saying was making me sick. Mechanically I picked at my sole. It might as well have been cardboard for all the enjoyment I got out of it.

'You're not eating,' said Cedric, 'which is a shame because you have become painfully thin. Try to eat, darling.'

'I want a divorce.'

The words were out before I could stop them, and the effect they had on Cedric was immediate and terrifying. His eyes

narrowed and his mouth thinned. Before I knew what he was
going to do he had leaned across the table and taken hold of
my hand. It was no lover's grip. He squeezed it. Hard. Painfully
hard. My wedding ring cut into the fingers beside it and I felt
a sharp pain at the base of my thumb, where it met the index
finger. It was all I could do not to cry out. Instead I sat there and
kept up the façade of calm good humour while he held my hand
in a way that to a casual observer would have seemed lover-like,
but which was slowly crushing the bones and sinews in my left
hand.

Why didn't I get up and walk out of the restaurant? Why
didn't I cry out that he was hurting me? The English hatred of
a 'scene' was part of it. Also, it was hard to comprehend that it
was really happening. Someone who knows about such things
told me later that in that moment I had reverted to the eight-year-
old child being bullied by her father and I was as powerless as I
had been then. All I know is that I sat there and let my husband
cause me intense physical pain in a restaurant full of people and
I did nothing about it.

Eventually he released me. I tucked my hand under the table
and rested it on my lap, where it throbbed painfully. Cedric
returned to eating his fish as if nothing had happened.

'You know,' he remarked, 'I was worried that Quag's might
have lost some of its style in the war, what with the rationing,
but this is really excellent.' His tone was terrifyingly even. 'No
divorce, darling. Only death will part us.' He smiled. 'Yes, really
excellent fish.'

The waiter took away our plates. Lamb kebabs were placed
before us. Cedric tucked in, while I sat looking at mine, trying
to conceal with a straight back and expressionless face that my
hand was so painful I doubted I could wield a fork. In any event
my appetite had entirely disappeared.

Why didn't I get up and stalk out and never see Cedric Ashwin
again? Looking back, I think I was in shock, unable to believe it
had happened. I simply couldn't believe that my husband, who

had impeccable manners and was a lover of women in every sense, could have caused me such pain. And so I sat opposite him and watched him eat.

Cedric laughed. 'I do share a love of good food with Churchill. Like him, my tastes are simple. I am easily contented with the best of everything.'

The lamb in front of me was removed untouched, as was my pudding. Cedric appeared to have enjoyed the meal enormously and had kept up a running commentary on the excellence of the dishes. As we sipped our coffee he informed me that I would be accompanying him to the Ritz that evening where we would be meeting old friends.

I began to demur, but he stopped me with a cutting gesture. 'Darling, I don't like to hurt you, but if you behave like a child…' He drew in a deep breath, and smiled as he exhaled. 'You are my wife, Celia. You will accompany me, because if you're not with me then I must make excuses for you, and I don't want to have to do that. I will not be embarrassed by my wife. Or by her absence. We've been apart for many months. I accept that it may be difficult to pick up where we left off. I'm willing to give you time.' He sipped his coffee. 'Good coffee, this.'

I desperately tried to think what I could do. Negotiate terms. Try to strike a deal, regain the initiative. My voice was harsh and higher than my usual pitch, but I thought I managed to sound calm and non-committal.

'What do you really want from me, Cedric?'

'I want you to act appropriately.'

'I don't know what that means. Cedric, I can't return to the marriage.'

'Pretend then. For a while.' He twisted the coffee cup around in its saucer. I will not be embarrassed by you, Celia. I need to re-establish myself in Society and to do that I need you by my side. I would … lose face, if it were known that you had deserted me.'

'But—'

'If you still feel the same way in two months, then I'll divorce you. I give you my word.'

'Two months?' My heart began to pound. 'I have your word on that?'

He held my gaze. 'You have my word. If you still feel the same way in two months, then I will take the usual steps to enable you to divorce me.'

'Let's be very clear on this, Cedric. On April the first, you'll provide me with the usual affidavit?'

'April Fool's Day. How apt. If you still want a divorce, on April Fool's Day I will swear an affidavit admitting my adultery.'

My hand was throbbing painfully, but I scarcely noticed. *A divorce. He had promised me a divorce*. I lifted my head and took a deep breath.

'I will be pleased to accompany you to the Ritz tonight,' I said, 'if it's really that important to you.'

'Good girl.'

'But Cedric, I will not live with you. Not even to allow you to save face, as you put it. No one need know that we're living apart.'

He didn't answer for a moment, but sat there eyeing me with a cool, rather clinical gaze in his ice-blue eyes. There were pale pouches in the skin beneath them, criss-crossed with fine lines. They had not been there before his incarceration and they gave him the look of an ageing roué. *Which is exactly what he is*, I thought.

I said, in a firm voice, 'I will accompany you to social events but am not prepared to live with you as your wife. Is that clear?' I doubted that he would want for female company if I weren't interested in obliging his needs. 'And I'm deadly serious about the divorce. I'll pretend to be your wife for two months, but on April the first I'll expect that affidavit.'

He stared at me while he considered this, and then he smiled. 'Come spring, all will be different anyway. Then you may find that you are very pleased to be Cedric Ashwin's wife.'

His smile became calculating. 'That boy. The one who was in your flat when I came to visit you?'

'What about him?'

'Eddie discovered his name. Leonhard Weitz, isn't it? It would be a shame if...'

He took another sip of coffee, and laid the cup back in its tiny saucer.

A thrill of fear rippled through my belly.

'A shame if what?' My voice was too high and strained, too obviously worried. My hand was still throbbing painfully and as I watched his face a thought flashed into my mind, *If he can hurt me, his wife, with such ease, what would he do to a small Jewish boy*? I took a small breath and lowered the pitch of my voice, made myself sound cool and calm.

'Whatever do you mean, Cedric? He is a child who wished to visit my pet parrot. What has the child to do with anything?'

He went on as if I'd not spoken. 'And that Jewish doctor you've been seeing far too much lately. He's the son of the banker Jonathan Levy, isn't he? They live in Montague Street, Eddie tells me.'

I stared at him. 'What are you saying, Cedric?'

'Why? What do you think I'm saying?' His look at me was veiled, but again I saw the hint of something swirling in the clear, pale depths of his eyes. 'So dangerous,' he murmured.

'What is?' The give-away tightness in my voice had returned.

'London, right now. There are so many dangers, it's a wonder anyone survives.'

Cedric motioned for the bill, which was brought to him by a waiter with a flourish.

'It's been delightful. So glad we had our chat. I'll pick you up at eight, shall I?'

His manner was now perfectly civil, even pleasant, but there was no love, no tenderness in the look he gave me. He had made sure that I would do what he wanted and now that he had, he would treat me with calm cordiality. So much for his protestations of undying affection, I thought.

'Wear something lovely,' he said. 'I want to show you off.'

I found myself longing for the bombers to arrive, because it seemed that nothing but a full-on air raid would allow me to avoid dinner with Cedric that evening. My hopes were dashed when by eight the weather had worsened and no raiders had appeared in the sky. As ordered, I wore my most stylish frock, a pale silver silk sheath, and I carefully applied my make-up. I did my hair with some difficulty as my hand was beginning to swell and discolour, but I thought there were no broken bones. It hurt to pull my evening glove on to the sore hand, but I managed. The best I could hope for was that I would be home early. *Head high, walk tall.*

Cedric arrived at eight in a taxi and I greeted him in the lobby. He leaned in for a kiss.

'Darling, you look exquisite. We could make a night of it. You could stay at the Dorchester with me tonight.'

'No, Cedric.'

He gave an elegant shrug and a smile. 'Can't blame a man for trying, darling. You do look ravishing.'

When we stepped outside it was clear why no Warning had sounded. Thick clouds hung low above us in a protective layer. It was a bitterly cold evening with sleety snow driven by a gusty wind. I shivered in my coat. For yet another night, London would be protected by the English weather.

I had rarely ventured out to the West End on a social outing since I'd begun my work with the ambulance service, and I had not been to the Ritz since the start of the war. When we arrived, it was almost shocking to find Piccadilly in utter darkness, because it had always seemed to me to be a place of light and laughter. Few people were on the streets. Silence was heavy around us and we found the entrance by the light of our masked torches.

Cedric had told me we were meeting another couple in the below stairs Grill Room, a place we had visited often before the war. I had read that it had been rechristened *La Popote du Ritz*. As we descended the stairs I saw why. *Popote* was French for army mess, and the old Grill Room had been altered to represent a stage setting of the Great War trenches. Instead of glittering chandeliers, a candelabrum composed of old bottles now dimly lit the dance floor, and it swayed above the sea of khaki and blue serge.

Sandbags packed the walls, kept in place by wooden props and naked metal struts. The ceiling was apparently shored up with mighty beams. Check tablecloths, rather than white linen, adorned the tables, and on each was set a candle pushed into an old bottle – champagne, brandy, liqueur or beer. The band was playing dance tunes on a large stage, in front of a panoramic mural of the Western Front in the early days of the Great War. A similar mural adorned the wall of the adjoining bar, where the Siegfried Line wound its way past caricatures of Hitler and Goering. To complete the illusion, graffiti – in the best of taste, of course – had been scrawled on the woodwork.

We were led to a table set against the wall.

'Who are we meeting?' I asked. 'Do I know them?'

'Yes, of course.' Cedric seemed preoccupied. 'We're meeting the Ramsgates. Archie has some clout in the War Office, I'm led to believe. Could be useful to me.'

I let my gaze drift around the room and was electrified to see Simon on the dance floor with a dark-haired girl in a WAAF uniform. It seemed at first glance to be the girl I had seen him dancing with at the Dorchester after Lily's wedding. There was a look of Lore Rosenfeld about her, so I thought it must be Miriam, his oh-so accommodating girlfriend. I gave a mental shrug. Who Simon Levy danced with was not my concern. I hoped he was very happy with the girl. I could only pray that Cedric did not see him, as my husband's veiled threats against Leo and Simon had been playing on my mind all afternoon.

'Ah, here they are,' said Cedric.

230

I turned to see that the Ramsgates, a couple we used to know quite well before the war, had arrived. Cedric rose and smiled and greeted them and deftly drew them within the circle of his charming presence. He greeted them like dear friends, but I remembered that he had always referred to them disparagingly as the Irish setters, because they were both tall and slender with strawberry-blond hair. Captain Archie Ramsgate MP was around Cedric's age, in his early forties, with a toothbrush moustache and a receding hairline. He greeted me with a hearty handshake that made me fear for my undamaged right hand.

'Beautiful as ever, Celia. You must be thrilled to have this handsome dog back where he belongs. Isolde and I always said how unfair it was that they sent him away for saying what all of us with any sense thought.' There was a pause as he glanced around. He raised his voice slightly. 'Thought at the time. Before the war, of course. Very different now, what?'

My murmured response was ignored as he turned to Cedric, who had been giving his full attention to Isolde Ramsgate. Her look of fierce longing at Cedric made me aware – I hadn't been before – that she must have been one of his many lovers. Isolde was a year or so older than I. She had a sulky mouth that men seemed to find attractive, but I had always thought that the deep lines from her nose to the corners of her mouth gave her a cross, ill-natured look. We had never been close.

'Are you still being unbearably brave, driving ambulances in air raids?' she asked, and flicked a glance at Cedric who was talking to Archie.

'Still driving ambulances,' I admitted.

As Cedric, Archie and Isolde began a low-voiced conversation about Cedric's months of incarceration, I looked around the dance floor. I couldn't see Simon at first. Eventually I located him at a table across the room. He seemed to be enjoying himself, or at least he and his friend were both laughing a great deal.

'I hear he spends every weekend at Chequers,' said Cedric. I turned my attention back to those at my table, thinking that Cedric was unhealthily obsessed with Churchill.

'But he's sure to be on the streets after a raid, trying to win the approval of the masses,' said Archie.

'He's a madman,' said Isolde in a low, intense tone. 'He wants to lock up anyone who disagrees with him, and he will let London burn rather than treat for peace.'

Captain Ramsgate's eyes flicked around the crowded room. 'Isolde,' he said warningly, 'not at all the thing to say in a place like this.'

'What is the general view of Churchill?' asked Cedric quietly. 'Almost the first thing he did when he became prime minister in May was to – to send me away. All I hear now is what a magnificent war leader he is. And yet, look at London. Look at our defeat in France. How can he be so respected?'

'He's very popular, old man,' said Archie, in a low voice. 'Adored, even. Don't speak out against him publicly, no matter what you think.'

My attention wandered. Simon was dancing again with the dark-haired girl. Their laughter never seemed to cease. Miriam's demeanour was at odds with a woman who was mourning David, I thought. And then I took myself to task. David had been so very *alive*. He would never have wanted or expected Miriam, or me, or Simon, or anyone who had loved him, to give up on life because he had died. David would have thought it risible to be seen as a ghost, tagging along with the living, dragging them down, preventing them finding happiness again.

'Didn't you, darling?' Cedric asked me.

'Please forgive me, I was somewhere else entirely.'

'We were talking about Cedric's return to politics,' said Isolde. 'I expect you will be very useful.'

'Useful?'

She gave me a look of surprise, and glanced at Cedric.

'Celia is charming and decorative. She is not at all a political creature, are you, darling?' said Cedric, cutting smoothly into the conversation.

I decided to say what Cedric obviously wanted to hear. 'No, not at all political. Cedric has never discussed such matters with me, and I'm really not interested.'

She frowned. 'But you should always be interested in such matters. Politics is the breath of life.'

Cedric leaned towards me and whispered, 'Your nose is shiny, darling. Why don't you...'

I took the hint by excusing myself and heading for the ladies' room, where I spent as long as I could, fixing my hair and then reapplying my lipstick. The familiar routine of doing my face and hair calmed me, although my hand had begun to throb painfully in its tight glove and I wished I could go home.

Eventually I could delay my return no longer. I pushed open the door into the lobby and entered into a sea of uniforms. A cavalry man with colourful stripes on his trousers and chain mail on his shoulders bumped my shoulder. He apologised profusely but I scarcely noticed because Simon and his companion were standing in front of me, apparently having just collected their coats. The dark-haired girl murmured something to Simon and I saw his shoulders stiffen. When he swung around he showed the expressionless mask he had worn when meeting Cedric on the dance floor at the Dorchester.

'Good evening, Simon,' I said, and I was annoyed at the high pitch of my voice.

'Enjoying yourself?'

'Why yes, I am,' I said lightly. 'You?' I flicked a glance at his companion, who gave me a slight, embarrassed smile.

When Simon said nothing further she held out her hand. 'I'm Miriam Rosenfeld,' she said. 'I believe you know my mother, Lore.'

'Of course.' I forced a smile and replied in a light, conversational tone, 'And you obviously know I'm Celia Ashwin. It's lovely to meet you. Your mother has spoken about you often. I'll be seeing her again on—'

'Won't your husband have something to say about that?' Simon's voice was cold but now his eyes were blazing and an expression of brooding bitterness twisted his mouth. My heart gave a sickening jolt, but I raised my chin and met his eyes squarely. *Head high, walk tall.*

'No,' I replied. 'My work at Bloomsbury House has nothing whatever to do with Cedric. We're estranged. You know that.'

He raised his eyebrow at that and gave me a look that was frankly disbelieving. And then my temper was up. I *am* red-haired after all.

'Whom I accompany to dinner is none of your business,' I fairly spat at him. 'None at all.'

'It is if my mother allows you to work in her charity and trusts her foster-child to your care.' His voice was low, tight and controlled.

'That's ridiculous. I—'

'So this is *dealing* with him is it?' His voice was no longer controlled. 'You don't seem very estranged to me. What did it take? A few compliments and an invitation to the Ritz? We trusted you, and all the time you were—'

'What? I was what? Just what are you implying? That because I am seen in public with Cedric, I have somehow betrayed you?'

He flushed. 'Not me. My mother. Leo. The children in my mother's charity.'

Out of the corner of my eye I saw Miriam slip away, out into the night. 'Your girlfriend's going,' I said, with as much of the grand manner as I could summon. 'If you're quick you might catch her.' I wheeled around to descend the stairs to the restaurant.

'Not so fast,' said Simon and grabbed my bruised hand to pull me back.

I gave a sharp yelp of pain. 'Don't,' I said, through clenched teeth, trying not to whimper. 'Please let go.'

Simon released my hand at once, but moved his grip to my upper arm, above my evening glove.

'What is it? What have you done to your hand?' His voice was now entirely dispassionate, a doctor asking a patient for information upon which to form a diagnosis. His hand was steady on my arm and his face showed no expression but cool interest. 'I'm sorry to have hurt you. What have you done to yourself, Celia?'

'It's nothing. Really. I hurt it. At work.'

'How?'

'It was, ah, crushed. In a door.' He began to unbutton the glove. I tried to break his hold. 'No, please leave it alone. The hand is very swollen. If you take the glove off I'll never get it back on again.'

Simon did not reply. Instead he pulled me through the crowd into a corner of the foyer where the light was better. He gently palpated my hand through the glove, then the wrist and asked me to move my fingers. I wriggled them obediently.

'I don't think you've broken any bones, but from what I can tell through the glove it seems to be badly bruised,' he said. 'When did this happen?'

'This afternoon.'

'You weren't on duty today.' His voice had an edge to it that I had not heard before. I looked up at him, met squarely the hot fury in his eyes. He was still holding my upper arm in a firm grip.

'I wish to return to my table. Please release my arm.'

Simon became very still, but high in his throat a vein pulsed in fast fluttering beats. He said, quietly, 'Was it your husband? Is that why you're here with him?' And even more quietly, 'Did he do anything else to you?'

'He hurt my hand but he did nothing else. I swear it, Simon.' I spoke quickly and urgently, because I had not seen him look like that before, like he wanted someone's blood. The last thing I needed was Simon marching downstairs to have it out with Cedric.

'Tell me what happened.'

'When we were dining this afternoon I asked him for a divorce. He squeezed my hand, hard enough to hurt me. He did it to teach me a lesson.'

'He won't divorce you?' Again my eyes were drawn to that fast pulsing vein high up in his throat. 'So he wants you to return to the marriage? You can't—'

'No. I can't,' I said firmly. 'I'm not going back to him. He knows I'm not returning to the marriage.'

The tension in his face lessened and he took a few fast breaths. Then his eyes narrowed and the corner of his mouth twisted into a sort of smile. 'I don't understand. Why are you here with him?'

'He – we made an agreement. I must talk to you about it, but I think he's having me watched.'

Simon thought about this. 'We'll talk about it tomorrow. When I bring Leo to see Bobby.'

'All right.' I hesitated. 'Simon, watch out for Leo, will you? I'm worried that Cedric might—'

'I can protect Leo.' He glanced at stairs leading down to the restaurant. 'Are you sure you'll be all right?'

I touched his shoulder. 'I'll be fine. Now, you'd better find that girl of yours, or she'll never forgive you.'

He seemed puzzled, then said, 'Oh. Miriam. Of course.' He glanced around. 'Where did she go?' I indicated the door and he gave me a shamefaced smile. 'As I said before, she's a forgiving sort.' He turned away, but immediately twisted around to say, 'Keep the hand elevated. Put ice on it. I'll look it over tomorrow.' He pushed through the blackout curtains and disappeared into the night.

'Celia, darling. It's been such a long time.' The voice was high and fluting, and sounded ever so slightly tipsy. I turned to see Peggy Needham, who had been a debutante with me. I smiled at her, as if she was my dearest friend.

'Peggy. Lovely to see you.' And I took her arm and walked her downstairs into the Grill Room.

236

As I explained to Cedric and the others when I returned to the table, 'You know the way it is with old friends. I'm sorry I was so long away, but Peggy simply would not stop talking.'

When the taxi pulled up outside St Andrew's Court, Cedric asked the cabbie to wait. He walked me to the entrance but did not open the door. Instead he put an arm loosely around my shoulder.

'Would you like a cigarette, darling?' His voice was light and I could hear a smile in it. Or was it a smirk?

'Thank you, no. I'm very tired, Cedric. And my hand hurts.'

'I did squeeze rather hard, didn't I.' Now his voice sounded mocking. 'But darling, you were behaving abominably.' His hand fell away from my shoulder to cover my right hand, the undamaged hand. Through my glove I felt the warm strength of his fingers as he squeezed softly. He released my hand and slid his arm up and around my shoulders again.

'Cold, darling? Let me warm you.'

I pushed back involuntarily and his grip tightened. I knew then that I'd have to pay the ferryman before I was allowed inside, so I made an effort to relax. The last thing I wanted was an undignified tussle on my front step. Two months. He had given me his word. For two months I could play along. Cedric breathed a laugh and pulled me towards him.

Cedric kissed me with practised ease. I let myself relax into it because I had no choice. He used all his tricks, the ones that in our early days had so dazzled me. I wondered how long I would have to stand there, submitting, and hoped that if I did nothing he might finish sooner. I knew he wouldn't expect much from me. When I had confronted Cedric about his infidelities, he had intimated that he needed other women because I was, in his words, 'rather wooden'. He had told me once, 'You really don't have much of a flair for this sort of thing, do you, darling?'

David had disagreed.

Eventually the kiss ceased. Cedric waited and for a moment I wondered what it was that he wanted. An invitation to spend the night in my flat? A declaration of undying love?

'You know I adore you, darling,' he said, at last.

'No, Cedric, I don't know that.' My voice was dry. 'You were constantly unfaithful when we were married, and that's hardly a sign of adoration. Then today you bruised my hand, bruised it badly. Once again, not really an indication of adoration.'

'Darling, I *married* you. Those other women meant nothing. I told you that. And I have already apologised for hurting you.' His voice became petulant. 'You hurt *me* when you asked for a divorce.'

The darkness of the blackout seemed to press into my body, my mind, my very soul and my voice was apathetic as I said, 'I would like to go now, please, Cedric.'

He leaned in towards me. 'Of course,' he said, and released me with a sigh. 'You always were peevish when tired,' he said. 'Off to bed with you, darling. I'll let you know when I want you again.'

# CHAPTER TWENTY-TWO

Simon rapped on my door at three o'clock that afternoon. When I opened it, Leo stood beside him, holding Simon's hand and bobbing up and down excitedly. His smile at me was the open, happy smile of an eight-year-old boy who was looking forward to a treat. I had the impression that Leo was somehow taller than he had been when I first met him. Then I realised that Leo no longer stood with his head pulled down into his shoulders as if he were expecting a blow. He had come a long way in a few weeks. I knew it was not just Bobby, although the bird may have helped. It was the love of the Levy family that was releasing the boy from his demons.

As usual, Leo's manners were excellent. He bowed to me and wished me a good afternoon, but his eyes were searching the flat for the parrot. I opened the door more widely and ushered him in. He barely took time to shrug off his coat before he went to Bobby's cage, opened the door and presented his arm. Once Bobby was on his shoulder he moved over to the window.

'Leo Weitz,' said Bobby, and snuggled his head into Leo's neck.

'Good bird,' replied Leo, in his accented English. 'Good bird.'

'How's the hand?' asked Simon.

I presented my hand for medical inspection. The discolouration had advanced to a lurid collection of reds, purples and yellows. He stroked it gently.

'I'd like to take a closer look at it.' He called over to the boy, 'Leo, Celia has hurt her hand and I want to examine it. We'll just be in here, in the bedroom.'

Leo and Bobby turned to look at us and Leo nodded gravely.

'I am now talking to Bobby in English,' said Leo to me. 'He likes it better than German.'

'Quite right,' I said.

Simon and I entered the bedroom and he was careful to leave the door wide open so we could keep an eye on Leo and Bobby. They were standing by the window and Leo was keeping up a constant low-voiced chatter to the bird.

'Rather a one-sided conversation,' said Simon. 'Leo is talking quite a lot at home now, too.'

'I'm so glad.'

'He is still very fragile emotionally. Wets the bed. Retreats into lengthy silences, or flies into quite terrifying rages over trifles. My mother is very patient with him. Actually, she's coping with it all much better than I had thought she would.'

'I suspected she might. She probably needs him almost as much as he needs her.'

'Leo adores that bird. Seeing Bobby seems to have helped him enormously.' He gave a laugh. 'I think he feels that he can talk to the bird, without worrying about the response.'

I hesitated. 'Simon, last night—'

'First your hand,' he said. I held it out to him.

His touch was gentle as he palpated the fingers. 'No broken bones, but he certainly made a thorough job of it.' His tone was light and conversational. 'I must say that I think your estranged husband is a bully, a coward and a cad.'

I matched his tone. 'And yet he dresses well and tips liberally.'

'The hallmarks of an English gentleman.'

'Oh, a right proper gent he is. Cabbies say so.'

Simon looked at me and raised an eyebrow. 'You do meet the oddest cabbies, Celia. I've never met one yet who discussed proper gentlemanly behaviour with me or mentioned the Devil's pants.'

I gave a gurgle of laughter. 'Not the Devil's pants, you idiot. The Earl of Hell's waistcoat. Because it was such a dark night.'

'I knew it was some form of diabolical underwear. Damned peculiar simile.' He smiled, then gave me a searching look. 'Last night.' He cleared his throat. 'I'm sorry to have misjudged you.'

'I can see why you did. It must have looked as if...'

'Did you ice the hand?' His voice was brisk and business-like.

'Yes.'

'Are you keeping it elevated?'

'Not really.'

'Good thing I brought this with me, then.' He reached into his tunic and pulled out a bandage. 'I'll use this for a sling.'

Simon folded the material expertly, knotted it around my shoulder and lifted my hand into the sling. As he did so I noticed that he had some bruises of his own, across the knuckles of his right hand. They were the sort of bruises that came with a bare-knuckled punch.

'Keep the hand in the sling whenever you can for the next few days.'

'Sir. Yes, *sir*,' I replied, as if I were a soldier who had just received an order. That earned me another raised eyebrow.

'Will you stop me going back to work?' I asked. 'Put me on light duties again?'

Simon smiled. 'I doubt I could stop you doing anything. Just be sensible, please. I doubt you can drive, though.'

'I'll be sensible.'

He crossed his arms and leaned back to rest his hip against my dressing table, which stood by the French doors that led to the balcony. I had pulled back the blackout blinds and pale winter sunshine flooded the room with light, making interesting shadows on the white walls. It lit Simon's tense face and accentuated the purple shadows under his eyes. He was pushing himself too hard, I thought.

'So Ashwin won't divorce you?' His voice was brusque.

'Oh, how can he divorce me,' I said lightly, 'when Hitler will adore me, and the Fuhrer so hates divorce.'

Simon gave a soft bark of laughter. 'I've no doubt Hitler would adore you, but when is he likely to meet you? Are you planning a trip to Berlin?'

'Of course not. But he … well, it sounds mad, but Cedric seems to be convinced that the Nazis will invade Britain in the spring. He talks about it as if there is a definite plan and he knows all about it. He says that Churchill is a liar and we didn't really win the air war against Germany. Also that the Royal Navy has been destroyed by German submarines.' I sat on the bed and looked up at Simon. A crease had appeared between his eyebrows and he was frowning.

'It's a line that's being pushed in America,' he said. 'Many Americans seem to think we're done for.' He gave me a smile. 'We're not. Really, Celia, we're not done for. I promise you that. The government may have exaggerated the Luftwaffe losses, but we clearly won the Battle of Britain and that's why Hitler is trying to annihilate London. It's sheer spite on his part. Believe me, the Royal Navy is as formidable as ever and war production is up, despite the Blitz. My father is a good friend of Leslie Hore-Belisha, and although Hore-Belisha may no longer be Secretary of War, he still knows what's going on.'

As Simon spoke in his calm, measured voice I felt my tense shoulders begin to loosen. Cedric had seemed to be so very sure of what he had told me. Although in my rational mind I knew it must be false, a small doubt had crept in.

'Do you think that Cedric is mad?' I asked.

He frowned. 'Because he sees invasion as a likely prospect? No. Hitler may still make the attempt, although we're much better able to withstand him now. But it's clearly irrational to hurt you so badly in such a public place. I wish you would keep away from him.'

'It's complicated.'

My voice trailed away as I looked up at him. His eyes were a lighter brown than David's eyes had been and were flecked with gold and green, like sunshine in a forest glade. A flutter

242

ran through my body. How had I not noticed that before? Had I simply not looked?

'How is it complicated?' His voice was brusque.

I started and looked away from him. 'We've done a deal. He's determined to re-enter society, and he wants to drag me about with him as he tries to do so.'

'Because you're more socially acceptable than he is?'

'I suppose so. He thinks it would be embarrassing if people knew I'd dumped him.'

Simon frowned, and said slowly, 'He probably wants you to be his wife again. This may all be an excuse to keep you close so he can win you back.'

'If he does want me back, it's not because he's in love with me,' I said bitterly. 'He didn't care in the slightest whether he broke my hand. He wanted my obedience, and he was willing to hurt me to get it. That's not the act of a lover.'

'Is that all he did to you?' Simon's voice had dropped and although it was without inflection, I glanced up. Our gaze met and locked.

'He threatened Leo,' I said. 'Nothing specific, but he made it clear that he knew where Leo lived. And...' I hesitated, unwilling to disclose that he had also mentioned Simon.

'And your charming husband also threatened to hurt me?' I shot him a surprised glance and he smiled. 'He tried. Or, rather, his minion did.'

My heart gave a thump, then began to flutter in fast, unsteady beats. 'When? What happened?'

'This morning that fellow from the Paramount was lounging around outside the house. The fair-haired one with the thick neck and no chin. He followed me and then tried to warn me off seeing you. What happened? I dealt with him. My brother Saul – and the army – taught me how to take care of myself.' He glanced down at his bruised knuckles and flexed his fingers. A quick breath of laughter and Simon was all business again.

I gave him a reluctant smile. 'And to think I've been worried about you. Your sparring partner is called Eddie Hollis and he's a blackshirt bully.' My smile faded. 'Be careful of him. Fists don't trump guns. He's just the sort who would use a gun or a knife against an unarmed man.'

'I'll be careful. Don't worry about me.'

'Cedric also played his trump card yesterday,' I said.

'And what's that?'

'He said that if I do what he wants for two months, then he will agree to a divorce. Give me an affidavit attesting to his adultery.'

Simon gave a derisive laugh. 'And you believe him?'

'I think I do,' I said slowly. 'He gave me his word. Simon, I'm desperate. So desperate that I'll do what he wants.'

Simon made a quick movement and I said, 'Go out with him socially. That's all. And always in public. He hurt me only because I annoyed him. I really want this divorce.' I looked up at him. 'But ... I'm worried.'

'You think he's a traitor.' Simon said.

'And when did you add mind-reading to your many and varied skills?' I asked.

'Of course Cedric Ashwin's a traitor. Or he'd like to be one. That's the reason they locked him up.' He frowned. 'The question is whether he's intending to do anything about it. Do you think he's a fifth columnist, trying to help the Nazis?'

I sighed. 'I think *he* thinks he's a patriot who hates Churchill and we'd be better off fighting *with* the Nazis against Russia. He also thinks that Hitler is preparing for invasion and he seems not to be appalled at the prospect. But to actively act as a fifth columnist and try to undermine the British war effort?' I shrugged. 'I don't know. I don't think so. '

Simon ran a hand through his hair, leaving it dishevelled. It made him look very young. 'Look, Celia, if you tell the authorities what he's been saying about the invasion it may convince them to gaol him again.' A pause, then Simon said lightly, 'I, for one, would be happier if he was back on the Isle of Man.'

I looked down at my hand, nestling in the sling Simon had made for me. 'But it would be a wretched thing to do, to turn him in when he hasn't actually done anything. It would be acting like a quisling.'

'Not if he really is a traitor.'

I grimaced, nibbled at my lip. 'But what if he's just misguided?' My voice became mocking. 'And if Cedric's in prison he can't divorce me, and I do want that divorce. I think he just wants to be important again. Influential, in the way he was before the war.'

'Won't happen,' said Simon. 'Churchill detests him.' He pushed away from the dressing table, stared at me. 'Celia, I – I hate the idea of you spending time with him. Being at his mercy. He hurt you once, he may do so again.'

My heart lurched. This was an intensity I hadn't seen him display before.

'Did you catch up with Miriam last night?' The words were out before I could take them back.

He swallowed and looked away from me. 'Eventually. She was waiting for a taxi in Piccadilly.'

'Was she very annoyed?'

'No. She simply thought it would be diplomatic to leave us to row in peace.'

'I must say that I think her attitude is remarkable.'

'Oh, Miriam's the very best sort of girlfriend.'

'Really?' My voice was dry.

'She never interferes with my social life, is available whenever I need a partner, and is very discreet about what I do in my spare time.' There was a smirk in his voice.

I turned away to look out of the French windows and saw that clouds now covered the sun. It was as if a soft grey blanket had fallen over London. My jaw tightened. I had always been discreet about Cedric's affairs and I had never interfered with his social life. It seemed that I had entirely misread Simon's character. He was just like Cedric. He abused Miriam's trust, and presumably her love for him, to go out with anyone he pleased, do whatever he wanted.

Simon gave a soft laugh. 'I think we need to talk about Miriam.'

'I have no wish to discuss the matter any further. I think I'll return to Leo and Bobby.'

His mouth tightened. 'Do you practise that hoity-toity voice and the ice-queen look, or does it come naturally if you're to the manor born?' There was no good humour in his voice any more. It was sharp and hard and annoyed.

I ignored him and turned away to gaze out over the grey rooftops.

His voice rose. 'You are determined to be counsel for the prosecution, judge and jury all rolled into one, aren't you?' he said. 'Ever feel lonely up there on that high horse?'

'I have no idea what you're talking about.'

'I'm talking about the aura of self-righteous indignation that has surrounded you since I mentioned that Miriam doesn't mind me doing what I please. You immediately assumed that I have been taking advantage of a poor misguided girl who has been blinded by her passion for me.'

*If the cap fits…* 'Your personal circumstances are none of my business.'

'Miriam doesn't give two hoots what I do because she is madly in love with Antoni Gnys, a Polish pilot who is stationed at her airfield. Tony's Catholic, of course, and Miriam is terrified that her parents will find out about him. We decided before I left for North Africa that I'd pretend to be seeing her so that her parents will leave her alone and allow her to discover if this rather mismatched love affair of hers has a real chance.'

'Oh.' My neck muscles loosened and I drew in a deep breath. 'Forgive me. I shouldn't have assumed you were a cad,' I said. 'But honestly, Simon. What was I supposed to think?'

His voice was clipped and bitter. 'Apparently the worst.'

I wheeled around to glare at him. 'I've said I'm sorry. Must I keep apologising?'

'Not all men are like Cedric Ashwin. *I'm* not like Cedric Ashwin.'

'I know that. I know you're not like Cedric. I'm truly sorry to have thought—'

He gave me a slight smile and shook his head, as if trying to reason out a puzzle. 'We always seem to grasp the wrong end of the stick, always think the worst of each other until we learn differently. Why is that, Celia?'

'I don't know.' I looked at him, into his eyes, and said tentatively, 'Perhaps we're so afraid of being disappointed that it's easiest to think the worst and hope for the best. '

'You've not disappointed me yet, so perhaps I'd better start by assuming the best in future.'

'Then again,' I said lightly, 'you began with such low expectations of me, that whatever I do is bound to impress.'

The corners of his eyes crinkled in a smile and again I was lost in the colour of his eyes, that hint of gold. The world seemed to diminish, to fold in on itself, until only Simon and I existed in a place somewhere else, far from London and from war and from the cold realities of life.

Simon cleared his throat and looked away from me, out over the rooftops. I sucked in a breath and let it out slowly.

'The state of affairs between me and Miriam suits us both very well,' he said, addressing Greater London. 'She is spared her mother's nagging to find a nice Jewish boy, and I am spared my mother's nagging to find a suitable Jewish girl.'

I gave a soft laugh. 'I can see the advantages for Miriam, but what if you meet someone yourself?'

'I'm too busy for romance. Suitable Jewish girls are thin on the ground, and right now all my time is taken up with my medical work, air-raid duties or my family. When I'm ready I'll find someone my parents will approve of.'

'What you need is a – a *shidduch*. Is that the word?'

He looked amused. 'Perhaps I do at that. How do you know about the *shidduch*?'

'Lore Rosenfeld. Simon, she and your mother are going to be very annoyed with you and Miriam when they find out that you've been deceiving them.'

'I'm able to cope with my mother and Lore Rosenfeld.'

I raised an eyebrow. 'Best of luck with that.'

He laughed. 'Let's return to Leo and Bobby.'

The bird was perched on the bookcase when we entered the room, and he was amusing Leo by walking up and down, sticking out his beak and making clicking sounds interspersed with the occasional whistle.

'Say Simon Levy,' said Leo to the bird.

'God Save the King,' replied Bobby, and Leo giggled.

Simon walked over to him and put a hand on his shoulder. The boy smiled up at him and said in his precise but accented English, 'Bobby still thinks that you are the King.'

'Very perspicacious, that parrot.'

'What does that word mean?'

'He's a smart bird.'

Leo giggled again and nodded vigorously. 'Bobby loves the music of Mozart.'

'As I said, perspicacious.' Simon looked at me. 'Leo also loves the music of Mozart; he told us so at dinner last night.'

'Because I have played it, on the violin,' said Leo eagerly. 'I played with—' He stopped speaking abruptly, and stood with his mouth open. A wave of scarlet washed up from neck to forehead and receded, leaving in its wake a pasty white, almost grey tinge to his face. The memory of some horror was in his dark eyes and it was terribly painful to witness it.

Simon acted quickly, putting his hand on Leo's shoulder and squatting down in front of him to look at him, eye to eye.

'I told you – didn't I, Leo – I told you that I love Mozart, too. And that I can play the viola.' Simon's smile was somewhat forced, but it seemed to comfort Leo, who gave him a little smile in return. 'Should we should tell Celia what we have planned?' asked Simon, and Leo nodded shyly.

Simon looked up at me. 'Mutti bought Leo a violin and Leo has promised to play a Mozart piece with me and Mutti. We decided upon the Kegelstatt Trio and Mutti has ordered the music.' His hand moved from Leo's shoulder to ruffle his dark hair. 'You will play violin, I'll play viola and Mutti will play the piano, won't she?'

Leo nodded. 'I do not know that piece,' he said softly. 'I must learn it.' He fell silent again.

'It will be good to learn a new piece in a new country,' I said. 'I love the Kegelstatt Trio. It's glorious.'

Leo looked up at me. 'Do you, Celia? Do you love it?'

'I most certainly do. It's an absolute favourite of mine.' I was trying to recall if I had ever heard the Kegelstatt Trio. Surely I had heard it.

'We will play it for you.' Leo's shoulders straightened. 'I am a very good violin player. I am one of the best in London.'

I looked at Simon and raised an eyebrow.

'Mutti says so,' Simon said, as Leo nodded.

'I'm sure it will be marvellous and I can't wait to hear you.'

'And you will bring Bobby to listen as well,' said Leo decisively. 'Mutti wants to meet Bobby. She told me.'

I looked up and caught Simon's eye and mouthed 'Mutti?' I was unsure whether it was a good idea to encourage Leo to see Mrs Levy as a replacement for his deceased mother. Simon gave me a wry smile and turned to Leo.

'It's time to leave now,' he said. 'Say goodbye to Bobby and to Celia.'

Leo gravely farewelled the parrot and then turned to me. To my utter surprise, he flung his arms around my waist and hugged me tightly. 'Goodbye, Celia,' he whispered. 'May I come back next week to see Bobby?'

I folded my good arm around his thin little body and hugged him back as hard as I could, ignoring the pain it caused in my left hand, now safely in its sling. 'Of course,' I said. 'Bobby would miss you if you didn't come. And so would I. We'll see you next week.'

He moved out of the shelter of my arm, and then abruptly turned back to hug me again. 'I hope your hand is better soon,' he whispered.

After Leo and Simon had left the flat I stood for some time, staring at the painted wood of my door. Leo had changed greatly from the traumatised little boy who had come into my life only a month before, but it was clear that the memory of past horrors lay close to the surface of his mind. I thought of how Leo must feel in coming back to the music of Mozart, music he had last played in company with his family, who might all be dead, and I felt a bitter rage at a world that allowed children to be so traumatised. It was then I knew with utter certainty that I would do anything to protect Leo, whether from Cedric, or from anyone or anything else that could hurt him.

I stared at the door and I whispered, 'Leo, I promise I will protect you. I give you my word on it.'

But in the end, I was unable to keep that promise.

# CHAPTER TWENTY-THREE

I woke to a cold, dark Monday morning with a swollen and throbbing hand. It was obvious that I wouldn't be able to control my bicycle and so I walked to the ambulance station. A gusty north wind was blowing as I set off in a fast loping stride, trying not to slip on the frosty pavement. Grey clouds lowered above me and it wasn't long before a sleety rain began to fall. My umbrella was no match for the weather and the icy raindrops burned when they hit my exposed skin.

Because time was pressing, I took the shorter route, the one that took me along Guilford Street, past Caroline Place where David had died. I felt an immense sadness when I passed the ruins, but for the first time there was no nausea. Perhaps the wound caused by David's death finally was growing a scab. His death had been inexpressibly sad, but in this war death plummeted out of the skies night after night. Here in London we were surrounded by death. I had lost my love, but there were so many other women who had lost as much and had had to find a way to get on with their lives.

I was in no doubt that I had loved David. And yet, I had scarcely known him. We had been so wrapped up in physical passion during our tumultuous affair that there had been little opportunity to spend time in the simple, peaceful enjoyment of each other's company. I realised with a jolt that in many ways I knew Simon so much better than I had ever known his brother.

Soon I was at the entrance to Coram's Fields, the former foundling home. It was where women who had loved unwisely used to leave their illegitimate babies to the charity of strangers.

*Charity*. Miss Marshall, who had been the best of my inadequate governesses, had taught me about love. Actually, she had taught me about the words for love. Charity, she had informed me, came from the Latin word, *caritas*, which was itself a translation of the Greek word *agape*. And *agape* was one of the words used by the ancient Greeks to describe the types of love that humans could experience.

'*Agape*,' I murmured. I had always liked the idea of *agape*, love for mankind. It was the selflessness and willingness to care for strangers that I had been seeing every day in the Blitz. It was what Simon showed to those in need, including me on several occasions.

I continued my trudge along Guilford Street and tried to remember the other words for love that Miss Marshall had taught. *Eros* was what David and I had shared. It referred to sexual passion and desire, love that leads to a sort of madness. *Philia* was the love that underpins deep friendship and shared goodwill, the deep, loving bond between comrades on the battlefield. *Ludus* described a playful and uncommitted love, such as was enjoyed by potential lovers before any real decision had been made about their future.

David and I had bypassed *ludus* and gone straight to *eros*. My all-too-brief time with David had comprised brief rendezvous marked by feverish desire, followed by deep discussions about what David thought was important for me to know. I had been like a sponge, soaking up his knowledge while revelling in his desire for me and consumed by my desire for him. Would *eros* have transmuted to something deeper, stronger between us? Into *pragma*, the word used by the Greeks to describe longstanding love, based on patience and tolerance and deep understanding?

I didn't know. It's not for nothing that Cupid is depicted as a blindfolded child. David had a particular brilliance that seemed to eclipse everything around him and the passion between us, once ignited, had indeed blinded me.

I rounded the corner at Russell Square, still pondering the true meaning of love. And, as usual, thoughts of David became thoughts of Simon, whom I now liked and trusted. But he was David's brother. There was no possibility of *eros* between us. My mind rebelled against the idea, and I recalled his look of loathing when I woke him after the Bank Station disaster. There was nothing lover-like in Simon's dealings with me. But it seemed to me that Simon and I were developing a real friendship. *Philia*? It was the best I could hope for.

I had by now reached Russell Court, where the ambulance station was located, and I headed directly to the common room to check the roster board. Moray had chalked the Ford sedan next to my name. I stretched out my fingers and felt the pain that came with any movement. Could I change gears? The cars were too valuable to trust them to an injured driver. Simon had said I should be sensible. I decided to tell Moray that I'd be on the phone tonight.

Maisie was in the kitchen, where I went next for a cup of tea. She noticed my hand at once, of course.

'Whatever have you done to it?'

'Caught it in a car door. It's badly bruised.'

'Ashwin is injured,' she said to Moray, as he walked into the room. 'Her hand.'

He looked at it, then at me and shook his head. 'Do you think you're able to drive?'

'Probably not without difficulty.'

'I'll take the Ford,' he said, as I had assumed he would, 'and you're on the phone tonight.'

I nodded.

'You're accident-prone, Ashwin,' he went on. 'To be frank, you look done up. Please take things more easily. Don't forget you're still not fully recovered from the incident with the parrot.'

I laughed. 'That's one way to describe it.'

'How is Bobby?' asked Maisie.

'Growing feathers. I think he's getting better.'

Nola Fripp came up to me as Maisie and Moray left the room. 'How marvellous,' she whispered, 'that your husband is out of prison.'

'Yes.' I flexed my hand and felt pain. 'Yes, he's been released.'

Her eyes shone. 'He's a great man. So many of us think it was outrageous that he was ever incarcerated. It was because of Churchill. He was jealous of Cedric Ashwin's popular appeal. And now we're facing invasion, all because of Churchill.'

I murmured an excuse and left the kitchen. There was no point engaging in a discussion with Fripp about Cedric or the war. In the common room I began to leaf through an old magazine as the crew for the shift arrived. It wasn't long before the conversation turned to the so-called lull in the Blitz that London had experienced over the past couple of weeks. There had been no heavy night raids on London since the one in mid-January that had caused the Bank Station disaster.

'It's the weather,' said Harris. 'Germany can't risk its planes in the fog and snow and freezing weather.'

'Nah,' said Squire, 'we've blown up all their airfields. You've seen the photos. We're whacking them even harder than they're whacking us.'

Fripp reported in a low, thrilling tone, 'We've not had big air raids because the Nazis are putting the final touches to their invasion plans.'

She sounded like Cedric. I said, sharply, 'You should know better than to spread such rot.'

'It's only what everyone has been saying,' she said, with a sniff and shrug.

Purvis shook his head. 'That invasion rumour has been debunked.' He glanced at Squire. 'As has yours, mate. It's in this morning's *Telegraph*.'

'As if they'd tell us the truth,' said Sadler, with a sneer.

'The Americans have warned our government to be prepared for invasion,' said Fripp, again warming to her subject, 'but Churchill is too arrogant to take any notice.'

'Don't you say a word against Winnie,' said Squire, jutting out his jaw and glaring at Fripp. 'If we get through this war it'll be because of him.'

'Churchill's to blame for the mess we're in,' said Fripp defiantly. 'The Americans know. They say the German invasion will begin with the resumption of daylight bombing. And guess what? Last week we had daylight bombing again.' Her voice rose and broke. 'We need to convince Churchill to begin peace negotiations now. We must—'

'Fripp. Might I see you in my office, please?' Moray's cool voice cut through her outburst.

She rose and stumbled past him into his office, but turned at the doorway saying, 'The Germans don't want to subjugate us, they want to be our friends. We should negotiate with Hitler.'

Through the window I saw her collapse on to a chair, weeping.

Moray followed her in and closed the door. I glanced around at the shocked faces and wondered if I looked as pale and if my eyes also were wide and staring.

'Our friends?' said Maisie. 'She says the Nazis want to be our friends. That's mad.'

'She's taken a dead set against Winnie.' Squire was incredulous.

'Her dad's in the Defence Ministry,' muttered Sadler. 'Maybe she really knows something.'

Purvis glared at him. 'If there is one thing we know about the Nazis it's that they thrive on misinformation.' He stared at each of us in turn. 'This war will be lost if the Germans are able to destroy civilian morale. Invasion rumours sap morale badly and that's why the enemy wants us to spread them. And it's why we shouldn't spread them, and why it's a criminal offence to do so.'

'Why'd we have those daylight raids last week then?' muttered Sadler.

To my surprise it was Harris who replied. Throughout the conversation she had been quietly knitting. 'Just like I said before, you silly ass. It's because of the British weather.' She put down her knitting and gave a laugh. 'How could any planes have flown at night with all that snow and stormy weather we've had since January? They'd have got lost and tipped into the sea. The Irish Sea, because they'd have overshot London completely.'

'And they don't do much harm in the daylight raids,' said Armstrong. 'A few dive-bombings and some bombs and incendiaries but it's nothing like last year's daylight raids.'

'It's all a lot of nonsense, this talk of invasion now,' said Harris, pulling more wool off the skein on her lap. 'But I agree that the incendiary attacks have been really annoying.'

And, just like that, the conversation turned to less fraught subjects, such as the best way to deal with incendiary bombs, the war in Africa and what was likely to go under the ration next. And I had the sudden realisation of how peculiar small talk was in wartime.

I saw Moray a little later in the kitchen when I was pouring myself another cup of tea.

'Fripp had better watch out,' I said. 'Someone will report her to the authorities if she's not careful.'

'It's not only that,' said Purvis, who came in as we were talking. 'She's lost her nerve, Moray. I'm sorry to say it but I think she's a liability to the station.'

He nodded. ' And that's why Fripp and I have decided that her talents will best serve the nation in a capacity other than ambulance driving. She'll be out of the station next week, maybe earlier.'

'I think it's wise,' said Purvis. He picked up his tea and left.

Moray said, as if it were of no consequence, 'I met your husband last week. It was easy to see why he was so popular before the war.'

'Yes, it is.' I said flatly. 'But he's not so popular now.'

'Some people still think he has his finger on the pulse. Charismatic men like him will always attract followers. You must be pleased to have him back.'

'Mmm.' I tipped the remains of my cold tea into the sink. 'I'd better return to the others.'

# CHAPTER TWENTY-FOUR

'Did you hear?' Maisie said brightly, when I arrived at the station for a shift later that week. 'Fripp's left us to go to a cushy job in the Ministry of Food, the lucky duck. All arranged by her Dear Old Daddy. You know D.O.D., he's the fellow who supplies Fripp with her seditious rumours. Whatever will we do for information now?'

I smiled. 'There's always Powell's Aunt Glad. And I loved the gas-beating knickers trick from Sadler's Aunt Millie.'

I followed Maisie into the common room, which was empty save for Purvis, whose head was deep in a book. He looked up as we entered and smiled.

'Fripp's not much of a loss,' I said.

'No, she's not. I drove with her a few times last week and she screeched like a scorched cat when the raiders were overhead.' Maisie laughed. 'An ambulance attendant who's scared of bombs – not much good in a Blitz.'

'Are you really envious of Fripp? Would you rather be in a cushy job in a ministry?'

Maisie's smile broadened. 'Of course not. I'd be bored to snores sitting at a desk. Give me a rip-roaring air raid any day of the week.'

'Me, too.'

Squire entered the common room. 'It's freezing out there. Too cold even for snow.' He smiled at me. 'Hullo, Duchess. How's the hand? You've ditched the sling, I see.'

'It's much better.'

The bruising was fading and I was able to use my hand without too much effort, which was just as well, because that night the weather cleared and a few raiders returned to bomb London. It was nowhere near the scale of what it had been in past months however, and we all wondered about the continuing lull in the Blitz.

Powell's Aunt Glad had a theory, of course. 'I've heard a rumour why we're having so few night attacks,' Powell informed us, as we ate our lunch, two days later.

'And why is that?' asked Purvis in a suspiciously grave tone. He loved to encourage Powell's more outrageous gossip.

'What I've heard,' she said, in a thrilling whisper, 'is that some of the German pilots we've brought down are much too young to have had any real training. Some were only sixteen years old, or even younger.'

'That's old news,' said Sadler, who was standing in the doorway.

'This isn't,' said Powell. She lowered her voice. 'These young pilots have been *doped*.'

'Why would they dope them?' asked Maisie.

Powell frowned, obviously unsure. 'To give them courage?' she ventured.

Maisie sat up straight. 'That's crazy. No one can fly properly if they're doped.'

'Exactly,' said Powell, as if Maisie had made a good point.

'And why would the doping of boy pilots cause the lull in the Blitz?' asked Purvis.

Powell bit her lip and considered the question. 'I think a lot of them must crash their planes before they get here to London. Because of the doping. And there's more. They're using *girls*. As pilots. It's shocking. And they're doping them, too. No wonder not many planes are getting through.'

Maisie shook her head impatiently. 'I don't believe they're doping their pilots and letting them crash. The Germans aren't that stupid. And if they're using girls as pilots I'm sure they're just as good as any man or boy. What about Amy Johnson? She never needed to be doped for courage. And Amelia Earhart.'

'The same Amelia Earhart who crashed somewhere in the Pacific a few years ago?' said Sadler.

'Amelia Earhart was a wonderful pilot. Anyone can have a bit of bad luck. It annoys me when people seem to think that women can't learn to fly, or drive properly. Look at what women have been doing in this war – taking over lots of so-called male jobs, and doing them marvellously.'

'Listen to the New Woman,' said Sadler, with a sneer.

Maisie rounded on him, 'And what's wrong with that? Give me a New Woman over an old man – over *any* man – any day of the week.'

Sadler put up his hands in mock terror, laughing.

Purvis looked up from his plate. 'The forecast is for clear skies tonight. They'll be back. Whatever pilots they're using, the raiders will be over tonight.'

I stood. 'Cup of tea, Halliday?'

In the kitchen she said, obviously annoyed, 'What's wrong with being a New Woman?'

'Absolutely nothing.' I handed her a cup of tea.

She smiled. 'Thanks, Ashwin. Sorry for the song and dance, but it really gives me the pip when men like Sadler go on about women. I happen to believe that women can do a lot of things that men think we're too stupid or too fragile to do.'

'I know for a certainty you're not stupid or fragile,' I said. 'And I've seen you do a lot of things men would have been afraid to do.'

'Fragile!' She slammed the cup into its saucer. 'I'd like to see Sadler dance for two hours straight, or learn a new tap piece. In the chorus line we practised for hours on end to learn a new dance and it's jolly hard work, I'll tell you. I'd lay odds that I'm a lot tougher than Sam Sadler. Where does he get off, acting so tough? Sometimes it's a lot harder to be softer. I mean, it's harder be kind and nice than to be rough and nasty.' She paused. 'If you know what I mean?'

I smiled. 'I think I do. Don't let Sadler annoy you. He's just a cynical spiv.'

The Warning sounded at eight that evening. Moray told us it was an intensive incendiary attack and we were sent out to collect burns victims, which was ironic as it was the coldest night of the year so far.

Another Warning sounded at ten o'clock. We all looked up as Moray appeared with a chit in his hand.

'It's not a heavy raid, five bombers so far. They've dropped high-explosive bombs behind High Holborn. Hit a shelter. Six casualties thus far, more expected. Ashwin, you're attending Halliday. Purvis, you've got the Ford sedan. Sadler, you're attending Harris.'

Maisie and I were held up by a detour and arrived late at the incident. Several houses had suffered direct hits and were in ruins, together with a group of small shops. As well as the usual smashed glass and plaster and bricks and twisted steel and wooden beams, we had to pick our way through tattered bits of haberdashery, books and what looked like household goods. The rotting-food smell of gas competed with thick smoke and the scent of cordite. Fires had taken hold and the galloping flames were so fierce they took the chill out of the night.

Maisie nudged me and I looked over towards the remains of what had been a large public house. All the bottles must have been smashed because alcohol was running into the gutter. A fireman crouched down, put a small tin cup into the liquid and drank.

'Why waste it?' whispered Maisie.

'I could use a nip myself,' I said, jokingly. 'Think he'd share?'

Maisie laughed. 'If you don't ask, you won't get. It's a wonder Sadler isn't here with a few empty bottles to fill. Then he'd try to flog them tomorrow with the story that they fell off the back of a lorry, or a mate bought them from a bombed-out publican.'

'Let's find out where our casualties are.'

We were walking towards the Incident Officer when we came across a figure standing still and somehow alone among the members of the rescue squads and the firemen who swarmed around the incident.

'That's Sadler,' said Maisie. 'Whatever is he doing?'

As we got closer it became clear that he was attempting to cradle a very young child in his arms. Her small body was coated in grey-white ash and there was blood on her face. She was squirming hysterically, arching her back and making an unceasing high-pitched keening sound, more like the shriek of a small, terrified animal than a crying child. I had heard similar sounds from dying mice as the stable yard cats toyed with them before the final mercy blow.

Sadler, the most cynical of all the officers in our station, the hard-faced spiv from the East End, who was as likely to make a sarcastic comment as he was an off-colour joke, was cooing and whispering to the child, obviously trying to calm her down. He watched her with what appeared to be frustrated pity as she continued her eerie wailing. Then he began to sing a nursery rhyme in a surprisingly fine tenor voice. Nanny had sung the same song to me when I was around the same age as the child in his arms.

'*London Bridge is falling down,*' sang Sadler, '*Falling down, falling down. London Bridge is falling down, My fair lady.*'

The well-known ditty seemed to slice through the thunder of the guns, the roar of the ruptured gas main across the road, the hiss of the fire hoses and the shouts of rescuers. The child continued to squirm hysterically, arching her back and striking Sadler's chest with hard little fists, and all the while making the awful, unearthly keening noise. Undaunted, Sadler continued his singing.

'*Build it up with wood and clay, wood and clay, wood and clay, Build it up with wood and clay, My fair lady.*

A nearby building collapsed with a deafening roar and flames shot up into the darkness. The child shrieked and arched her back until I was worried it would break. She kicked her little legs into Sadler's stomach and continued the high-pitched shrieking. Sadler took the blows, held her closer and continued to sing.

'*Wood and clay will wash away, wash away, wash away, Wood and clay will wash away, My fair lady.*'

Maisie and I were near to him now. Sadler looked up and saw us.

'I can't take her to Harris like this,' he said in a tight, frustrated voice. 'She's out of her mind, poor little devil, and she'll do herself an injury. I don't want her to be restrained in the ambulance – can't bear the thought of tying her up – and we can't dope her if we don't know what injuries she has. So I'm hoping she'll snap out of it. Not a word about this at the station, mind.'

We nodded, and he bent his head to the child and continued his crooning.

'*Build it up with bricks and mortar, bricks and mortar, bricks and mortar, Build it up with bricks and mortar, My fair lady.*'

'*Bricks and mortar will not stay, will not stay, will not stay, Bricks and mortar will not stay, My fair lady.*'

I remembered that in his off time Sadler was a bandleader, and thought that this might account for the sweetness of his voice. The child continued to fight him but now with less fury. He held her against his chest and rocked her like a baby. The child's awful keening became a series of hiccupping sobs. She reached up and wrapped her arms around his neck and buried her bloodied little face in his chest.

'I'll take her to Harris now,' said Sadler. 'Poor little devil lost her mum. I found her with the body.'

Still holding the little girl close and rocking her gently, Sadler walked away from us through the mud and ash and wreckage, picking through the broken wooden beams and cracked pieces of plaster and all the usual detritus of bombed buildings, stepping over steel girders that had been bent and distorted by the heat of the fires. He was backlit by the roaring flames and he sang as he went.

'*Build it up with iron and steel, iron and steel, iron and steel, Build it up with iron and steel, My fair lady.*

'*Iron and steel will bend and bow, bend and bow, bend and bow, Iron and steel will bend and bow, My fair lady.*'

Maisie sighed. 'I should have known. People are always much more complicated than you think at first.' She gave me a wink. 'That includes you, the Honourable Celia, and your Dr Levy also.'

# CHAPTER TWENTY-FIVE

I returned to St Andrew's Court after my shift on a bitterly cold Saturday morning to find that a note had been delivered the previous afternoon. It was from Cedric. He informed me that my company was required that night at a dinner party to be held by our old friends, Sally and Harold Beamish, at the Hungaria restaurant. He was sure I'd be thrilled to accompany him.

'Thrilled, my foot,' I muttered, and seriously contemplated tearing the note very slowly into tiny pieces and letting them flutter to the floor, like an actress in a bad melodrama. I didn't. I decided to keep to my plan. I would do what Cedric wanted until April while I made sure that Leo and Simon were safe and that Cedric was not a real danger to my country.

And so I stood in the lobby holding the note, pondering what to wear to a dinner party held by friends who had barely acknowledged me since Cedric's incarceration.

'Bad news?'

I looked up. Katherine Carlow was standing in front of me and I threw her a perplexed smile. 'What does the well-dressed girl wear to a dinner party at a smart restaurant these days?'

'Nothing too ostentatious,' she said. 'There's a war on, you know.'

'I had noticed.'

'Bright colours are in vogue, because they are cheerful in dark times.' She tilted her head, looked me up and down and said, 'If I were you I'd wear that dark green woollen number I saw you in last May. Your hair is bright enough provide good cheer to all.'

'You remember what I was wearing in May last year?'

'I always remember clothes, especially when they cause me a jolt of lustful envy. It's a gorgeous frock.'

Albert the caretaker and doorman popped up from his basement flat. He was a wizened little Irishman with ginger whiskers, who was always immaculately dressed and liked to wear the Queen's South Africa Medal, awarded to those who had served in the Second Boer War, as a decoration on his hat.

'You'll be wanting Bobby,' he said.

Albert had taken to looking after the bird when I was away from the flat for any length of time.

'Do you mind keeping him until tomorrow? I really need to sleep, and I'm going out tonight.'

Albert grinned. 'Not at all,' he said. 'He's a grand bird, that Bobby.'

'I'll pick him up tomorrow morning. Leo's coming to visit him in the afternoon.'

I fell asleep as soon as I dropped into bed, and woke five hours later feeling unrested with gritty eyes and the beginning of a headache. But I dressed carefully in the green woollen frock and I fixed my hair and applied my make-up to look as glamorous as possible. Cedric was waiting for me in the lobby when I descended that evening.

'Darling, you look washed out,' were his first, cheering words. 'You should join me at the Dorchester. One is scarcely aware that a raid is in progress. You'd get a better night's sleep with me.'

I doubted that. 'We're in a lull, Cedric. There have been no heavy raids for the last few weeks. You've never experienced a heavy raid – I'm sure that even in the Dorchester you'd know about one of those.'

'Poor darling,' he murmured, as he ushered me out of the building, 'you're working too hard. Makes you fractious and ill-humoured.'

A taxi was waiting by the kerbside and once we were settled it rattled off in the direction of the West End.

'Harold and Sally Beamish have barely given me the time of day since you were—' I paused, and glanced towards the cabbie. 'In the past months. I'm surprised that they invited us to dinner.'

'It's a celebration for Sally's birthday.' He held up a small, wrapped package. 'I managed to find some scent for her. You were presented with Sally, weren't you, darling? She's quite a friend of yours, so Helen tells me.'

'Ye-es,' I said. 'She used to be.' I had caught a false note in his voice, a hesitation that hovered beneath his usual certainty. It was so unusual for Cedric to be uncertain of anything that I looked at him sharply. 'Cedric, we have been invited, haven't we? I've heard nothing about this.'

'Helen and Rory were invited,' he said smoothly, 'but I convinced them to let us go in their stead.' He held up an invitation card. 'After all, you were presented with Sally. You're more her friend than Helen is.'

'But why? Why are we pushing into their celebration?'

'I told you. I want to re-enter Society, re-establish my political influence. I want to position myself to be of use when...' He also glanced at the cabbie. 'When things change.'

'So we're barging in on a private party?'

'They'll be delighted to see us, I'm sure.'

My face became hot at the thought of turning up uninvited to a birthday celebration. *Head high, walk tall.* I'd suffered worse than being socially embarrassed in the past few months.

Of course, Sally and Harold were too polite to throw us out. Harold, who was in the uniform of the Coldstream Guards, and Sally, who was in the blue Wrens uniform, greeted me cordially and Cedric with cool courtesy.

'Poor Helen,' said Sally, as Cedric gave the excuse for the absence of my sister and her husband. 'A nasty cold is just awful. Please give her my best, and Rory also. We're delighted you and Celia could come instead.'

She leaned forward and gave me a quick kiss on the cheek. 'I've missed you, Celia. It's been so fraught lately that I've had little time for old friends. I hear you're doing marvellous work driving ambulances. And aren't you involved with Jewish refugees? Well done. Do let's catch up soon for tea.'

'I'd like that,' I said.

Cedric beamed at me as we walked away. 'Well done,' he said, echoing Sally. 'Do renew your friendship with her. Her father is close to Kingsley Wood and others in Churchill's war ministry. I want to meet him, offer my services. Make them understand how Churchill's grandiose idiocy will destroy this country.'

'Please keep your voice down,' I said. 'And I seriously doubt that the Chancellor of the Exchequer will agree to meet with you, Cedric.'

He made a gesture with his hand, as if brushing away my comment as a mere quibble.

As I walked by his side, greeting acquaintances in the crowd, I thought I understood why Cedric was so anxious to have me with him. Although no one wanted to know him, they were polite enough to me, and it was fairly clear that he would not have been tolerated without me. Towards the end of the evening we were standing near a major in the uniform of the Scots Guards, who was holding forth about Hitler.

'He overran the greater part of Europe because he was aided by treachery,' said the major, waving his pink gin like a banner. 'But, as Churchill says, at last he's abandoned the attempt to defeat Britain in the west.'

'The Americans claim that invasion of the British Isles is imminent,' Cedric put in smoothly.

'What? Nonsense.' The major looked more closely at him. 'I say, aren't you Cedric Ashwin? I thought they'd locked you up.'

Cedric inclined his head. 'And they let me out. So you don't accept what the Americans are saying?'

'I most certainly do not.'

And with utmost deliberation he turned his back on Cedric and continued his conversation. 'It's bad news about Bulgaria. But the important thing is that trouble in the Balkans keeps the

Nazi invasion army well away from us.' He raised his voice and declaimed, 'What we need to worry about are Nazi-loving quislings.'

Cedric stood behind the major for a beat or two, staring at his back. Then he whirled around, taking hold of my arm as he did so. He dragged me through the crowd towards the buffet table, where he picked up a plate.

'Would you care for some potatoes?' he asked me. 'Chicken?'

I nodded woodenly and he filled a plate before handing it to me.

'Fools,' he said, in a low, conversational tone. 'They'll learn. Come spring, they'll learn.'

The following afternoon while Leo communed with Bobby, Simon and I sipped tea, ate Mrs Levy's stollen and dissected the war news.

'I heard someone say that Hitler must choose either a blitz in the Balkans or an attack on England,' I said, as I poured tea into Simon's cup. 'Cedric remains convinced that we're facing German invasion within weeks.'

Simon glanced at Leo who was giggling as Bobby pushed his feathery head under the boy's chin to nuzzle his neck.

Once he was confident that Leo was not listening to us, Simon said quietly, 'Who knows? We're talking about Hitler. To get to Greece he'd have to embark on a serious Balkan campaign. He might decide it's better to start his delayed-action invasion of Great Britain instead.'

'He can't do both?'

'It would be difficult with his commitments in his occupied territories. He needs to keep his occupying army in adequate strength.'

'But there are millions of men in the German Army.'

'And those men must garrison Poland, Denmark, Norway, Holland, occupied France, and...' His lips twisted in a bitter smile. 'I've forgotten the other countries he's subjugated.'

'Belgium, Czechoslovakia, Luxembourg and our own Channel Islands.'

'Thank you. And he also has to keep enough troops in Germany to protect the fatherland. Given all of that, even Hitler would find it hard to embark on a tough campaign in the Balkans *plus* a full-length invasion of Britain.'

'Which would be the better move? Tactically, I mean.'

Simon sighed. 'Hitler's a gambler. A successful invasion of Britain would allow him to end the war at one supreme stroke.'

It was exactly what Cedric had been saying. 'And we just have to wait and see what he decides.'

'Pretty much. All we can do is to keep up war production and morale and deal with the air attacks. He'll not find us a pushover. An invasion attempt on Britain could well destroy him.'

I sighed. 'Wouldn't do us much good either. Think of the civilian casualties.'

'It's war,' said Simon. His face lightened and he threw me a maniacal grin. 'But you'll be fine either way, beautiful Celia. I have it on very good authority that Hitler will adore you.'

I hoisted the teapot. 'And I have it on the best authority that hot tea poured in the lap will cause nasty damage.'

Leo looked up in surprise. I winked at him, and he smiled.

'How sad,' Simon declaimed to the room, 'that the face of an angel should hide such vicious tendencies.' Another grin. 'Must be all that red hair.'

'You do like to live dangerously, Dr Levy,' I remarked, and put down the teapot.

I glanced at Leo, who had gone back to chatting comfortably to Bobby about Mozart, and looked again at Simon. Perhaps Cedric was right, and Hitler would adore me. I may well comfortably survive a successful Nazi invasion, but it would be entirely different for a little Jewish boy and a Jewish doctor. Our futures were dependent on the whim of a cruel dictator, who was perhaps also a madman. And I had no idea if Cedric had a part to play in any of it.

'How is your delightful husband?' asked Simon.

'Mind-reading again?'

Simon put down his cup and looked hard at me. 'Are you seeing much of him?'

'Last night we gatecrashed a birthday party because the birthday girl's father is well connected to Churchill's war cabinet. Is that suspicious?'

'It's poor form, but I'm not sure it's suspicious.'

'I wish I could refuse to see him, but I want that divorce, and I'm still concerned for Leo. It was all said rather obliquely, but Cedric definitely threatened Leo.' The enormity of what I had just said hit me like a sledgehammer.

'I need to see you,' I said. 'About that thing. In the bedroom. *Now*.'

Obviously perplexed, he followed me into my bedroom.

'What's up?' he said.

'Should you continue to bring Leo to my flat, given Cedric's threats? Should I give him Bobby now? Would your mother accept the bird? I know he's not attractive with so many bald patches, but he seems to be growing new feathers.'

'Don't get ahead of yourself. I think you should wait until Bobby is fully recovered before you give him to Leo. I don't want him and my mother coping with a sick bird. Or worse, a dead bird. Leo'd blame himself and—'

'Should we find him a parrot of his own? A young healthy parrot.'

'I think only Bobby will do, but I could ask him.'

'No-o, you're right. He really seems to love Bobby.' I straightened my shoulders. 'I'll keep the bird until he's well enough to go to Leo for good. But please keep a close eye on Leo.'

He leaned towards me and whispered, theatrically, 'I can protect Leo.'

In a normal voice he said, 'Stop worrying about Leo and tell your swine of a husband to leave you alone.'

'It's only for another seven weeks.'

'You trust Cedric Ashwin?'

'I have to. I want the divorce.'

I rubbed my tired eyes and followed Simon back into the sitting room. Leo had extracted a piece of shrapnel from his pocket and placed it before Bobby.

'It was red hot,' he said to the bird, pointing at the small piece of shattered metal. 'And Mutti said I shouldn't pick it up, but I did. And I burned my hand. See. There is the mark. Simon put salve on it but it still hurt.'

'And so you won't pick up red-hot shrapnel again,' said Simon. 'Will you, Leo?'

Leo shook his head obediently. Then he turned to the bird saying, in a hissing whisper, 'I will. I am making a collection.'

'God Save the King,' said Bobby, watching Leo with bright little eyes. He bobbed his head, fluffed his feathers and stretched out his neck. 'God Save the King. Leo Weitz. Good bird.'

# CHAPTER TWENTY-SIX

Cedric insisted that I accompany him to various dinners, nightclubs and parties whenever I had a night off during the following fortnight. He seemed convinced that Hitler wouldn't take him seriously unless he had a formal position in the government and he was worried that time was running out and Hitler would have invaded before he could do so. So he pulled in favours, made veiled threats and used his very real charm on anyone he thought might help him. Despite all his attempts, and to his chagrin, no one of any importance or with any real influence wanted to know him.

One Thursday night in late February he insisted that I accompany him to a little nightclub in a narrow lane off Greek Street in Soho. Inside, it was small and dark and reeked of cigarette smoke. Small tables were set too close together and there was a rather tawdry floorshow and a minuscule dance floor in front of a small swing band. I realised, as the band moved into 'Oh, Johnny', that the bandleader was none other than Sam Sadler. He was a good ten to twenty years younger than the 'boys' in his band, probably because all the younger musicians had been called up, but they had real rhythm and Sadler kept them tight. I thought that Simon would have approved of the sound they were making.

I found myself remembering how gentle Sadler had been with the child on the bomb site. When I first began working at the station, during the phony war, he had often made excuses for avoiding duties. But since the Blitz began Sadler had never missed a shift and he had saved as many lives as any of us at the station. I knew that in his own way Sadler loved London just as much as Simon did, even if he saw nothing wrong in taking advantage of the chaos of the Blitz to make a little money from its inhabitants. I tapped my feet to the beat and I thought that this war made for strange bedfellows.

As was now usual, Cedric began drinking as soon as we arrived. He downed a double Scotch and ordered another. I sipped my pink gin slowly.

'I'm fully convinced,' said Cedric, in a low voice, 'that the invasion will come in March with the better weather. There will be – simultaneously – a push into England and Ireland and a drive through the Balkans towards Greece, Turkey and Suez.'

'Simultaneously? Not even Germany has that many troops and resources.'

His eyes narrowed. 'You know nothing about it. Who's telling you these things?'

I shrugged. 'I can read. It's in the newspapers that Hitler does not have the capacity to invade both Britain and Greece.'

'That's whistling in the dark. The British authorities know what they're facing and they're terrified.'

The upward notes of the Warning sounded outside, muffled in the nightclub by the sound of the band and the noise around us. When the Blitz began in September 1940, the manager would have come on to the stage when the Warning sounded and pointed out the nearest air-raid shelter. Now it was accepted that no one would take shelter during a raid unless it looked like annihilation was imminent. Most clubs had spotters on the roof to let them know when raiders were directly overhead.

'I am willing to accept the hard truths,' said Cedric. 'Germany is too strong for us to withstand alone. A properly brokered truce will leave us in a position of power—'

'Brokered by Cedric Ashwin?' My voice was scornful.

'Yes, why not by me? I've met Hitler. He likes me. I can negotiate terms with him that will be beneficial to this country. Why can't they see that?'

'Because they think we can win this war, Cedric. And I do, too.' I repeated what Simon had said. 'An invasion attempt on Britain could well destroy Hitler, but it won't destroy Britain.'

Cedric's handsome face twisted in a snarl and his hand twitched, as if he wanted to strike me.

'You're parroting nonsense. Is that what the Jewish doctor tells you?'

My temper was up and red hair defeated prudence. 'Yes. It is. And I think he's right. We can beat Hitler.'

He half rose out of his chair, glaring at me. I tried to face him down, but his fingers had curled into a fist.

'Hullo, princess.' I looked up to see Sadler standing beside the table. 'Looks like your old man's in a bit of a temper.' Safe on his home ground, Sadler's tone was nicely balanced between annoyance and contempt. 'We don't put up with that sort of thing in this club. Or with his sort, actually.'

'Who the hell are you?' Cedric lowered himself into his seat, took a few breaths and said evenly, 'I'm having a discussion with my wife. Please leave us alone.'

Sadler ignored him. 'You okay?' he asked me.

'Thank you,' I said, and smiled at him. 'I'm fine. It's good to see you, Sam.'

'Me and the boys,' said Sadler, 'we see everything in this club. You get worried about anything, anything at all, mind, you just crook your finger.' He glanced again at Cedric. 'You want him out?'

I smiled again. 'No. But thanks.'

He walked back to the band to start another number.

'Who was that?' Cedric was fuming. 'He looks like an East End thug.'

'He works with me,' I said. 'He's someone I misjudged.'

'Sometimes I think you try to provoke me,' said Cedric. 'It isn't a sensible thing to do, darling.'

I decided upon discretion and said nothing in reply.

'Ah, here they are,' he said.

Archie and Isolde Ramsgate were wriggling through the press of people towards us.

'Good of you to come,' he said, as they sat down.

Isolde gave a low laugh, and her tone turned sarcastic. 'I like your choice of surroundings. Is the floor show worth waiting for?'

'Archie asked for somewhere dark and crowded,' said Cedric. 'I obliged.' He ordered drinks and when the waitress had left us, turned to Archie. 'Anyone would think you were ashamed to be seen with me. Any news?'

'Sorry, old man, but you're rather *persona non grata* at present. No one in the Cabinet is willing to speak to you.'

'Fools.' Cedric spat out the word with real venom. He gave me a narrow look, as if daring me to respond. I sipped my drink and let my gaze drift to the dance band, got a wink from Sadler and raised my glass to him.

'They'll need me to negotiate with the German High Command,' said Cedric.

'Steady on, old man.' Archie made a calming gesture, but his eyes seemed to dart about the crowded room. 'No need to let the world know our business.' He gave another glance around, before saying softly, 'I may have found someone, though. Someone who could be useful to you. Admirer of yours. Works in the War Office.'

Cedric smiled. 'Then I should meet him.'

'Name's Fripp. Arthur Fripp.'

'Does he have a daughter?' I asked. 'I used to work with a Nola Fripp.'

'Couldn't say,' was Archie's reply.

'Yes, he does,' said Isolde. 'Mousey little thing. Wouldn't say boo to a goose.'

'That's the one,' I said. 'She's recently transferred out of the ambulance service.'

'All the better.' Cedric looked very pleased with himself. 'It's good to have a personal connection. It takes time, but one

275

by one, they'll come back to me.' The entire room jarred as a bomb fell somewhere outside. Cedric shook his head. 'We need to begin negotiations now, while there is something of London left.'

'We have to go,' said Archie nervously. 'Another engagement.'

Cedric looked interested. 'Something I should know about? Who'll be there?'

'The usual crowd. Sorry old chap, invitation only.'

They left and Cedric sat in his chair fuming. 'It's Churchill. He's behind this. He wants me out of society. He's afraid of me.'

'Why don't we leave?' I suggested.

'You go,' he replied. 'I'll stay a bit longer.' He downed his Scotch and raised his hand to order another.

I left him sitting there alone.

The following Sunday afternoon, when Simon and Leo arrived as usual for Leo's visit with Bobby, I was shocked to see that Simon's face was a mess of grazes and bruises. My first thought was that Eddie had attacked him again.

'What happened?'

'Got caught in a raid. I'm fine.'

As he always did, Leo rushed over to Bobby to tell him about his week. Some of Leo's words seemed to jump out at me.

'And then Simon was *begraben*...' Leo looked at Simon. 'What is the English for *begraben*?'

Obviously flustered, Simon said, 'Don't worry about that. Bobby doesn't want to hear about it.'

I glanced at Simon, at the bruises and grazes on his face. Then I looked at Leo.

'Bobby wants to know all about it,' I said firmly. 'Bobby wants to hear *all* the details about Simon being *begraben*. You must tell Bobby *everything* about Simon being *begraben*.'

'I really don't think so,' said Simon, just as firmly, 'Bobby doesn't need to know about it. There's no need to tell him anything.'

Leo looked across at Simon and me. 'I do not understand. Why are you angry?'

I was immediately contrite. 'It's just adults being silly, Leo. We're not angry.'

Simon sighed. 'Of course we're not angry. You tell Bobby whatever you think he wants to hear.' He flopped into a chair and looked up at me. 'Buried. That's the English word, Leo. You tell Bobby that Simon was buried in the rubble of a bomb site and a big rescue worker hauled him out by his feet.' He flicked me a glance. 'It was quite amusing, really. Leo laughed when I told him about it, didn't you, Leo? You laughed to think of a big rescue working pulling me out by my feet. You tell Bobby what a lark – *ein witz* – it was.'

'Mutti didn't laugh,' said Leo.

My mouth had become very dry and the air seemed thin. I pulled in a shaky breath. 'You were buried? For how long?'

'Not long.' He stood and said, in a conversational tone, 'You were going to show me that thing. You know, that thing in your bedroom.'

I stared at him. 'Oh. Yes. The thing. I'll show you it to you now.'

We left Leo chattering to Bobby, and once we were in my bedroom I turned to Simon, 'Why wouldn't you tell me?'

He ran a hand across his face, winced. 'Because I'm fine. I didn't want you to make a fuss.'

'What happened?'

'A single raider, what they call a cloud snooper, dropped a single bomb. One bomb. Only it hit a railway arch near London Bridge that was being used as a shelter. One plane dropped one bomb.' His face twisted as if he was in pain. 'Dozens of people died. Many more were injured. I thought I heard someone calling. I went in to help them and part of a wall collapsed on me. A rescue worker hauled me out. That's the whole story.' He touched his face. 'It's not as bad as it looks. I'm a bit stiff, but I won't even be left with an interesting scar.'

I sat on the bed and looked through the door at Leo and Bobby, at something sweet and wholesome that might take away the picture in my mind's eye of Simon being buried under a pile of rubble, crushed and choking for breath until a big rescue worker hauled him out by his feet.

I turned back to Simon and said, in a tight, thin voice, 'Are you ever going to stop taking such insane risks, Simon?'

'Probably not.' He looked at me, laughed, and held up his hands in a defensive gesture. 'My dear Ice Queen, cease that freezing look right now, please, because words such as pot and kettle and black spring to mind.'

'Oh, that's—' I gave him a reluctant smile. '*Touché.*'

He sat next to me, and the springs of the bed squeaked under his weight. 'I'm fine. Really. I think your cosy meetings with your fascist husband are a great deal more dangerous than anything I do on a bomb site.'

'Oh, that's nonsense. It's all rather sad, actually. He drags me along with him and we're snubbed and frozen out.' I shook my head. 'Cedric's nothing if not persistent. A lesser man would have given up by now.'

'He is facing the loss of everything – wife, social position, political influence. He's a cornered rat, Celia, and they're very dangerous indeed.'

'I can handle Cedric,' I said, and we returned to Leo and Bobby.

Miss Marshall, the governess who taught me about the Greek words for love, also taught me about the Greek word, *hubris*. It refers to the sort of excessive pride that annoys the gods, and leads to your own destruction. Cedric's deluded belief that only he could lead Britain into its new future as a Nazi dominion was *hubris*.

As was my deluded belief that I could handle Cedric.

# CHAPTER TWENTY-SEVEN

It happened because Moray changed our shifts. Just before Christmas we had moved to three twenty-four-hour shifts per week. Since then I had worked from seven-thirty each Monday, Wednesday and Friday morning until seven-thirty the following morning, with a full day off on Sunday. Then Moray decided it was time to change our rosters.

When I arrived at the ambulance station on the first Monday in March I was told that under my new roster I would start work at seven-thirty every Sunday, Tuesday and Thursday morning, with Saturday free, beginning at the end of the week. That meant my cosy Sunday afternoons with Leo and Simon would have to cease.

Cedric had already given me my orders for the weekend. We were to join Archie and Isolde at the Café de Paris nightclub on Saturday evening, where we would meet Mr Arthur Fripp and his daughter, Nola. I was to be ready at eight, which would give me, I thought, enough time to see Leo and Simon on Saturday afternoon before Cedric arrived to collect me. As the Levys weren't practising Jews, I assumed that there would be no religious objection.

So I sent a note to Mrs Levy, and her reply came by return of post.

*Dear Celia,*
  *Of course Leo must visit his friend Bobby on Saturday. Simon is on duty at the hospital that day, so my husband, Jonathan, will bring Leo to you at three o'clock. I hope*

*that you have no objections to entertaining the boy alone, as Jonathan is otherwise engaged for the afternoon. Simon will collect Leo at his convenience. He apologises, but sometimes he cannot be sure of leaving the hospital at a given time. If this is suitable to you, I look forward to your confirmation.*

*With best wishes,*
*Elise Levy*

Jonathan Levy arrived with Leo promptly at three o'clock on Saturday. When I opened the door, Leo was jiggling with excitement. He pulled Mr Levy over to Bobby's cage, where they both stood, gravely examining the bird.

'If I hold out my arm,' Leo explained, in his careful English, 'he will walk up my arm and sit here.' He pointed to his left shoulder. 'And he does this to my hair.' Leo ruffled the dark hair over his ear. 'Once he put the side of *meine Brille* in his beak—'

'Your spectacles,' said Mr Levy. 'That's the English word.'

'Yes. My spectacles. But I said, "Bobby, let go," and he did.' He stared up at Mr Levy. 'He is a smart bird. Simon says so, too.'

'He's obviously a very smart bird,' agreed Mr Levy.

'Stand back.' He gave Mr Levy a little push and opened the cage door. 'Now he will walk up my arm.'

Bobby performed exactly as expected, clawing his way up Leo's sleeve to sit on his shoulder.

'Say Simon Levy,' ordered Leo.

'God Save the King,' said Bobby. 'Simon Levy. God Save the King.' He whiffled Leo's hair, making Leo giggle, and then disgraced himself by saying, 'Bloody hell. Simon Levy.'

Leo's eyes went wide with dismay and filled with tears. 'No, Bobby. Don't say that, or Mutti won't let you come home, ever.' His lip quivered.

Mr Levy glanced at me, then squatted down in front of Leo, just as Simon had done when he was upset. 'Mutti will let Bobby come to visit. I promise.'

Leo sniffed and blinked away his tears. 'I have a plan,' he whispered. 'If I think Bobby is going to say that word, I will say, very quickly—' His voice rose almost to a shout. '*Cover your ears,* Mutti.'

Bobby fluttered off his shoulder to land on the bookcase by the window.

Mr Levy laughed. 'I can see you've given it a great deal of thought. I suspect Bobby will behave like a gentleman in front of Mutti. Even so, I'll warn her that a certain word might slip out and I'm sure she'll pretend that it's not been said.'

Jonathan Levy ruffled the boy's dark hair and stood up. 'And I must leave you now.' He looked at me. 'Simon hopes to be here around five to collect Leo, but he said to warn you that he can't give any guarantees. He'll let me know if he can't make it by six, and if so I'll come myself.'

Leo was chatting to Bobby as I accompanied Mr Levy to the door and handed him his hat and coat. He paused in the doorway. A sharp crease had formed between his eyebrows and he seemed lost for words. He looked so much like Simon at that moment that my breath seemed to catch in my throat. It did so again when he cleared his throat gently, exactly as Simon often did.

'My mother, Mrs Cora Levy, is staying with us at present. I believe you met her some weeks ago?'

'Yes, I did.'

'She wishes to see you again. Elise has suggested that perhaps an afternoon next week may suit.'

'Your mother wants to see me? Whatever—' I blurted out the words, recollected my manners, and spoke in a more measured tone. 'I'd be delighted, of course.'

Jonathan Levy smiled.

'Do you know why she wants…?' My voice trailed away.

'I have no idea.' He added dryly, 'She knows nothing about you and David, if that's what concerns you.' He shrugged. 'My mother's motives are usually unfathomable.'

'I'm free on the afternoons of Monday, Wednesday and Friday next week.'

I wished I knew why Simon's grandmother wished to see me again, and I was afraid that she had indeed heard about David and me. *Head high, walk tall.* If she had I'd simply have to deal with it.

'Elise has a second motive for your invitation,' said Mr Levy. He laughed. 'And a third, actually. She, Simon and Leo have been practising a Mozart piece and Leo is anxious for you to hear it. If you brought the bird, my mother could see you again, Elise could meet the remarkable Bobby and the three musicians could give a recital.' He glanced back at Leo. 'I must say, the boy is a talented violinist. Elise is already working out how best to nurture his talent.'

I also looked at Leo, who was humming to the bird. When he saw us watching him he said, 'Bobby is learning how to sing Mozart. *Ich sumpte* – what is the English, please?'

'Humming. You are humming the tune to him,' said Mr Levy, 'so that he may learn it.'

'I am humming to him *Eine Kleine Nachtmusik*, and he is learning it for our Mozart concert. You are coming, Celia?'

'Yes, I'm coming. I can't wait to hear you.'

I said to Mr Levy in a lower voice, 'I can't guarantee that Bobby will be a gentleman with his language.'

The bird had revealed a few more words in the last week or so that were not at all acceptable at a polite gathering.

He smiled at me. 'People seem to delight in teaching parrots to swear, don't they? Elise can cope with a bit of language. Because she's not a native English speaker swearing isn't something she worries about overmuch.' He took his hat and gave me a nod of thanks. 'Thank you for looking after Leo. Elise will correspond with you about a suitable day.'

He left and I turned back to Leo, who was doggedly attempting to teach Bobby to mimic Mozart.

In just under two hours my world would be shattered into tiny pieces.

It began at four-thirty with a sharp knock at my door. I assumed it was Simon, come early to pick up Leo. I was entirely off my guard and that's why he was able to enter the flat so easily.

I opened the door with a smile, expecting Simon. Cedric was standing there. He returned my smile and pushed past me into the flat.

'What are you doing here?' I asked, standing in the open doorway behind him. 'You're not due until eight.'

'Darling, that's no way to greet your husband.'

'I'm busy at the moment.'

'Never too busy for me, darling.' I had not offered to take his coat. He removed it anyway and laid it across the arm of the sofa, placing his hat on top.

'Cedric, you're not staying. Come back at eight.'

He ignored me. Instead he turned to Leo.

'You must be Leonhard Weitz.'

Leo nodded gravely, then he stood and gave Cedric his little bow. His dark eyes were bright behind the lenses of his spectacles, and in his serious little face I thought that both his intelligence and his innate sweetness were clearly apparent. I was annoyed and upset at the obvious contempt in Cedric's scrutiny of him.

Cedric turned away from Leo and smiled at me. He seemed buoyant, but also edgy. It was a strange combination in a man who prided himself on his insouciance. He walked over to me, leaned in and whispered, 'It's all about to begin. Now that the weather has cleared there will be an aerial attack on Britain that will dwarf last September's blitz.'

I could smell the alcohol on his breath, and when I looked closely at him the hints were there. The edginess, a glassiness in his eyes and the slight hesitation in his movements. Cedric had always been able to hold his liquor, but I knew the signs. My husband was profoundly drunk.

'Why would you say such a thing?' I pulled away from him.

'Now, darling,' his voice was gently amused. 'I was merely speculating. It's what many people have been saying. As for me, I've been getting things ready.'

My body tightened into wariness. 'Ready for what?'

He met my look blandly. 'For our new home. I've rented a charming town house in Chelsea. You'll adore it.'

'I won't see it. I'm not returning to the marriage, Cedric. I told you that. And you promised to give me my divorce. In three weeks, on the first of April. You promised.'

His tipsy good nature was unalloyed. 'When the troops parachute in you'll join me soon enough. I'll be an influential man in German-occupied Britain. These fools in the government may treat me with contempt now, but they'll regret it.' He flicked a look at Leo. 'What about your little Jewish friend? How can you hope to protect him without my influence?'

'There will be no invasion.'

'I do wish you'd not comment on things you know nothing about,' he replied snappishly, walking back to me. 'I thought you had more sense.'

Before I realised what he was about he took hold of my left hand and squeezed it hard. It was all I could do not to whimper, but Leo was watching us, so I managed to smile. Cedric released my hand.

'Wear something lovely tonight. I like that silver frock. Wear that one, would you, darling?'

I pulled away from him and surreptitiously rubbed my hand. It seemed clear that he had lied to me and did not intend to give me the divorce after all. I lost my patience.

'You're behaving like a boor. Will you please leave? I'm not going out with you tonight. I want a divorce. How many times must I repeat it? I want a divorce.'

His handsome face twisted in a snarl and his hand snapped up as if to strike me. I put up my arm to protect my face and braced myself, but the blow didn't fall. Cedric lowered his hand.

'You really shouldn't provoke me, darling,' he said, and smiled.

I turned to look at Leo, who was huddled in his chair watching us. 'Don't worry, Leo,' I said, and managed a smile at the boy. 'It's just adults being silly. Nothing for you to worry about.'

Leo nodded gravely. '*Genau wie du und* – I mean, like you and Simon,' he said.

My heart gave a thump.

Beside me, Cedric stiffened and became very still. But when he turned to Leo he was full of smiling bonhomie, a favourite uncle or a beloved schoolteacher, someone with whom it would be easy to talk to, easy to share confidences with. Shy little Leo, who craved affection, smiled back.

I began to speak, but Cedric spoke across me, asking Leo, 'Do Celia and Simon talk often? Are they often silly like this?'

Leo nodded.

'And I suppose he sometimes holds her hand.' He took my hand again and this time he stroked it gently, like a lover.

I pulled it out of his grip, but did so with a smile because I did not want Leo to be upset.

'Cedric, Dr Levy treated my hand.' My voice was level, and although I sounded a little piqued at Cedric's implication, I was clearly more bored than annoyed. I had to work very hard to get that tone when my heart was thumping like an express train over tracks. I caught Cedric's eye and raised an eyebrow. 'You remember how I injured my hand, don't you?'

His lips tightened, but he ignored me to ask Leo again, 'Does Simon do that, Leo? Does he hold Celia's hand?'

Leo nodded.

'Ah,' said Cedric. His smile widened. 'And I expect they go into Celia's bedroom together, and spend time in there. Just the two of them.' He took my hand again, and held it in a tighter grip. I tried to pull free, but his hold was like a vice.

Leo looked at me and then at Cedric, obviously confused. Then he nodded.

A muscle began to twitch in Cedric's temple. He had been holding his jaw tightly clamped, and now it began to slide back and forth. I knew it was entirely unconscious and also that it only happened when he was enraged.

'A Jew?' he snarled, turning to me. His face had darkened and a vein throbbed in his temple. I seemed unable to tear my gaze away from that throbbing vein. 'A Jew? I thought better of you.'

'Nothing happened between us.' I spoke firmly and with patience. 'Dr Levy treated my hand. That's all.'

Cedric hit me hard across the cheek, a blow painful enough to rattle my jaw and make me see stars. The pain filled my eyes with hot tears and the room dissolved. When I could see again I looked at Leo. He was cringing back in his chair, head pulled down into his shoulders, watching us with a fixed, frightened stare.

Cedric said, as if speaking to himself, and as if it were a simple statement of fact, 'I will kill Simon Levy.' He glanced at Leo, then looked back at me with eyes that showed no emotion whatsoever. 'Should I kill the boy as well? He won't last long after the invasion. It may be a blessing to the child if he were to go quickly.' His gaze narrowed. 'And you really must be punished for this.'

'No,' I said quickly. 'Please, Cedric.' As I spoke I was thinking furiously. If I screamed who would hear? The flat on one side of me was empty, like so many flats in London nowadays. Katherine Carlow's flat was on the other side, but she had gone out earlier that afternoon. *No one will hear me if I scream.* Could I get Leo outside, away to safety? Cedric stood between Leo and the door. *There's no escape that way.* Cedric was drunk, but could I still reason with him?

'You must be punished,' he repeated.

'Then punish *me*, not a child. I'm sorry I was so dismissive. Of course I'll go out with you tonight.'

He smiled, and turned towards Leo.

'But you must be punished,' he repeated.

'Why would you do that?' I asked, taking his arm in a tight grip. 'He's a child. Utterly defenceless. There's no honour in such an act.'

His smile widened. 'He doesn't matter. Don't you see? He's Jewish. He's nothing.'

'Cedric, you can't—'

'Everything is going to change. In few weeks we'll be a part of something much greater. This child is a way of punishing you. And you really must be punished, darling.'

'If you touch him I will kill you,' I said, in a low voice I scarcely recognised as my own.

There was a glint of amusement below the heavy eyelids, and the arrogant tilt of his chin betrayed his formidable confidence. Beneath it all I could sense his alcohol-enhanced excitement and allied to it was a brutality flickering beneath his smooth and polished persona, his veneer of civility.

He shrugged, smiled more broadly. 'No. You won't. And, Celia, I'll have no more nonsense about us living apart. You're my wife. From tonight you'll live with me as my wife.'

The atmosphere in the room had become charged as if with electricity. Cedric looked at Leo, who was crouching in his chair, small and so very, very vulnerable. Bobby had flown up to the curtain rod and was watching the scene unfold with his round yellow eyes. Would he fly at Cedric if he tried to hurt Leo? Use his sharp beak to rend flesh and his claws as talons? He was not a match for Cedric. Neither of us was.

'Guns are so noisy,' said Cedric. 'I won't use the gun. Knives are messy, guns are noisy. Best to wring his neck like a chicken, don't you think?'

Terror had me in its chill and nauseating grip, and for want of a better plan I launched myself at him, pulling at his arm, trying to scratch his face, his eyes. I remember very little except my blind panic for Leo's safety. Cedric laughed throughout, seeming to enjoy the fight. And, really, there was no contest. I was no match for superior weight and strength and training. I scarcely landed a blow. After a short struggle he pushed me down into the sofa and stood over me, still laughing. Then he straightened up and looked at Leo, who had wrapped his arms around his thin body in a protective gesture. I grabbed Cedric's arm again and tried to use my weight to desperately pull him back, keep him away from Leo.

The Warning sounded.

The banshee wail echoed through the flat to tell us that raiders had been sighted and were on their way. Cedric flinched at the noise and stood absolutely still, wide-eyed and staring at the window. His breathing had quickened.

Almost immediately came the rumble of an aeroplane, the push–pull sound of a Heinkel engine, coming in low.

And it was as if a switch had been pulled in my brain, as if I had heard that small, still voice, the one that our vicar spoke of when he gave his sermon about Isaiah in the cave. All at once I knew exactly what to do. I had two cards to play. Cedric was extremely drunk, and he was not used to air raids. We'd been in a lull since he had arrived back in London and anyway, the noise of an air attack was muted almost to silence in the Dorchester. I had a minute at most, I thought, maybe two.

I screamed.

When I had Cedric's attention I spoke in a voice that throbbed with fear. 'We've got to take cover. There's a shelter in the basement.' My voice rose to become a high-pitched wail. 'I was trapped for hours in a bombed building. I can't go through that again.'

Cedric hesitated. He shook his head as if to clear it. I screamed again, jumped up and took his arm to pull him with me towards the doorway. He came with me, step by hesitant step. We were close to the door now. The sound of the Heinkel was louder.

My voice was high, terrified. 'We must get away from the windows. Shattered glass rips exposed skin into shreds.'

He flinched, raised a hand protectively to his face. I pulled the door open. The corridor lay beyond.

'We've got to get out,' I repeated, louder. 'We'll be killed, maimed, scarred for life. Oh, Cedric, if you'd seen what I have seen in the past few months—'

There was confusion in his eyes. 'How long do we have?'

'Not long. They're directly overhead.' I spared a look at Leo. He was sitting up in his chair now, staring fixedly at Bobby, who was perched high on the curtain rod above the window.

Next came the ghastly swishing, shrieking noise a bomb makes when it is plummeting to earth. It always seems to be heading directly for you and, believe me, it is a terrifying sound. Cedric ducked down, tucking his head into his shoulders, much as Leo did when he was afraid. Imminent death is a great leveller, I thought, with a touch, just a touch, of contempt. But it *was* satisfying to watch all Cedric's careful insouciance flee at sounds I'd had to cope with, night after night, for months.

Cedric thrust himself through the doorway first. I had a wild hope that I could escape him, but he grabbed my arm and pulled me with him out of the flat. As he did so I called back to Leo, 'Stay inside the flat. Don't open the door to anyone.'

There was a sound like crashing thunder as the bomb exploded. The door slammed shut behind us. I made sure of that. It was a solid door and made a satisfyingly loud thump as it closed. And then I was standing with Cedric in the silent corridor and Leo was safe behind the locked door.

That is how Bobby the African Grey parrot saved Leo Weitz. Would Cedric really have murdered a child? He had killed before, of course, when fighting in the Great War, but it is a leap, even if drunk, to go from killing an enemy soldier to murdering a child. The point is, when I thought Cedric was about to kill or at the very least hurt Leo, I was powerless to protect the boy. It was Bobby who saved Leo and he did so with an imitation air raid of epic proportions.

'Has the raid finished?' Cedric seemed confused.

I swallowed. 'Sometimes they are very short. The daylight raids in particular. One or two planes only.'

He glanced at the door. 'And I suppose you forgot your key?' His cool composure had returned and a small smile played around his mouth, under his carefully cultivated moustache.

'He's a small boy, Cedric. He's of no consequence. Leave him.'

'Do you have your key?' he said, his tone sharpening. 'My coat and hat are in there and it's very cold outside.'

'No.' I held my arms out. 'Feel free to search.' I was wearing a thin woollen frock and there were no hiding places or pockets.

Thoughts raced through my mind. Leo was safe for the moment, but he was alone and scared in my flat. What if he left his place of safety and came looking for me? And what of Simon? *Simon.* If he arrived to collect Leo then Cedric would try to hurt him. Maybe he would kill him. Cedric had mentioned a gun.

'Tell him to open the door.' His voice was louder now. 'I won't hurt the child. Honestly, Celia, do you really think I'd have murdered that child? I wanted to frighten you and I did. The child was always perfectly safe.' He moved his neck from side to side as if to loosen tense muscles. Frowned at me. 'Tell the boy to open the door, please.'

'No.'

His eyes narrowed. 'Is your Dr Levy expected back soon?'

'I was to return the boy to his home,' I lied. 'It was all arranged. Dr Levy is not coming here.'

'Celia, it's cold outside and I need my hat and coat. This is ridiculous.'

He took a step towards me, smiling. It was a charming smile, but his fist was clenched. I felt a shiver run up my spine and my heart began to hammer in my chest.

We both started at a clanking, shuddering sound, the sound of the lift as it stopped at my floor. My heart gave a painful jerk. *Simon.* The cage was pulled across. Katherine Carlow emerged and began to walk along the corridor towards us.

Katherine gave me a smile and Cedric an appraising look.

I nodded at her, murmured, 'Good evening, Katherine.'

'Good evening, Celia,' she replied. As she came closer surprise registered in her face, then her eyes narrowed. 'Hurt your cheek?' she asked.

Cedric's face twisted as if in pain and he turned away from her. I put up a hand to rub my cheek. It was very sore from Cedric's blow and as my skin is very fair I knew the bruise would be already colouring up splendidly. As I said before, Katherine is quick at picking up social nuances and she is very observant.

'I'm fine,' I said. 'My husband is just leaving.'

Katherine nodded and carried on walking along the corridor to her door. She looked back at us, turned the key and entered her flat. A few seconds later her head popped out of the doorway.

'Do shout out if you need anything,' she said. 'Anything at all. My hearing is excellent and I'm sure to hear you.' She shut the door behind her.

Cedric inhaled slowly and as he exhaled the tight muscles in his face loosened. He gave me a tentative smile.

'This *is* ridiculous.' His expression was now one of amused frustration. 'I cannot believe that you, even for a moment, thought I'd harm that child. We've been married for three and a half years. Did you ever, in all those years, know me to be violent?'

'Your followers were violent. You hurt my hand at Quag's. Just now you struck me. And you terrified Leo.'

He shook his head. 'You can't hold me responsible for my followers' actions. As for me... Celia, you must know I'd never have hurt the boy. I was angry and I wanted to frighten you. I struck you because I was enraged.' He grimaced. 'It was unforgivable, I know, but the thought of you and that Jew – I've never felt such rage before. Celia, I love you. How am I supposed to respond to news like that? As for your hand, I had no idea I'd hurt you so badly at Quag's. You made no sound, gave no indication that I was really causing you pain. I'm so sorry that I did.' He seemed calm and very sincere, but the glitter of inebriation was in his eyes.

I found myself thinking. *Surely Cedric wouldn't have hurt a child. Not even a Jewish child. He couldn't have meant to hurt Leo. He only wanted to frighten me.* Because the thought that once I had once loved, married and shared a bed with a man who could hurt a child made me feel sick.

Common sense reasserted itself. Even if Cedric wouldn't really have hurt Leo, he had frightened us both half to death by pretending that he would. It was not an honourable act, and I despised him for it.

'Do you really have a gun?' I asked. 'You said you had a gun.'

He shrugged and gave me a sheepish smile. 'It's in my coat. Which is in your flat with a young child. I should think the boy's in more danger alone with a loaded gun than he ever would be from me. Tell him to open the door, darling. I'll pick up my things and leave immediately. Please, darling.'

'Don't call me that. Never call me that again.' I said. 'No. I won't ask him to open the door until you have gone.'

'Then we have a conundrum,' he said. His manner was calm, somewhat amused and somewhat annoyed. 'I need my coat and hat, and my gun, and it seems that you no longer trust me in the slightest.'

I glanced at my watch. It was nearly five o'clock. I was relieved to hear that the gun was with Leo in the flat and I assumed that was why it hadn't appeared before now. I did not for a moment believe that Leo would look inside Cedric's coat, but I was worried that Simon would arrive at any moment. He would be angry when he saw my bruised cheek and the thought of Cedric and Simon engaged in a fight over me was abhorrent.

So I sighed and turned to Cedric. I was holding my hands so tightly that my nails were digging into the palms, but my voice indicated my calm acceptance of his right to his possessions, my annoyance of the fact that his actions had brought us to this situation and my hope that all could be amicably resolved.

I said, 'I will bring your coat and hat—' He began to speak, and I talked across him. 'I won't bring the gun. I'm keeping that, but I'll bring your hat and coat to the Dorchester this evening. But Cedric, please leave now. I won't ask Leo to open the door to the flat until I know you've actually gone.'

He looked at me, as if trying to gauge how serious I was. I returned his gaze steadily, pushing aside my fear that Simon would arrive, trying to show that I meant every word I had said. I was pleased that Katherine was close by and had made it clear that she was looking out for me. Her timely arrival meant that Cedric knew his Gestapo tactics wouldn't work. If I screamed then he'd be dealing with two angry women, and knowing Katherine she'd emerge with a fire-iron ready to swing at his head.

Cedric's eyes held an indefinable expression and a shadow of unease was evident underneath his nonchalance. I thought he was annoyed and trying hard to hide the fact, but surprising to me was the lingering unhappiness underneath the annoyance. It seemed close to misery.

'That would be kind of you,' he said at last. 'But please bring them to the Café de Paris. Please darling. The man who's coming with Archie and Isolde, this Arthur Fripp, he may be the one who holds the key to my future.'

He held out his hands to me in a gesture of supplication. 'I gave you my word that I'd allow you to divorce me, if you still wanted it, and I'll keep my word. But darling, for pity's sake, help me now. Fripp wants to meet you. He made a point of telling Archie that. I need your help. Please, darling.'

There was a bleakness in his eyes that I had never seen before in my husband, usually the most self-confident of men.

He seemed calm and sincere. Cedric had lost everything he treasured – his social position, his political influence and me. For the first time in my life I pitied him. And so it was pity that led me to take the decision that in a few hours would hurl me into the abyss.

I blew out a breath. 'Very well, I'll deliver the hat and coat to the Café de Paris tonight. I'll drop them into the cloakroom and I'll come down to say hello to your guests. But Cedric, then I will excuse myself. I won't stay for the evening.'

'Thank you,' he said. 'You were always kind. I never appreciated how—'

'And please understand, I won't see you any more after tonight. Our marriage is over.'

His voice became wooden. 'If that's what you really want, then so be it. I'll tell my solicitor to take the steps to prepare for divorce.'

'Thank you.'

A minute or so later and we were standing on the St Andrew's doorstep. The wind, scented with brick dust from the ruins of London, whipped past my cheeks and made them sting. I shivered in my thin woollen frock. It was a cold evening and very dark, but I knew that it wouldn't be long before the full moon would rise. A bombers' moon would sail the skies tonight in a clear sky and London would be fair game to the Luftwaffe.

Cedric turned away from me without a word and walked down Gray's Inn Road, heading, I suspected, for the Tube station near Russell Square. His arms were wrapped around his body for warmth, as mine were, to give some protection against the arctic wind. I felt cold, shaky and sick, and I suddenly wanted to cry.

Instead, I sucked in a deep breath and was about to turn and re-enter St Andrew's when the shuttered headlights of a small car came along the road from the south. I waited as the car pulled up outside the building and the engine was turned off. A door opened and slammed shut. The thin beam of a masked torch bobbed its way around the car and across the footpath towards me. Torchlight fell on the front step, then my shoes, and bounced upwards to illuminate my face.

'You're late,' I said.

'Celia?' Simon sounded astonished. 'What the devil are you – it's freezing. Come inside.' He bustled me through the door and into the lobby, saying in his usual offhand manner, 'Sorry I'm late. Got caught up at the hospital. Has Leo behaved himself?'

A lower, harsher note came into his voice when he saw me in the dim light of the lobby. 'What happened to your face?'

# CHAPTER TWENTY-EIGHT

Leo opened the door at once when Simon asked him to do so. As Simon was calling through the door to the boy, Katherine poked her head out. She saw Simon, waved and smiled at us both and returned to her flat.

Once Simon was inside Leo clung to him with a fixed rigidity and hid his head in Simon's chest. That I had the almost overwhelming desire to do the same, I put down to the aftermath of my fright.

Simon lifted Leo up into his arms, carried him into the sitting room, and sat with him on the sofa, still holding him close. They remained like that for some time, with Simon murmuring to Leo. I couldn't hear what he said. Leo said nothing in response. It wasn't until Bobby, who was perched on the curtain rod, called out 'God Save the King' that Leo began to loosen his grip.

The parrot squawked again, 'God Save the King' and added, 'Good bird.'

At that Leo's head came up, and he looked at Bobby and then at Simon.

'The *braunhemd* hit Celia,' said Leo, 'and then Bobby made sounds like a bomb and the *braunhemd* was afraid and he ran away.'

'Bobby's a very clever bird,' said Simon.

'Then he made *scheisse* – what is the English?'

'Never mind.'

'He did it on the *braunhemd*'s coat.'

I looked and, sure enough, a large white and green smear now decorated Cedric's black cashmere overcoat. Bobby was house-trained and it was almost certainly an act of defiance and distain on the part of the bird.

Simon glanced at the coat. 'As I said, he's a very smart bird.' Leo giggled.

At that my legs gave way and I sat – no, I collapsed – into a chair. And stupidly, helplessly, I began to cry, hiding my face behind my hands. It was the relief, of course. Knowing that Leo had not retreated into silence again, and that despite all that had happened because of my stupidity in allowing Cedric into the flat, Leo was able to laugh.

I was pulled up out of my chair and Simon's arms wrapped tightly around me. I hid my head in his chest just as Leo had done, breathing in the scent of him, feeling his thudding heart against my ear. My stupid sobbing would not cease. Leo hugged me also, wrapping his thin arms around my waist and resting his head on my back, saying something in German to me, over and over, in a soothing tone as if I were the child in need of comfort. I remember thinking, *All I need now is the parrot on my shoulder, nuzzling my neck.* At that, tears gave way to bubbles of inappropriate laughter and it wasn't long before I pushed away to loosen Simon and Leo's hold.

'I'm all right,' I said, avoiding Simon's eyes. 'It's not hysteria. It's just some sort of reaction to it all.'

I sat on the sofa and Leo climbed on to my lap. I found it enormously comforting to hug the boy. Simon sat opposite us. I looked up and met his gaze.

Simon took Leo home in his car, leaving me alone with the parrot and Cedric's richly and rather ripely decorated overcoat. He insisted I wasn't to leave the flat until he returned, and said that we'd work out what to do with Cedric's coat and hat then. I had the firm impression that his preferred option was to throw both coat and hat into the Thames.

I hadn't been able to reveal much to Simon about what had happened because Leo, snuggled on my lap, was listening to every word we exchanged. The boy had agreed to go home only because he was hungry and because Simon said that he would be able to 'Tell Mutti all about what Bobby did.'

I strongly suspected that my invitation to attend the Mozart recital and see Simon's grandmother would be revoked once Elise Levy heard the news.

The thought of having to recount the events of the afternoon in detail to Simon on his return was something I dreaded, and after Simon and Leo left I spent a long time sitting on the sofa just staring at Cedric's coat, trying not to remember how terrified I had been for Leo's safety. My thoughts turned to Simon and his gentleness with Leo and then with me, holding me so close that I could hear the beating of his heart. Annoyingly, tears filled my eyes, overflowed and rolled down my face. I hated that I had become the sort of woman who so easily turned to mush. My handkerchief was nowhere to be found and I wiped ineffectually at my face, wincing as I rubbed the bruised area on my cheek.

What shocked me out of my self-absorbed misery was a fluttering of wings. To my delight, Bobby flew down from his high perch to sit on my shoulder. He nuzzled his feathery head into my neck and made clucking, cooing sounds. I spent a while stroking his feathers and I scratched his head at the spot I knew he liked to be scratched. His body was warm and soft and comforting.

'You're a smart bird all right,' I said to him. 'I owe you a great deal, Bobby.'

'Simon Levy,' he replied. 'Bloody hell.'

'As usual, right on the money. *Such* a smart bird.'

I scratched Bobby's head again, then stood up. He flew over to the bookcase and watched as I walked across to Cedric's coat. I felt the need to be busy, and obviously I would have to sponge the coat before I returned it. As I picked it up I made a firm decision. I would return the coat and hat to Cedric, briefly meet his guests tonight, and never speak to him again except through lawyers. And then we would be divorced and I could carry on with my life.

The overcoat was one that Cedric had had tailored for himself just after our marriage. It was black cashmere, beautifully cut. First I looked for the gun. It was tucked into the inner breast pocket, a Webley revolver. When I cracked it open I saw it was fully loaded. With hands that shook slightly I placed it in a drawer of my writing desk. Out of sight, out of mind, at least for the time being. Then I quickly checked the coat again for any other hidden surprises, but the pockets were empty.

Bobby's 'message' in white and khaki green was like an abstract painting splashed across the front of the coat. As coats of that quality had become unobtainable and I didn't want Cedric to be able to complain about my pet ruining it, I decided to try to deal with the stain the best I could before I returned it.

I picked up the garment and took it into the bathroom where I wet a flannel, wrung it out and began sponging the stain over the basin. It was messy work, but the droppings were fresh and I managed to clean off the worst of it. I spread out the now relatively clean coat out on my bed to dry.

Simon's knock at the door came soon after, but I'd learned my lesson. I put my ear against the wood.

'Who is it?' I hissed.

'Simon. Open up, please.'

As he walked in I felt an odd sort of constraint, which I put down to embarrassment. After all, I'd nearly been the cause of his foster-brother's death or injury. He walked over to the electric fire and stood, looking down at the red bars. His hands were thrust deep into his pockets and his forehead was creased.

'Now, supposing you tell me what happened,' he said, turning to look at me. 'All of it.'

I told him. He listened in silence, watching my face. When I had finished he took a deep breath and let it out slowly.

'Thank God for Bobby,' he said. 'Do you think Ashwin really would have hurt Leo? It seems pretty drastic, even if he was furious about our supposed affair.'

'I keep asking myself that question, and I really don't know. At the time I thought he would. Now I'm not sure.' I paused. 'Simon, what does *braunhemd* mean? Leo called Cedric the *braunhemd*.'

'Brownshirt. We think his brothers were killed by Nazi brownshirts, or assaulted and then taken away by them. We think Leo saw it.'

I stared mutely at Simon and licked my dry lips and said, 'I am so sorry that Leo—'

'*Did* he have a gun?' Simon spoke across my inadequate apology.

I walked over to the desk, took out the gun and handed it to him, handle first. He broke it open. 'Fully loaded.' He looked up at me. 'Why would he be carrying a loaded gun?'

'Who knows? Paranoia?'

'Any other little surprises in the coat?'

'Not that I could find.'

'Are you serious about returning his hat and coat to him?' he said. 'Because I happen to think it's an amazingly stupid notion.'

I met his gaze. 'I gave my word I'd return his coat and hat. Making that promise got him out of the flats and away from Leo. Cedric has promised to divorce me if I do this last thing for him, and I need that divorce.'

'It makes no sense. Why would he give you that promise just for the return of his hat and coat?'

I felt the heat in my cheeks. 'It's more than that. Cedric's meeting a man from the War Office at the Café de Paris tonight. It's one of his supporters who he thinks can help him. He wants me to charm the fellow. I said I'd only stay a minute.'

Simon's expression was almost comedic, his eyes wide and staring and his mouth open. 'You're willing to meet – to *charm* –

someone who wants to put Cedric Ashwin into a position of influence?'

'Arthur Fripp can't help him into any position of influence. The man's a junior civil servant in the Ministry of Defence who pedals silly rumours and wants to seem more important than he is. I'd *never* help Cedric if I thought it would harm my country.'

'Why do anything at all for Cedric Ashwin? I don't understand you, Celia. Do you feel sorry for the poor fascist without any friends?' A strange little smile was playing around his lips now, but his eyes had a blank, dead look. 'Are you sure you want out of your marriage?'

'There's no need for sarcasm. And yes – I'm absolutely sure I want a divorce. But – and it's difficult to explain – in a way I do feel sorry for Cedric. He's an unpleasant man, but he's lost everything. Including me.'

Simon's anger showed in the angle of his brows and the way his lips were twisted in a mirthless smile. 'He's a despicable brute,' he said bitterly, 'and a traitor to this country. A dangerous man, a liar and a bully who is willing to hurt you in public to get what he wants. Grow up, Celia. He'll never divorce you. Instead, he'll use your pity to persuade you to help him. If persuasion doesn't work then he'll hurt you, and if that doesn't work he'll threaten those you care about. He'll do anything he can to keep you in his power.'

'I think you're exaggerating,' I said, hoping I believed it. 'Cedric's no Hitler. He's trying to work out how to live in a world that has passed him by. One in which he has no place any more.'

Simon shook his head. 'You're wrong. He's using every trick he has to keep you with him. He threatened Leo, for God's sake. Stop playing his games.'

'I gave him my word. And he promised me the divorce. *He promised.*'

There was a perceptible hardening of his features. 'If you go to Cedric Ashwin now then there's no hope for – whatever it is – between us.'

'There's nothing between us,' I whispered.

'You know that's not true.'

I felt a painful jolt, somewhere deep in my chest. 'David—'

'Is dead. I loved him. You loved him. But he's dead, and we have to find a way to live without his memory stopping us from giving whatever this is a chance.' His eyes were gravely intent, holding mine, giving me nowhere to hide. 'David doesn't stand between us; your fascist husband does.'

I could not deal with what Simon had said, not then, when my bruised face was throbbing and my chance of obtaining a divorce was so close. Not when I had no idea what to think.

Simon left the flat, and I didn't try to stop him.

I readied myself for the Café de Paris with slow, almost mechanical movements. *Whatever it is between us.* My skin felt tight, stretched thinly over bone and sinew, and my cheek hurt as I brushed powder over the bruise. *There's nothing between us.* I coated my lashes with mascara. *You know that's not true.* My lips trembled as I applied my lipstick. *David doesn't stand between us; your fascist husband does*. I shrugged on my coat and picked up my handbag. *Stop playing his games.* I put Cedric's coat over my arm and held his hat tightly. *If you go to him now there's no hope.*

I dropped Bobby off at Albert's flat and walked to Theobald's Road, where I found a taxi. I asked it to take me to the Café de Paris. Above us a bombers' moon was rising, cold and bright in a clear sky. *No hope.*

# CHAPTER TWENTY-NINE

*Saturday 8 March 1941*

The taxi made quite good speed though the darkness and dropped me off at Piccadilly Circus. From there I followed the bobbing light of my torch along Coventry Street towards Leicester Square. The night was one of moonlit beauty and chilly darkness and the only sounds were the chatter of other pedestrians braving the blackout for a night out in the West End.

'This is like the good old days before the Blitz,' a woman exclaimed. 'I don't think they'll come over tonight. They're hitting the ports instead of London now.'

'They'll come,' said her companion. 'Moonlit night, you see. And London is their prize target.'

As if to prove him right, the Warning sounded just before I reached the Lyons Corner House and I increased my pace, because the last thing I needed was to be caught outside when the bombing began. The ornate Rialto Cinema was in sight, and tucked away next door was the entrance to the Café de Paris. I pushed through the thick blackout curtain and entered the restaurant.

Just inside was a uniformed doorkeeper. 'I suspect it's going to be rough tonight,' he said, 'seeing as how we've not had a proper raid in weeks.' And then he began what must have been his usual patter. 'But you're safe at the Café de Paris. It's all under the ground, you see. Safe as a Tube station.'

The cloakrooms were at street level. I handed over Cedric's coat and hat and received the ticket. I checked my own coat separately. Then I squared my shoulders and lifted my chin as

I descended the straight flight of stairs to the nightclub foyer. *Head high and walk tall.* Once I was divorced from Cedric, then I could work out what I felt for Simon and then we could decide whether there was any chance for us.

The Café de Paris restaurant was decorated in opulent shades of red and gold, and its gilded ceiling glittered in the light of chandeliers. Mirrors lined the walls and threw back fluid and somewhat kaleidoscopic images of luxury and gaiety. Something in the roof caught my eye and I looked up again. Beyond the chandeliers was a small glass dome, painted over to comply with the blackout, which was about the size of a large sunshade. *Not entirely underground*, I thought.

The Café de Paris comprised two lower levels, the foyer where I was standing and a lower floor, in which were the main restaurant and the stage where the band and floorshow performed. The foyer was a more like a balcony, as it overhung and encircled the deeper chamber. David had told me once that the lower floor of the Café de Paris had been a bear pit in past centuries. Now it was the place to be if you were young and smart. Those without influence or the foresight to book a table on the lower floor had to make do with tables in the foyer. I looked around for Cedric, but couldn't see him, so I decided he must have been fortunate enough to snaffle a table downstairs. So I went to the edge of the balcony, which gave a splendid view.

Beside me a divided staircase curved in two gold and crimson arms to the floor below. A circular stage nestled between the arms of the staircase. On it a Caribbean dance band, which I recognised as Snakehips Johnson and his West Indian Dance Orchestra, played with syncopated gusto under a flood of light. The dance floor in front of the band was heaving with couples. The men were mostly young and in uniforms of khaki and blue. Many women were also in uniform, or they wore fine evening gowns. The couples milled around under the floodlights like a swarm of fishes in a splendid fishbowl.

Only the first row of tables downstairs was illuminated by the floodlights on the stage. I couldn't see Cedric at any of them. The second row was more in the shadows and I caught glimpses only, of the ruby notes of a lifted wine glass, the glint of silverware and the sparkle of jewels on white fingers. Further back, beyond the floodlights and behind the row of pillars supporting the balcony, nothing was visible but the small shaded lamps on each table. It looked as if I'd have to check each table on the lower floor to find Cedric, give him his ticket and smile at Mr Fripp. And then I'd leave him forever.

The dance music ceased and the dance floor cleared. A drum roll announced a troupe of barely clothed cabaret girls who seemed to glide on to the stage with a rhythmic swinging of their hips. A high-kicking routine ensued, complete with fixed smiles, flashing eyes and shimmying limbs. I descended the steps to the dance floor as the girls kicked up a storm.

The roar of planes was now loud overhead, competing with the thundering reports of the ack-ack guns and the ominous crump of bombs hitting the ground. The restaurant shook each time a bomb fell. A few conversations around me briefly paused, but then carried on as if nothing was happening outside.

I found Cedric's party at a table for six in a dark corner. Archie and Isolde were chatting to a thin, middle-aged man with a toothbrush moustache. Next to him was Nola Fripp, and she was gazing at Cedric as though he had hung the moon.

'Good evening,' I said, and five pairs of eyes turned to look at me.

The men rose. Cedric smiled. 'Darling. I was just telling our guests that you'd been unavoidably delayed.' He introduced me to Mr Fripp, and Nola and I smiled at each other as if we were friends. I sat beside Cedric and when I passed him the coat check ticket beneath the table, he smiled again.

'I can't stay long,' I said, and was about to proffer an excuse when I saw Cedric's face change. He half rose out of his chair and his eyes seemed to flicker.

'You—' Cedric sat down again.

I turned. Simon stood by the table watching Cedric with anger and more than a hint of bitterness in his eyes. Again I felt that single, painful thud in my chest. Without even realising I had arisen from the table, I found myself standing beside Simon, my arm brushing his, allying myself with him against the others.

Cedric frowned. 'This is a private party, Dr Levy.' He flicked me a look of fury. 'Sit down, Celia. You're making a fool of yourself.'

The planes above us were very low now and very loud. A bomb landed nearby and the cutlery on the table shook.

'It's madness,' said Simon, in his deceptively light manner, 'to try to stab a man through a greatcoat, a tunic and a shirt. But he's not the smartest of assassins, is he?'

'Who?' asked Cedric.

'Your man. Hollis.'

My mouth was very dry. I tried to make sense of what Simon had said. It made no sense. And then I realised.

'Eddie Hollis,' I said, in a choking voice that I barely recognised as mine. 'Cedric asked Eddie to kill you?'

'Yes,' said Simon. 'And he botched it. And now he's with the police, who were happy to hear about your husband's orders to murder me and his threats towards an eight-year-old child this afternoon and his assault on you. And his unlicensed gun.'

I swung around to him, clutching his arm. 'Are you all right?'

'He barely touched me.'

Cedric looked bored. 'I have no idea what you're talking about. Did Eddie say that I asked him to hurt you? It's nonsense. I don't like you, but...' He lifted his shoulder in a dismissive shrug.

'You told me you were going to kill Simon,' I said.

'I was angry. It was a meaningless angry threat.'

'But Eddie would have assumed it was an order.' My voice was high, incredulous. 'You know that, Cedric. Did you say it to him? Did you tell him you wanted Simon dead?'

A bomb landed nearby with a thundering crash and the room seemed to clench like a fist. A fork fell to the floor with a clatter and, as if released from a spell of immobility, the others at the table began to stir. Archie and Isolde exchanged glances and rose, murmuring excuses. Mr Fripp dragged Nola up with him, saying in a prissy voice, 'Well. It's been a fascinating evening, Mr Ashwin, but we must be running along.'

In a minute the four of them were gone, practically running up the stairs to the foyer. How ironic, I thought later, that such social cowardice probably saved their lives.

Cedric was looking at Simon now with undisguised loathing. He said to me, 'Celia, sit down at once. You're making a fool of yourself, clinging to that—'

Clinging? It was only then that I realised I had Simon's arm in a tight grip. It didn't seem to bother Simon, and I didn't let go.

Behind me, on the stage, Snakehips and the band had begun a jazz number. The music swelled and Snakehips sang, 'Oh, Johnny—'

There was a blinding blue flash, then a deafening roar. Everything went dark as the world exploded and I was blown backwards off my feet. There was a second flash and a second explosion and I went back further. Something landed on top of my chest and shoulder, something very heavy but chillingly soft.

For a second, the world held its breath. Then the silence was shattered by groans and shrieks and voices calling out in fear. I felt disoriented, lonely and lost in the darkness. The air was thick and choking with dust and smoke and the smell of cordite, and beneath it all, the sweetly sour smell of fresh blood. Something wet was trickling down my neck. People crawled around me, knocked whatever was on top of me. It was large and heavy and pinned me down from my chest to my lower legs.

I pushed ineffectively at whatever it was that was crushing me, but I seemed to have no strength in my arms. 'Simon,' I cried out, 'Simon, where are you?' It was a second or so later I realised that I had said nothing. Everything had slowed. I closed my eyes and began to drift, slowly, as if in a pool of thick treacle.

Someone trod on my hand and the pain drew me back sharply into consciousness. '*I'm not dead,*' I thought, with some surprise. And then I remembered what had happened. It was difficult to breathe in the smoky, dusty air, but I called out his name. 'Simon. Simon, where are you?' My voice was merely one of many in the darkness. Around me others sobbed and moaned and cried out names and supplications to God.

I pushed again at whatever was pressing down on me, but it didn't move. I now suspected it was a human body, but I couldn't be sure if it was dead or merely unconscious. *Oh, God,* I prayed. *Don't let it be Simon. Don't let him be dead.*

'Help,' I called. 'Help me.' I gulped in air and pushed at the body pressing down on me. I felt it shift, but not enough to release me. My head ached, every part of me ached, and I felt weak and shaky, flattened by the dead weight on top of me. Surely it was too heavy to be Simon. *It couldn't be Simon.* He had to be alive, because I had to tell him what I now knew, that there was more than something between us, there was *everything* between us. I had to tell him that I loved him in every way that the Greeks could describe that emotion.

I pushed again at the weight above me and it seemed to give a little, but not enough to allow me to slide out from underneath it.

'Help,' I screamed. 'Help me.'

Little lights had begun to move about in the darkness. Tiny will-o-the-wisp flames of cigarette lighters and matches, slim beams of pencil torches and a few brighter lights that I thought were flash lamps. One of these came close and hovered over me.

'You all right?' It was a man's voice.

'I need to get out from under—'

I stopped, rendered mute, because the lamp had moved away from my face to reveal that the headless torso of a black musician was lying across me. The lamp abruptly went out and I heard the sound of retching. A wave of mindless panic engulfed me and I pushed in desperation at the body. It barely moved.

I gathered my thoughts, forced myself to accept the horror of my situation. I'd seen sights as terrible in my months as an ambulance driver. *It's just a body. I can cope with bodies.*

So I called out to my unknown rescuer, in what I hoped was a bracing voice, 'You can do that later. Right now I need him off me. *Right now*, please!'

'Sorry,' he mumbled, in a now raspy voice. 'I'm so sorry. It's the shock, seeing him like that.'

The lamp flicked on again. When he put it down to help me it illuminated the front of the corpse, lit up the shiny buttons of the white jacket the dead man was wearing. I had a sudden vision of the band, dressed in matching white suits with those shiny buttons, as they played with verve on the stage. All smiling. Not more than fifteen minutes ago, I thought, this man had been up there, making music and smiling. My neck was wet and sticky with what I now knew was the musician's blood. I swallowed convulsively as saliva filled my mouth, refusing to give into nausea. A distraction came when my rescuer said 'Push.'

I pushed as hard as I could, and he pulled.

'It's moving,' he said, and I felt the weight on top of me lessen. 'See if you can slide out from underneath.'

I gave a desperate, scissoring thrust with my legs and at last I was free. I lay still for a few seconds, sucking in the dusty air and shivering at the horror of it all.

My rescuer helped me to stand up. 'Are you injured?'

'No. I'm fine.'

'Then I'll carry on looking for survivors,'

'Wait! Have you seen a doctor? Not for me. He – he was with me when the bombs hit. He'd be helping if he could.'

'It's a shambles down here. I'm sorry.'

Heavy footsteps were on the staircase. Rescue workers had arrived. I stood still, waiting as they set up arc lights, and then began my search for Simon. As the area became illuminated the full hideousness of the scene was apparent. In the past six months of the Blitz I had become used to horrific sights, but what I saw as I stumbled forward turned me cold. The Café de Paris looked like a charnel house. The walls and the mirrors lining the staircase were splattered with blood. Tables and chairs, bodies and body parts were scattered across the room.

I scrambled over debris, frantic now and praying with incoherent desperation that Simon had been spared. I saw the corner of the stage and used it to orientate myself, to work out where the table had been. And then I saw it, upturned, with two men beside it. Cedric was lying unconscious on the floor. His face was black from the blast and his clothing was drenched in blood and his breathing appeared to be laboured. Simon's face was also blast-blackened and his uniform bloodstained. He was kneeling beside Cedric and applying pressure to his brachial artery.

I think I cried out, said something as I stumbled towards them. Simon glanced up, saw me, and seemed about to speak. Instead he just looked at me. It was the look Jim had given Lily as she came towards him in the register office. It was a look I'd waited a lifetime for.

'You're late,' he said, when I reached him. His voice trembled. 'Spent a decade or so hoping you'd arrive in one piece.'

'Sorry. Got held up ... or pushed down, if one wants to be crass about it.'

'Not your blood, then?' He had reverted to his usual offhand tones.

When I glanced down, I saw that the bodice of my silk gown was a mess of dried blood. I thrust away nausea, gulping in air and swallowing convulsively.

When I could speak, 'No, not my blood.' I gestured at his bloodstained tunic. 'Not yours, then?'

'No. I'm fine.' He glanced at Cedric. 'His blood.'

Simon's hand was keeping a firm pressure on Cedric's artery and thus keeping him alive.

'You do know who that is,' I said.

At that he almost smiled. 'Of course I do. My patient.'

I looked at Simon, desperately trying to save the life of Cedric Ashwin, a man he detested. Simon knew that Cedric would happily see him dead, and yet he would fight his hardest to keep Cedric alive. I felt again that strange, sweet, painful thud in my chest.

Simon's gaze fell to examine my evening gown. 'I hope you're not partial to that frock. It's badly stained and bloodstains are devilishly hard to remove.'

'What—?'

'Sorry, blethering. I need a bandage to try to stop this bleeding. Could you lop off an inch or so off the bottom? If you reach into my breast pocket I've some little scissors.'

I reached into the pocket of his tunic, just over his heart, and found a small leather pouch. When I flipped it open it had scissors, tweezers and a tiny scalpel. I looked at Simon and raised an eyebrow.

'Always prepared,' he said. 'Like a boy scout.'

The little scissors were sharp. I cut the fabric and tore off a two-inch strip. Three more strips and the frock finished above my knees. Then I started on my silk slip, which gave me another four strips. I held up the makeshift bandages.

'Stout fella,' said Simon. 'Let's change places.'

I held my hand over the throbbing artery in Cedric's arm while Simon packed the wound and bandaged it.

Cedric's eyes fluttered open. He seemed to want to speak, so I leant closer.

'Bit of a mess,' he said. His breathing was laboured and his voice rasping.

'You'll be fine,' I said in the sort of bracing voice I used in my ambulance.

'Looks like … no need for divorce.' I began to remonstrate, but he shook his head. He glanced up at Simon, who had moved away to give us some privacy. Cedric glanced at him, then back to me. 'Told me—' he sucked in shallow breath. 'He told me … was keeping me alive … just to annoy me.' His chest moved in a silent laugh.

That sounded like Simon. I smiled.

'He's a good man, Cedric. You rest now. Save your strength.'

'Think … think I might die anyway.' He gave another choked laugh. 'Just to annoy *him*.' When he looked at me his pale eyes seemed clouded. He clutched at my hand. 'Only ever wanted the best … for this country. Shame I didn't see…'

'Didn't see what?' I said gently, but he had lapsed again into unconsciousness.

'Need a stretcher?' Two ambulance officers had arrived. The man glanced at the caduceus on Simon's shoulder. 'Any instructions, sir?' he asked.

Simon stood up. 'Patient's name is Cedric Ashwin. He has a ruptured brachial artery and has lost a lot of blood. It's a make-do sort of bandage, so take care with the wound. I'm also worried about blast lung because his breathing appears to be compromised. Where are you taking him?'

'Charing Cross hospital. The dead go to the Rialto Cinema next door.'

'Let me help you lift him,' said Simon. With great care, he and the man lifted Cedric on to the stretcher.

As they did so I asked his female attendant which station they were from.

'Number forty-one, in Bruton Mews. It's been quite a night. Buckingham Palace was hit again. And there was a frightful incident at Garland's Hotel in Suffolk Street.' Her voice shook. 'This is the worst, though. I've never seen anything like this.'

'New to the job, are you?' I asked. I *had* seen incidents as bad, and the realisation made me feel old and tired.

She didn't answer. Instead she took her end of the stretcher. She and the man hoisted it and left with Cedric, picking their way carefully over the debris still scattered across the floor.

I turned to Simon, who was looking at the carnage that surrounded us. His features might be hidden under the layer of soot and blood, but nothing could disguise his air of self-command and purpose, the quiet and unassuming dignity with which he surveyed the devastation to see if anyone else needed his help.

*It is your innate kindness that defines you*, I thought.

He turned, caught my eye and gave me a puzzled smile. 'What? What's that look?'

'You do know that I love you, Simon. So very, very much. More than anyone, ever.'

Simon's expression became at once bashful and exultant. 'I had an inkling. I love you too, of course. Have done since … probably for ever. Seems like for ever.'

He rubbed at his blackened face and flicked another glance around the room. 'Not the time to discuss it, though.' I thought he looked ready to collapse, but he said, 'I want to stay a bit longer down here. See if I can help.'

I reached out to touch his arm, felt the wool of his tunic, gloried in the fact that he was alive and I was alive and we were together.

'Of course you do,' I said.

Simon ran a finger gently down my cheek. 'You should go home. You look done in.'

'Chance would be a fine thing. Not while I can help, and not without you.'

We walked towards the wrecked stage, where the Incident Officer seemed to be giving instructions. I slipped on a patch of liquid and stumbled over a body, a young man in a RAF uniform, who groaned. Blood had pooled on the floor under his head.

'Dead men don't groan,' said Simon. 'Let's take a look at him.'

Simon knelt beside the body, oblivious to the bloody floor, and shone his torch at the man's head. He grunted when the deep penetrating head wound was revealed.

'The rescue workers must have overlooked him,' I said, and handed over a couple of the strips I'd cut from my silk dress. Simon folded one into a pad and used the other to bandage it in place. He stood, looked around, called a stretcher party over and told them off for missing the man.

'It's a bloody shambles in here,' the man said. 'He seemed to be dead.'

'Dead don't bleed. He was dripping blood.'

After that, Simon insisted on checking every body we saw, of course. I was happy just to be with him and followed him around like a puppy, until we were both stumbling with fatigue.

Time seemed to have shifted, stretched. There was always more to do, more patients to see, more people to declare dead.

I was not the only woman that night who cut up her evening dress for bandages and Simon was not the only person there to continue beyond the limits of endurance. The lower floor was filled with firemen, wardens, nurses, first-aid workers, doctors, stretcher-bearers, police and others, giving what they could to help those who could be helped and deal fittingly with those who couldn't. But with the heights come the depths. I began to notice men running around and bending over the dead, sometimes over the wounded. At first I thought they were listening for a heartbeat, but when I saw one of them pocket a wallet, I realised they had come in from the street and were looting.

I jumped up and ran over to the man, grabbed his arm, and called out, 'Here's a thief.' He shook off my hold and disappeared into the gloom before anyone could help me.

'Sorry I wasn't fast enough, miss. Where'd he go?' A policeman, a big man with tired eyes, had appeared beside me.

'Over there.' I pointed into a gloomy corner beyond the pillars.

'They're like rats, these Soho thugs. They scurry away into the dark. What'd he take?'

'A wallet, from that man there.' I pointed to the corpse.

'They've done worse than that,' he said, and rubbed at his eyes. 'It's impossible with the dead, the injured, the firemen and wardens and everyone everywhere down here, it's impossible for us to know who's who. Easy for them to snap off a necklace, cut away a finger for its ring.' He silenced my exclamation with, 'It's awful, of course it is. This is my beat and nothing surprises me here. But, miss, you have to remember that the Soho rats are outnumbered – far outnumbered, down here – by those who just want to help. Like your young man there, and that nurse.'

The policeman pointed to Simon, who was helping a nursing sister to bandage a woman's leg wound. *My young man.*

'Where did you get the bandages?' I asked the sister.

'They're field dressings. Got them from the Scots Guard soldiers who've cordoned off the entrance. They're trying to keep out looters and hold back the crowd.'

'Crowd?'

'Ghouls,' she said, dismissively. 'Watching the smart set come out with their finery in tatters.'

Eventually, Simon realised that exhaustion was making him a liability to the rescue efforts. We clung to each other as we ascended the staircase to the lobby where we rifled through the cloakroom for our coats. It seemed a long way up the stairs to the entrance. We pushed aside the curtain and, at last, escaped into the night.

Far above London the moon was tranquil and almost unbearably beautiful. When I looked back, the untouched doorway to the Café de Paris was clearly illuminated by moonlight. It gave not a hint of the horror inside. The air raid had ceased, but the inevitable fires had taken hold and we stood in a pink landscape that changed every so often to a throbbing red, like arterial blood. The acrid smell of smoke was thick around us. A morbid crowd had indeed gathered outside in the chilly darkness, and their faces shone white in the moonlight. The cordon of Scots Guards kept them back.

Simon and I slipped through the cordon and entered the crowd. We used our elbows to force our way through and we tottered along Coventry Street until we reached Leicester Square. There we clung to each other in silence. When I lifted up my head, Simon kissed me. He tasted of ash and dust and blood, and I gripped him with a fierce energy that belied my exhaustion. Eventually, we pulled apart and stood, just looking at each other in the ruddy firelight.

'We'll never find a cab,' he said, in his careless way.

'Shanks's pony then.'

He gave me a smile and kissed me again, hard and quick. Then he put his arm around my shoulder and wheeled us both around, so we were facing up Wardour Street. And we began our long trek home to Bloomsbury.

# CHAPTER THIRTY

We arrived at St Andrew's Court with the dawn. Albert gave us a look that was so astonished it was almost comical. I could understand why. Simon's uniform was filthy and bloodstained, his face was blast-blackened and a crusty-brown rivulet of dried blood ran from his forehead to his chin. I knew my face was also black with blast, plaster had whitened my hair and under my coat my silk evening gown had been lopped off until it reached an inch or so above my grubby knees.

'We've been at an incident,' I said, in my most imperious tones. 'I've offered Dr Levy a bath.'

Simon brushed at his uniform and rubbed at his face. 'Which is much needed,' he said. Albert gave him a grin in reply.

When we arrived at my flat Simon took off his tunic, hung it on the back of a chair and sat on the sofa in his shirtsleeves.

'You have first bath,' he said.

I opened my mouth to protest, when he cut across me. 'Don't even begin to be unctuously polite and suggest that I must bathe before you. Because I'll be fine, sitting here on your ludicrously comfortable sofa until you've finished. And, frankly my dear, you stink.' He yawned.

I blew him a kiss and went into the bathroom. While the water filled the tub to the regulation five inches, I peeled off my dirty, blood-soaked clothes and dropped them on the floor. Then I slipped into the hot water with a moan of utter bliss. I wasn't satisfied until I had scrubbed my entire body and washed my hair. I drained the now black bathwater, refilled the bath and climbed in again. Only then did I feel clean and only then did I relax. I poured in a heady concentration of bath oil – Simon's remark about my odour rankled – and luxuriated for ten minutes or so until guilt about Simon got the better of me.

When I climbed out I was scented with attar of roses. I left the water in, as I thought Simon could use it as a first wash, and then refill with fresh water as I had done. I combed my wet hair back from my forehead and when I checked my reflection I thought I'd pass muster, even if my right cheek was discoloured by Cedric's bruise.

*Cedric.* The events of the past day flooded into my mind. Had Cedric really intended to kill Leo, or was it merely a drunken show of strength to punish me? He had asked Eddie to kill Simon. Or had Eddie misunderstood what was simply a muttered, meaningless threat? Was Cedric still alive? I didn't want freedom from the marriage by his death and I smiled to think of Simon telling Cedric that he would keep him alive to spite him. No. Divorce was my way out of the marriage. Cedric would have to agree. I would make him agree.

I made an entrance, wafting into the sitting room in my best silk pyjamas on a cloud of attar of roses. Simon was fast asleep on the sofa, lying on his side in an uncomfortable-looking half-crouch. He didn't wake when I removed his shoes and lifted his legs up so that he was lying along the sofa. I went into my bedroom and pulled a couple of pillows off the bed along with my bedspread. I returned to Simon, gently lifted his head on to one of the pillows, and dropped a rug over him. I put the other pillow on the floor by the sofa, wrapped myself in the bedspread and fell asleep on the floor beside him, listening to him breathe.

I awoke some hours later, swimming up from a pleasant dream that slipped away as I drifted back to consciousness. I had the impression that Tom and David and Nanny had been in it, all smiling and happy in the bluebell glade beside the river. I lay for a minute or so, disorientated, then realised I was lying in my bed, under my bedspread. The sound of running water was not the river, but was coming from the bathroom and was accompanied by splashing. It seemed that Simon was washing away the grime of the night before. I lay still, listening sleepily, enjoying the sounds and the relaxed warmth of my body. The bathwater was let out. Then came soft splashing sounds and softer swearing. I could only assume that Simon was using my razor, the one I used for my legs, to shave his face. I drifted back into a doze and woke at a soft knock on my bedroom door.

'Come in,' I said.

I turned sleepy eyes towards the door. It opened to reveal Simon standing in the doorway with a cup of tea. His hair was wet and there were spots of blood on his cheeks from a hasty attempt at shaving. He was wearing his uniform.

He walked across and put the cup and saucer on the bedside table. When he sat on the bed it heaved drunkenly under his weight.

'I hauled you over from the sitting room,' he said. 'Thought you'd be more comfortable here. Feeling better?'

'Better for seeing you,' I said. 'You've dressed. Your uniform must be in a state. I was going to sponge it for you.'

'I sponged the uniform myself,' he said. 'Ruined one of your flannels. Sorry.' He tilted his head up to look at the ceiling. 'I thought it would be – safer – if I was dressed. I really am crazy about you, Celia. I love you and I want you, but not when you're still married—'

'To Cedric Ashwin,' I finished bitterly.

He shook his head. 'To anyone.' He said, in his cool way, as if it didn't matter, 'Call me old-fashioned. Let's wait for the divorce.'

'Simon...' I began, and stopped, unsure of how to tell him what he needed to know. 'I think we must talk about David.'

He became very still, and a fluttering pulse began to throb in his neck, but he said nothing.

'David changed everything for me,' I said, haltingly. 'I had always thought I was stupid, but David refused to believe that. He – he taught me so much. In many ways I was still so young, unformed, unsure of almost everything, and David forced me to think for myself, to be more than I had been.' I hesitated, plucking at the sheets, my face flaming. There was no nice way of putting it. 'It was more than that, though. Cedric had led me to believe that I was – was frigid. But David...'

'Proved you weren't?' Simon put in dryly.

'Yes.' I reached out and took his hand. He flinched when I did so, and I became very still. 'Does it matter so much?'

Simon looked down at the rumpled sheets. David had never been to my flat, but he couldn't know that.

'He was my brother, Celia. Of course it matters.'

'I was infatuated with David. How I feel about you – it's entirely different. It's so much more than anything I've felt before.'

Simon sucked in a shuddering breath, then looked up and gave me a slight, twisted smile. 'When I first met you I was surprised at how young you seemed. I knew nothing about you, really, except that you were married to Cedric Ashwin and you had had an affair with my brother and treated my parents shamefully. I'd expected—'

'A *femme fatale*?'

His smile became less forced. 'Yes. I'd expected a shallow sophisticate who had ensnared my brother with her beauty.'

'And you found me.'

'I found *you*. A frightened girl trapped in a ruined house and a loveless marriage, tormented by the deaths of those you loved, including my brother. Facing what life threw at you with understated, possibly unconscious, bravery. You were nothing at all what I had expected.' His face softened. 'You were so much more.'

He leaned across, cupped my face between his hands and kissed me in an intense, almost furious way. He released me and leaned back on his elbow, looking at me. The give-away was his breathing, faster than usual. 'And I fell in love with you.'

'I do love you, Simon,' I said. 'More than *anyone*, ever.'

He smiled at me, stood, and walked to the doorway. 'We'll make it work. Somehow we will make it work. But right now, I must be off. I'm due at the hospital in...' He looked at his watch. 'God, in fifteen minutes.' He ducked out of the door.

I lay, thinking about what he had said. Hardly daring to believe it.

Simon came in again, walked over to the bed and bent down to me. Again he kissed me, making my senses whirl and my heart race. When he pulled away he gave me his infectious smile. 'My family will hate this.'

'No more than mine will.'

'A plague on both our houses. We'll work it out somehow.'

And then he really did leave the flat.

I went back to sleep, but this time I had the first of many nightmares about the Café de Paris bombing. The dream shifted abruptly into the scene in my flat when Cedric threatened Leo. I woke when someone cried out. It took me a few seconds to realise it had been me.

The horror of the nightmare had vanished and now I felt invigorated. Simon loved me and we would work it out somehow. There was no point worrying about how this would be achieved, I told myself; I just had to believe that it would.

It was ten o'clock and I was very hungry. The hour was long past breakfast but too early for lunch, but I thought I could sweet talk the cook in the service restaurant into giving me at least some bread and margarine. I also had to telephone Jack Moray at the Ambulance Station to explain my absence.

In the kitchen, my luck held. Agnes, the cook, took pity on me and gave me a late breakfast, saying, 'I wouldn't do this for everyone, miss, but I do admire you ambulance drivers.'

Feeling refreshed after three cups of tea and a decent breakfast I left the dining room and headed for the telephone booth in the foyer. Albert caught me before I picked up the receiver. He had a worried expression and was carrying a telegram.

'Mrs Ashwin,' he said hesitantly, 'this arrived a few minutes ago.' He shoved the envelope at me. 'I do hope it's not bad news.'

I thanked him, took the envelope and pulled out the flimsy telegram paper. It had been sent earlier that morning. Its message was short and simple and changed everything:

REGRET TO INFORM YOU CEDRIC DIED THIS MORNING CHARING CROSS HOSPITAL STOP HORACE ASHWIN

Horace Ashwin was my father-in-law.

# CHAPTER THIRTY-ONE

Cedric's funeral took place a week later. I remember little about it, except that he was buried in the rain. I had thought that I wouldn't cry, but as the coffin was lowered into the wet earth, I did cry. My tears mingled with the raindrops on my face as I thought about what Cedric could have been, but wasn't. I wept to think of all the wasted potential of that charming, charismatic man who had chosen to follow his dream of what Britain should be, even after the Nazis' subjugation of Europe had shown so clearly that the dream was in fact a nightmare.

In the following weeks Cedric was proved wrong. The German invasion did not come with the spring, or indeed at all. As Hitler's army became embroiled in the Balkan and North African campaigns, we shelved our fear of invasion and got down to the business of coping with yet more air raids.

As I had feared, Mrs Levy's attitude towards me cooled after she heard of Cedric's Gestapo-like behaviour towards Leo, and Eddie Hollis's attack on Simon. Also, I suspected, because Simon had told her about our romance. She found an excuse to prevent Leo from visiting my flat on the Saturday after Cedric's death.

'Really, Celia,' Lore Rosenfeld said, when I turned up at Bloomsbury House the following week, 'you cannot expect her to be pleased about Simon announcing he loves you. But she will come around.'

'How do *you* feel about it?'

She gave a shrug. 'I am disappointed for my Miriam, but she explained that she and Simon were only ever friends. As for Leo, the incident with your … with Cedric Ashwin has affected him badly. Many problems that Elise thought Leo had overcome have returned. Bedwetting, nightmares and such. Elise is merely trying to protect the boy by keeping him away from the place where it happened.'

'She's being a guarding dog?' I suggested.

Lore smiled. 'You remember that unfortunate phrase? Yes. Leo is one of her boys now. She will try to protect him, as fiercely as a guarding dog.'

'And Simon?'

'Simon can protect himself. He is just as strong-willed as Elise.'

It turned out that Leo, also, was very strong-willed. When I opened the door to Simon the following Saturday afternoon Leo was standing beside him. He wrapped me in a hug that squeezed the breath out of me.

'Simon said the *braunhemd* is dead,' he whispered. 'Now you are safe, Celia.'

At his appearance Bobby squawked 'Leo Weitz. God save the King', and delighted the boy with a vivid impersonation of a Heinkel engine flying low above the rooftops.

'I told Mutti I would not play my violin if I could not see you and Celia,' Leo informed Bobby, once the bird was on his shoulder. 'And I would not eat.'

'He starved himself for a day,' Simon whispered. 'She gave in when he also refused breakfast the following morning. I was most impressed. If he can win a battle of wills with my mother, I predict great things for that boy.'

One afternoon, a month after Cedric's death, Simon arrived at my flat with an envelope addressed to me in spiky, old-fashioned handwriting. Inside was a letter that had been written by his grandmother, Mrs Cora Levy. She begged my attendance at a recital the following week, at the Levys' home. She also wrote that she wished to discuss 'a matter of importance' with me. I looked at Simon and raised an eyebrow.

322

'Why would your grandmother want to see me?'

He shrugged. 'I think you made quite an impression on her when she met you.'

'But will your mother be happy if I come?'

'If my grandmother wants to speak to you, she'll do it eventually. She's formidable. I think my mother accepts that.' He smiled. 'Besides, Leo talks of you and Bobby all the time.' He gave me a quick grin. 'Mainly talks about Bobby, but often refers to you as well.'

I laughed. 'That puts me in my place.'

'She knows he'll be devastated if you don't hear him play.'

'I'll come, then. And I'll bring Bobby. It's time he went to Leo for good, actually.'

Simon lifted the viola to his shoulder with a practised ease and looked at his mother, who was seated in front of the piano. He lifted his bow and began with a flourish. The piano supported him and picked up on the tune. Then Leo joined in with his violin and the entire piece soared. Simon barely kept pace as the instruments flowed in and between each other. Leo's talent was obvious.

I thought there was a sublime innocence to the piece. In it, Mozart seemed to describe friends coming together to make music and enjoy each other's company. Leo's playing picked this up, toyed with it and, I thought, transmuted it into a longing for loved ones not present but not forgotten. I watched his face as he played and I knew that he had left the Levys' drawing room and in his mind was somewhere else, somewhere beautiful where no one could touch him. His own bluebell glade, made of music.

The piece finished with a note that seemed to linger. After a second's silence we clapped furiously. Bobby, who had been listening from his cage in the corner, gave a loud whistle and clicked his beak. Everyone laughed.

Leo, flushed with his success, put down the violin carefully on a chair and ran to Elise Levy to give her a hug and be told how wonderfully he played. Leo then ran to me and clambered on to my lap.

'Were we excellent?' he whispered.

'You were all wonderful, but the violin was my favourite. You played marvellously.'

Leo gave a sigh of pure joy and announced to the room, as if it was the last word on the subject, 'Celia says I was the best.'

Mrs Levy's lips tightened. 'Over here, Leo. Come and have something to eat, *hertzchen*.'

Leo patted my cheek, clambered off my lap and returned to Mrs Levy, who handed him a plate piled with food. I suspected it was to keep him firmly by her side. I looked up and caught Simon's eye. He gave me a wry smile. Elise Levy had made it plain, in an exquisitely mannered way, that she did not approve of me at all and wished I'd never arrived at the recital.

I sat quietly, watching Leo as Mrs Levy fussed over him, wishing he was back with me, on my lap and chattering in his precise English. I looked away to scan the room. It seemed that Simon's grandmother had disappeared. Mrs Cora Levy had greeted me warmly when I arrived. Then she had terrified me by reminding me that she wished to speak to me later.

Lore Rosenfeld was also there, with her husband and with Miriam. She had greeted me warmly with a quick hug, kissed my cheeks and introduced me to her husband as 'the invaluable Celia'. When she went on to say, 'I don't know how I could cope without her in the office,' I had demurred.

Lore had smiled. 'It's true. I am so happy you still work with me.' Then she had glanced at Elise Levy.

Simon brought a plate of food and sat next to me, ignoring his mother's cool look as he did so.

'Miriam looks happy,' I said.

'She's told them about Antoni and they've met him. He agreed that any children may be raised as Jews, and they've agreed to the marriage.' He gave his lazy shrug. 'Under Jewish law, any children born to a Jewish mother are automatically

324

Jewish. But it is important to the Rosenfelds that they are raised in the faith.'

'I'm so glad for Lore. And for Miriam.' I looked at him. 'Only a Jewish mother? What about children with a Jewish father and a Gentile mother?'

He frowned. 'The Nazis think that one Jewish grandparent makes you a Jew. But under traditional Jewish law – the *halacha* – Jewishness is passed down through the mother. So, it's only if your mother is Jewish, that you are too.'

He must have seen something in my face, because he took my hand and said, in an urgent whisper, 'It doesn't matter to me. Really, Celia. None of that matters to me.'

'Celia.'

I started, then realised that Mrs Levy had come across to stand by us, leaning heavily on the stick she now used instead of crutches. 'My mother-in-law wishes to speak to you in the library,' she said. 'I will take you to her.'

'Thank you,' I said. Simon squeezed my hand as I stood, and Mrs Levy frowned at him. *Head high, walk tall.*

When I was alone in the corridor with Elise Levy she looked me straight in the eye and frowned. 'I believed that you wanted to atone for your actions after David's death. And so I accepted you into my children's charity. Now I am expected to accept you into my home, perhaps into my family? I cannot do it, Celia.'

'I am very sorry to hear that.'

She raised her hand, as if to block the sight of me. 'Seeing you distresses me. You are here today at my mother-in-law's insistence. But also Leo wanted you here, and Simon.' Her voice rose. 'And Jonathan. And Lore Rosenfeld. They are all against me on this. You and Simon, it's—' She dashed away a tear and straightened her back. 'Have you heard of Lilith?'

'No.'

'There is a legend that Adam had a first wife, before Eve. A red-haired demon who now enters into men's dreams and tempts them to sin.'

I stared at her, appalled. 'And that is how you see me? As a demon?'

She shook her head, dabbed a handkerchief to her eyes. 'I don't know – I don't know what to think of you. First you and David. And now my Simon. You bewitched both my boys. How can I approve of this?'

I stopped walking and turned to her. Tried to think of what to say, but my brain seemed woolly. I blurted out, 'You think I'm the very worst person for Simon to love? Is that what you mean? Because I'm not Jewish, and I was married to Cedric Ashwin, and – and because David and I…' I sucked in a breath and said more calmly, 'What you're saying is that you'll never accept me and Simon.'

Mrs Levy shook her head, seemed troubled. 'You were very young when you married Cedric Ashwin. Simon explained that. And he gave us some idea of how difficult your life was with that man. Although I would greatly prefer Simon to marry a Jewish girl, it is not the most important thing. *Who* he marries is the most important thing. And you are not who I would wish…'

I said, woodenly, 'You think I'm not good enough for Simon?'

What could I say to that? I was inclined to agree.

She didn't answer. Instead, she drew in a quick deep breath and seemed to collect herself. Her voice became brisk. 'This is the library.' She knocked on the door, then opened it and ushered me in.

In a chair by the window Mrs Cora Levy was sitting. She looked me up and down as I entered, and nodded.

'Leave us please, Elise. I will talk to the girl alone.' Mrs Levy was dismissed with a wave of the hand.

When the door closed behind her, Cora Levy gave me a searching look. 'You are very lovely, my dear. I can see why Simon – but tell me, how is your grandmother? I knew her quite well when she was a girl.'

'Which grandmother?' I wondered how this fierce little Jewish matriarch could have met either of my grandmothers.

'Your mother's mother. She was Célia Bernard when I met her in Toulouse. That would have been in… in 1875, I think.'

'Grandmère usually lives in Hampstead, but has moved to Cornwall for the duration. However did you meet her?' I was bemused that Simon's grandmother might know my French grandmother.

'I met her when I was visiting relatives in the area. We were both fourteen and girls have intense friendships at that age. Cesia – we all knew her as Cesia – was such a pretty girl, full of mischief.'

'Grandmère doesn't speak much about her family. All we know is that they were Huguenots who had textile mills in Toulouse.'

'Yes. Her family owned textile mills there.' She shook her head. 'They were not Huguenots.'

'I don't understand.'

'Cesia's family was Jewish.'

I became very still. 'You think my grandmother is Jewish?' I smiled politely. 'I'm afraid you are mistaken.'

'I met her in synagogue. They were not a very religious family, but the Bernards celebrated the traditional holidays. I remember it well. It was *Yom Kippur*. Cesia and I became fast friends and corresponded regularly after my return to England.'

When the old lady looked at me I was put in mind of Bobby's ferocious little yellow eyes.

'You really look nothing like her,' she said accusingly.

'I take after my father.' Again I shook my head. 'I know nothing about a Jewish family connection.'

'Oh, I'm sure it was never mentioned once Cesia arrived in England. Her parents died soon after her marriage and she was an only child. She knew no one in this country but me, and she wrote as soon as she arrived to ask me not to reveal her origins. It seems that her husband wished her to forget about them. Cesia never saw me or wrote to me again, and she soon moved in circles far distant to mine. I didn't care. By then I had my own family to concern me.' The old lady smiled. 'I had no idea that she had concocted the Huguenot story. How silly. The Huguenots left the area a long time before she was born.'

'But she's a staunch Protestant.' My mind was whirling with memories of attending Christmas Day services with my little French grandmère, who was so very devout.

'Cesia was always thorough. I have no doubt that she is a Christian now. But her family were Jewish. She is Jewish. She cannot deny it.' Her smile became ever so slightly malicious. 'If she tries to deny it, tell her I kept the letters.'

'So you can prove it?' I laughed, a trifle hysterically. 'I'm sure Father had no idea. Perhaps Mummy does, but if so she never revealed it, not even when Father was so horribly disparaging about... Or when Cedric...' I looked up at the old woman. 'You've told me this for a reason.'

'So you know the truth. Your mother's mother is Jewish, your mother is Jewish, and so are you.'

I shook my head. 'I'm a Christian. I was baptised and confirmed in the Church of England.'

She made a dismissive gesture. 'You are Jewish by blood, by law.'

I felt a sense of unreality. Helen would be furious to know that the Jews she so despised counted her as one of their own. One Jewish grandmother. If Helen and I were now in France, then Hitler would have arrested us and made us wear yellow stars of David.

'Mrs Levy – I don't understand. Simon said...' I hesitated. 'What does it really mean?'

'That you are Jewish. Your children will also be Jewish. Use that information as you will. I will tell no one unless you wish me to. Simon isn't devout, but of course that may change as he gets older. It often does.'

I wanted to respond but I couldn't. Instead I just sat, gaping at her.

'The heart leads where it will,' she said. 'Elise will come around to the idea eventually.'

Mrs Cora Levy kept her word. When Simon asked me to marry him two weeks later, he had no idea of my grandmother's Jewish background. I told him, just before our wedding in September 1941, and he said it made no difference whatsoever, but I think he was pleased to learn that I was – albeit unwittingly – part of his tribe.

Helen wasn't in the least happy to hear of it. Nor was she happy to learn that I was to marry Simon a mere six months after Cedric's death. It was her husband, Roly, who silenced her objections in an unusual show of defiance.

'I know his father, Jonathan Levy,' he had thundered, 'and he's a capital fellow. I think you should be happy for Celia. Just look at the girl. She's positively glowing. A new girl entirely.' He kissed my cheek and whispered to me, 'Young Levy's a much better husband for you than that Nazi. Much better indeed.'

My grandmère took the unmasking of her deception in her stride, and re-established the friendship with Cora Levy that had stalled more than sixty years before. When I approached my mother about it she gave one of her elegant shrugs. 'Of course I knew of my mother's background,' she told me, as she settled her ermine stole more securely over her shoulder. 'Quite frankly, I never saw a reason to mention it, not to you children, or to your father. What would you like as a wedding present? Silverware?'

I gave her a considering look. My mother had exquisite taste in clothes and was always beautifully and expensively dressed. 'What I'd really like, Mummy, is fabric for a pretty dress. One of your old evening gowns?'

She smiled, and I found myself hoping that I'd inherited her bone structure. She was remarkably beautiful still, her hair dark and glossy and her complexion pale and flawless. 'And my veil?' she asked.

'Probably too fussy. It's to be a registry wedding. Simon's not devout and I'm only Jewish by blood, not faith. We thought a registry wedding was the thing to do.'

'Thank God. I assumed a synagogue and dreaded the thought. I'd be a duck out of water in a synagogue, and I do so hate feeling ill at ease.'

I doubted my supremely confident mother could ever be ill at ease.

'You'll need to get used to it,' I said, 'because, although I'm not intending to convert, the children will be raised as Jewish.'

She shrugged. 'Darling, I couldn't care less. The mere thought of grandchildren is horrifying enough and I don't intend to waste any concern about how they will be raised.' She laughed. 'Don't worry. I'm sure I'll dote on them when they arrive. One of my old frocks?' She seemed to consider the matter. 'I have a pretty silk jersey frock with a bolero that could be reworked quite nicely for you. It would be perfect for a simple wedding outfit.'

In the months leading up to the wedding, Elise Levy's attitude towards me remained cool. I confided to Lore Rosenfeld my concerns about never being accepted by my future mother-in-law.

'Give Elise time,' she said with a smile, 'and – most importantly – give her a few grandchildren. All will be well. You and Simon will be very happy together and soon Elise will come to love you. You'll see.'

Lore Rosenfeld is a very wise woman. She was right, of course.

I married Simon Levy in the local register office on a warm September day in 1941. I wore a pretty day dress in cream silk jersey with a lace bolero on which was pinned a small posy of sweet peas, Simon's favourite flowers. Leo played his violin as I walked into the room. Simon was standing in front of the registrar and when he turned towards me, I thought, *Never in my life have I ever been so happy.*

And then he smiled.

# ACKNOWLEDGEMENTS

Thanks, as always, to my wonderful husband, Toby.

Thanks also to my ever-supportive Australian agent, Sheila Drummond, and Anna Carmichael in London. And to the team at Ebury Press, especially Gillian Green, Katie Seaman and Katie Sunley. Also to Justinia Baird for the lovely cover and Justine Taylor for her sympathetic editing.

Thanks to my dear friends in Perth and in Oxford – you know who you are. And to Lisa Fagin Davis. A special thank you to my Australian GP, Sue Rogers, who has always been willing to answer my medical questions in each of my novels. In this one she gave me insight into the effects of concussion and the treatment of wounds in the pre-penicillin age.

Finally, I dedicate this novel to all the men and women who gave their time and sometimes their lives, to help others in the Blitz. The word *agape* is not enough to encompass their bravery and selflessness.

# FURTHER READING

I could not have written the novel without recourse to the work done by others. As always, I acknowledge my debt to the digitised newspapers on the National Library of Australia site, Trove.nla.gov.au. And I spent many happy hours in the Bodleian Library Upper Reading Room devouring information about the Blitz. The following books stand out as invaluable:

Beardmore, George, *Civilians at War: Journals 1938–1946*, London: John Murray, 1984.

De Courcy, Anne. *1939: The Last Season*: London, Phoenix, 2003

De Courcy, Anne. *Diana Mosley*: London, Chatto & Windus, 2003

De Courcy, Anne. *Debs at War 1939–1945: How Wartime Changed Their Lives*. London: Weidenfeld & Nicolson, 2005.

Freedman, Jean R. *Whistling in the Dark: Memory and Culture in Wartime London*. Lexington: University Press of Kentucky, 1999.

Gardiner, Juliet. *The Blitz: The British Under Attack*. London: Harperpress, 2010.

Harris, Jonathan Mark and Deborah Oppenheimer. *Into the Arms of Strangers: Stories of the Kindertransport*: London, Bloomsbury, 2000

Hodgson, Vere, *Few Eggs and No Oranges: A Diary Showing How Unimportant People in London and Birmingham Lived Throughout the War Years*. London, Persephone, 1999.

Hutton, Mike. *Life in 1940s London*: Stroud, Amberley Publishing, 2003

Nicholson, Harold. *Diaries and Letters*, London: Fontana, 1969–1971.

Nixon, Barbara. *Raiders Overhead.* London: Lindsay Drummond, 1943.

Raby, Angela, *The Forgotten Service: Auxiliary Ambulance Station 39, Weymouth Mews. London.* Battle of Britain International, 1999.

Sweet, Matthew. *The West End Front: The Wartime Secrets of London's Grand Hotels.* London: Faber and Faber Ltd, 2011

Ziegler, Philip. *London at War 1939–1945.* London: Sinclair-Stevenson, 1995.

Read on for an extract from:

# AMBULANCE GIRLS

## Also by Deborah Burrows

Available now

EBURY
PRESS

# CHAPTER ONE

*Tuesday 15 October 1940*
*London*

Blood, warm and sticky, was trickling down my forehead. Something sharp must have nicked me as they pushed me through the narrow gap. Never mind, I was inside.

'Hullo,' I called out. 'Anyone there?'

The words disappeared into the darkness as my torchlight flicked over the mess of plaster, wood and debris. In the fug of soot and dust and ash, my breathing was shallow and unsatisfying, which added to the sense of impending doom that had gripped me the moment they shoved me inside.

The trickle of blood on my forehead had become exquisitely itchy. When I lifted my gloved hand to wipe it away, the leather was harsh against my skin and felt gritty. Now my face was bloody *and* dirty; I probably looked like any child's nightmare.

*Whatever was I – Lily Brennan, schoolteacher from Western Australia – doing here, crawling into the ruins of a bombed house, playing the hero, when the children were most likely already dead?*

But what could I do? Really, there was no choice.

I had arrived with my ambulance partner, David Levy, to find a familiar scene of devastation, bleached to aquatint by the moonlight. Piles of rubble stood in the middle of what had been a row of Victorian dwellings. They towered in gaunt ruin against the sky, between shapeless wrecks of masonry that showed the signs of a direct hit. Men's voices, brisk and business-like, emerged from the gloom, between whistles and the occasional shout. Short flashes of torchlight appeared and vanished in the darkness, as rescue workers sought doggedly for signs of life in the ruins.

When I emerged from the ambulance, the warden had looked me up and down as if I were a prize cow at the Royal Show. As he did so, the letters on his tin helmet had stood out brightly in the moonlight: 'ARP'. They stood for air raid precautions, and I had felt inappropriate laughter bubble up in my chest when I got a good look at him. How could this small man protect anyone from the destruction London had suffered in the past five weeks of air raids? And yet there was a quiet authority in his slow nod to me, and in the way he had then turned to throw a cryptic comment to the men standing behind him.

'She'll do; she's thin enough.'

Levy, who had come to stand beside me, laughed at that, saying, 'I think she might prefer to be described as slim.'

There had been no answering smile from the warden. Instead, he gestured at the ruins of what had been a house. 'We've got two infants buried under the rubble there,' he said. His clipped, precise voice did not at all obscure the horror of those words. 'At least one's alive – or was alive until a half-hour ago – because we've heard a baby crying. We understand they were left sheltering under a solid kitchen table before the bomb hit. Problem is, the place is just holding together. If we disturb the site too much it'll bring the rest down on top of them. It looks like someone slim – as slim as you, miss – could squeeze through. You'd need to crawl through to the kitchen at the back, find the kids and bring them out. Think you can do that?'

Levy knew I had a horror of tightly enclosed spaces. 'I'll go,' he had said. 'I'm good at squeezing through ruins. I've done it before.'

'There isn't the room. You'd never get in.' The warden sized me up with another quick glance and challenged me with his eyes.

I had always been small for my age. Even now, at twenty-five, I could still be mistaken for a schoolgirl. I always suspected that was because I had been born too early and never really caught up. I was so small when I was born that I really should have died, like the three tiny babies who had slipped away in my mother's arms in the years before I arrived in the world. And that was why my mother took one look at my little wrinkled body and turned her face from me, unwilling to engage in another losing battle for a child's life. That I survived was due to my father. He was a fighter, and he fought for me.

A woman who had helped at my birth told him the best chance to keep me alive was to carry me next to his skin, where his strong heartbeat would teach my heart to keep beating when it forgot. So Dad fashioned a pouch for his tiny joey and for two months, until I could suckle and had grown into my skin, he carried me everywhere, pressed against his heart, just as the woman had said. I was no bigger than his hand and he fed me my mother's milk from an eyedropper, like a little bird. When I was old enough to hear the story he told me that the moment he saw me he knew I would live, because he could see that I was a fighter too.

Most people cannot see that in me. Because I am small and slender people often mistakenly assume that I am fragile. Not the warden.

'I think you could get to the children,' he said to me. 'Get them out. Willing to chance it, miss?'

I had smiled and said, 'Of course.' What else could I do?

Now on my hands and knees, crawling over the rough, debris-strewn floor, I took comfort in the thought that, after five weeks of driving an ambulance in this relentless Blitz, I had learned to push fear aside when attending an incident.

Served me right for being smug. Without any warning, my torch dimmed and failed. Darkness enfolded me. My heart thumped painfully and my chest tightened. I tried to breathe my way out of the almost overwhelming panic, but my breaths were shallow and too rapid, and my thoughts would not stay still, so that I couldn't settle into a plan of action. Snatches of a song, a poem, memories of home came unbidden and left as quickly to resolve into one, dreadful realisation. *I'm entombed. I'll die here, alone in the darkness, far from home.*

Then there was anger at my own defeatist thoughts. I pushed them away and shook the torch violently, once, twice, and on the third shake it flickered back into life. As the beam strengthened I exulted in the simple fact of light.

My slow crawl began again and optimism reasserted itself. I would find the children alive and I would get us all out of here. They would probably be afraid of me, with my dirty face and goggly eye shields under the steel hat, but in my three years as a country schoolteacher I had learned how to soothe frightened children. The important thing is to keep calm, speak with authority and show a sense of humour. I used the same tactics in dealing with the injured adults I transported in my ambulance.

The air was dusty, and I sneezed. That immediately reminded me of home and I let my thoughts drift into childhood memory, anything to take my mind off this interminable crawl into darkness. It was always dusty in Kookynie, the tiny gold-mining settlement on the edge of Western Australia's Great Victoria Desert where I grew up. It was dusty also in the Wheatbelt town of Duranillin, where I had taught in a one-room school and saved the money to make my escape to Europe. My students had been bush kids, independent, cheeky and often rambunctious. I had loved teaching them, probably because I had been just like them myself – until my mother took note of that fact and sent me to boarding school in Perth.

'Lily needs to learn how to live in *society*. She's thirteen and it's time she learned how to act like a *lady*,' she had said, as if

Perth were some cosmopolitan centre of civilisation, and her own grandfather had not been convicted in 1850 of stealing a cow, and transported to Western Australia for ten years of penal servitude.

My mother hated people to know of her grandfather's convict past, but I was proud of what he went on to do with his life after such troubled beginnings. After receiving his ticket of leave, he became a government schoolmaster and a respected member of the community. His son became a bank manager and his grandson – my Uncle Charles – was a judge. Life is often ironic in Australia.

A sharp pain in my knee brought me back to the present as I bumped into something that gave a loud crack. My entire body jerked, and I froze, heart pounding, praying I had not disturbed the precarious jumble around me.

Silence and, except for the narrow band of my torchlight, darkness. I sneezed again and I crawled a few feet more, slowly and more carefully. I wished I were not so alone. My hands were sweaty and sticky inside the thick gloves. I stopped to stifle yet another sneeze as best I could, and I gazed at the destruction exposed by my torchlight.

Splinters of cabinetry, shards of glass and crockery, and pieces of plaster with torn wallpaper attached. The wallpaper was a cheerful yellowy colour scattered with a design of orange berries, the sort of paper that would brighten up a kitchen. Small children would barely notice it as they drank their milk and ate their meals. It would have been there in the background in a room they had thought was as permanent as the Rock of Gibraltar, but was now a shattered mess.

'Hullo? Are you there?' I called out again, making my voice calm and firm. 'Please tell me if you are. I'm Lily and I'm here to help you.'

There was no reply. If the children were alive I did not blame them for hiding from a stranger who was waving a torch around in the ruins of their lives. It would be better if I could call them by name, but I did not know their names. So I listened hard for anything that might be a sign as to their presence: a whimper, a sob, a moan. Silence pressed in, broken by creaks and groans from the settling ruins. I could not see the kitchen table they were supposed to have sheltered beneath.

It occurred to me to recite some poetry. My students had loved Edward Lear's poetry, which is nonsensical enough to surprise and delight small children. A frightened child might be intrigued.

'Those who watch at that midnight hour,' I declaimed, 'From Hall or Terrace, or lofty Tower, Cry, as the wild light passes along,' – and here I let the torchlight play around me – '"The Dong! – the Dong! The wandering Dong through the forest goes! The Dong! the Dong! The Dong with a luminous Nose!"'

'That's silly.'

It came distinctly, the piping voice of a small child. *Oh, God, please let them both be all right. Oh, God, please let them be together and unhurt.*

'It *is* silly, isn't it?' I said into the darkness. 'Are you hiding? You're doing a super job at it if you are.'

'I'm waiting for Mummy. You go away you Dong.'

'Your mummy sent me to get you,' I said. 'She's waiting for you outside. She wants you to come with me.'

It was a lie, and I hated to use it. They had told me the mother had gone off in another ambulance. I didn't even know if she was still alive.

I shone the torch in the direction of the voice and from the jumble of wood and plaster a small white face squinted into the light. It belonged to a bright-eyed little boy, about three years old, who was hugging a big torch to his chest. I supposed he had turned it off when he heard me approaching. Grey dust coated his hair and the blue striped pyjamas he was wearing; he seemed to be in a cave, until I realised that he was in fact under the kitchen table. It had saved him when the walls came down on top of it, but I wondered how much longer the table would hold with the ton of rubble it bore.

The boy shook his head. 'I'm looking after Emily, our baby. She's asleep.'

*Oh, God, please let her not be dead.* I had seen too many dead children in the past weeks.

'It's all right, sweetheart, I've come to take you both to Mummy,' I said as I crawled across the rubble towards him.

It wasn't until I was almost at his sanctuary that my torchlight revealed the baby lying on her back on a blanket in front of him. She looked about nine months old and was, just as her brother had said, fast asleep. With a sense of wonder I watched the quick and regular rise and fall of her chest.

'Emily cried and cried,' he said. 'But she's asleep now, you mustn't wake her up.'

I reached out a hand to the infant and the boy immediately tried to push me away. 'Mummy said to wait here. Go away you Dong.'

I backed off a little. 'How are you, old chap,' I asked. 'Are you hurt anywhere?'

He shook his head and shrank back, but said nothing more as I gently felt along Emily's body to see if there were any indications of injury. She woke as I did so, and gave a high mewling cry of surprise. Her little body was firm to the touch, but her eyes were sunken and she seemed lethargic. I assumed she was dehydrated and prayed that was the worst.

I reached into the hiding place and picked her up, tucking the blanket around her. Her arms wrapped around my neck in a tight, trusting grip that brought hot tears to my eyes. I had thought I was hardened after seeing so much horror and I felt oddly happy to know that tears could still come.

'Leave Emily alone.'

The boy's voice was sharp, imperative; he was close to hysteria. He was also confused and probably hungry and thirsty and certainly terrified.

'You've been such a brave boy,' I said. 'And you've looked after Emily so well. Your mummy will be very proud of you.

But it's time for us all to go now. I'll carry Emily. Can you crawl behind me while I carry Emily?'

'Like a baby?' He sounded unenthusiastic. I could not force him to come out, but I could not carry both of them, and neither could I leave him behind.

'No. Like a—' My mind was blank. I hugged Emily closer. She had my neck in a stranglehold, but she was too quiet and it worried me. The creaks and moans of the settling ruins above us worried me more, though. The panic I had kept at bay was threatening to engulf me again and I needed to get out. *Now.*

'Like a train,' I said, sparked by a sudden, ancient memory of the game I had played with my younger brother, Ben. 'Let's play trains. I'm the engine and Emily is the driver, but we need a coal truck. Could you be a coal truck, d'you think? Grab my ankles and we'll set off.'

With my right arm tight around baby Emily and gripping the torch, I cautiously turned myself around to face the way I had come. A loud sob sounded behind me. He was close to losing control; I was taking his sister and he was terrified of being alone in the dark. *We're all frightened of that*, I wanted to tell him, *in a war we're all afraid of the dark.*

I shone my torch down and back towards my feet, dipping Emily as I did so. 'Quick, grab my ankles. The train must leave on time, but it can't run without coal.'

Instead he switched on his own torch.

'Leave your torch,' I said, 'and take hold of my ankles. Mummy will pick it up later.'

He looked very uncertain.

I raised my voice and made a train sound. 'Woo-oo-oo. All aboard that's going aboard. The train to Euston station is ready to go.'

'You should say that it's about to depart,' he whispered in a mournful little voice.

I repeated obediently, 'The train to Euston station is about to depart. All aboard. Where's my coal truck? Unless there's coal for the engine we won't get far. Is there a coal truck around here?'

'I'll be the coal truck,' he said, and I heard the note of excitement in his voice and knew I had him.

Small hands grabbed my ankles. I turned the torch to light our way and slowly, painfully, we began to crawl through the debris of his shattered home, puff, puff, puffing as we went.

'Woo-woo,' I said. The smell of dust and charred wood and soot was almost suffocating and I coughed.

He sneezed.

'My knees hurt,' he said.

'I know,' I said. 'Not much further now.' My knees felt as if they were on fire, and baby Emily was becoming unbearably heavy in the crook of my arm, which was cramping painfully. When I tried to shift her weight a little she whimpered.

'Let's put more coal into the engine, shall we?'

'Engines can't run without coal,' he whispered and held tighter to my ankles, a dragging weight behind me as I crawled.

I felt my heart jump when at last I saw the circle of light ahead of me. It was not daylight yet, of course. They would have set up arc lights and erected a tarpaulin to hide them from the bombers. We crawled towards the light and now I could hear the generator. But as they pulled us out I heard a more ominous sound, the growling roar of planes overhead and the heavy thump of ack-ack guns. The raiders had returned.